"Endearing . . . Ros[...]ove, loss, faith, and rede[...]s of earnest contempora[...]*ekly*

"*Glory Falls* was a wonderful heartwarming story line that pulled on many different emotions: love, tragedy, manipulation, friendships/family, and happiness."

—The Reading Cafe

PRAISE FOR
WILDFLOWER ROAD

"*Wildflower Road* is a beautifully written novel about two lost souls seeking their path to redemption that find each other on their way. I would most definitely recommend reading this emotionally moving contemporary novel that touches on a lot of deep topics but still keeps true to being a clean romance."

—Harlequin Junkie

"What a powerful story of redemption! . . . If you enjoy your romance with a more serious edge, *Wildflower Road* is a well-written story that shows the darkness in man—to emphasize the light!"

—Among the Reads

PRAISE FOR
THIS WANDERING HEART

"A heartwarming novel that embraces all the wondrous elements of romance: love to last a lifetime, family values, loyalty, forgiveness, and second chances."

—Catherine Anderson, *New York Times* bestselling
author of *Huckleberry Lake*

Aspen Crossroads

A Whisper Canyon Romance

JANINE ROSCHE

JOVE
New York

A JOVE BOOK
Published by Berkley
An imprint of Penguin Random House LLC
penguinrandomhouse.com

(Penguin colophon)

Copyright © 2021 by Janine Rosche

Scriptures taken from the Holy Bible, New International Version®, NIV®.
Copyright © 1973, 1978, 1984, 2011 by Biblica, Inc.™ Used by permission of
Zondervan. All rights reserved worldwide. *www.zondervan.com* The "NIV"
and "New International Version" are trademarks registered in the
United States Patent and Trademark Office by Biblica, Inc.™

ISBN: 9780593335758

First Edition: August 2021

Printed in the United States of America
1   3   5   7   9   10   8   6   4   2

Book design by Daniel Brount

This book is dedicated to the survivors and all those fighting to end human trafficking.

AUTHOR'S NOTE

This novel deals with topics that may be sensitive to the reader, including sexual assault, childhood sexual abuse, homelessness, and sex trafficking. It should be noted that the reality of what survivors of sex trafficking have experienced is far grittier and darker than what is portrayed within these pages. To learn more about how you can help stop human trafficking and provide support for the survivors, visit hundredmovement.com. The Hundred Movement provides free counseling services to survivors of sex trafficking and training for foster parents of survivors.

If you need help for yourself, or you suspect someone might be in a trafficking situation in the United States, please call the National Trafficking Hotline at 1 (888) 373-7888 or text "BeFree" to 233733.

If you have experienced sexual violence in the United States, you can receive confidential help twenty-four hours a day, seven days a week through the National Sexual Assault Hotline by calling 1 (800) 656-HOPE (4673).

Chapter One

As Haven slipped through the farmers' market crowd, the side-eyed glances scrawled decades-old Haviland family gossip across her skin. She should've grown used to it, but these days it felt far more personal. And after all she'd done to help them. Or tried to help them, anyway. That was over now, though, thanks to her foolishness.

"Just like her mother," Mrs. Vermillion whispered loud enough to reach Haven's ears.

"All those Haviland kids are, in one way or another." Sandy Hugh, her mother's onetime best friend, tsked and shook her head. "Their poor father."

Haven fidgeted with the neckline of her blouse. Despite the heat, she tugged it up to her clavicle.

"Don't mind them, Haven. They only *think* they know our family." Her sister Rarity adjusted the scarf tying up her ebony tresses. With her capris and halter top, today's look made her appear as an extra on a sixties teen beach movie. Rarity handed each woman a three-by-five flyer advertising her vintage dress shop. "Ladies, bring this card into Fringe and Lace for thirty percent off your purchases." Unlike Haven, Rarity welcomed the attention—good and bad—and was determined to make a living off it. Rarity linked her arm through their brother's. "Daniel doesn't let the whispers bother him, do you, bro?"

"What was that?" Daniel kept his eyes laser-focused on a petite blonde selling honey from a tent directly beneath the grossly outdated *Welcome to Whisper Canyon: Arrive a Stranger, Stay a Friend* sign.

Haven's stomach clenched. Leave it to her twin brother to find the one girl on Main Street he hadn't already dated. On second thought, *dated* wasn't the right word. At least Haven wouldn't be seeing this one on her office couch in a few weeks. Maybe if she'd heeded the term *conflict of interest* before, she could've saved herself a whole lot of heartache. Haven blew out a breath and gathered her chocolate-brown hair in front of her right shoulder. Colorado shouldn't be this hot in early August, especially not in the mountains.

Rarity combed the loose strands with a gentle touch. "Everyone's just curious why their favorite counselor closed her practice. You've been the confidante for everyone in town as long as I can remember."

"Haven, you know what you need?" Daniel's voice was as smooth as his perfectly coiffed waves of hair. Her brother was too good-looking for his own good. "A date. One nice forget-your-troubles good time with a guy you'll never lay eyes on again."

Haven allowed herself two blinks before she opened her mouth, making sure her judgment didn't stretch across her face. "A man is the last thing I need right now."

"And your advice stinks worse than your cologne." Rarity turned her focus back to Haven. "You can talk to me, you know. Whatever you're carrying, you don't have to do it alone."

Just as she had her entire twenty-seven years, Haven molded her lips into a pleasant smile. Her family had been through the wringer. They certainly didn't need to fret over her. "I'm fine. Really."

"If you say so. I think I'll find some flowers for Mom's grave. Anyone want to join me?"

Nearby, two dogs barked a greeting to each other as their owners mingled over soy candles—a welcome distraction as Rarity's question hung awkwardly among the three of them.

Daniel looked over his shoulder toward the blonde. "I think I'll go sample the local honey."

Was there any point in trying to dissuade him these days? "Be careful, Daniel."

Her brother neared and kissed Haven's cheek. "You know me." Then he was gone.

"What about you, Haven?" Rarity asked.

A welcome breeze dipped into the canyon, cooling Haven's face. She and Daniel had taken after their mother in appearance. Their skin bronzed quickly in the sun. Still, at this altitude, Haven shouldn't risk it. "I need some of that sunscreen Delaney sells. I'm sure whatever you pick out will look great. I'll go with you to the cemetery, okay?" Haven put steps between them quickly, lest she give in. Those women were right. Nina Haviland had passed more down to Haven than just her skin tone, and Haven didn't feel much like memorializing her mother for it.

Half the town seemed to fill Main Street, just like every Saturday morning in summertime. And as always, the crowd split in two. On the east side of the street, where the high-end boutiques sold the finest apparel, jewelry, and handbags, the weekenders meandered with their fat wallets and designer sunglasses. On the west side, local artists hawked their paintings and goods while a group of young folks—probably drifters—sat on the pavement in front of a man who wore his blond hair in locs and picked a folk tune on his guitar. Haven walked straight down the center line, keeping her chin steady despite the stares from both sides.

She stopped at Delaney's skin care booth to peruse the product-filled tables. Reality burned brighter than the

Rocky Mountain sun when Haven spied the sticker on the sunscreen. The bottle was smaller, and the price was higher. Too high for someone three months unemployed.

Something brushed Haven's hip. On her right, a tall man peered down at her. And while his smile was friendly, his eyes seemed to be canvassing her figure. Again, his hand swept against her side, not accidentally.

As gooseflesh rippled over Haven's arms, a woman on his right turned. When she noticed the person on whom her husband's unflinching gaze was focused, she dropped the lotion she'd been holding.

Haven swallowed hard, ignoring the heat in her cheeks. "Mrs. Singleton, how are you?"

Ramona Singleton brushed her bangs to the side as the man excused himself. "Hello, Haven. Pardon my husband. He's not himself today. It's the heat, I think."

"Perfectly understandable. It's getting to a lot of people, it seems." Haven gripped the strap of her purse tightly as she pondered what to say next. "I've been hoping—"

"I meant to call—"

Haven and Ramona exchanged awkward grins. "Go ahead," Ramona said.

"I've been hoping to hear back from you about the job at the preschool."

"Yes, about that . . . I have someone else in mind for the position. I'm sorry."

"Oh." Haven breathed in deep. "You've already filled it?"

"Not quite." Ramona backed out from under the tent. Her gaze darted nervously about the crowd.

Haven followed. "Is it my lack of teaching experience? My salary expectations? I'm willing to work hourly—"

"It's not that." Ramona sighed. "Some parents heard you were interviewing and . . ."

Haven nodded for her to continue.

"The mothers were nervous about you teaching their children. They've heard rumors. No one wants their husbands, well, you know . . . I can't say I blame them. I'm sorry." Ramona patted Haven's shoulder. "Some risks simply aren't worth taking."

She was a risk? And one not worth taking? Before Ramona could see the tears forming in her eyes, she slinked past her until a teenager stepped in her path.

"You look like a gal who loves adventure." The boy shoved a paper in Haven's hand. Pictures of crystals, stalactites, and stalagmites surrounded the words *Whisper Canyon Caverns and Cave Tours*. He must be a college kid working with Bo Radford for the summer. Whisper Canyon was ideal for that sort of thing, with its hot springs, outdoor sports, and adventures.

"You've pegged me wrong."

"You can't know a town until you know what's beneath the surface. We've got hour-long tours and half-day excursions." This guy was selling it well. Bo would be happy.

"No, thank you."

When Haven moved aside, the boy followed with promises of experienced guides and the highest safety precautions.

"I'm not interested." Haven thrust the advertisement into his chest and then ducked into a fully curtained booth. The smell of pine replaced the kettle corn from outside, and an artificial light cast a glow across the space. Two men negotiated prices in the corner, but Haven's focus went to the chirping little fluffballs hopping around a baby pool lined with wood shavings. Five of the chicks gathered on the far side, leaving one all alone nearest to Haven.

She kneeled to get a closer look. "Hello there. Aren't you sweet?"

The chick peeped.

A glance over her shoulder assured the men weren't paying her any mind, so Haven scooped up the solitary little chick, sheltering it between her hands and stroking its baby-fine feathers. "You are darling."

The chick kicked her feet, but something was off. On

one foot, the toes stretched wide, forming a star shape, but on the other, the toes curled in on themselves. "Oh, sweetheart, is that why you're over here all by your lonesome? Have they cast you out? Poor thing. I think you're perfect. In fact, you are so perfect that I dub you Audrey."

"Excuse me, miss. I have a question for you. Are you planning to buy that Ameraucana?"

Instinctively, Haven drew the chick close, holding her against her chest. The other chicks now peeked out of a cardboard box, their heads bopping about in time with their chirps. Beyond the box, a pair of legs donning work boots and jeans rose vertically until the light over the baby pool washed out the rest.

"Because if you aren't, I'd like to." The voice was masculine enough to stir up a few flutters in her belly. Then the owner of the voice bent down into a crouch. The light caught the striking lines of his face. A strong jaw and straight nose played against the tuft of sandy hair peeking out from his backward baseball cap, creating a playful combo of boyish and manly. He wasn't from around here. Haven would remember him.

"I . . ." Haven started, peering down at the chick in her hands. "I hadn't thought about it." She had no coop. She had no house, either. At least not one of her own. With all Dad had going on, the last thing he needed to worry about was a pet chicken. "I guess not."

The cute guy watched her for a long moment. If he was in a rush, he wasn't showing it.

The chick wiggled against her palms.

"She has an injured foot."

His brow furrowed, and his lips dipped into a frown. He rose, then stepped around the pool to join Haven. When she stood, the man towered a good half foot above her. For some reason, she thought of the hickory armoire in her childhood bedroom at her dad's house. "It's sturdy," Dad had said the day he gifted it to her. Now as she stood in a darkened tent with this handsome stranger, all she could think about was that dumb piece of furniture.

"Sturdy."

"What?" he asked.

"Um, the chick. I don't know how sturdy she'll be as she grows." Haven opened her hands to give him a view of the animal.

Yet the man waited two feet away. "May I?"

It took a second for Haven to realize what he wanted permission for. A gentleman? Now she was sure he wasn't from Whisper Canyon. Haven gave a quick nod, and he moved in to inspect the chick. He allowed the warped toes to wrap his fingertip. He was gentle as he thumbed the tiny bones and talons. With his other hand, he stroked the chick's head. With each movement, he brushed Haven's hand, forcing her to train her thoughts on the animal—not the man whose ocean-clean scent threatened to buckle her knees.

No wedding ring. So much for training those thoughts. But she'd learned that was the most attractive trait a man could exhibit. Well, that and a habit of honesty, which was rare these days.

"I can try to splint those." His voice dove to a deep, lulling timbre. Was he trying to soothe the bird? Or her? "Hopefully, it's only cosmetic. If so, she'll still be plenty useful to me."

Haven closed her hands and twisted away from him. "Are you planning to eat her?"

His smile cracked. "Ameraucanas aren't meat birds. But I do plan to eat her eggs. Is that all right with you?"

The panic eased out on a breath. "I suppose."

He held out his hands. They were calloused but clean, and Haven liked the look of them. Sturdy.

Again, with that word. Haven placed the chick in his hands, his rough skin catching slightly on hers. Following her father's advice, she looked the man straight in the eye to let him know she could hold her own. Not that the guidance had worked for her so far. Here she was, unemployed with no job prospects, covered in salmonella, and debating custody arrangements for a chicken.

"Thanks, miss. I'll take good care of her."

"Audrey."

His forehead wrinkled. "Thanks, Audrey."

"No, I'm not Audrey. The chick is Audrey. Hepburn."

Confusion turned to amusement. "How about Audrey *Hen*burn?" His eyes pierced hers. She couldn't tell their color in this light, but they crinkled at the corners and warmed her straight through. An image of the two of them sitting beneath a tree as the chicks hopped around their legs appeared in her head, but she quickly dismissed it. Her judgment, or lack thereof, was troublesome these days. A man, especially one like this, was the last thing she needed.

"That'll do." She stepped away from him and searched for words as he loaded Audrey into the box with the others. "Make sure the others are nice to her."

"I have a strict no-bullying policy in my coop. I even have a friend that knits sweaters for them. Audrey will get the nicest one."

The reality of his words jabbed Haven right in the gut. "Tell your *friend* to make Audrey a pretty black one. Maybe add a string of pearls."

"Will do." He had a great smile.

Haven spun on her heels and ducked out of the tent before she made more of a mess in her life.

Chapter Two

Jace Daring placed the box of chicks in the back of his pickup truck next to the potted rosebush and the wooden tractor toy for Elijah. That's who he needed to think of. Elijah. Rosalie. Jillian. Sonny. Not the brunette in the chick tent. He didn't come to Whisper Canyon to flirt with pretty girls. He had a job to do. Once he'd accomplished that, he'd shake this town's dust off his boots and never return. At least he hadn't been dumb enough to get her name. It was bad enough that he'd remember her whenever he saw Audrey Henburn. To think he had to promise to take care of her. As if he didn't have enough people relying on him to keep them safe. Now he had to add a chicken with a bum leg. He stared down at the peeping box, then brought it to the cab of the truck with him. He set it on the floor in front of the passenger seat. The engine roared to a start, and Jace fussed with the air conditioner so it wouldn't blast Audrey and friends.

His phone buzzed, and he retrieved it from his pocket. Terrence, calling on a Saturday. Jace didn't mind. The guy was much more than a boss, and Jace owed him everything.

"Hey, Terrence," Jace answered. "Don't you ever take a day off?"

"Do you?"

"Good point." Jace checked the time on the dashboard's display. This farmers' market trip had taken longer than he'd planned. Now he'd be making up for the lost time after sunset.

"Did you get a meeting with the mayor?" Terrence asked.

"Wednesday at nine. I can only imagine what tricks he'll try now."

"Jace, if I'd had any idea you'd face so much opposition, I wouldn't have sent you to Whisper Canyon for this assignment."

"Yes, you would've. You aren't you if you aren't barging in on my life somehow."

"Eleven years so far, with no plans to stop. Speaking of, have you learned anything about your mom?"

"No, and I won't."

"Jace, you have the opportunity to learn where you came from, what happened to your mother that led her—"

"What good could come from that, huh?"

"I don't know, Jace. Family? Home? Belonging?"

Jace scoffed.

"What exactly are you afraid of?" Terrence asked with the subtlety of a cattle prod.

"Right now? Not getting today's tasks done. If I don't get this operation up and running, I'll have to stay in this town even longer than I planned."

"Okay, okay. I tried."

Jace ended the call and set his phone on the center console next to the laminated picture. In the shot, he was eight or nine with ratty hair that likely hadn't been cut in months. He saw the oversize thrift-shop T-shirt and dirt on his skin from a few days without a shower. Back then, he'd known only that his mother—and his mother alone—loved him.

The box chirped. Would she be proud of him for taking in a wounded chick? Yeah, she would. She would've done it herself, and like the girl, she might've given it some silly name.

Movement through the windshield caught his eye. Farther up the street, the girl—the one from the chick tent—headed in his direction from the market. She walked beside a raven-haired woman who wore something kitschy. But his girl was the real deal, dressed simply in shorts and a sleeveless blouse. Boy, she was pretty. The thought made him grit his teeth. He needed to be better than other men.

Jace prepared to shift his car into reverse, but a man appeared from an alleyway. The women startled, and the retro-dressed one dropped a bouquet of flowers. The man lunged at the chick girl, seizing her.

Adrenaline propelled Jace from his seat, and seconds later, he was on the sidewalk running. The man looked back at Jace, then released his hold on the girl just in time for Jace to plow into him. The force pinned the man's back against the brick wall of a storefront, and Jace held his forearm to the guy's throat. Jace and the man were about the same height and build. Even if he couldn't keep him long enough for the cops to get him, a few seconds would allow the women to escape.

Except they weren't escaping. In fact, the girl he'd met tore at Jace's arm. "Stop! Please, stop!"

But Jace didn't stop. "You like to hurt women, do you?"

A blow nailed Jace's cheekbone, making him fall back. A pair of arms circled his neck, choking him. The other girl?

His girl pressed her hands against Jace's chest. "Please! He's my brother!"

Jace breathed hard as he unsuccessfully tried to unpeel the other woman's arms from around his neck.

"Let go, Rarity. I know him," the girl said to the one giving the choke hold.

"You know this jerk?" The brother shook out his fist.

"Yes. No. Not really," the girl said. "We met in the hatchery—with the chickens?"

As soon as the arms around his neck released, Jace found his voice. "This guy is your brother? He was hurting you." An only child, Jace didn't know about sibling relationships. This couldn't be normal, could it?

The girl rolled her eyes. "Twins." Her hands relaxed against Jace's chest but didn't move otherwise. "And he didn't hurt me. He was messing around."

"Of course I wasn't hurting her. Go back to where you came from, Captain America."

Ignoring the taunt, Jace leaned a bit closer to her. "If I walk away, you'll be safe?" How many times had he asked women across the country that exact question?

Her hands slid off him. She nodded.

"I'm sorry," Jace said to the man, then peered down into the girl's soothing eyes. "I'm sorry."

"You're already forgiven," she said quietly. "Thanks for looking out for me. I'd forgotten nice guys existed."

He lingered in her gaze longer than he should. Then, embarrassed, Jace turned and trudged back to his truck.

"You never told me your name," the green-eyed, chick-naming girl called from behind him. For a split second, Jace allowed himself to imagine what it might be like to meet a normal girl like this one, date her, care for her, and maybe even love her. To settle down somewhere with a couple kids and a chicken named Audrey Henburn who wears sweaters and pearls. But the picture of his mother flashed before his eyes. Then the faces of Sonny, Jillian, Rosalie, Elijah, and countless others like them. No, that dream—family, home, belonging—was for someone else. Looking back, he took a mental snapshot of her and allowed the ache of *what if* to claw at his very soul. "That's probably for the best."

So," Rarity said, tapping her spoon on the edge of her bowl of minestrone, "are we going to sweep today's rumble under the rug?"

"Yes." Daniel's answer flew across the dinner table quicker than Captain America's shield.

"Of course you don't want to talk about it. You got shown up," Rarity countered.

"I want to hear about it," Valor, Haven's oldest sister, said.

At the head of the table, Haven's dad left his bread half-buttered. "There was a rumble? I thought you kids had grown out of that."

"Dad, it wasn't a big deal. And it wasn't between us," Haven was quick to reassure him.

"Yeah, just another case of the Havilands against the world," Rarity said. "Basically, Haven nabbed a man while she was buying fried chicken or something. I don't know the details, but the guy must be half in love with her already because he saw Daniel messing with us, and he came charging. He slammed Daniel against the wall, all to save his fair Haven."

Dad turned his concerned focus first to Daniel, who insisted it "didn't even hurt," then looked Haven's way. The compassion she'd inherited from him was etched deep into his forehead wrinkles. "Love?"

Her father's pet name for his daughters made her grin. "I don't even know his name. Don't worry about me." If only the pat she gave to Dad's hand could implore him to mind her words. He would worry over her if he knew she'd also inherited his inclination to fall for liars and cheats.

"That's the thing. No one knows his name. He's a big mystery," Rarity said, waving her spoon in the air. "Delaney said she first started seeing him when the farmers' market opened for the season back in March. He goes to the market every Saturday but keeps a low profile. She thinks he lives south of town. Remember where we used to go pick pumpkins when we were kids?"

Dad rapped his knuckles on the table. "Oh, uh, the

Creightons' old land. Aspen something or other. Used to be a dairy farm long before that."

"Aspen Crossroads. Supposedly, he lives there, but no one knows what he does. I heard he's got, like, ten women living there with him in some polygamist cult thing."

"He wasn't wearing a ring," Haven said softly.

"Okay, so maybe it's just a harem," Rarity said.

No, Captain America . . . whatever his name was, wouldn't be a part of anything like that. He was too sturdy. Ugh. A master's degree and she couldn't think of another word? There was more to a man than the width of his shoulders. And not all of it promised warm, fuzzy feelings.

"Well, I've gotta go. I have a date." Rarity rose from the dinner table.

"Who's the lucky guy?" Valor asked. "Not another football player, is it?"

"Heavens, no. This guy does performance art."

Daniel chuckled. "I think performance art is a fancy way of saying he's a street mime."

"One can only hope." Rarity pretended to use an invisible rope to pull herself from the dining room.

Her father's home quieted with her sister's exit. Soon, Valor and Daniel would head back to their apartments. Dad would fall asleep watching a movie on TCM, and Haven would spend the night wondering what on earth to do with the rest of her life. Maybe she could become a mime. Mimes helped people, didn't they? Bringing joy and laughter and all that. She could help, not harm. Piece of cake.

"I hope she doesn't marry him. Mimes creep me out," Valor whispered out of their father's earshot.

So much for the mime idea. The makeup would probably cause her skin to flare up anyway.

Valor nudged her. "Any news on the job search?"

"Only more dead ends."

"You know, there are rumors going around about why you closed your counseling practice."

Haven pinned Valor with a questioning look. "Do you believe them?"

"Absolutely not. Although others in town might, especially after what Mom did. It might be hurting your chances at landing something new. Maybe you should tell everyone the reason you quit."

Her breath caught. Which reason? The real one or the one she'd told her family?

Valor tucked a curl behind Haven's ear. "Burnout is a very real thing in the helping professions. You don't have to be ashamed."

"Thank you, Val. Right now, I just need a paycheck. I don't want to burden Dad, especially when his shop is struggling so much."

"I grabbed this." Valor dug into her back pocket and withdrew a tiny slip of paper. "It's from a flyer on the town bulletin board. It was a job ad for a home behavioral specialist. Must have experience working with trauma survivors. Must have a clean history. Background check required. Or something to that effect."

Must have a clean history? Haven forced a swallow. Before she could loosen her throat to speak, her sister had taken her hand and forced the phone number onto her palm and curled her fingers around it.

After waving Daniel and Valor off, Haven hugged Dad good night and retired to her bedroom for the evening. Upon entering the room she'd lived in her entire life, she placed the phone number on her desk. The only person who would call about this disturbingly vague job description would have to be out of their mind. It was something her siblings would do. Not her. And then when it blew up in their faces, Haven would be their shoulder to cry on. Always.

She leaned against the hickory armoire, welcoming its cool kiss on her forehead. Memories of her tween years frolicked past her mind's eye. How many times had she stood in this very spot and imagined what it might feel like to slow-dance with a boy? And how many times had she looked up and imagined catching the boy's glance just before he leaned in for a kiss? A laugh escaped beneath her breath. She'd probably even kissed the thing once or twice, hopeless romantic that she was. Practicing for that magical moment when she'd have her first kiss.

Now those imaginings were long since passed. And first kisses weren't so magical. They'd all brought her right back here. She pushed off the dresser and straightened. It wasn't much taller than her anymore. Just half a foot or so. But still just as sturdy.

Minutes of fitful sleep alternated with hours watching the shadows tiptoe across her room. And thinking, always thinking. Thinking about the mysterious man at the market, the unrelenting rumors about her family, and her dreadful mistakes. Twice in her life—only twice—she'd taken risks. The first time, it destroyed her family. The second time, it destroyed her career, her reputation, and her integrity. When dawn broke, she groggily climbed out of bed. On a sigh, she crumpled the paper strip in her fist and dropped it into the wastebasket. Risk, like love, costs far too much, and Haven couldn't afford to lose anything else.

Chapter Three

From where he sat on his porch, Jace thought his fields might've caught hold of the sunrise and shattered it into ten thousand pieces, enough for each stalk, leaf, and blade of grass to enjoy a sliver of its own.

Let the fields be jubilant, and everything in them; let all the trees of the forest sing for joy.

Jace dropped his gaze back to the worn book that folded over his palm, back to the story of David spying on Bathsheba as she bathed on her rooftop. The coffee he'd enjoyed moments ago churned in his stomach. He knew what would happen next and he didn't need to read it. He had seen it play out countless times. And every day, he worked to heal the scars David's sin left in its wake.

Now, if only Mayor Garrison would stop getting in the way of that work. Jace prayed for the right words to say during their meeting later that morning to convince him that his team was not a threat to Whisper Canyon's economy or virtue. The way Garrison talked about the place, you'd think no sin had ever been committed within the town limits. Too bad Jace was living proof *that* wasn't true.

Over at the farmhouse, the familiar groan of the front

door across the driveway announced the first sign of life. Good. There was much to be done if the restaurant was going to open before kingdom come, and he certainly couldn't do it all himself. At some point, the women would have to step up and claim it and this farm as their own or he'd never be able to leave this town.

He half expected to see Elijah in his footie pajamas come running out to collect the eggs for breakfast. Jace didn't have the heart to tell him they'd be waiting awhile for this new batch of chicks to provide. Perhaps he could put a few of the eggs he'd grabbed at the store in the coop for him to find. Like that one Easter egg hunt Jace had done when he was young. Where was that anyway? Could've been in a dozen states or more, considering how much he and Mom moved around.

But it was not Elijah who stepped through the doorframe, unless Elijah had stretched in height and traded his footie pajamas for a silky thing that left absolutely nothing to the imagination.

Jillian took a statuesque pose against the porch post and ran a hand through her hair. Like Jace had been doing moments ago, she stared out over the fields.

Jace shut the Bible on David's story and rose from the rocking chair on the porch of the small cabin he called his temporary home. He turned to head in through the back door.

"Morning, Jace," Jillian called. She waved to him with one hand before placing it on her hip, inching her slip up a bit more on her thigh. Jillian and her games.

He tossed a hand up in greeting and disappeared inside. He should say something about these ploys of hers, but what? Anything he scripted always fell into two columns: shaming or rejecting. For Jillian, Sonny, Rosalie, and all the other women he'd helped leave the sex industry, those were the last possible things they needed to feel more of. All he could do right now was pray that the right person would see his job ad on the town's bulletin board and call. But it had been six weeks, and none of the callers had gotten past the phone screen. At this rate, he might never find the right mentor for the women in the farmhouse. What would he do then?

Two hours later, Jace stepped inside Whisper Canyon Town Hall, pausing to remove his Stetson hat and kick the dust from his boots. Not that the show of respect or the state of his attire would make one lick of difference to a mayor dead set against Jace and his plans. However, the office building had recently finished a restoration project. As the project manager of another renovation, he had to respect freshly tiled floors.

His gaze trailed the length of the floor, past the offices, meeting rooms, and Town Hall auditorium, to the back wall, which had always been covered by plastic sheeting. Until now. His hat slipped from his hand as a wave of nostalgia stole the breath from his lungs. At the sight of the larger-than-life grizzly bear carved into the stone wall, Jace was knocked back twenty-five years or more.

He'd been hiding behind his mother, gripping on to her coat as she spoke to someone. She was scared, too, he'd thought. Who wouldn't be terrified at the huge claws and snaggled fangs? Jace had been certain the bear would break through the stone and charge at him and his mother. He'd begged his mother to leave, until finally she'd scooped Jace up in her thin arms and run him outside, away from the beast.

"This town is full of evil. If we stay, we'll be eaten alive," she'd said as she forced him into their car. "Promise me, Jace, that you'll never come back here."

Now that Jace stood at six feet, the grizzly statue didn't look anywhere near as tall. Still, that same fear bristled his nerves. *This town is full of evil.*

"Ol' Sixclaw. That's his name."

Jace turned toward the voice, finding Trent Garrison approaching from the direction of the restroom. The mayor stretched his hand out. After a slight hesitation, Jace accepted the handshake in the spirit of cooperation. Gross. Garrison's hand was wet—hopefully, from sink water. Nevertheless, Jace wiped his hand on his pant leg.

"He's a legend around here. Most ferocious bear ever to roam these mountains." Trent crossed his arms and stared up at the bear's open jaws, poised in a roar. "He was first seen in 1861. Folks still claim to find his distinctive prints in and outside of town. See his front-right paw? Six claws, not five."

Jace couldn't stomach small talk about local legends. Not with this guy. "Thanks for meeting with me. I'm hoping I can offer you some reassurance that my team and I aren't out to destroy your town."

Trent's focus remained on the bear looming over the hall. "You'd be wise to learn more about this town's rich history before you try to change its future." He bent down and retrieved Jace's hat off the floor. Turning it in his hands, he examined it.

Terrence had gifted that hat to Jace long ago, when Jace had been a wayward young man, simply trying to survive. It was more than a hat. It was a sign of trust. A sign that at least one person in the world thought Jace worthy of a calling. Having Trent Garrison hold that in his hands made Jace grit his teeth. Rather than ripping it away, Jace squared his shoulders toward the mayor and held out his hand.

After a prolonged and certainly intentional pause, Garrison gave Jace back his hat. "Let's take a walk, shall we?"

"What about our meeting?"

Garrison didn't answer. He strolled to the door and held it open for Jace.

The pride Jace attempted to swallow lodged in his throat. Sonny. Elijah. Jillian. Rosalie. He needed to put them first.

Humbly, he retraced his steps from minutes before, back through the front door.

As with most of that summer's mornings, Whisper Canyon was awash with sunlight, making Main Street seem almost incapable of keeping its secrets hidden from view. But where there was sunlight, there were shadows. Jace would be wise to remember that, no matter what Garrison had cooked up.

"This was a great place to grow up," the mayor began. He pointed his polished shoes to the north where, past the stretch of storefronts, his absurdly flashy mayoral mansion abutted the town's park. He spread his arms wide, nearly hitting Jace in the process. "Our community has long come together for festivals, concerts, car shows, parades, and holiday celebrations. Did you know that the day after Thanksgiving, Santa Claus and his reindeer lead a parade of children from the visitor center to the dance hall?"

"What's your point?"

"In the six years I've been mayor, we've added more festivities. We host races every summer and fall that draw runners from around the world."

"Which is why our organization chose Whisper Canyon for The Mill Restaurant. In every location—"

Trent held up a single finger. To silence Jace? Not on his watch.

"In every location, Secondly's restaurants, bakeries, and shops have stimulated the local economy. They are tourist draws. At June's town council meeting you stated your intentions to bring more tourism to the town. In your next breath, you fought the zoning change to allow us to turn the abandoned gristmill into a restaurant."

"When families come to Whisper Canyon, they expect clean, wholesome experiences."

"And you assume The Mill won't offer that? That's why you fought Secondly's purchase of the gristmill, the approval of the site plans, the zoning change, and the construction permits. We should be getting ready to open. Instead, we're way behind schedule."

"And my only regret is I wasn't able to shut down the project completely." Garrison waved to an elderly man sitting on a bench across the street, all while maintaining a sculpted smile. "I thought I should give you fair warning, man-to-man." Garrison's gaze locked on to two females jogging through the park. They were too far away for Jace to recognize—not that he knew many here in town, but their stature and dark hair were enough to remind him of the brunette from the farmers' market. And the way Garrison watched them like a cat might watch a canary heated Jace's blood to boiling. "Look, Daring. Since the town's founding, the Garrison family has occupied the office of mayor for one reason—to protect the residents of Whisper Canyon. It's my birthright to fight tooth and nail so people like you don't destroy it."

"What do you expect me to do? Let the fields at Aspen Crossroads go to weeds? Pack up and restart in a new town?"

Garrison spun around to face him. He puffed out his chest and confronted Jace. His steel gray eyes narrowed, and his smile melted into a sneer. "That's precisely what I expect."

O kay . . . spill it," Valor wheezed on two exhales, then charged forward into Haven's periphery.

"What do you mean?" Haven asked.

"You always run a . . . faster pace . . . when you're troubled."

"Sorry." A deep breath filled Haven's pumping lungs, and she cut her stride by a few inches.

"Much better. Now tell me what's up . . . or you'll need a new running partner."

Haven buttoned her lips a moment. God placed her on earth to be there for others, not the other way around. "I'm feeling strong. That's all." Ugh. She hated lying, especially to her family.

Valor tossed her a quizzical glance. "Does it have to do with that job I told you about?"

Over the past few days, Haven had removed the phone number from the trash several times, only to put it back in when she regained her sense. "No, it doesn't."

"Can't say I didn't try to help. Let's cut through the cemetery. You may feel strong, but my legs feel like they're full of sand."

Haven stopped. "I don't want to. It feels disrespectful."

Valor turned left into the cemetery despite Haven's objections. She waved, urging Haven to follow. Perhaps it was the paramedic in her sister, but Valor saw death as a logical consequence to living. To her, a cemetery was no more holy or consecrated than a passed-on person's home or office. "Come on. No one's even here."

Haven peered over the lines of stones. No mourners to be found. She clenched her jaw but followed her big sister's lead. The single drive split the cemetery in two. The Haviland family section took up a significant portion on the south side. As they neared, a heaviness pressed in on Haven's chest. Seeing her family name on tombstones was always sobering, but one struck harder than most.

Closing in, Haven's breath spilled out with a whimper. The granite slab for Nina Haviland, *beloved wife and mother*, had lost its shine. A film of some kind covered it. Upon closer inspection, Haven understood. Someone had thrown their coffee against her mother's stone. The empty to-go cup from Jailhouse Roasters lay empty next to the flowers Rarity had purchased from the farmers' market.

Haven sank to her knees on her mother's grave. The dried liquid was sticky to the touch. "Who would do this?" she asked before untying her long-sleeve shirt from around her waist. She wadded the fabric in her hand and wiped the stone.

Valor came to a stop above her. "A number of folks. Mom hurt a lot of people in her time here."

"She doesn't deserve this. Do you have any water left?"

Her sister placed the small plastic bottle from her hydration belt in Haven's hand. "She slept with half the town."

Haven shook her head while she soaked her shirt with the water. "Not half." She scrubbed at the stone until her biceps burned.

"She broke up several marriages. And every time, she hurt Dad in the process. She hurt us."

As the town's only counselor, Haven was all too familiar with the damage her mother left in the wake of her affairs. She also saw the damage at every family dinner in the way her siblings carried the heartache, the abandonment, with them, all in various ways. The wrinkles that burrowed deep into her father's kind, trusting face. And every time she looked in the mirror and recognized her mother's olive skin, dark hair, green eyes, and full lips. *The spitting image*, she'd heard all her life. No wonder the town believed the stories that Haven acted like her mother as well.

Once Haven's arm gave out from exhaustion, Valor took over the scrubbing. "She came back because she knew we were the only ones who would care for her in her last days. And she never said she was sorry. Not even to Dad. And yet, she's buried here, next to Nana." Out of breath, Valor sank onto her heels beside Haven. "Do you think she ever would have changed? If she had a longer life to live, I mean."

Haven shrugged. "I'd like to believe she would have. Everyone deserves a chance to make up for their mistakes."

"That's why you're the counselor. You see past a person's mistakes. You see the future they could have. Maybe that's why I thought of you when I saw that ad. Whether you wanted the job or not, you were the official Haviland home behavioral specialist."

Once again, Haven pictured the number in the wastebasket. She nearly had the thing memorized by now. She tensed against the urging both from her sister and inside her own heart to take the chance.

"You, sweet sister, have a heart for helping the hurting and the vulnerable. If Mom did anything right, it was giving you the name Haven."

One phone call. That's all it was. What harm could come from one call? On the other hand, what good could come from one call? A chance to make up for her own mistakes?

As dusk rolled in, calling for an end to a long day, Jace returned to his house. He made sure he was alone before stripping off his T-shirt that bore the sweat of a hard day's labor. Jillian and even Elijah had surprised him more than once inside his house, as if the boundaries he was trying to set meant nothing.

On the dresser's top, his phone vibrated. The screen showed a 970 area code. Probably a contractor working at the restaurant.

Jace cued the speakerphone then began kneading his tired neck muscles. After that morning's disastrous meeting with the mayor, he'd chosen the most difficult tasks on the farm to work out his anger. "Hello?"

No one replied.

He bent over his phone. "Anyone there?"

"Yes, hello. I'm calling about the ad for a home behavioral specialist. If that position is still available, I'm interested in learning more."

The woman sounded young. Too young. He'd hoped for a woman in her fifties or sixties who could offer a wealth of advice on how Sonny, Jillian, and Rosalie could rebuild their lives with this farm-to-table restaurant providing their income.

"It is still available, but as you saw on the ad, the uh, uh, home, uh . . ."

"Home behavioral specialist?"

"Yes," Jace said, rolling his eyes. He'd written the ad himself and even he couldn't remember the title he'd made up. "A home behavioral specialist. Because of the population we work with, confidentiality is our highest priority, so unfortunately, until we're farther along in the hiring process, I can't tell you much more."

"Well, I'm not looking to be murdered today, so thank—"

"Whoa. Hold on. No one is going to be murdering anyone on my watch. If you pass this phone screen, I'll be able to tell you everything before you accept the job. All right?"

The woman sighed. "What would you like to know about me?" Her voice played tricks on his brain. He hadn't spoken to many people in town since he'd arrived in February. Most of those conversations were with construction workers, most of them men, or people at the permit office, so why did she sound so familiar?

"Maybe your name?" Jace searched his bedroom for a piece of paper. Nothing. He grabbed his laptop off the spindle chair in the corner.

"Haven Haviland."

"That's unique," he called out in the direction of his phone.

"You should hear the names of the rest of my family."

Jace placed the laptop next to the phone, then booted it up. "And what is your experience?"

"I'm a licensed professional counselor in the state of Colorado. I ran a practice for four years and treated everything from suicidal thoughts, eating disorders, behavior management, trauma, physical abuse, sexual abuse . . ."

As she continued, Jace's thoughts ran wild. Age aside, this woman would be perfect for this job. Although with her qualifications, she might need more than the salary he'd had in mind. He could talk to the boss, or even give up a portion of his own salary. It would be worth it if the women could get the guidance they needed. That way, he wouldn't have to feel guilty heading to the next location in November. There'd be no repercussions when he left. Not like last time. He couldn't bear that again. He'd found his saving grace and her name was—

"I'm sorry," Jace interrupted. "What was your name again?"

"Haven Haviland." She proceeded to spell it, and Jace typed the name into a search engine.

The first thing to pop up was the website to her now-closed counseling practice, and then her picture. Jace rocked back on his heels until he found his breath. Haven Haviland was the girl in the chick tent.

And Jace Daring's simple world just got way more complicated.

Chapter Four

Daniel steered their father's 1967 Shelby Mustang GT500E down the curved drive, flinching each time a speck of gravel sprayed the precious car. When Haven snickered in the passenger seat, her brother shot her a glare. "Sure, go ahead and laugh now, but you're going to help me buff out any nicks later."

"It's not even your car. Dad just lets you drive it sometimes."

"It will be mine one day, remember?"

"When Dad passes on in thirty years."

"Think about how much more valuable it will be then—if it survives this jungle."

The car rocked as the front tire dipped into an unavoidable rut. As Haven's weight leaned against the passenger door, the cockeyed *No Trespassing* sign nailed to the tree out her window almost looked straight. "Why didn't you bring your truck? There's been no sign of life in this forest for twenty years. Were you expecting a smoothly paved road?"

"When you asked me to go with you to see about a job,

I figured it would be somewhere more professional." A lurch of the car forced the last word to sound more like a groan. "And I have a date after this."

"That explains why you smell like the set of an Axe body spray commercial. Who's the unlucky girl?"

"Her name's Melissa. No. Marissa. I met her in front of the deli counter at Foley's."

"And now the three pounds of sandwich meat in Dad's fridge makes sense."

"Yep. It took a while to get her number. One of her college friends kept interrupting and calling me a player."

"What would you call yourself?"

Daniel lowered his chin until his brow shaded his eyes. Classic deflection. As much as her heart pitied the deli counter girl, it ached for her brother even more.

"You've never spoken about what happened with you and Grace. If you want to talk—"

"I don't."

"Or about what Mom did?"

"I've told you. I'm your brother, Haven. Not a client."

The Shelby cleared the den of trees. Once Haven's eyes adjusted to the flood of sunlight on the windshield, she made out the shape of a dilapidated building three stories tall. The first story was composed of stone and formed a base for the wooden structure stretching above it. Off to the left, a tower reached even higher into the sky.

Beside her, Daniel expelled a breath. As an architect, he had a fondness for unique buildings. This one, even with its decrepit appearance from the gravel lot, had the potential to steal her brother's focus. "Check out that fieldstone foundation, the gabled roof, and the cupola up there. I heard someone had bought this old gristmill and was fixing it up, but I had no idea *this* was back here."

With Whisper Canyon's history as a ghost town, it wasn't too surprising to stumble upon remnants of the past, but this one was much bigger than a horseshoe or boot spur. Quickly, the hint of excitement within her fell to an overwhelming sense of dread. She double-checked the note she'd made on her phone as if the address she'd been given could match anything she saw here.

"Wait. Your interview is at this place?"

"I didn't see any other buildings on the driveway."

"And the guy gave you no details about the job?" Daniel drove over what appeared to be a recently cleared and groomed section of dirt.

"Not really. *Home behavioral specialist* could mean a million different things. I wasn't expecting this, though."

"I don't like this. What if the man you're meeting doesn't even own this property?" Daniel swung the car around to the side of the mill where a car or a person could easily plunge down the embankment into the rocky bed of Whisper Creek. What looked like a medieval torture device jutted out to the side, partially submerged. Given its broken spokes, the waterwheel had seen better days. "That's the perfect place for a serial killer to dispose of a body."

"Hold on." Haven pointed to a truck parked on the far edge of the lot, in the shade. "See that truck? Serial killers wouldn't drive a truck that nice."

"I'm not going to let you find out."

"Daniel." She covered his hand where it gripped the gear shift. "I need a job. I've almost depleted my savings, and I don't want to be a burden to Dad forever."

"Then reopen your counseling practice. How long does burnout last, anyway?"

"It's not that simple."

"Fine. Let me cover your expenses for a while."

"Just park the car."

"No way."

"I knew it might be a ruse. That's why I brought you. I'll let you come in with me."

Interest arched his brow, but he seemed to think better of it. "So he can get two victims for the price of one? I don't think so." He turned the wheel back toward the driveway to leave. "I'd never forgive myself if something happened to you, and I could've stopped it."

"Please, Oak?"

The name stopped the car's motion at once. After a long moment, he faced her. "Fine. I'll go in with you but remember, call me Daniel or nothing at all." The green in his eyes slid to near-black.

She squeezed his hand, hoping he couldn't feel the chill in her veins. "All right, Daniel. Let's go see what this is about."

After they parked near the front door, Haven attempted to exit the car as smoothly as possible in case her future employer was watching. Where had she seen that gray truck before? She chided herself as she slid her palms down over her slacks. That same nondescript F-150 could be found at every intersection, especially when the second-homers were in town.

"Do I look okay?" Haven brushed some lint off her blouse sleeve.

"Very professional, especially for a murder scene."

The rustic wooden door contrasted against the neon yellow *Caution: Enter at Your Own Risk* sign attached at eye level. So not helpful.

Haven resisted the urge to hang on Daniel's arm. "I guess we knock?" She rapped her knuckles on the wood to the beat of her heart battering her sternum.

Heavy footsteps approached them from inside. At the sight of the door's labored movement, Daniel stepped in front, protecting her but also blocking her view. All she could see was Daniel's spine straightening. "It's you," Daniel growled.

Curiosity forced Haven onto her tiptoes to see over Daniel's shoulder. Squarely facing them and donning a hard expression, the man from the farmers' market nearly filled the doorframe. Even as the man and Daniel prepared for a second brawl, the sight of him relieved all her worries. She scrambled between them. "It's you." The skyward lilt of her simple words spurred a flush that heated her cheeks.

The man met her gaze with his, and the smallest of smiles greeted her. He extended his hand. "I'm Jace. Jace Daring."

Haven slid her hand into his, relishing the warm skin of his palm against hers. A firm handshake might command respect, but that didn't seem necessary with this man. His hand looked strong enough to crack a stone, but he held hers with gentleness and restraint. They may as well have been back in the hatchery holding Audrey between them. "Haven Haviland."

"Jace Daring? Sounds like a fake name." The annoyed huff behind her brought her back to the present.

"You remember my brother, Daniel. He accompanied me so—"

"She wouldn't be killed. What kind of guy invites a woman to some abandoned mill in the woods? Let's go, Haven." Daniel gripped the crook of her elbow and tugged her.

Jace held tight to her hand. Or maybe she held tight to his.

"Please don't leave," he said before releasing his hold. "I told you during the phone screen that this job deals with sensitive information. I don't have the luxury of meeting potential employees in public places. Daniel can stay if it'll make you more comfortable."

"Haven, I don't care what job he's offering. You aren't working for this jerk."

"I want to at least speak to him. You don't have to protect me anymore. We aren't fifteen." It was all she needed to say to break through his heroics.

He angled his furrowed brows in her direction and heaved a sigh. "I'll battle you for it."

"This is ridiculous." Haven turned her back on Jace and rested her right fist on the open palm of her left hand. Daniel did the same, and together they whispered, "Rock, paper, scissors, shoot." Haven scissored the first two fingers of her hand, whereas Daniel spread his hand paper-flat. "Ha. Scissors beats paper. Now that we've settled that, Mr. Daring, I'm ready for my interview."

C all me Jace," he said, even as wisdom and something else battled inside him. Attraction? He had to watch it, especially if he might hire this woman. People, even beautiful women, were rarely what they seem. He stepped back from the door, welcoming her in.

"And you can call me Haven." She moved past him, carrying with her the sweetest flowery scent, so light he wondered if he'd just imagined it. But that smell was quickly overtaken by the stench Daniel brought with him. Did the guy bathe in cologne? And with the way he eyed Jace, his attitude stank just as bad. They were twins, she'd said that day. How on earth? Sure, they shared the same green eyes and tanned skin, but even now, Haven glanced around the beat-up building with wonder and grace. The same way she'd beheld that chick with the crooked toes. Her brother's face displayed only disgust, either with Jace, the mill, or both.

"My brother told me this used to be a mill."

"We're renovating it into a restaurant, aptly named The Mill."

"You've got a long way to go," Daniel interjected. He headed straight for the newly built staircase and stomped his foot on the first step.

Jace sniffed the air. With remnants of perfume and cologne gone now, the scent of new lumber mingled with the stench of musty rotted wood surrounding them. One task at a time. "Sure do. We finished that staircase yesterday. Now we can reach the second-floor dining area."

"Daniel's an architect. He loves poking around old structures."

Jace did a quick run-through in his head. Rosalie and Jillian were working the farm today, and Sonny had already left a half hour ago. All their personal information was sitting right here on this table. What harm could this guy do? "Feel free to check the place out. Just watch out for weak floorboards." Jace pulled a second chair up to the single table in the room. Binders leaned against the wall and loose papers hung over the edge of the table's surface. He should've organized his makeshift desk before she'd arrived.

"And leave you two alone?" Daniel scoffed.

"I'll be fine," she said. "Go explore. We'll be right here when you're done."

Once the guy fastened one last glower on Jace, he climbed the steps. Good. Jace wouldn't have to be as secretive about the job's details if the guy was out of earshot.

"I'm sorry about my brother. He's a bit protective of me."

"I'd be protective of you, too." Jace squeezed his eyes closed for a few seconds. "I mean, if you were my sister." Jace gathered the papers into a stack, not just to give her a clear space to sit, but to keep as much detail about Secondly's work hidden as possible. Haven was on a need-to-know basis.

She appeared unfazed by his words. "I thought I'd be working at a home of some sort, not a restaurant. I have to say, I worked as a waitress for one day, and it wasn't good."

"Let me guess. Two male customers brawled over you?"

"Pssh. No. That was a first. We used to have this seafood place here. On my way in, I'd named this one lobster in the tank. It had this marking on his face that looked like a mustache. My customer requested that one for his dinner. I quit right then and there." A childlike flicker danced in her eyes with the memory. A hint of innocence that breathed fresh air into this stale building and Jace's very soul.

"What was the lobster's name?"

"Clark Gable. If you can't tell, I love classic movies."

"Ah. I haven't seen many of those." Jace took the seat across from her.

"Your parents never made you watch them?"

"It was just my mom, and we didn't even have a television until I was fourteen."

"I'd be happy to share some of my favorites with you." She pressed her lips into a tight line, her expression soft and unreadable—a honed counselor skill? "I didn't mean it like that. Professionalism is extremely important to me."

Jace couldn't help but grin. "It's important to me as well. And I'm not looking for your help at the restaurant. This is connected to a larger mission. You would be helping my colleagues in this venture at another location. Mentoring them, essentially."

Haven tilted her head. "What might that entail?"

"My colleagues come from difficult pasts. They haven't always had the best opportunities or role models. I was trying to take that on but I'm in over my head with this renovation, and eventually I'll need to move on to a new town. That's why my boss approved the creation of this position. Your job would be to help them develop goals for themselves, aid them with schooling, and provide moral guidance."

"Moral guidance?"

"They have trauma they're working through. Essentially, I need someone to be there for them. It can't be too different from counseling. Could you tell me more about that experience?"

Her eyes shifted right to left and her manicured nails dug into the worn table. "I ran that practice for four years. My clientele ranged from children to the elderly." She perked up. "I was voted Whisper Canyon's favorite counselor four years in a row."

"That's impressive."

Was she blushing? "Not that impressive. I was the only counselor in town. Before that, people had to drive to Breckenridge. I guess they have to do that again." She quieted. The words she swallowed appeared to catch in her throat, and she gulped them away.

"It sounds like you loved helping your clients."

She nodded slowly.

"And then you closed. Why?" The question felt far too personal, but he needed to ask.

"My mother . . . She died in June. Cancer."

Her admission punched Jace straight in the gut. "I'm sorry."

"Thank you. She had a complicated place in our family. When she died, I wasn't myself. I needed a break."

"It must've been hard to walk away."

"Really hard." The sheen overtaking her eyes was so familiar. How many women had he seen with that same wistful regret worrying their brow? But this was different. Instead of wanting to help rescue Haven, he wanted to hold her. She maintained eye contact for a couple moments longer before she scooted her chair back a few inches and seemed to right herself. "But I'm ready to get back to doing what I do best. Being the person everyone leans on."

"A haven?"

"Yeah." She laughed. "My mom was a bit of a free spirit. She called each one of us *baby girl* or *baby boy* until she got a feeling for our gifts. Around age two she'd hold a ceremony for us. Only then would she give us our names. She said I had a way of bringing peace into the room. Even when my mother would have one of her episodes, she'd seek me out to settle her."

Jace could rest on that reassuring smile of hers, similar to the way Rosalie sometimes relaxed on the hammock. "I can see that about you."

"I get that sense with you, too." Her eyes pinched closed,

and her head gave a small shake. "Have I earned the right to know exactly what I'll be doing if I get this job?"

He didn't want to tell her. Not yet. This work wasn't for the faint of heart. After eleven years, Jace wore the exhaustion like a second skin. And if he told her and she fled, she was a liability.

Daniel descended the steps. "Haven, are you good?"

"We're fine. Jace was telling me more about the job." She slipped Jace a side-eyed glance, daring him to disagree.

But he wouldn't mutter a word with her fool of a brother lurking about.

"Can I check out the back?"

"Sure," Jace said.

"I was asking my sister."

"For the last time, I'm *fine*." Once Daniel had disappeared behind the staircase, she squared herself to face Jace across the table. "Now, tell me. You have no idea how many secrets I've had to bear in my work. I've never shared a single one. You can trust me, Jace."

He grasped for a deep breath. "As a counselor, I'm sure you have a strong sense of ethics and professionalism, but we ask everyone who learns the specifics of our work to sign a confidentiality agreement." He slid the printout toward her, along with a pen.

She stared at the paper a long time. Nearly long enough for Jace's heart to burst through his chest and push the pen into her hand. When she finally signed the agreement, relief washed over him.

"Thank you. I work for a group called Secondly. We go into places and offer sex workers and sex trafficking survivors a way out." He paused a moment, giving that truth a chance to sink in, but Haven didn't flinch or shy away. "Most don't take it. The ones who do, we offer them protection, refuge, and opportunities for a new life. There are all kinds of different avenues open for the women—coffee shops, bakeries, salons, bookstores, but all involve education, health care, and other resources. The avenue I offer them is the chance to start up and manage a farm-to-table restaurant."

Haven leaned forward in her chair.

Again, Jace caught that whiff of flowers. Tonight, he would sniff every bloom on the farm to see if he could place it. "All three of my colleagues are child sex trafficking survivors. Their personal histories include suffering and abuse. I want to help, but my hands are full. They need solid guidance from a female who can be a good example in all areas of life."

Haven's elbow slipped off the table. When her wrist hit the edge, the binder fell from its place, scattering the stack of papers onto the floor. Haven dropped to her knees to gather them. "I'm sorry. I'm really sorry." Her hands flitted about, scrambling to gather the fallen documents.

Jace joined her on the ground. "It's all right. Not a big deal."

Nevertheless, Haven moved about furiously trying to clean the mess. "I'm not the best example. I've made mistakes—"

He touched her hand—her trembling hand—and she stilled. "Neither am I."

She sank into a seated position, then raised her eyes to meet his.

"I need help, Haven. To give these women the best possible chance to make a good life. You don't have to be perfect. You just have to be there for them."

"You're in luck. Being there for people is my greatest skill."

"Hence the name, right?" Jace reluctantly pulled back his hand. Together, they gathered the last of the papers and reclaimed their seats. "Our farm is called Aspen Crossroads. The team lives in the main house. My cabin is a stone's throw away. There are three women. Sonny, Jillian, and Rosalie. Sonny has a three-year-old son named Elijah, who lives with them. That farmhouse is where I'd expect most of your work to take place. But Haven, the women, well, they're tough. This won't be the easiest job."

"I can hold my own. You've met Daniel and Rarity, and they're only half of my family."

Jace allowed himself a grin, but it fell as quickly as it appeared. "This isn't without risk. There's always a fear that someone from their former life will find them, and there has also been serious resistance from the powers that be in Whisper Canyon. Your involvement with us might tarnish their view of you."

At once, she folded her arms protectively across her stomach. "It's hard to tarnish something that didn't shine to begin with," she said in a mousy voice he could barely hear over Daniel's returning footsteps.

A curt nod was all he could muster. What was he thinking putting Haven in harm's way? All so Jace could get a few hours of sleep each night? So he could keep a rigid boundary? So he could keep from repeating past mistakes? But what choice did he have? He leaned back in his chair and stared hard at the ceiling, where a perfect hole the size of a corncob sat square between two rafters.

Please don't let this cause her harm, he silently prayed. Would God listen to him? The same God his mother told him about at the shelter or in the backseat of their car before she'd head out to earn their keep?

He scribbled Secondly's website on a scrap piece of paper, along with the generous salary the donors had contributed for the first year, and handed it to her. "Take a few days to think it over. I know I'm asking a lot of you. Maybe too much. I wouldn't ask if I weren't desperate."

After a moment, she stood and smoothed her shirt and

pants with an air too polished for this place. "Thank you for this interview. I would like some time." She reached for the slip of paper, and this time, when their hands touched slightly, neither one of them pulled away until Daniel stepped in.

Chapter Five

My fingers hurt, Mommy." Jace's teeth knocked together, fast and loud, like a train chugging down the tracks.

"I'm sorry, baby. I'm sorry." Mommy lifted his hand from beneath the blanket and then pressed his fingertips to her lips. Her breath formed a cloud that slid past his fingers and floated up until a shadow with long horns on the roof of the car ate it up. Jace puckered out his bottom lip and tried not to cry. Five-year-olds were supposed to be brave and strong. Except he didn't want to be brave or strong. He wanted to be warm, and he wanted Mommy to be warm.

Outside, the parking lot was dark except for some windows in the 'spensive hotel Mommy said they couldn't afford. He couldn't even see those anymore because the car windows were covered by tiny ice stars.

"I don't want to sleep in the car no more."

"Neither do I, but it's colder outside. Let's thank Jesus for the car."

Jace wanted to tell Mommy no. He wanted to thank Jesus for a room and a bed and a warmer blanket and hot chocolate and a big bowl of mac 'n' cheese. But that would make Mommy cry and he didn't like when that happened.

Outside, the wind whistled, and the shadows grabbed at them. One of the monsters scratched on his door, and he hid himself under the blanket. Even though he tried really hard not to, his body started to shake.

Mommy held him tighter against her chest. "Lord, thank you for this car. Without it . . . well, just thank you. And thank you for the crackers and juice to fill our bellies. Please help us through this cold night."

You died on a Sunday," Jace said to no one that could hear him. He took another step away from the safety of the path and toward the edge of the mountaintop. The toes of one boot reached over the drop-off. A few thousand feet beneath him, tiny cars filled the community church's parking lot just off Main Street. Hypocrites. Filling a stained-glass sanctuary and pretending their town is immune to the sins of man. They were wrong, and they'd been wrong for more than thirty-one years. Something happened down there. Something his mother never wanted to talk about.

This town is full of evil, she'd said that day. Why had she brought him here to her hometown? Was she looking for help or confrontation? Jace had been too young to understand. Other than a few sparse memories of the stone bear, an orange door, and that promise, he recalled nothing about Whisper Canyon.

"Forgive me, Mom." Jace's promise to her had broken into a hundred shards the moment he stepped foot in this canyon. Every day he felt those shards piercing him from the inside out. When Terrence first revealed he'd chosen this town for the next Secondly site, Jace had refused the job. Yet, after offering to walk alongside Rosalie, Jillian, and Sonny toward a new life, he'd felt responsible for their protection, at least until they got their footing. He couldn't put their safety in the hands of an inexperienced operator. He just couldn't.

After all, his mother had taught him what the Bible called *true religion*: to care for the widows and orphans. To love others who, like him and his mother, wouldn't be welcome in a church building by a church crowd. No, he'd let those people down below plan their picnics and sing their pretty hymns while wearing their finest attire. Meanwhile, he'd pray. He'd read scripture. And he'd defend the helpless.

"And what happens if I do find out who hurt you, Mom?" Jace forced the seethe of anger back down his throat.

His mother didn't believe in vengeance. *Turn the other cheek*, she'd say. And yet, she'd given him her surname—Daring. She'd wanted him to be brave and courageous. But how could he do both that and turn the other cheek? It was the latter advice that had left him orphaned sixteen years ago. If he'd fought instead of turning away from a threat, she'd still be alive.

His eyes burned, and he squinted against the hot tears that threatened . . . Jace lifted his eyes to the sun bursting through the morning's clouds and sucked in a lungful of chilled air.

"Jace, what are you doing?"

Lizzie Sautter held an armful of roses the color of her blood-drained face. The sight of her frightened eyes was enough to urge him back to safety.

"Sightseeing."

"If you don't mind, please sightsee from the path. No one wants to have their wedding on a mountaintop where someone died."

He shrugged. "Technically, I'd die down there, not up here."

Lizzie had been Terrence's first contact when he'd researched the town. She'd singlehandedly raised enough funds to finance the first-year salaries for the women and Haven, should she accept the job. All while preserving the specific details of Secondly's work. She'd become a friend of sorts to Jace over the last six months. Like him, she was a bit of an outcast in town.

Jace glanced over his shoulder at the sunken town of Whisper Canyon. "I hope you don't mind. I've never seen anyone here on Sunday mornings before."

"I don't mind. However, you do know there are churches in town, right? Ones that actually perform services and have Mass."

"I prefer this." He nodded to the small stone chapel crowning the top of Chapel Peak.

"Suit yourself. I'll be gone in a few. The florist is too sick to deliver the flowers for this afternoon's nuptials, so I said I would."

"The work of a wedding chapel owner is never done, I see. Let me help you with those flowers." Jace made his way to the open back door of the late-nineties Cadillac. He retrieved a stack of pungent boxes. If these were full of the same white roses Lizzie was carrying, then he could eliminate that from the list of flowers Haven smelled of. Nasty things. Why did girls like them so much? He carried as many boxes as he could to the back door of the chapel.

Jace stopped short of the door's threshold and waited for Lizzie to meet him.

"Thank you. Don't these smell heavenly? Roses are so romantic." She sighed, staring off into space like the blonde in that *Tangled* movie Elijah watched. "And don't you start about romance being the stuff of fiction again. I won't hear it."

"I won't as long as you remember that not all men are out to fall in love. Most only want one thing. How do you think the women at Aspen Crossroads ended up where they are? And before Aspen Crossroads, the women in Cheyenne, Ruidoso, Fargo, Tucson . . . Romance is a sure way to end up—"

"Working the streets?"

"I was going to say that romance is a sure way to end up with a broken heart. I want better for you."

"Thanks for looking out for my best interests, but I'm sure there are good men out there. Like my grandpa. Like you."

Jace felt light-headed, and he couldn't blame the altitude. He'd been through this before. "Lizzie, I'm not looking for—"

"Oh, gracious, Jace. I know you're married to your work. And besides, I want a man who will write swoony love letters and dance with me in the rain. A man who will see me across the room and has a smile just for me." Lizzie disappeared inside the chapel.

Jace leaned back against the stone to take in the mountaintop scene. Married to his work. Nothing wrong with that. Better than being conned by love.

"That's it," she said as she reemerged. "I can keep it unlocked if you want to go inside."

"Nah. I'd rather stay out here."

"Suit yourself. Any more calls about the job?" Lizzie closed the back door and then inserted the key in the lock.

"Yeah, I offered it to someone. Do you know the Haviland family?"

Her hand stilled. "Of course. Michael Haviland—the father—gave a generous gift when I was looking for donors. And he isn't exactly wealthy. Simply a great guy." A curious look crossed her brow. "Which of his children did you hire?"

"Haven. Did I make a mistake?"

Lizzie grinned. "No. Haven will be perfect."

"Are you friends?"

"No, but I don't have many friends under the age of sixty. The twins were two years ahead of me—Haven and Daniel." Lizzie seemed to lose her breath a bit on the brother's name. "From what I know, Haven is level-headed and dependable. The only thing . . ."

"What?"

"It's gossip. And it probably isn't even true, so forget it."

Jace straightened up. "Lizzie, I'm hiring her to be a mentor. It isn't too late. I can still recant the offer."

"Don't do that. There are rumors about why she closed her practice. That maybe she fell for a client, became obsessive over him, even though he was married."

"Not possible."

"I don't believe it, either," Lizzie said.

Jace scratched at his neck until it burned. "What client is the rumor about?"

"I shouldn't have spoken. I'm sure it isn't true. It goes against everything I know about her. The ladies at my grandpa's senior center love to gab about anything and anyone, whether it's true or not."

"Who was he, Liz?"

"I've gotta go. If I hurry, I can make the next service and be back before the bride's family begins setup." She dashed past him toward her car.

"Lizzie, please. I know you don't want to spread gossip, but if there's any possible chance this rumor could harm Jillian, Sonny, Rosalie, or Elijah . . ."

She stopped, then slowly turned to face him. "The mayor."

Chapter Six

No one in the congregation so much as coughed as Mayor Trent Garrison addressed them from the pulpit. His pressed button-down glared a harsh white against the black leather Bible he held in his hands. As with his public speeches about town affairs, the words from the Sunday-morning reading sailed from between his lips.

Haven heard only his lies. Her breaths felt far too shallow to keep her upright in the pew, but she didn't dare inhale any deeper while sandwiched between her sisters.

At Trent's side, his wife, Elaine, caressed her ever-rounding belly and gazed at her husband lovingly, foolishly. Haven knew the feeling. Once Trent closed the Bible, he smiled at Elaine. She spread her hands wide and said, "Let us pray." In her well-manicured, former Miss Colorado voice, she led the congregation in prayer.

But between the words, Haven felt stares searing her bowed head. She sneaked a glance up front, where Trent focused hard on Haven.

A swell of heat climbed her neck, and the shame she'd been trying to hide for months slicked her forehead with perspiration.

God forgive me.

Once the service let out, Haven welcomed her father's arm around her shoulder as they exited the church. She plastered on a smile and skimmed the crowd, keeping her focus two inches above everyone's heads. Confident and invulnerable.

Until she recognized Elaine Garrison's voice greeting Valor. Haven became all too aware of Trent standing on her right, that expensive cologne roiling her stomach. And to think, that had once smelled good enough to melt all reason in her brain.

"Valor, I have an idea about honoring the town's first responders. I'd love to run it past you," Elaine said. With soft features and a sweet smile, she was beautiful, and far too trusting to be married to a man like Trent. For the five hundredth time, Haven debated whether she should share the truth with Elaine, even if it would break the expectant mother's heart.

Trent angled toward her and her father. "And Michael, I have some thoughts about next summer's car show. I want to make it even bigger. You, Bo Radford, and I need to set up a meeting."

"I'd like that," her father said.

"And I need to get an est—"

Rarity stepped between them. "I'd like to meet with you about your so-called mission to 'clean up' Whisper Canyon. Do you plan to get rid of all the unique shops on Main Street or only the ones you haven't invested in?"

Trent smiled. "Miss Haviland, you can call my assistant and set up a meeting. I'll tell you about our auspicious plans to make Whisper Canyon an even better place to live and work. Perhaps your sister could sit in with us. She and I share the desire to help everyone in our town, don't we, Haven?"

"Dad," Haven said. "I feel like walking back to the house. I'll see you there in a bit."

Concern deepened the lines in her father's forehead even more than usual. "That's quite a walk."

"I wore my comfy sandals. I'll be fine." Haven kissed his cheek, never once looking in Trent's direction, before heading north on Main Street.

The street got quieter the more space she put between her and the church. As she waited at the crosswalk, she noticed a man peering into the front door of the library, a cowboy hat in one hand and a short stack of thin books in the other. Jace Daring's sandy blond hair was even lighter in the sunlight, but it was him, all right. When the *Walk* sign appeared, Haven crossed the street toward the library on the corner.

"It's closed on Sundays."

He twisted his body toward her voice. When he saw her, the smile that appeared on his face set something inside her to bloom. "I'm picking up on that. I have some books to return." He jogged down the concrete steps to meet her.

Haven scanned the book spines. "Big fan of Clifford the Big Red Dog?"

"They're Elijah's—Sonny's little boy. But, yeah. Clifford's cool. I prefer Elephant and Piggie, though."

"Hmm. I'll have to look them up."

"You should. Mo Willems is ahead of his time."

"All the great ones are. There's a drop-off box over here." She led him to the receptacle and then held the door open while he slid the books inside.

At the light, one car honked. The light had turned green and yet a Land Rover driven by Wendy Hollingsworth, a childhood neighbor, didn't move. From the driver's seat, Wendy stared at Jace and Haven, all while laughing. To be nice, Haven gave a small wave just as the car behind Wendy's honked again. The Land Rover took off and something that sounded like *homewrecker* sailed from the windows.

Haven nearly choked on her sharp intake of breath. After a moment, she was able to collect herself, all the while hoping she hadn't lost her ability to dismiss all emotion from her face, save compassion.

Jace, however, didn't carry that skill. He wore troubled like it was made by Maybelline.

"You came from church?" he asked.

"Yes. I decided to walk home. I live over there on Copper Kettle Way." She pointed toward the park, where Main Street came to an end at a traffic circle.

When she turned back, Jace was still staring at her with full intensity. He must have heard either Wendy's shout or the rumors surrounding Haven and her family. Was this the part when he retracts the job offer? What would she do then? She couldn't stay unemployed forever. Yet the idea of leaving Whisper Canyon to head somewhere mistakes couldn't follow simply wasn't an option. The last time she'd left her family had been catastrophic. Instead, Jace looked up and down the street before settling his gaze on hers. "Would you like company?"

A dash of hope tap-danced on her heart. Haven bit her bottom lip and nodded in the direction of her dad's house.

As Jace joined her side, he moved his hat from one hand to another. "Does your whole family go to church with you?"

"No. Only Valor, Rarity, and my dad. My little sister, Dash, does, too, when she's in town."

"Valor, Rarity, Dash, and Haven?"

"I told you we have interesting names. Daniel's first name is Oak, but he made us stop calling him that a while ago."

"I see. Does Daniel go to church with you?"

"He used to, but after my mom left, he stopped," Haven said. That, of course, was only the beginning of her family's troubles, but Jace didn't need to know all those details.

"I thought you said she passed away in June."

"She did. She abandoned us when I was sixteen to start a new life. In October, she returned with a terminal diagnosis. I guess no one in her new life was willing to care for her in the end."

"Hmm."

"Too much information. Sorry."

"Why are you sorry?"

Haven shrugged. "I shouldn't burden others with my problems."

"You can burden me." His eyes, the color of the clear Colorado sky, shot wide open. "Not that it's a burden at all. It isn't. I mean, we both know what it's like to live without our mothers. My mom died when I was fifteen."

"I'm sorry. What from?"

Behind them, the church bells clanged, announcing the eleven o'clock hour. Jace was silent for all eleven chimes. Once they quieted, he glanced at Haven. "She was killed."

"Oh, Jace. I . . ." Haven's tongue tangled on words until Jace reached over and yanked her against his side. She expelled a breath, only to realize he'd saved her from colliding with a park bench.

"Didn't want you getting hurt," he explained.

"Thank you."

"You're welcome." He flustered a bit. "My mom grew up in Whisper Canyon."

"She did? Is that why you chose this location?"

"I didn't choose it. My boss did. I think it was his way of making me confront my family's past."

"And you don't want to?"

Again, the hat switched hands. "I don't think my mother's time here was all that great. In fact, she never talked about her life here even though we talked about everything." At that, he fit his hat to his head, pulling the brim low.

"I see. I could always help you find out more—"

"I don't want to."

His curt response sent a chill over Haven's skin. She rubbed her hands on her arms to smooth the gooseflesh.

He stared down at her. Concern replaced the scowl. "Are

you cold? Would you like my jacket?" Before she could answer, he shrugged it off.

"I'm fine."

"You have goose bumps." His hand moved to touch her arm, but he must have thought better of it because he snapped it back. Instead, he stretched the jacket wide and placed it around her.

The leather sagged, since his shoulders were much broader than hers, not to mention his muscles. Although the jacket lacked the correct fit, it bestowed immeasurable warmth, and not only the physical kind. Haven inhaled the rustic and masculine scent of a man who had bigger concerns than dousing himself in cologne, and yet it took all of Haven's self-control to not bury her nose in the jacket to fully appreciate it.

Focus, Haven. "Jace, it was your answer, not the weather, that gave me chills. I didn't mean to pry."

"Oh." His face fell. "That sounded much harsher than I intended." He wet his lips as he prepared an explanation Haven had no right to. She was about to say as much, but he spoke first. "My mother was only sixteen when she left Whisper Canyon. I believe she was forced to leave. I'm not sure. All I know is my earliest memories are of homeless shelters and sleeping in cars. She did whatever she had to do to take care of me. I don't want to know what happened to her for that life to be the better option."

Haven clasped her hands in front of her so she wouldn't grab his. This guy made her want to break all her counseling rules. Again. Words were all she'd let herself offer. "It sounds like she loved you very much."

He nodded. "I'm sure your mom did as well."

Haven tried a smile, but Jace didn't seem to buy it. She almost didn't mind. Something about Jace Daring made her feel like she could be honest. How great would that be? To find a haven in someone else.

And not one that dissolved at the end of every counseling session. She glanced down. There was a time Trent would've offered her his jacket. He had offered her everything else—a shoulder to cry on, a listening ear, a soothing touch. She'd been such a fool.

Behind them, a vehicle approached, but didn't pass. Haven's nerves devolved into a tizzy even without a glance. Please, not Wendy again. Then Haven realized they were almost to the park. And behind that? The mayor's mansion.

The engine revved, and the black Escalade sped down the street. In the side mirror, Trent watched them.

"Another friend of yours?" Jace was eyeing her. Reading her.

"Not in the least."

"He's been our biggest opponent in buying the farm and mill. He's one of the few that knows about our organization's mission, and he's adamantly against us 'sullying his town,' to use his words." Jace peered at her through expectant eyes.

Unfortunately, she pulled no weight with the powers that be in Whisper Canyon. "I'm sorry. I can't help you."

He looked down at his boots.

Was that his reason for offering her the job? So she could butter up the town for the sake of the restaurant? Was he using her the same way Trent used her? A lump formed in her throat at the very idea. On instinct, she stripped the jacket off and handed it back to Jace without even a thank-you. She steered them west down Copper Kettle Way. Who was she kidding? She didn't have the luxury of saying no to this job offer, no matter what his intentions were. Besides, soon enough he'd realize she wasn't in a place to butter anyone up, thanks to those rumors.

It wasn't until her father's house came into view that either of them spoke again.

"You're turning down the job?" He looked more than disappointed. He looked . . . hurt.

Haven slowed, gripping his arm to turn him toward her.

"No, Jace, I want the job. I was going to call you this afternoon. I meant I can't help with Trent—the mayor."

His eyes seemed to brighten to a more crystalline shade of blue. He lurched forward the slightest bit, almost like he'd meant to hug her, but he didn't, of course. That wouldn't be professional. Instead, he shuffled his feet back. "Thank you, Haven. Truly."

Chapter Seven

"Any news on Momma Daring?" Sonny finished rolling out the dumpling dough for supper and dotted her floury fingertip on Elijah's nose. The boy's eyes crossed as he peered at the smear of white against his tawny skin.

Jace carried the cutting board over to the stove and, using the knife, scraped the diced onions, celery, and carrots into the stockpot. He set the board and knife by the sink, then grabbed a wooden spoon from the drawer closest to the oven. "Nice try, Sonny." Although she was six years younger than Jace, she had the big-sister role nailed down.

"If you don't start researching her, I'm gonna do it for you."

Jace struck her with a glare.

"Don't roll those baby blues at me, Jace Daring. I'll put you in timeout. Isn't that right, 'Lijah?"

"Jace is sassy," the boy said, clapping his hands and sending up a cloud of flour into the air above the kitchen island. "Look, Mommy, a cloud." He giggled, then sneezed.

"Oh, baby, no. Don't sneeze on the dumplings," Sonny said.

Jace snickered. "It's fine. It adds protein. But when we

get the restaurant going, we might need a no-flour-cloud rule in the kitchen, eh, 'Lijah?"

Elijah pretended to sneeze again and looked at Jace.

"Now you're just being goofy," Jace said. The melted butter bubbled, begging for a stir, and he obliged.

"What if you have family here? Maybe they're one of the millionaires up in the hills, just waiting for an heir to bless."

"Or maybe they're looking for another family member to scorn."

Sonny sighed. "Sadly, that's probably true. Not many of us came from loving homes."

Speaking of those with a terrible childhood . . . "Where's everyone else?"

"Rosalie discovered John Hughes. She's in her room bingeing every eighties teen movie."

"She should be studying for her GED test."

"That's what I said. Jillian's probably out tanning. I tried to tell her that pale skin of hers will never do anything but fry in the sun, but she won't listen to me or Rosalie. Stubborn as the night is long, that girl."

"True, true. I picked up a journal for her."

Sonny shook her head. "If you keep buying her nice things, she's going to try to pay you back the only way she knows how."

"It's a journal. I got Elijah that truck, you that set of knives, and Rosalie—"

"You know Jillian, though. You're her knight in shining armor. Are those onions clear yet?"

"Clear?"

"Step aside," Sonny said, shooing him with a wave of her hand. "Just watch yourself. I've seen men more innocent than you give in to their cravings, and I don't mean for chicken and dumplings."

"That brings up an important point. I've hired someone to take over the mentoring stuff."

Sonny's spoon stopped stirring at once.

Jace sighed. It was bad enough he was still having to convince himself hiring Haven was a good idea. Now he had to convince Sonny. "Hear me out."

"I'm doing great," she said.

"I know you are. But Jillian and Rosalie—"

"I can take care of my own. That includes them."

"You need to focus on Elijah. And besides that, Jillian and Rosalie don't always listen to you, remember?"

"Elijah, go on and play with your trains in the other room. Mommy's going to give Jace here a piece of her mind."

The boy didn't waste any time hurrying down from the stool and out of the kitchen.

"Sonny, you know I'm moving on to Austin in November. Haven is well connected. She's lived here her whole life. She'll help you all settle in and form roots. Isn't that what you said you wanted that day we met on the street? Roots for you and 'Lijah? I can't give you that. Maybe Haven can."

"Haven? That's not even a name. It's a paint color in a Pottery Barn magazine."

"Sonny, give her a chance. For me."

She held the spoon out toward him like a sword, only to surrender moments later. "When is she starting?"

"Monday."

"Like five-days-from-now Monday?"

"I wanted to give you a few days to get used to the idea."

"Can't believe I signed up for this," she muttered. "Hand me that bowl of chicken stock."

After he did as she asked, Sonny held the liquid above the sautéed vegetables. "But you know I'm not the one you've gotta worry about. It's Miss Thing out there. I can guarantee she won't be too happy sharing you." At that, she poured the stock into the pot and the contents screamed as a plume of steam reached the ceiling.

Chapter Eight

"Dad, you in here?" Haven heaved open the door to her father's shop. Funny how the familiar combination of paint and grease could be so welcoming. An old Brooks & Dunn song streamed from the CD player. "She Used to Be Mine." *Oh, Dad.* He was a glutton for punishment. He hadn't deserved what her mother did.

"Over here, love." A hand waved above the far side of a windshield.

"A 'Vette? What year?" She caressed the rich blue hood that had seen better days.

"It's a '72 Stingray. I'm finishing up an estimate and project outline for a full-car restoration."

Her dad scrawled on a notepad as he sat in the driver's seat. "When I'm done, how about we grab a pizza?"

"You shouldn't eat pizza, Dad. Your heart."

"I'll get a salad to go with it. Deal?"

"Deal," she said. "So, I found a job."

"Did you?" He glanced up at her, a proud smile beaming. "A counseling job?"

"Sort of. More like mentoring or life coaching."

"Where's your office?"

"Not an office. It's a farm. Aspen Crossroads."

"The one—"

"Yes, Dad, the one. But you don't have to worry. It isn't a harem or anything like that. The owner's name is Jace, and I think you'd like him very much. Lots of integrity and a real desire to help people."

"And he's your boss?"

"Colleague is more like it. We're both working for Secondly—an organization that helps people get back on their feet."

"At that restaurant, right? That Sautter girl—Lizzie— came by back in spring. She was looking for financial support for it."

"And did you give any?"

"What I could."

"You're the best. It's money well spent, I assure you. I'm not at the restaurant, though. I'll be working at the farm."

His jolly laugh shook the vinyl convertible top.

Growing up, Haven wasn't exactly outdoorsy. "I know what you're thinking, and no, I won't be doing farm chores unless I need to. I'll do whatever it takes to earn my clients' trust."

Her dad climbed out of the car. "That won't be hard. You are the kindest soul I know. Your care and compassion shine through all you do. That's what makes even the hardest hearts come to you." He made his way to the sink, wet his hands, and began lathering them with soap. "Even your mother. You were so good with her, right up until the end."

"It wasn't easy." Haven let her eyes roam the room, finally focusing on the neon *Open* sign.

He tossed the paper towel in the trash bin then put his arm around her. "I'm proud of you for taking on this new challenge. You aren't you if you aren't helping someone find their way."

"Thanks, Dad," she said, leaning into his embrace. "Jace's family is from here. Did you ever know any Darings?"

"Doesn't sound familiar. Sorry, love." He checked his watch. "Almost closing time. Let me finish writing up this estimate real quick, then off to dinner we shall go."

A not-so-quick calculation led to a cost that made Haven raise her brows. "I thought you said people around here had fallen out of love with classic cars."

"Many of them have. If they have the money, they buy new, and then I don't get any work. As you know, it costs money to live in Whisper Canyon and run a business. That's why this big job is a blessing. Not only that, but it will be free advertising for the shop."

"Oh yeah?" Haven kneeled to pick up her dad's Maglite flashlight off the floor before he stumbled on it. "Who's the lucky customer that gets to benefit from your magic touch?"

The shop's heavy door swung open, and the sound of dress shoes clacking on concrete echoed around her.

"Hello, mayor," her dad said.

When Haven stood, the flashlight slipped from her hand and clattered loudly on the cement floor.

"What's the damage, Mr. Haviland?" Trent moseyed between her and her dad. "Hello, Haven. It's good to see you, as always."

Haven nodded but caged her litany of middle school swear words behind her teeth.

Her dad stapled the sheets of paper before handing them to Trent. "Here's my evaluation. You won't find a lower price anywhere in Colorado for this amount of work. But once I'm done with her, I guarantee she'll be able to win any of the NCRS events."

Trent laughed. "Chump change. Could you have it completed before the election? I'd like to use it for my victory parade."

"Victory parade? Aren't you running unopposed?"

"I am. That's a reason for celebration as well. Would you mind if I came by every now and then to learn from you?

Maybe even help?" Even though he spoke to her father, his stare was locked on her.

Haven needed air. "Dad, I'll take a rain check on that pizza."

"Why is that, love?"

"I didn't get my run in this morning, but maybe tomorrow night."

An hour later, Haven rounded the corner to head back toward her dad's house. It had turned out to be a nice night for a run. Cool and mostly quiet until now. Sassy's Saloon was hosting a street concert, and Haven was happy to distance herself from the lights and sound. She passed Haviland Restorations, the *Open* sign now darkened in the front window.

When she stepped in front of the alley, a figure reached out and grabbed her, pulling her into the narrow divide between buildings where no moonlight or streetlight dared touch. A cry sprang from her throat, but a hand muffled it as her kicking feet dragged through the gravel.

"Shh, it's me. Don't scream." The hand fell from her mouth and the arm loosened enough for her to face the man. Trent Garrison's stupidly gorgeous face was barely recognizable without light, but his cologne provided proof of who stood before her, dangerously close. "I've missed you."

She opened her mouth to protest, but he covered it with his, pressing a hot, needy kiss against her lips. When Haven pushed off his chest, he followed until she was pinned between his body and the brick wall. Had there really been a time when she'd welcomed such kisses?

Haven clenched her teeth, nearly biting him in the process, but at least he pulled back enough to let her breathe. "Get off me, Trent."

"You don't want that." He thrust himself forward again.

Haven turned her cheek to him, and the same slimy lips that had spun her into his web of lies slid down to her neck. Summoning all the anger from the past few months, Haven shoved Trent back.

Trent held up his hands in surrender. "Okay, okay. I get it. We'll pick that up later."

"Not a chance. Have you forgotten what you did to me?"

"Have you forgotten what you *do* to me? You fell for me, too. Admit it."

"Only because you lied. You said you granted your wife the divorce she'd demanded, so long as she kept it hidden until after the election. For six months, session after session, I listened to you talk about how heartbroken you were."

"How do you know the divorce wasn't finalized?"

"She's carrying your child."

"It's probably not even mine. I don't love her. I love you. My heart is broken for you."

"You lied, and you took advantage of me in my most vulnerable time. You cost me everything."

"Hey, I didn't make you close your practice."

"I broke the professional code of ethics for counselors. I had to shut my doors. It's called integrity, and you should try it sometime."

"I wish you hadn't. I miss our sessions. It's been too long." Again, he crushed her against the wall, pressing his mouth against hers so hard her lips stung, and she tasted blood.

"Trent, no."

"Maybe I'm not getting a divorce. The people in this town would never accept a divorced mayor." His fingers trailed down the side of her throat and paused on her clavicle, but his eyes kept going down from there. "That doesn't change how I feel about you."

"It changes how I feel about you." Haven shoved him off. "Don't touch me again, or I'll tell everyone what you did."

"Need I remind you who your mother was? Don't turn this into a game of he said, she said. No one would believe the daughter of Nina Haviland didn't seduce the mayor away from his loving, pregnant wife." His voice, full of gravel, scraped down her spine. A shadow traveled across his face, sharpening the lines of his brow, nose, and jaw. The small scar on his cheekbone that she'd once found handsome now cut a threatening arrow in her direction. "What about the rest of your family? What about your father? He's restoring a car for me. If you say a word about me, he may find himself on the other end of a lawsuit over unethical business practices."

"My father runs a clean business."

He leaned closer. "And proving that in a court will bankrupt him. Then there's Rarity's shop. And Daniel's work with the town's planning and development office. I could destroy your whole family. But I don't want that. I want you."

"No."

"Okay. What about Aspen Crossroads?"

Heat raced into Haven's face. "What about it?"

"When a nonprofit wants to come into our town, raise donations, buy up farmland, and build a new restaurant, they come to the mayor."

"And?"

"I saw you talking to Daring. Is he the reason you don't want to keep seeing me?"

"There are a million reasons I won't keep seeing you."

"And I *won't* have this town associated with prostitution. It will heap humiliation on Whisper Canyon. My ancestors would roll in their graves. A Garrison won't allow it." He seethed between his teeth, so close to Haven she worried he might kiss her again, or maybe do something worse.

She may not be the bravest, most adventurous Haviland, but she wouldn't be intimidated, either. "Perhaps it's time for someone other than a Garrison to lead this town."

He pointed a finger in her face. "Stay away from Jace Daring, or you'll regret it."

"Then I can add it to my list of regrets."

"You don't want me and him to engage in battle. I always win. Always."

"Go home to your wife, Trent."

He expelled his breaths so loudly, Haven thought he might start to howl. He reared back his hand and swung it toward her face. She flinched, but his hand flattened against the wall next to her head. "You're as crazy as your mother if you think I'll let him take you from me without a fight."

She stood at her full height, although she wondered if her scream could even be heard over the concert, should he lose his control. Thankfully, before she had to test that, he took off down the alley and disappeared.

Haven fell back against the wall and pressed her hand to her mouth before the sobs she'd been holding back for months reached her lips. How had she been so dumb to fall for Trent's lies? A quiet divorce? She should've known better. And then to give him all of herself, despite everything she believed?

Now she'd put her family in the man's crosshairs. Maybe she wasn't any better than her mother. Would her foolish actions cause trouble for those she loved? And what about Aspen Crossroads and The Mill? What about Jace?

Chapter Nine

Jace knocked a quick three times on the door and waited, cursing himself for taking time away from the farm to deal with such matters. He'd started this Monday hopeful. Everything was in place for success. Haven would swoop in and help Rosalie, Sonny, and Jillian, and he could concentrate on the farm and the restaurant. They'd be in good hands when he'd pack his things and leave for Texas in November.

Then he'd listened to her voice mail. Although he'd tried to put it and Haven out of his mind for his morning work, he couldn't. *Angry* didn't describe the feel of his fevered blood racing through his veins. He'd confided in her about their purpose, the women's pasts, his mother . . . He'd invited her in, and she'd teased him into thinking she was reliable. Just like Marjorie had. Had he learned nothing since he was sixteen years old? If Haven was going to pull this, she'd have to say it to his face.

He knocked again. From inside the house, the floorboards creaked. The curtain blocking the door's windowpane pulled back enough to allow a sliver of Haven's face to appear. The door rattled then gave way to reveal Haven dressed far differently from her church dress or farmers' market casual. While the top of her body was cinched into a plain, fitted tank top, the lower half was drowning in wide-legged pants that pooled extra fabric around her feet. Her curls frizzed, and a cowlick lifted one section of hair on her crown high enough that he might have laughed in other circumstances.

"Hi, Jace." She kept her puffy eyes low and chewed her lip the same way Elijah did when he spilled his juice.

Be firm. He held up his phone. "A voice mail? That's all I get?" The question came out broken as if it were spoken by someone less self-assured and self-reliant than he was. "I mean, sure, we don't know each other that well, but I think I deserve more than a voice mail if you're going to get my hopes up, only to leave me in the lurch."

The sight of her pretty lips bowing into a frown shattered any remaining frustration inside him.

"Was it me? Something I said or did?"

"Of course not. It was me and a situation I got myself into."

He nodded—an invitation for her to continue.

"There are things from my past that would jeopardize Aspen Crossroads and all the good work you're doing there. I won't let that happen."

The rumor. *Jesus, don't let the rumor be true*, he prayed. "Tell me what it is, and we'll figure out a way around it."

"Jace . . ." Her gaze flitted to the porch roof, and she blinked a few times.

Please, no tears. Jace never knew how to handle tears.

"You better come inside." She stepped back and held the door for him.

Inwardly, he cringed. What use was it getting drawn even deeper into her world—emotionally and physically? He should cut his losses and leave now. Take his chances that he could handle the rest of the Whisper Canyon job without anyone's help. So why on earth was he now bending down to untie his boots?

Minutes later, he was standing in the Haviland family room and waiting for the glass of water she'd offered him. The home was modest, like most of the homes built against this part of the canyon wall. Perhaps a bit too small for . . . How many Haviland children were there again?

He scanned the shelves surrounding the television. In an oak picture frame, five children circled two adults. One face captured his attention first. Dark curls, green eyes, and the gentlest grin were instantly recognizable. Other than the braces and the fuller cheeks, Haven's appearance hadn't changed much since that picture was taken.

"Don't look at that," she said, stepping between him and the family portrait.

"Why not?"

"Talk about an awkward phase. I used to eat a lot of ice cream."

"What's wrong with that? Sounds kind of ideal."

"Not if you get made fun of at school for being on the heavier side. Meanwhile, Daniel was Mr. Popular, as always. Dash was the talented one."

"Wait. Dash Haviland, the soccer player?"

"The darling of the U.S. Olympic team? You got it. See? Dash was the talented one. Valor was the star student. Rarity was . . ." She glanced over her shoulder to where a teenage girl sported an oversize beehive hairstyle and exaggerated eye makeup. "Rarity was the eccentric one. This was taken during her Amy Winehouse phase. And I was just there."

"When was this?"

"Um, 2007, I think. I was thirteen."

"So that makes you twenty-seven now?"

"Yeah, in January. And you're . . . ?"

"Thirty-one. Although I feel a whole lot older than that."

"I'm guessing that's a hazard both of our professions share. We absorb lifetimes of tragedy and sin, so the people we help don't have to." She placed the glass of water in his hand, and his fingers slid between hers. Instead of allowing the touch to linger—a habit of theirs, he'd discovered—she let go and moved to the couch. Haven scooped up a throw pillow and hugged it against her chest as she sat on one end of the sofa.

Jace lowered himself on the other end, keeping a full seat between them.

"What I'm about to tell you is something that no one knows. I don't confide in people. They confide in me. In fact, I'm only telling you because it's become a threat to you." She took in a breath and released it slowly. "I had a run-in with the mayor last night." In her lap, Haven's hands clutched the edges of the pillow until the veins bulged beside her strained knuckles. "Trent—the mayor—we have a past."

Jace turned in his seat to face her more squarely. Lizzie had warned him about this, yet Jace wanted to hear it from Haven. "What kind of past?"

The answer to that question declared itself in the way her brows knit together. She worked her jaw, but still, her chin trembled slightly. In his line of work, he'd seen the way shame seemed to live in the irises of the human eye.

"I see."

"He was a client of mine. He'd claimed his wife divorced him, and he was distraught. For six months, we had weekly sessions. He said they were waiting to make the divorce public knowledge after the upcoming election. God help me, I believed his lies."

Haven heaved a deep breath. "During the same time, my mother was dying, and my family was a wreck. For the first time in my life, someone let me confide in *them*. Trent made me feel loved, cherished, and I let down every guard. The week after my mother died, I gave in completely."

His gut clenched. "You slept with him?"

She gave a tiny nod. "Just once. Not that it matters. Then, they announced their pregnancy. I broke things off immediately and I never told a soul. Still, there are rumors."

Jace chugged a couple of gulps of water, hoping to wash away the image of Haven with Garrison. But it remained.

"I should have been honest with you from the start. That was why I closed my practice. I couldn't keep it open knowing I'd gone against my personal and professional code of ethics. I'd always planned to wait until I was married, but I was in such a bad place. Nothing mattered anymore."

"He preyed on you. For six months, he spun lies."

"Longer than that. He once told me he'd wanted me in his bed since I was sixteen. He was always sending me e-mails and notes, inviting me to do internships at his office when I had no interest in politics."

"How old was he then?"

"Maybe twenty-nine or thirty?"

"A predator, in every sense." Jace recognized the signs too well. "You shouldn't blame yourself."

"Well, he saw us talking yesterday. He demanded I stay away from Aspen Crossroads and you. Or else."

The muscles in Jace's shoulders pulled tighter than a tractor's fan belt. He tilted his head to one side, then the other to stretch out the muscles. He scooted closer to Haven on the couch. "I've faced worse threats than him. I can handle Trent Garrison."

"What about me?"

Jace smirked. "Like, can I handle you?"

Her eyes widened, and for one slight moment, the guilt, shame, and worry slipped away on an audible breath that made Jace chuckle.

"Sorry. Not a good time for a joke. We need you at Aspen Crossroads, especially due to the opposition. If this venture fails, where will the women go? It must succeed. Failure isn't an option in this game." Jace peered deeper into her eyes. "And in the meantime, I'll do everything I can to protect you from Garrison. But why haven't you said anything?"

"Because no one would believe me. My mother had a

reputation. She cheated on my father . . . a lot. She actually did wreck several homes. Everyone in town knew about it. Ever since, people have pitied my father, but it's like they are waiting for my sisters and me to turn out like her. This would only make it worse. Plus, my dad's business is struggling, and Rarity's lease is coming up . . ." Haven squeezed her eyes closed.

"Haven, it's okay." He covered her hand with his and squeezed. "I still want your help at Aspen Crossroads. What do you say? Is Aspen Crossroads' success worth the risk?"

Chapter Ten

Aspen Crossroads was almost five miles south of town, and Haven relished the hum of her car's wheels zipping down the highway but never quite reaching the fifty-five-miles-per-hour speed limit. Safety first. Once she drove past the water tower, where most of the other teens in town had their first kiss, she slowed and flicked on her blinker to turn right on Cavern Drive. If she kept going for a half mile, she'd see the private drive where the interview had been last week. Although there weren't a ton of businesses on this end of Whisper Canyon, the restaurant would be on the main stretch in and out of town. Hopefully, that meant success.

Steering the car onto the gravel road, Haven rocked in her seat with every rut. In all her years in Whisper Canyon, she'd taken this road only once. And that ill-fated field trip to the caverns left her with a lapful of her regurgitated breakfast. Haven rolled down the driver's window to let in fresh air so she wouldn't repeat that nightmare.

The road was barely two lanes wide, with concentrated aspens and pines stretching their branches toward her car from both shoulders. She paused at the four-way stop but considering the weeds towering high above the gravel, no one had ventured along the cross street in weeks if not months. A split rail fence led to the propped-open gate and driveway Jace had described. Although the gate itself was rusted and old with the words *Aspen Crossroads* barely readable overhead, a garden of sunflowers welcomed her. Maybe she wasn't setting herself up for another disaster after all.

Rolling fields hid all but the roof of the farmhouse ahead. When Haven breached the top of the highest hill, a picturesque mural spread across her windshield. A two-story brick farmhouse with a small wooden porch stood facing a cabin similar to her family's. Must be Jace's home. On the right, a small shed and large red barn abutted what appeared to be the edge of the property. Beyond the structures, rows of corn and who-knew-what other plants bled into the mountains—the perfect homestead.

Haven parked her fifteen-year-old Civic next to Jace's truck. No one greeted her as she stepped out of her car. Perhaps they were at the restaurant. She turned in a circle. No one. She moved toward the fields. The closer she got, the more she was able to see how meticulous the farm was. Each row was marked with stakes identifying each vegetable. Jace and his team knew what they were doing. She'd be sure to keep her plant-murdering hands far away from the crops.

She walked toward the barn, where a tractor and trailer stacked with hay were parked in front of the open door. Jace rounded the trailer and heaved a hay bale off the pile, then carried it into the barn. A fly buzzed around Haven's neck, and she shooed it away. Perhaps perfumed lotion wasn't the wisest choice for her first day of work. Then again, she hadn't expected to be outside. She hadn't known what to expect at all.

A breeze ruffled her blouse, a soft pink color that paired well with her black slacks that fit slim against her legs. A pair of flats completed her professional ensemble.

"That's quite the outfit for storing hay." A feminine voice came from behind Haven and stopped her steps. "Where'd you get it? Talbots?" The voice's owner bypassed her and headed straight for the barn, swaying her short shorts–clad backside with each step. Just above her waistband, a strip of pink skin met the frayed edge of a tank top. Twin strawberry blond braids trailed down the girl's back.

"I'm not here to store—"

"Hey, babe, I brought you lunch," she called into the barn.

Jace stepped into the sunlight. "Jillian, please don't call me b—" His focus landed on Haven, and the corners of his lips went heavenward. "Haven."

"Hello, Jace."

Jace removed his leather work glove and outstretched his hand but pulled it back almost instantly after taking in the full sight of her. Sweat and hay dust glazed his tanned skin, and his worn jeans and old T-shirt showed the signs of a full day's work although it was only noon. "I don't want to dirty you up."

The girl scoffed loudly. She was pretty with a killer body she was clearly proud of. Like Jace, her clothes and skin were smudged with dirt and dust, and a pair of matching leather work gloves had been tucked into the waistband of her jean shorts. In her right hand, she held a plate with a basic sandwich and potato chips. And in her expression, she leveled disdain directly at Haven.

Jace stepped back, splitting the distance between both women. "Jillian, this is Haven Haviland. She's here to—"

"Do my taxes?"

"Remember? We talked about this. She's here to help you reach your goals."

Jillian smirked. "Yeah, all right. Do you want this, or should I give it to the pig?"

"We don't have a pig on the farm," Jace said.

Jillian lowered her glare on Haven, and she felt it cut

straight through. Thanks to her running regimen, Haven was fit. Still, no one would call her skinny. And she certainly didn't have washboard abs like Jillian was showing off.

Jace spun toward Jillian and spoke to her quietly. Haven heard nothing except for the occasional grunt or hiss. While she stood by, she willed herself to maintain composure. Keep her chin steady and her eyes soft. She'd been insulted by clients before, but always in her office, not on someone else's turf.

And Jillian's turf was now littered with slices of bread, cheese, deli meat, and chips.

"Jillian," Jace said in a most fatherly tone. If Haven had to guess, Jillian didn't see him in a fatherly way at all. Why would she? Jace was strikingly handsome, and from her few encounters with him, he had shown a courageous heart and kind soul. He'd be easy to fall for, especially if he'd come to a girl's rescue.

"I best get back to work." Jillian shoved the empty plate into Jace's stomach, and he grabbed it. She pushed off him and sauntered her way into the barn, never glancing back.

Once she was out of sight, Jace bent down and gathered the flailed food back onto the plate before depositing it on a bale of hay. He faced Haven. "I'm sorry about that. She can be immature."

She held her palms out toward him. "No apology necessary."

He nodded. "How about a tour? Fair warning: your shoes might get dirty."

"I can handle dirty shoes."

Jace led her around the tractor. In front of them, acres of land, dressed with the foliage of crops Haven didn't recognize, flitted in the light wind. The farm was much larger than she'd thought.

"So, back there in the barn, we store the hay. Some of it gets used for the small animals, but we'll sell most to ranchers for winter feed. We have painted mountain corn over there, which we can eat fresh, feed to the chickens, or grind into flour for the restaurant. Sonny makes amazing spoon bread with it. And this field is for pumpkins, spinach, lettuce, and root vegetables. That's mostly all we can grow well in this climate. We have some tomatoes, peppers, and so on, but only enough for our team's needs."

"How will you sustain a restaurant?"

"We're in a partnership with several farms that are better able to produce other crops, along with the dairy and meat. We pledge that none of our food travels farther than five hundred miles."

She stumbled on a stone but found her footing before Jace had to put his rescuing to work on her. Still, he stepped back to retrieve the offending rock and chucked it into a thicket of aspens. For good measure, he found three more stones in front of her and kicked those out of her path.

"You don't miss a chance to be a hero, do you?" she asked.

"Maybe I just don't want you to twist your ankle. Then I'd have to carry you to my house."

"Something tells me Jillian wouldn't appreciate that."

"No, she wouldn't. Believe it or not, Jillian has her nice moments. And she's got a great work ethic." Jace directed Haven to turn across a grass strip bisecting the fields. "There's nothing going on between us. She'd like for there to be, and she does all kinds of antics to try to make there be, but there's not. I'd never cross that line or take advantage of Jillian, Sonny, or Rosalie."

"Good. I suppose that will make my job easier."

"My goal is to keep things as professional as possible with everyone here in Whisper Canyon. Everyone."

His extra emphasis might have made Haven laugh before this summer. Now? She had a new appreciation for professionalism.

"Jace!" A little boy zoomed around the edge of the cornfield. His long blond curls bounced with each flat-footed step. His eyes were even more blue than Jace's, and that was saying something.

"Little man," Jace said, reaching his arms out. When the boy got near enough, Jace snatched him up like he weighed no more than a butternut squash and sat the boy on his shoulders. "Elijah, this is my friend Haven. Haven, this is Sonny's little boy."

"Hi, Heaven!"

Jace laughed. "Not heaven—"

Haven wagged a finger at him. "Don't you dare correct him. Hello, Elijah. How old are you?"

Above Jace's head, the boy held up all five fingers and bent two down with his other hand. "Three," he said, replacing the *th* with an *f*.

"You gotta hold on tight, buddy," Jace said, prompting Elijah to squeeze his arms tight around Jace's eyes. "Where's your momma?"

A woman followed the boy's exact path, although she looked far more annoyed than excited, judging by the way she pressed her hands on her hips. "There you are. You still have two chicken nuggets left to eat." She shared Haven's hair color, although the woman wore it in a pixie cut that emphasized her petite features.

"Sonny, this is Haven. Haven, Sonny," Jace said, able to peek one eye open between Elijah's hands.

"It's nice to meet you." Haven added her most pleasing smile to her greeting, but the nicety wasn't returned. Rather, any excitement Haven might have had about meeting her clients ricocheted off Sonny's granite-hard expression.

"If you're hungry, we've got sandwich meat and two cold chicken nuggets," Sonny said without a hint of humor.

"I've already eaten, but thank you."

"You'll probably be wanting to meet Rosalie, huh? I know she wants to meet you. She's barely given me a moment's peace about it all morning. She ran to the grocery, but she'll be back soon."

Haven caught Jace's eye, and he grinned.

Sonny reached for her son. "'Lijah, time for your nap."

"I wanna play with Jace," the boy whined.

Jace angled his head so he could see Elijah's face. "After you wake up, you can help me start building your swing set." He bent his legs and lowered his shoulders for Sonny to take the boy in her arms.

As the two walked back toward the house, Elijah waved back at them. "Night night, Jace. Night night, Heaven."

"Night night," Jace called. When he caught Haven watching him with amusement, he gave her a questioning look. "What?"

"What was all that talk about keeping things professional?"

Jace shrugged. "Elijah doesn't count."

Throughout the remainder of the tour, Haven grew quiet. Perhaps she was put off by Jillian's and Sonny's less-than-enthusiastic welcome. She was likely regretting ever agreeing to this job. Suddenly the idea of her walking away drained him of the energy he needed for the afternoon's tasks.

"I guess that's enough for today. I can show you the rest tomorrow."

Haven looked disappointed. "Where's Audrey?"

The chick? How had he skipped the coop? If anything might make her stick around, it would be the small animals.

"This way." He led her back around his cabin to a large shed with six-foot-high fencing on either side to form pens. On one side, two goats watched them from the raised planks that he and Rosalie had built back in June. The other pen was deserted except for the rooster and the new wooden coop.

"This is quite a setup," Haven said.

"It has to be. A coyote got into it a couple weeks ago. The goats were locked inside the shed, but the only fowl to survive was the rooster."

The look of horror that crossed her face made him want to laugh and simultaneously offer her comfort. "It won't happen again. I won't let it. That's why I built this fortress."

"How did the rooster survive?"

"Not sure, but knowing him, he probably fought back. The chicks are in the shed. I'll keep them in here for the next five weeks while they grow." Jace unlatched the shed and welcomed her into the chick nursery. Inside a cardboard box, the six chicks hobbled around on wood chips.

Her eyes immediately went to the Ameraucana with a blue sandal on her foot. "How is she?"

"Her toes are taking longer than I thought to straighten. Every few days, I make a new splint."

The noise Haven made was more like a balloon leaking air than any human sound he'd ever heard. "She's so big!"

"They grow fast, don't they? You can hold her if you'd like. Rosalie hand-feeds them, so they're used to being handled, especially Audrey, since she needs special care." Jace rested his knee on the ground, and Haven crouched unsteadily beside him, keeping her pants off the dirt.

"Oh, Audrey, your shoe is fantastic." Haven slowly ran two fingers down the chick's fuzzy back. "Is it designer?" That smile of hers could add light to the sun and shine to the stars, as his mother used to say.

"You remind me of my mom. She loved animals. She promised me we'd get a dog once we got a house of our own."

"Did you?"

"Nah. The guy she married when I was fourteen wouldn't let us."

Haven waited for him to continue, but Jace tried to avoid thoughts of Gus if he could. "Did you grow up with one?" he asked.

"A dog? No. Valor's allergic to pet dander." Haven shrugged, but a wistful look remained on her face.

Jace couldn't help but wonder how many times in her life she'd shrugged off her own desires for the good of those around her. Again, just like his mom.

"I would like to have met her—your mother. Did you take after her?"

"Appearance-wise, yeah. Same hair and eyes. But personality-wise, I don't know. She was more trusting and way less bitter." Too much. He forced his lips into a smile.

Her lips parted, then closed again.

"Go ahead and say it, counselor." He put his hands in front of him, palms up, and gave her the old give-it-to-me gesture.

"You've invited me here. That takes a good deal of trust. For all you know, I could be the coyote in the chicken coop." If it was intended as a joke, it was a terrible one. Haven wasn't smiling. She merely locked eyes with him.

The crow of the rooster pierced the air and knocked Haven off-balance, and she fell forward on her knee.

"As you can see, he doesn't know his morning from his afternoon." Jace helped her back to a stand. Her sharp black slacks were now dusty with farm dirt.

"Thank you." She glanced down, then back up at him. "If I'll be spending time on the farm, I might need to get some different work clothes. Now I really look like a pig."

"Listen, Haven," he said, leading the way out of the shed. "Jillian and Sonny are guarded. They've had to be, after what they've seen."

She nodded. "Patients with past trauma need time to open up. I know how to do that in an office setting, but out here?"

Jace spread his arm wide to show the farm. "Try to think of this as your new office. Spend time with them. It won't take long for them to tell you their story."

Haven bit her lower lip for a few seconds. When she released it, a rich rose color pooled into the fullness of it. "I'll do what I can."

"I'm sure you will. And for the record, you don't look like a pig. You look pretty." Jace cringed at his own words. "Pretty professional, I mean."

He held her gaze until they'd both stopped smiling. What on earth was wrong with him? He hadn't felt this way since—

"Is this her?" Rosalie's yelp sprang from the driveway, where she'd haphazardly parked the minivan. She'd had her license only one week, and it showed. She skipped through the grass, and when she reached them, Rosalie threw her arms around Haven and hugged her. "Hi, Haven. I'm so happy to meet you!"

Haven peered at Jace over Rosalie's shoulder.

"This is Rosalie."

Rosalie pulled back and grabbed both of Haven's hands. "Oh my. You're so beautiful. Are those your real eyes or contacts? I've always wanted green eyes. Do you want to come inside with me? At the store, I got froyo."

"Froyo?" Jace asked.

Rosalie rolled her eyes. "Jace, you're such an old geezer. Frozen yogurt. But you're not invited. I want girl talk. You can catch up with Haven later." She hooked her arm around Haven's, and as they walked toward the farmhouse, he overheard Rosalie say, "We're going to be BFFs. I just know it!"

Chapter Eleven

I t makes sense this used to be a jailhouse. It feels like doing time," Jillian pronounced while glowering at Haven across the high-top table.

Haven looked away, sipping her latte. Beside her, Elijah was lapping his cup of whipped cream the way a puppy might. At least he was enjoying their coffee date at Jailhouse Roasters.

"This place was built in 1871?" Rosalie asked.

"She already said that. Then it burned down, and they rebuilt it. Don't ask any more questions, Rosie, or we'll be here all day." Jillian's cool demeanor had refused to warm even slightly toward Haven the past three days. None of her usual counseling tricks had worked, so she'd stayed up late each night studying the latest techniques in trauma-informed counseling. And for what? So Jillian could lance her with glares and curses. Sonny wasn't much better. She never wasted an opportunity to make Haven feel like an unnecessary speed bump on the road she was traveling. Rosalie, gracious as she was, chattered on and on about everything surface-level and nothing else.

"Why is everyone looking at us?" Rosalie asked.

"Because they have nothing better to do." Jillian didn't have a problem staring voyeurs down. If they lingered here too long, Haven was sure the girl would turn her sharp tongue on them.

"They're curious. And when people in Whisper Canyon are curious, they talk. You're new here. Of course they're interested in learning more about you."

"Funny. The only whispers I've caught mention you." Jillian gazed out the window. "Tell me. Does the term *stalker* mean the same thing here as it does in Denver?"

"Can we go yet?" Sonny asked.

"Yes, but I have two more stops in mind before we head back to the farm." Haven stood, ignoring Sonny's frustrated sigh and Jillian's headshake. She waited for everyone to gather their belongings, then led the way out.

Ahead of her, the door opened wide. Trent.

"Haven." The way her name slithered from between his lips made Haven's stomach roil. And that slick smile? She was speechless, even when the others joined her on the stoop.

"Hello, ladies. I don't believe we've met. Any friend of Miss Haviland's is a friend of mine. I'm Mayor Garrison."

Sonny crossed her arms and glared. "You're the guy that keeps wreaking havoc for The Mill."

Trent's eyebrow lifted. "You're the, uh, *ladies* of Aspen Crossroads, I take it." His inspection raked up and down Sonny, but Haven stepped in front of Jillian and Rosalie before he could do the same to them. "I'm simply working for the best interest of my town. You're professionals. You understand."

"Come on, ladies. Let's go before I say or do something I'll regret." Sonny lifted Elijah onto her hip and hurried past Trent, shouldering his arm enough to make him wheel back and drop what he was holding. A stack of metal sheets clanged as they hit the sidewalk.

Haven looked closer. "No loitering? Where are those signs going?"

"Up and down Main Street."

"I thought you wanted to boost the local economy, yet you don't want people near the shops?"

"I don't want the wrong people lingering near the shops."

"The wrong people?" Haven didn't have to ask. In Trent's mind, the wrong people included anyone who didn't look, dress, act, or spend like he did.

"How about we set up a meeting to discuss it more thoroughly?" The glint in his eye assured Haven he was offering much more than a meeting.

"I'd rather not. Excuse me." She rushed to catch up to the rest. Once she did, Jillian drilled her with an accusatory stare that Haven wouldn't quickly forget.

They made it to the bookstore without any more unfortunate run-ins. It felt good to duck into the warmth of the familiar space with its wall-to-wall dark woodwork and rows upon rows of colorful spines. Sonny was less impressed, especially when Elijah squirmed against her hold. "What's this about?"

"My sister learned about this game up in Montana. It's a get-to-know-you game. Everyone picks three books that made an impact on their life. It's called burn, bury—"

Jillian walked straight to the shelf marked *Classics*, ignoring Haven completely. Rosalie beamed as she looked toward the back of the shop where a boy—the reverend's son—was playing a solitary game of chess at a table. He tried to wave, and the motion knocked over some of the pieces. Seconds later, she was at his side, chatting away.

Elijah grunted as he tried to get free from Sonny's arms. When that didn't work, he turned into a jellyfish and his limp body slid to the ground.

Sonny relented but kept a death grip on his hand when he tried to squirrel away. "I'm sorry, Haven. I don't have time for games. Elijah needs his nap, and I'm meeting with the electrician this afternoon. Can we go?"

Haven's heart sank deeper into her chest. So much for their girls' day out. While Sonny dealt with Elijah's tantrum, Haven turned away in time to see Jace walk through the doorway of the bookshop. The breadth of his muscled shoulders blocked most of the sunlight from the street.

His focus landed squarely on Haven, and he greeted her with a tilted grin. Haven caught herself holding her breath. She let it spill between her pursed lips, nearly whistling in the process.

"Hey," he said, closing the distance between them. "I was coming out of the hardware store and saw you."

"Oh good. Girls, Jace is here," Sonny said. "We have to get back. Could you stay with Haven? She's got some game you can play." She didn't give Haven or Jace a chance to answer. "Rosalie, you have the keys to the van, right?"

"Yes." Rosalie avoided Jace's eyes but paused at the door to look back at the boy another time.

Sonny wrangled a now-crying Elijah against her chest. "Jill, let's go."

Jillian shelved the book she'd been reading and followed Sonny's call. Of course, she didn't miss the opportunity to sear Haven, then Jace, with a glare.

The door shut, leaving the two of them, and an eavesdropping cashier, alone in the front part of the shop. Jace waited until the women were gone before speaking. "What game was she talking about?"

"It was nothing. A dumb idea."

"No, we can play. I didn't get to play many games when I was a kid."

Haven shook her head.

Jace leaned in close for her to feel his breath wisp the baby-fine hairs at her temple. "Hang in there. It's only been a few days. I believe in you."

At least one of them did.

"I have a little bit of time before I'm needed at The Mill. What else did you have planned?"

"It's silly."

"I doubt it. You put thought into it. It's got to be good. Now, their loss is my gain." Jace rubbed his hands together. "So where are we headed?"

"The Whisper Canyon Historical Center?" Jace feigned enthusiasm as he read the sign.

"I thought learning more about the town's history might help the women understand the place a bit more. It's pretty interesting, and my family goes back to the very beginning. We may be able to find photos of the gristmill in its heyday. You know what would be cool? If we could get copies of those pictures to display in the restaurant." Her eyes lit with excitement at the idea.

Funny, how she was still able to find pride in her hometown after all the trouble her family had been through.

Meanwhile, Jace's disdain for the place only grew this morning when he'd seen Trent talking to Haven outside the coffee shop. Even though the run-in had ended without incident, he'd wanted to check if Haven was holding together, given their history.

Now he was supposed to ooh and aah over the town at this shabby museum? Yes. Because Haven had brought him, and for some reason, he couldn't bring himself to add more discouragement to her soft heart.

At his hesitation, her smile fell. "If you don't want to go in, it's fine. I understand." She spun on her heels, then marched back to the passenger door of his truck. "Rosalie wants to teach me to knit sweaters for the chickens anyway."

She was doing it again—covering her disappointment with a pleasant expression.

Jace scrambled around the front bumper and caught her hand before she could pull the door closed. "Haven, I want to go in."

"No, you don't."

"Visiting museums is my favorite way to spend an afternoon."

Her expression called his bluff.

"Okay, you got me. This wasn't on my list of places to visit. But I bet it won't be so bad if you're my tour guide."

Her gaze dropped to their hands, resting together still on the inside of the door.

Jace tore his hand from hers and pocketed it, in case it chose to act on its own again. He had a persistent itch to learn more about the woman in front of him. She didn't share much about herself, so every detail felt a bit like he was Indiana Jones discovering a new treasure.

After some arguing—Haven could be as stubborn as Jillian—Jace was pulling open the door of the center. An unearthly stench smacked Jace in the face hard enough to make him rear back. Haven coughed and held her fist up to her nose. "Oh my. It . . ."

"Smells like someone died with rotten pickles in their pockets?" He glanced around. The center's breezeway—a misnomer since there was definitely no breeze in or out of this place—consisted of only a ticket window and a closed door.

"Seriously, though. It smells like a skunk broke in dragging a cornucopia of dead fish."

Haven turned toward Jace, her features pinched in a partial grimace and . . . was that a smile?

"It's like—"

"No more," she pleaded with a shake of her head.

"—a baby ate a jar of sauerkraut and filled its diaper."

She released a noise that might be considered a laugh if people laughed through their nose.

"You okay?"

"Of course not. My eyes are burning," she said.

"You're lucky." He grimaced. "I can taste it."

Haven slapped his arm before wiping tears away. "We can go."

"No way. I can tell this place is going to be good." Jace approached the ticket window. Behind the Plexiglas a man sat motionless in a desk chair, his eyes closed. After a moment of observation, Jace whispered in Haven's ear, "Is he dead? I was joking about the pickles thing."

After another look, Haven whispered back, "He's asleep. See his mustache going up and down?"

"I thought that only happened in cartoons."

"Apparently not. See? We're already learning new things."

Yeah. Like how much he liked being this close to Haven. "This history center thing was a great idea." Funny. Even in the ugly yellow light above, her eyes remained a startling shade of green, with rays of gold radiating out from the pupils. Was she even wearing makeup? Her dark lashes looked feather-soft.

"Should we knock on the glass?"

"Oh. Yeah. Sure." Jace tapped his knuckles on the window. Nothing. Haven nudged him and he knocked again, harder this time.

The man bolted upright. He looked around as if he had no idea where he was. "What do you want?"

Jace looked behind him. "To see the historical center. You're open, right?"

"For nine dollars, we are."

"You said nine dollars? How big is this place?" he asked.

"Nine dollars per person."

"Ouch."

Haven unzipped her purse, but Jace caught her hand before she could reach her wallet.

"I got this." Before she could argue, he withdrew his wallet and dropped a twenty in the dish below the window.

The employee counted out the change and slid it back along with two tickets, a map, and about fifteen brochures. Finally, the man stood from his chair and slowly disappeared. The knob on their right unlocked and the door creaked open. "Come on, then."

Jace followed Haven into the museum. The funk remained, but either it wasn't as strong, or he'd habituated to it. It was his eyes that were most afflicted now.

Dead animals. Everywhere. And although Jace wasn't an expert on taxidermy, he was pretty sure these wouldn't make the hall of fame. Above them, a bighorn sheep's head was missing an eye.

"The rules are on the back of the map." The man held out a plastic grocery bag. "Phones."

"Sorry?"

"No phones allowed, buckaroo. They could damage the exhibits."

A polite smile was all Jace could muster. From the look of things, people in the past must have taken *a lot* of pictures. Haven took her phone from her bag and held her empty hand in front of Jace. He complied but only because of the way Haven peered up at him. The next thing he knew, Haven had tugged his shirt sleeve. He moved to follow her, and his boot kicked something dark and glassy that rolled under a souvenir penny machine.

"What was that?"

"Just an eyeball. It's fine." He pointed up at the sheep. "He didn't need it anyway. You know, if it was his nose he lost, I might be jealous."

She hooked her arm through his. "Let's go before he makes you get it out from under there."

Quickly, they ducked inside the first room. The longest wall featured a timeline, complete with black-and-white and sepia pictures. Haven pointed to a small, antique photo at the earliest moment. "This is my great-great-great-grandfather, Alva Haviland." The man looked young enough, but bushy eyebrows and a heavy beard filled most of the tintype.

"Ah. I can see the family resemblance."

She cocked her head and fit her hands to her hips.

"I'm kidding . . . kind of. Tell me his story."

"First thing you should know is my family has a history of being mischief-makers. Alva grew up in the South but he was a staunch abolitionist. It's believed he burned down a pro-slavery newspaper office and then fled west to avoid the gallows. But he left behind a heartbroken fiancée, Hester Garrison."

"Garrison? No!" he said.

Haven grinned mischievously. "Scandal, right? So he finds this uninhabited canyon in the Mosquito Range of the Rockies, and he settles it. After about a year, he gets lonely and heads into Denver to find a wife, which he does. Only while he's there, he's discovered by Hester's uncle Prescott Garrison, who has been on the hunt for the man who broke his poor niece's heart. He follows Alva to the canyon, fully intending to drag him back to Mississippi or wherever, but once he's there he sees a business opportunity. He threatened to turn Alva in for his crime until Alva offered to sell Prescott a large portion of his land." Haven stepped to her right, next to a picture of a dusty business building.

"Garrison Mining Company," Jace read off the barely legible sign.

"Prescott discovered a silver mine. The canyon filled with miners and a town popped up almost overnight. Garrison got rich, meanwhile Alva and his family had to sell more of their land to get by. Eventually, Garrison declared himself mayor, and a Garrison has remained mayor ever since. He named the town Hester Canyon, just to dig at Alva. But miners swore you could hear the wind whisper things if you listened close enough. Soon, Hester Canyon became known as Whisper Canyon."

"Have you ever heard the wind whisper?" he asked.

"Not yet, but I still listen whenever the wind picks up."

Jace spied a painting above the next mark on the timeline. In red, orange, and yellow strokes, fire blazed from the roofs of wooden buildings. "And this?"

"Fast forward to 1885, there was the Great Fire. With the mines dried up and the businesses destroyed, everyone left, except for the Havilands and Garrisons, of course. Whisper Canyon became a ghost town, until people made their way back in the twenties."

"What caused the fire?"

"No one knows. The most common belief is that Jacob Haviland, my great-great-grandfather, was feuding with Prescott's son, Barrett, over a girl, so he set the mining office on fire."

"Ooooh."

"I told you—mischief-makers." Haven held her hands palms up and shrugged.

"Was anyone killed?"

"Fortunately, no. Here's where it gets kooky. Legend has it that a grizzly bear ran through the streets, like crying out. It woke up everyone in time for them to get to safety."

Jace cocked his head. "Did that bear happen to have six toes on one paw?"

"How'd you know?"

"I've heard the legend of Ol' Sixclaw. Have you ever seen him or his tracks?"

With a shake of her head, Haven faked sorrow.

"You haven't heard the wind whisper or seen the six-toed ghost bear? What kind of tour guide are you, anyway?" He bumped his shoulder against hers gently.

She bounced right back and bumped his. "That's why there's so much animosity between the Havilands and Garrisons. Very Hatfields and McCoys, right? My grandfather and Trent's grandfather finally called a truce in the seventies, but what's done is done. The Garrisons still hold all the power and the Havilands are still barely getting by."

"For what it's worth, you don't seem like a mischief-maker to me," he said.

"Are you calling me boring?" she huffed playfully, and came nearer. "Because you never know, I could have trouble up my sleeve this very moment."

"You better not. Gramps over there will kick us out."

She brought her lips close to his ear. "Only if he sees us. Follow me." She disappeared through a curtained doorway.

Jace raked a hand through his hair as his flesh demanded he comply. Mental images of what she could have in store behind that curtain formed, and in his mind, it wasn't more taxidermy. Okay, so he was attracted to her. With that face and those curves, any man would be. And if he were one of *them*, he'd pursue her with the speed of an avalanche. But he knew better. Haven, like Jillian, Rosalie, and Sonny, was more than how she might please a man. And he was more than how he might please her. Both of them deserved more respect and more care than they'd been shown in the past.

She peeked through the curtains, one brow lifted high. "What are you waiting for, Daring?" She spoke his last name as if it was a challenge.

Lord, lead me not into temptation . . .

Chapter Twelve

"Wax figures, dust mites, and folklore, oh my," Jace said as he held open the truck's passenger door while Haven climbed in.

Haven burst out laughing for what seemed like the hundredth time. In the past two hours, she and Jace had dressed like nineteenth-century miners to search a fake cave for fool's gold, watched a movie about the legend of Ol' Six-claw, and practiced their best pickup lines on creepy wax figures, all while repeatedly getting asked, "You doing all right, buckaroo?"

Jace shut her door, then crossed the front of the truck, the sun glinting off his golden hair and perfect profile. Her stomach did a flip-turn, just as it had the multiple times she'd caught him staring at her or when he'd jumped out and grabbed her by the waist during their game of hide-and-seek. In normal circumstances, she'd be tempted to think he liked her. And she might be tempted to admit she liked him back. In normal circumstances . . .

She reached into her purse, and once he'd settled into the driver's seat, she pulled out the bag of popcorn. "You sure you don't want any more?"

He shuddered and his horrified gaze shifted from the popcorn to her eyes. "Why in the world did you keep that? Grossest popcorn ever. Why were the kernels wet?"

"I don't know. Should we go back in and ask Gramps what his recipe is?"

"For the love of Ol' Sixclaw, no!"

A snort prompted her to cover her face with her hand. Still, her shoulders shook, and her stomach muscles ached from laughing so much. It took a moment, but she finally composed herself. "That was fun," she said.

Again, Jace watched her, a glassy look in his eyes and a contented grin, as he rested his head against the seat back. "It was. It really was. I haven't laughed that much in . . . I don't know how long."

"Me, neither. A downside to our professions?"

"I guess so. It's nice to find someone that I can"—he seemed to search the roof of the truck for words—"let go with. You know what I mean?"

She nodded, her own words missing now.

"We should do it again sometime. Just maybe not here," he teased with a wink.

A wink.

The taste of the awful popcorn returned to her tongue, and she felt her smile fall flat. She was doing it again—falling for a man's good looks, flirtations, and charm. Would she never learn? Haven pushed open the passenger door and hopped down from the cab. The fresh air filled her lungs as she walked to the trash bin and dropped the popcorn inside. Keeping her focus on the pavement, she returned to Jace's truck.

When she climbed in, Jace stared straight ahead, through the windshield, and a thousand miles away. "That sounded like I meant it as a date. I didn't."

"No, no." She waved her hand. "I didn't think you did. We are coworkers, after all. Total professionals."

"Total," he agreed. He moved to start the car but paused.

"Thanks for bringing me here, Haven. It was nice to see that this town isn't completely vile."

Her heart squeezed. "Is that what you thought? Because of what your mom might have gone through?"

"I thought that because of what my mom told me." Jace stammered. "She brought me here once. I don't know why. I was probably five, so I only have these flashes of memories about the trip. In one of them, she told me this town was full of evil, and if we stayed, we'd be eaten alive."

"Oh, Jace." Haven forced her hands between her knees, trapping them in case the desire remained to touch his arm, or worse, stroke the short hair above his ear.

"Funny thing is, she told me that after she showed me the statue of Ol' Sixclaw at Town Hall. I thought she was warning me about a bear." Jace chuckled. "Then I promised I'd never step foot in this town again. I think of that broken promise every day I wake up in this canyon."

"You were five. She wouldn't have expected you to keep that promise. What else do you remember about your visit? Did she talk to anyone?"

In his hesitation, his brow danced to a somber tune, and he blinked rapidly. If she were a stronger believer, she might ask God to help him work through those warring emotions. Yet, despite twenty-seven years of steady church attendance, she'd never felt worthy enough to approach the throne of God on her own. And that was before she'd given herself to Trent. God might downright smite her now.

"We stopped at a house. I remember a man opening an orange door and speaking to her. I don't know what was said, though. I was still buckled in the car. But I was sad afterward because my mom was sad."

"Do you remember what he looked like?"

"He was older than my mom. Gray hair. That's all."

"Anything else?"

Enough sadness was relayed through Jace's gaze for her to regret the question. "Another time, then. Maybe when we return for our next visit to the historical center. Lucky us. I believe our nine dollars got us season passes."

Jace turned his focus to the steering wheel and started the engine. But a slight uptick at the corner of his lips turned the roar of the ignition into a joyful noise if she'd ever heard one.

Do you think Haven will be a bridesmaid in my wedding one day?" Rosalie sat on Jace's porch railing, swinging her crossed legs forward and back.

"Do you have a boyfriend you haven't told me about?" Jace said as he flipped the chicken breasts on the grill. She better not. No boys allowed.

"No, *Dad*, I don't. But when I do, Haven will be right there next to me."

"I'm glad you like her. What do you two talk about?"

"Mostly, my GED class and my future. She tried to help me review for the test, but I said no."

"Why? Rosalie, it's on Thursday. You should review as much as you can in the next six days. That test isn't easy. You need to take it more seriously."

"I know everything on the review, and I've aced every practice test. Anyway, did you know Haven hated math, too? She told me that in college, you only have to take lots of math classes for certain majors."

"I wouldn't know."

"How come you didn't go to college?"

Well, if that wasn't a question with a million answers . . . "No time. I've been working since I was fifteen."

"With how you nag about the importance of education, you should make time." As she spoke, she braided a section of her glossy dark hair. Although she was eighteen, Rosalie had the look of someone much younger, which sadly made her a desired commodity.

Nausea replaced Jace's appetite.

"I like it here," she said. "It's quiet, and it never gets too hot. Don't you like it?"

Jace turned his full attention back to the grill, willing the chicken to cook through. Where was she going with this line of questioning? "I do."

"I bet the kids who grow up here have it made. There's no crime, so you can't get into trouble. Everyone has money, so there's no reason to sell anyone off." The words fell from her lips too easily. No one should know the evil she'd seen during her life.

Using the spatula, he tried to lift one of the chicken breasts, but it stuck to the grill. He pried it off, only to leave a layer of flesh behind. He placed the chicken breast on his plate.

"They're all so nice." Rosalie lost herself in a trance for a few moments and sighed. "I want to live in Whisper Canyon forever. I wish you could stay here with us, too. It's starting to feel a bit like a family. Haven's the cool aunt. Sonny's the sister that bosses me around. Jillian's the sister who's kinda mean but I love her anyway. You're like our overprotective dad."

"You know I can't stay."

"Yeah, I know. Wishful thinking."

He hated the way her frown tugged at his heart. He was getting too close. Letting himself get too involved. It was so hard not to. In many ways, Rosalie was still the young woman shivering in the backseat of his truck, afraid he was one more man out to hurt her. Even though she'd since shown her strength and resiliency, the memory of her thin, bruised arms reminded him why he needed to keep those boundary walls high. Someone had to protect those who couldn't protect themselves. He couldn't do that if he stayed in one place forever. There were too many out there like his mother to quit now.

* * *

The whispers slithered through the darkness to his bed in the shelter. Jace looked at the cot next to him, but his mother was no longer there. Sitting up, he looked down the two rows of cots. Other than a few restless folks, nothing stirred.

Panic pooled in his chest until he felt like he was drowning. If Mom was in trouble, he'd do everything he could to help. He might be only ten, but he could throw a punch that would at least stun a full-grown man for a few seconds. What did he care if he got knocked around as a result? It wouldn't be the first time. He didn't like men getting in between him and his mom and they didn't like Jace getting between his mom and them. The way they touched her pretty hair made him angry. And although he didn't understand what most of their comments to her meant, he knew they were wrong because Mom never smiled after they said them. But soon, she'd disappear, often leaving Jace alone with only a pocketknife to defend himself if anyone bothered him. He reached into his duffel bag and withdrew the knife from the side pocket.

"It's all right, boy."

He shifted until he could see the face of an old lady. The same old lady who had been watching him ever since they'd arrived at this homeless shelter two nights ago. Only now, instead of her black hair showing streaks of gray, it glowed red, thanks to the light from the *Exit* sign. "Where's my mom?"

"She's workin'. I told her I'd keep watch over you while you slept. Now, what do you got there in your hand?"

Courage pushed him to stand. He needed to find Mom. He darted to the exit door, escaping the lady's reach. For all he knew, she was one of the shadow monsters. He wrenched the handle and pushed against the heavy door. Stairs, leading up and leading down. After the door closed with a thud, he listened for any sound. Nothing for ten Mississippis, then a sweeping noise. Whispering? Then, swish, swish, swish. The same steady rhythm Mom made when she cried late at night. Jace crept up the concrete steps. The noises grew louder. Jace readied his knife, willing it to stop shaking. If a monster had Mom, he'd need at least one good stab to save her.

He saw the soles of a man's shoes first, then a mismatch of fabric shifting about. Then he saw his mother's hand, clenched, fingernails digging into the hard floor. Jace burst up the last steps, holding the knife in front of him. A terrible shriek hurt Jace's ears from the inside out. His shriek.

He waited for the knife to sink into the monster's flesh. Instead, the knife was smacked out of his grasp. Then Jace was pummeled in the stomach and he was flying to the side. His shoulder hit a wall and his face scraped the concrete.

"That's my son!"

"That punk came at me with a knife."

"He didn't know—"

"Tell him to scram or forget the money."

Her eyes pleaded with Jace. "I'm okay, Jace. Go back to bed. I'll be there soon."

"Mom?" He sounded like such a baby. Probably looked like one, too, with those tears burning the cheek he'd landed on.

"Back to bed. Go on. We don't have a choice."

Jace raced by them, speeding down the steps and jumping over the bottom ones. He yanked the door open and spilled onto his cot. With his face pressed tight into the pillow, he felt a soft hand sweeping over his hair.

"It's all right, boy. It's all right."

Chapter Thirteen

Haven parked in the restaurant's lot, which had fortunately been paved since her interview. A temporary sign had been staked into the bare ground next to the front door. It read *The Mill Restaurant* in the same orange spray paint that marked the concrete waste area. At least there was progress. That should make Jace happy. She saw him sitting in the front window where his makeshift desk had been before. His head was down, and he was furiously scribbling something in a notebook. Just hours earlier, she'd seen him out in the field harvesting tomatoes. And before that, he'd been patching the roof on the barn. The man never stopped working. When he noticed her, he sat back in his chair and lifted his hand—probably surprised to see her here.

She'd spent the morning with Rosalie, mapping out all the possible paths she could take once she received her GED. Haven's head spun with the myriad of online educational opportunities the young woman considered. Nursing, teaching, hospitality management, creative writing, pharmacy, kinesiology . . . Four hours of that was enough for one day. Luckily, Rosalie needed to do some work with the animals. One glare from Jillian, as she stabbed a pitchfork into the hay, led Haven to seek out Sonny, and she'd come to The Mill.

Haven let herself in the front entrance.

Jace rose from his chair like a perfect gentleman. Next to him, Elijah sat with a fistful of crayons and coloring sheets. He looked up at Jace, then copied him by climbing down from the chair and standing to face Haven.

"Hey. Is Sonny here?"

"She's in the kitchen. Straight ahead past the stairs, down the hallway, and turn right."

"Got it." She headed that way, glancing back once to see Jace still watching her. What nasty flaw was he hiding behind those blue eyes and handsome smile? It had to be something. She scolded herself. It wasn't her job to figure out Jace Daring. *Focus on the women.* She pushed open the door to the kitchen. Haven stepped around an oscillating fan to where Sonny was kneeling on the ground with a paint roller in hand. "Hi, Sonny."

The woman didn't spare a look, but her shoulders fell on a sigh. "Hello, Haven."

"I was hoping to chat with you for a few minutes this afternoon."

"Was Jillian busy?"

"She was stabbing things with a pitchfork, so I'd say yes."

"Probably wise you stayed away, then."

As Sonny kept on painting, the only sound in the kitchen was the hum of the fan. Sonny clearly wouldn't open up easily. Haven had an idea. She glanced down at her outfit. She'd left her jewelry at home today, but she couldn't quite bring herself to dress too casually. After all, she needed them to respect her. That wouldn't happen if she showed up in her sloppiest clothes. She'd have to deal with the consequences of her next action. A brush sat next to the pail. Haven took it and dipped it in the paint, then scraped off the excess.

"Goodness, girl, what are you doing?"

"I'm helping. I may not be the handiest, but I can paint." In the corner, Haven moved the brush up then down in smooth strokes. "It's looking great in here. When will you get the appliances delivered?"

"Twelve days."

"Did you get to pick them out?"

"Yes. I'm in charge of the back of the house and kitchen, so I think that was my right."

Haven went back to the paint can to recoat her brush. "Have you been cooking a long time?"

Sonny huffed. "Since I was young."

Out of habit, Haven gave the counselor nod, but Sonny remained focused on the task at hand. Haven extended up onto her tiptoes to reach as high as possible on the wall without a ladder. "Who was it that taught you?"

"Look, I know what Jace hired you to do, and it isn't to counsel me. I'm doing just fine."

"I can see that."

"I've got my high school diploma and an associate's degree. Now I'm twenty-five years old and the executive chef at a restaurant. How many folks can say that?" Sonny dropped the paint roller onto the tray and stood facing Haven.

"Not many. It's quite an accomplishment." Haven turned her focus on Sonny across the empty room.

"I've got a job and my baby. And I'm not like all those other girls Jace has saved. I rescued myself two years before he even came around. Once I found out I was pregnant, I made the decision to get out of that world. It was a struggle, but I did it for 'Lijah."

"I had no idea." Progress. This was progress.

"So excuse me if I'm a bit resistant to getting life advice from some privileged lady who can't paint without covering the whole side of her shirt with it."

As the words remained pitted in her stomach, Haven perused her shirt. Sure enough, a swath of white paint dappled her blue satin blouse.

"You can leave the paintbrush on your way out. I've got this job covered," Sonny said.

Haven swallowed against the lump in her throat and balanced the brush on the top of the paint can. She refused to look at Jace as she beelined out the front door.

"Wait up! Haven!"

She didn't slow her steps until she got to her Honda and grabbed the door handle. "Go back inside, Jace."

"What happened?"

Haven braced herself and spun toward him.

His gaze immediately fell to the paint she wore. "Oh, your shirt. Don't be upset. I can reimburse you."

"Jace, I'm not upset about my shirt."

Concern creased his forehead, and his eyes softened. "Then what?"

Haven shrugged her shoulders. "What am I doing here? Sonny and Jillian want nothing to do with me, and I'm not helping Rosalie with anything that Google can't do."

"Not true. Rosalie idolizes you, and you're showing her what her future could be. Don't discount that. And Sonny and Jillian need time to adjust. In their lives, people, even women, aren't easily trusted. It's a defense mechanism."

She nodded, as if she could ever understand what they'd experienced.

Jace placed a gentle hand on her shoulder and somehow managed to press comfort into her skin. "I know you won't believe me, but you're doing great. Hang in there. It'll get better." His thumb moved across the fabric in a calming back and forth motion. Such a tender touch for someone as strong as he was. And it had the desired effect.

"Well, it can't get much worse, can it?"

The stick of wheels on fresh asphalt turned their attention to where a black Cadillac pulled into the lot. All the peace Jace's words and subtle touch had provided dispersed the moment Haven recognized Trent Garrison's SUV.

"Oh, great." Jace dropped his hand from her shoulder as

the car parked a few spaces away from them. "I should probably figure out what he wants. You go on home. I'll see you tomorrow."

"Mayor." Jace nodded to the man, but Garrison didn't see the greeting. The guy's attention remained glued to Haven's car as it left the parking lot. And Jace didn't like it. "Can I help you?"

The mayor turned back to Jace. "You must not have gotten my letter."

"Oh, I got it. I just thought it was better put to use as kindling."

"Look, Daring. Stop making this so hard. We don't want your people here."

"We? Who exactly do you speak for? You were granted exclusive knowledge of our staff. I still have the confidentiality agreement you signed."

"I know the people of this town better than I know my own brother. They want virtuous, righteous, and pure. They are a godly people, and prostitutes aren't who they want as neighbors."

"If they are godly people, then they'd know that no one besides Christ is perfectly virtuous, righteous, or pure. If they own a Bible, they'd understand that Christ didn't mind eating or spending time with *prostitutes*, as you continue to call them," Jace said, adding extra emphasis on the derogatory term. "And once again, my colleagues never chose that profession and they are no longer in that profession, so why does it matter?"

"You aren't an educated man, are you, Mr. Daring?"

Jace clenched his jaw.

"If you were, you'd know that when a town begins letting in questionable businesses, the quality of visitors plummets. Since tourism is our biggest attraction, we can't risk that."

"We're building a top-of-the-line restaurant here with fresh flavors that your town lacks."

"Tell me. When people buy dinner at your restaurant, will they get a special dessert for free?"

In an instant, Jace was directly in front of Garrison. Close enough that he could see the sweat on the man's upper lip. "You will not disrespect those who work at this restaurant." A dozen threats ran through Jace's mind, but Garrison was a public official, after all, and threats probably weren't brushed off, especially in a small mountain town like this.

Garrison blinked once. "You aren't going to heed my suggestion that you take this business elsewhere?"

Jace's fists burned. "No. We like it just fine here."

"All right, then. You leave me no choice but to take other actions. Ones that won't be so polite." Garrison backed away, returning to his car. He took one more look at the entrance to the parking lot where Haven had driven minutes ago. "One more thing, Daring. You'll keep your hands off the locals if you know what's good for you."

Chapter Fourteen

Haven placed the bookmark in her novel and set it on the dashboard. A yawn stretched her mouth wide as she laid her head back against the driver's seat of her car. She checked the time on her phone. It should be another hour before Rosalie finished the four-part test, and Haven needed some coffee from Jailhouse if she was going to make it through the remainder of this workday without a nap.

She stuck her key in the ignition, but a sight out the front windshield caught her attention. Rosalie strutted toward the car, swinging her ponytail with each step and waving excitedly at Haven. She jumped in the passenger seat, sporting a wide, toothy grin.

"You're done already?"

"It was easy! High school is finito! Let's celebrate!"

"Okay, then! What are you in the mood for?"

"Let's get ice cream, but can we get it to go? I want to tell the fam all about it!" Rosalie said.

Once they'd gotten six sundaes from ZuZu's, they returned to Aspen Crossroads. While Rosalie skipped inside to find Jillian and Sonny, Haven walked to the side of Jace's cabin, where he and Elijah were bent over in front of some new burgundy mums they must have planted. Quietly she crept behind them and peered over their shoulders. Jace held a handful of dirt, and an earthworm squiggled across.

"Hi, Wormie!" Elijah said. "I wanna hold him."

"Okay. Be careful." Jace allowed some dirt to avalanche onto the boy's palms, and the earthworm followed suit.

"Ew. Can I squish him?"

"No, we need him to break up the soil, so our plants grow. Besides, squishing him would hurt him. We don't want to hurt anyone, do we?"

"I'll be gentle."

Jace watched Elijah as he examined the worm closer.

Haven cleared her throat, and Jace glanced up at her.

"Done already?" he asked.

"Yeah. And we got ice cream."

Elijah yanked his head up and dropped the dirt and the worm back on the earth. He jumped up. The soles of his shoes narrowly avoided becoming Wormie's final resting place. "Ice cream!"

Jace rose to his feet and watched the boy run to the farm-house.

"You're so good with him."

"He makes it easy." Jace dusted off his hands. "Was today a better day?"

"Definitely, but I basically sat in a car reading a book the whole time. Sonny's still giving me the cold shoulder, but this morning when I picked up Rosalie, Jillian said she'd teach me how to cook fresh tomatoes down into marinara sauce for the restaurant tomorrow."

Jace didn't share her enthusiasm. "She did?"

"I'll have a whole afternoon to talk with her. Isn't that great?"

"Yeah," he said, although it sounded far more like a question than an answer.

"What's wrong? I thought you'd be happy about that."

"I am. Just surprised, is all. That doesn't sound like the

Jillian I know. But no matter. Thank you for driving Rosalie to her exam today. I bet it helped to have you in the parking lot supporting her. How does she think she did?"

"She passed."

Again, confusion twisted Jace's facial features, yet didn't mar his handsomeness. "How does she already know? When I got mine, it took nearly twenty-four hours to get the results back. Of course, that was eleven years ago."

"I don't know. She was pretty certain she'd passed."

"Hmm."

"What?"

"Nothing. Now, where's that ice cream at?"

The next day, Jace and Sonny spent the morning directing contractors at the restaurant while Jillian and Haven bonded over pasta sauce. More than once, he sent up a silent prayer that Jillian wouldn't pull any tricks. When they returned to Aspen Crossroads, Jace took a gander around the farm. Haven's car was still in the drive, so Jillian hadn't run her off.

While Sonny unbuckled a slumbering Elijah from the child safety seat, Jace climbed the farmhouse steps and knocked on the door. The farmhouse was the women's home—honoring that was essential.

Jillian opened the door, greeting him with her smooth grin. "Hey, you. Come on in."

Perfectly pleasant. Something wasn't right. Jace looked for the hidden camera before crossing the threshold.

By the stove, Haven stirred the contents of the large stockpot that, like most of the furnishings, came with the house. When her eyes brightened upon seeing him, Jace felt slightly taller for some reason.

He stopped short of her and sniffed the steam rising from the lumpy red sauce. "It smells great."

"Doesn't it?" Haven said. "Jillian truly knows her way

around the kitchen. She taught me how to flash-boil the tomatoes to remove the skin, and now I'm cooking them down while we talk."

"Talk, talk, talk, talk, talk. You know me," Jillian said as she retrieved two sodas from the refrigerator. She offered one to Haven.

Strange. Jillian was not a talker. Most of her communication came through surprise caresses, eye rolls, and smirks. "That's great. Is it too much to ask for a taste test when it's finished?"

"If there's enough. Now skedaddle and leave us women to the kitchen work," Jillian said with enough sarcasm to choke a horse.

"All right, then. I've got work to do anyway." Jace excused himself and went to the barn. The grass around and between the fields needed mowing, or soon it'd be taller than Elijah.

Almost an hour later, when he passed between the two homes on the lawn mower, Jillian hopped off the porch and flagged him down. Jace cut the ignition and removed his ear protection. "What's up?"

"Not much." Jillian rocked her hip to the side. "I just wanted to thank you for bringing Haven to Aspen Crossroads." Her lips formed a heart shape—sugary sweet and completely questionable.

"What are you up to?"

"Nothing. Haven wanted to know everything about my life, so I told her."

"Told her what?"

"About how I was on the street, and you came driving up in your Lotus. After one night, you offered me three thousand dollars to stay the whole week. Then you fell madly in love with me, and now we're living our happily ever after."

Jace's mouth went dry. "What are you talking about? None of that happened."

Jillian snickered, then her pale gray eyes went cold. "Did you honestly think I was going to spill my soul, or lack thereof, to some prissy townie? Fat chance, Jace."

"I need to set things straight with Haven. You know, Jillian, not everyone is out to hurt you. Some people want to help. Stop making it so difficult."

The words knocked Jillian's hand off her hip. Was that a flicker of genuine emotion on her face?

A shriek sounded from the farmhouse—a distinctly feminine shriek that sent an electric shock through every one of his nerves. And one that sent Jillian into a roar of laughter.

"What did you do?" Jace didn't wait for the answer. He jumped off the lawn mower and covered the distance to the farmhouse porch in a half-dozen strides. This time, he didn't knock, but flew through the door.

In the kitchen, red threads streamed down the front of the white cabinets. Starbursts splotched the ceiling and dripped onto the kitchen counter around the topless blender still billowing steam. Beside it, Haven stood frozen with her arms splayed out. Her white shirt displayed new orangish-red polka dots. "I'm—I'm sorry."

Jace rushed to her. Up close, he saw the liquid sheen of the sauce on her arms, hands, and face. "Did it burn you?"

She gave a quick nod, and Jace pulled her to the sink. He knocked the cold water handle and thrust Haven's arms under the faucet. She flinched when the stream of water hit her skin, but she didn't pull back. Jace grabbed a clean dish towel from a drawer and wet it. "Look at me."

Haven squared her shoulders toward him, allowing her wet hands to dangle at her sides. Her chin quivered, and Jace touched the towel to it. "It's okay. Let me help." Stroke by stroke, he wiped the splatter off her face with as much gentleness as he could garner. Her otherwise flawless skin now sported pink welts. Jace moved closer to her. He smoothed the towel down her temple, over her cheekbone to her jaw-line. Her eyes, greener than ever with unshed tears, stared wide at him.

Jace swallowed hard and spurned the impulse to lean nearer. He'd known protectiveness before. He'd felt it every time he met a man, woman, or child who had been mis-treated. But this was something else entirely. "You have some in your hair."

As he toweled her hair lightly, she dipped her chin. For a brief moment, he wondered how it would feel to welcome her against his chest. *Keep it professional, Jace.*

He took a small step back. "I don't think you'll have any blisters, but those spots will burn for a while."

"I thought I had heard you shouldn't put hot liquids in a blender, but . . ."

"Did Jillian tell you to? She knows not to do that."

Haven released a heavy breath. "I thought we were mak-ing progress. She was talking to me."

"About that. The story she told about me paying her money to spend a week with me—"

"—was a lie. I know the plot to *Pretty Woman* when I hear it. And you might be cute, but you're no Richard Gere." The corners of her lips lifted.

"Did you just insult me? Now we've both been burned." Jace smiled, but his fury toward Jillian remained.

"What a disaster! Good luck cleaning that up." Jillian's eyes narrowed on Haven.

"Jillian, how about you grab a mop, since this was your teaching?"

"Yeah, right. I have to tend to the animals. Except the pig. It looks like you've got that covered."

"Jillian!" Jace moved to follow her, but Haven's damp hand caught the crook of his arm.

"Let her go. It doesn't hurt much anymore. I'm fine."

"Why do you do that?"

"What?"

"Act like nothing bothers you when it clearly does."

Haven searched his eyes. "When you've had so many people in your life leave, you do everything you can to make them want to stay."

A lock of hair fell across her brow, and Jace's hand itched to sweep it off her face. Until he remembered Austin. In a few months, he'd be leaving her, too.

"How about we clean up the kitchen together. We'll turn on some music and make an afternoon of it."

"Sounds like a plan."

After Haven found a country music playlist on her phone, they got to work, sponging the kitchen from the top down. An hour later, the kitchen gleamed. Jace grabbed two spoons from the drawer and dipped them both in the remaining sauce in the blender. He held one out to her.

She came around to his side of the island and accepted the spoon with a nod.

They clinked them together, then tasted the sauce.

"Excellent job," he said. "Tastes like the end of summer. And it's cool enough to blend now."

"I'll take your word for it." She ducked past him, but he caught her around the waist.

"No, you don't. You need to see this through."

"Jace." She dragged his name out into two long, whiny syllables.

"We'll do it together, okay? Stand behind me."

After some hesitation, she did as he said, hiding from the blender. Jace fit the lid to the top and held it in place with one hand. With the other, he gently stretched her arm around his side and positioned her index finger on the lowest-setting button.

Haven tucked herself against his back, shielding herself. Jace couldn't help but smile. "Ready?"

"Yes."

Before he pressed her finger down, the front door slammed. Rosalie stood just inside the entryway, her shoulders rising and falling rapidly. Even from the kitchen, Jace spied the streaks of tears.

"I failed my test. All those plans I made are useless. Thanks for nothing, Haven."

Chapter Fifteen

On Saturday night, Haven moved through the crowded restaurant with two sodas in hand. Sassy's Saloon was slammed with tourists tonight after the morning's half marathon. With every step, Haven was bumped and bristled by runners eager to "rehydrate" after their race.

"Excuse me," she said to the man blocking the way to her table.

The man looked over his shoulder at her. His smooth smile torqued his entire body toward her in an unsmooth motion. "Hello, baby doll. Is one of those for me?" He leaned quite imposingly over her as if that were supposed to be attractive.

She opened her mouth to begin her speech about how *baby doll* was an offensive term for a grown woman he'd never met before, but an arm slung around her possessively.

Her brother, Daniel, clapped the man hard on the upper arm. "It's for me, flatlander."

As the man's smile dropped, Daniel escorted her around him and back to their table.

"Flatlander? Nice insult."

"That's what they get for spilling into our mountains for a race and looking for a one-night stand with my sister."

"Give me some credit."

Valor rose from the bench. Haven scooched in to reclaim her seat next to Wesley Stalling, a lifelong friend of their family who ran a pediatric practice on Main Street. Through the years, he'd been like a second brother to Haven, Dash, and Rarity. Valor's relationship with him? Well, it was more complicated.

"Mission accomplished. Haven's virtue remains intact," Daniel joked.

"Word to the wise, Oak. Don't refer to a woman's 'virtue,'" Wes said with a wink. He was the only one who could get away with calling Daniel by his first name. And the only one who had the right to speak wisdom into her struggling twin's life. Daniel didn't heed the advice, of course, but Haven hadn't given up hope.

Daniel took a swig of Coke, then aimed his annoyance at Haven. "Where's the Jack?"

"Don't ask me to order you a drink if you're going to complain about what I get you. You can survive one Saturday night without liquor."

Haven's phone screen lit up where it sat on the table next to her napkin. The sight of Jace's name in the text notification box released a flurry of emotions. Embarrassment over her failure to help Rosalie, Jillian, and Sonny. Disappointment because, as a result of her failure, she hadn't been able to make his work easier. And although she knew it was wrong, excitement that in this moment on a Saturday night, he was thinking about her.

JACE: Not trying to be annoying. Wanted to check in. How are you?

Haven pulled her phone between her stomach and the table ledge in case her siblings got nosy. She tapped a response.

HAVEN: For the 10th time, I'm fine. You warned me
this job would be tough. I wish I could break
down their walls somehow.

JACE: You'll think of something. If you want, I can
call, and we could brainstorm ideas.

HAVEN: I can't right now. I'm out at Sassy's.

JACE: Gotcha.

HAVEN: You could join us, if you want. I'm here with
my siblings.

JACE: Nah. Thanks, though. We can talk on Monday.
Just wanted to check in.

HAVEN: You already said that.

Before she sent it off, she added a winky-face emoji.
Goodness. Now she was the one winking at him.

JACE: Mischief-maker.

HAVEN: Buckaroo.

"What are you smiling about?"

Her phone slipped to her lap. "Nothing."

Valor grinned. "I bet it has something to do with a certain superhero you work with."

"My lips are sealed," Haven stated with a nod.

Daniel groaned from across the table before looking at the empty seat next to him. "This isn't for him, is it? If so, I'll go find someone to fill it."

"No, it isn't, so don't you dare," Valor said. "I met someone the other day. I don't think she has a lot of friends, so I invited her out with us."

"Who is it?" Haven asked. For a second, she imagined Jillian traipsing in and flaunting her curves in front of Daniel. That wouldn't be good for anyone.

"Lizzie Sautter."

At the name, Daniel sobered a bit. "Elizabeth Sautter?"

"Yeah. I think she went to our high school."

"Funny," Haven said. "Dad mentioned her the other day. She helped get local funding for the organization I'm working for."

As if their words had called to her, the girl appeared, only to be stopped by the flatlander. Daniel stiffened at the sight, but no further action was needed. Lizzie put her head down, clutched her purse to her chest, and pressed past the man.

"Lizzie, over here," Valor shouted.

She looked much the same as she had in high school. Soft blond hair that likely needed no dye. A delicately pretty face devoid of heavy makeup. A skirt and cardigan combo that made Haven's counselor attire look fit for a Denver nightclub.

"Hello," she said.

"Thanks for joining us," Valor said. "This is Wes, and my sister Haven. And finally—"

Daniel stood abruptly. "I'm Daniel."

"Yes, I remember." A faint mottled rash of pink crept up her neck.

Daniel pulled Lizzie's chair out for her, and Haven braced herself for the inevitable. Her brother would spend the rest of the night trying to woo the poor girl into his bed, and the rest of them would helplessly try to keep her from making a huge mistake.

While Lizzie accepted the seat, she kept her focus away from Daniel as the conversation proceeded around her work running the mountaintop wedding chapel. Although she seemed willing to share about her life, she was more interested in diverting the conversation to the others.

"Haven," she said, "I heard you're working at Aspen Crossroads."

"I am. How'd you know?"

"I know Jace."

A sickening feeling overtook her—one that Haven might mistake for jealousy if she saw Jace as anything more than a colleague. Whatever it was, she saw it mirrored in Daniel's face. Haven could only nod.

"He's a great guy," Lizzie continued. "I love what he's doing at the farm and the restaurant."

Lizzie had helped make Aspen Crossroads possible. Jace must have major respect for her. Plus, she hadn't had an affair with a married man. Despite Jace telling Haven it wasn't her fault, she still couldn't quite believe him.

The only one more put off by the Lizzie-Jace connection was Daniel. He'd made it clear in multiple texts and phone calls that he didn't like Haven working with the guy. And now, hearing Lizzie talk about him, too, appeared to wash all color from his face. As conversation veered toward Valor's work as a paramedic, Daniel remained uncharacteristically quiet. Eventually, he excused himself from the table and left Sassy's with no explanation at all.

As the evening wound down, Wes and Valor sought out an old college friend across the room, leaving Haven and Lizzie alone at the table.

"How did you meet Jace?" Haven asked.

"My grandpa has been donating money to Secondly for a few years now. When he found out they were planning to bring the operation here, he offered to help find more donors. That was all well and good, but my grandpa has a progressive form of dementia. He was hit with it last summer, and he's been rapidly declining in health."

"I'm sorry to hear that."

Lizzie swiped at her eyes. "I took over for him. I reached out to those at the senior living center who have a lot of money and big hearts. I also went to a few businesses that have a history of donating to good causes, like your father's shop. They came through, even without knowing what they were funding."

"You and Jace must work pretty closely, then." It was part statement and part question, and a strange quiver in Haven's throat made the words come out warbled.

A small smile crept across Lizzie's face. "He's a good friend. That's all we are. How are things going with the women?"

"Honestly? It's been rough. They don't want to let me in, and I can't blame them. I don't know what they've been through. I'm someone who shows up in the morning and leaves at four thirty. And all the while, they're going on with their tasks on the farm and at the restaurant. It's far different from my counseling experience. Do you have any ideas for me?"

Lizzie thought a moment. "You go to Whisper Canyon Community Church, right? Do you remember the Easter service?"

Haven nodded slowly.

"There was something the pastor said that stuck with me. He said the people who could appreciate Jesus's resurrection and the people most likely to experience new life were the ones who met two criteria. First, they felt like they had fallen farthest from grace. Second, they knew him and were known by him."

"What does that mean for me?"

"Do what Jesus did. Move into their neighborhood."

Chapter Sixteen

By nine a.m. on Monday morning, Jace had been awake four hours, and he'd thought about Haven for each one. He hadn't seen her car yet. She assured him in their multiple text exchanges that she was fine, but Jace couldn't help but worry the women had finally scared her off.

Ten minutes later, he glanced back toward the house from the cornfield but couldn't see anyone. He adjusted his cowboy hat and climbed down from the tractor. It was nearly harvest time for the corn. After snapping a cob off the stalk at the edge of the field, he pulled back the dried-out husk and silk. Almost ready. Which meant he needed to finish building the corncrib as soon as possible.

The restaurant was due to open in just under four weeks, and there was so much left to do. At least Sonny was on top of things with the back of the house. The kitchen would be set up two weeks from now, and Sonny could begin training sous chefs. She'd been testing out menu options for the last month, and the dishes were divine. But he and Jillian still needed to design the layout, order the tables and chairs, decorate, stock the freezer and pantry, plant the landscape. Oh, and get the approval to open. No pressure.

Jace rubbed the back of his neck as he returned to the tractor. Enough wasting time. One more look toward the house stopped him in his tracks. Haven approached, strolling between the two main fields. She wore jeans, a T-shirt, and—were those boots? Heaven help him.

"Sorry I'm late. It took me an extra couple of minutes to gather my things."

"Things?"

"I came up with an idea. The farmhouse is a five-bedroom, right?"

"Five small bedrooms, yes," he said.

"If it's all right with you, I thought I'd move in."

After Jace lifted his jaw off the grass, he grinned. The thought of having Haven right across the drive from him twenty-four hours a day warmed him more than he should admit, even to himself.

"I thought that maybe if I lived their lives right alongside them, the women might learn to trust me. I packed a lot of my small things, but I left my furniture back at my dad's house until I spoke to you. I would've called, but I only officially decided last night at about two in the morning."

"You know you could've called me at two in the morning," he said. "Is your dad okay with you moving out?"

"Are you kidding? He's been praying for this day. I should've moved out a long time ago, but my dad had no one else at home. I didn't want him to be lonely."

"I get it. If I could have lived with my mother a few years longer, I certainly would have. I'm glad you've decided to take this step, though."

"So you'll let me move in?"

"I think it's a great idea, but I never would've asked you to do it."

"What do you think Sonny, Jillian, and Rosalie will say?"

"Rosalie will love it. Sonny and Jillian? Not so much.

On this topic, I'll have to make the executive decision. What happened to your professional clothes?"

"That's the other thing. If I'm going to be living here, I need to pull my weight and get my hands dirty with something other than tomato sauce."

"Sounds fair. Can you drive a tractor?"

"I may need you to show me."

"Climb up in the seat."

Though nervous, Haven did as he requested, and he explained about the glow plugs, clutch, gear shift, and throttle. He liked lingering over her shoulder a smidge closer than necessary and covering her hand with his to help her move through the gears.

Jace hopped down onto the grass. "When you're ready, go ahead."

"What if I lose control, and you're way back here?"

"It's a tractor. How fast do you think you're going to go?" When that didn't calm her fears, he climbed back up. He sat on the fender beside her.

"Oh, no way. Haven't you seen that movie, *The Man in the Moon*?"

"With Jim Carrey?"

"No, Reese Witherspoon."

"Never saw it."

"Clearly. Because if you did, you'd have more respect for tractors, Mr. Daring. You may think you're strong with all those muscles of yours, but you aren't invincible, you know."

"Well, Miss Haviland, if I can't walk alongside the tractor and I can't sit on the fender, then the only other option is for one of us to sit on the other's lap. I'm not sure we're ready to take this partnership to that level."

"Good point."

He fit the muffs to her ears, finding himself way too comfortable being this close to her face. Her eyes weren't entirely green, he noticed. A faint golden sunburst radiated out around her pupils before fading into the same soft blue-green of an Ameraucana hen's eggs. Set between dark lashes, they were the prettiest eyes he'd ever seen. He mouthed, *Can you hear me?*

"What?" she yelled loud enough to make him flinch.

He pointed to the key, and she started the engine exactly how he'd directed her.

The tractor lurched forward, and Jace nearly lost his seat as his weight shifted. Haven's cheeks rounded in amusement.

"You did that on purpose."

"I can't hear you," she said with a big grin.

D on't you dare walk away from me again, Jace Daring," Sonny said as she climbed his porch steps the next morning. She assumed a power pose, hands on her waist, elbows out wide. If Jace didn't know the soft heart she carried inside, the coffee in his mug might have trembled. "You've been avoiding me and Jillian for the past twenty-four hours."

Jace took a sip of his coffee—his third since five a.m.— and leaned against the porch post. He'd better dig in for this conversation. Sonny wouldn't leave until she had answers. "Maybe I didn't want to get the third degree from you all."

"You moved her in! I thought you said that was *our home.*"

"It's still your home. But there was a spare bedroom in there that no one was using. And it was her idea."

"In what counseling handbook does it say *Move in with your clients*?"

"It makes sense to me. This way, you'll have to get to know her. Please give her a shot. And keep in mind that this probably isn't the easiest job she's ever had."

"She shouldn't be here."

"And she wouldn't have to be if you would step up and help me with Jillian and Rosalie."

"I've tried. You can't mentor someone like her."

"Jillian?"

Sonny bristled, but at least she dropped her hands to her sides. She retraced her path and sat on the steps facing the farmhouse. "Jillian's one of those girls who's always going to sell herself to men. She doesn't want any better for herself. She gets power from bringing men to their knees and shoving their lust in their faces."

"When I met her, she told me she wanted out. I didn't have to drag her, kicking and screaming."

"A nice-looking man like you? Of course she came along. But there's no mistaking. She was hoping to replace one handler with another. And every time you don't give in to her tricks to bed you, she's got one more toe out the door. One day, she'll go right back to her old life."

Jace's stomach soured. With a flick of his wrist, he dumped the remaining coffee over the side of the porch rail. "That's why I think it's a good idea to have Haven right there in the house. And not only to help Jillian. Rosalie, too. She . . ." Jace's thoughts hitched a ride on the breeze that seemed to carry Haven over the hill on the drive leading to their homes.

Her jogging motion swung her dark ponytail side to side until she slowed near the fence line. She rested her hands atop her head and paced in a slow circle. After a moment, she stopped and stood on one leg, holding her heel to her backside in a quadriceps stretch. Her body wavered a touch until she extended her free arm to the side and achieved perfect poise, displaying such strength in her form—an attractive balance to the vulnerability she'd shown him.

"You've got to be kidding me," Sonny growled, startling Jace back to their conversation. "Now I see what's up. You like her."

"Who?"

Sonny shot him a glare. "I know the look of a man who's attracted to a woman."

"It's not like that. I have total respect for her."

"You know, I thought I was in love once, too."

"I don't love her."

"Not yet, but give it time. From what I've seen, you don't do anything partway." Sonny sighed and rose from her seated position. "I should get back. 'Lijah is probably waking up."

"Sonny, I don't see her like that."

Sonny laughed. "I'll give Haven a chance. Mostly because the longer she sticks around, the more likely you are to get some action. It'd be good for you to kiss somebody. You could use loosening up."

Jace shook his head. "I'll let you think whatever you want. Thanks, Sonny." After he watched Sonny cross the drive and disappear into the house, Jace turned to go inside his cabin, but his hand froze on the door. Footsteps on the gravel seemed to be tracking straight across his chest. He didn't see Haven like that. Or more accurately, he *shouldn't* see Haven like that.

"Good morning." Her breathy greeting wrenched his focus away from his door. Her dark hair was slicked back with sweat. Her face sported a rosy flush. How on earth was she even more attractive after a run?

"Morning. Nice run?"

"Yeah, the downhill on the way back is great. And the water tower gives a good visual to let me know how far I still have to go." Haven kicked out her right leg in front of her and sank back into a runner's stretch. "You're welcome to join me sometime."

"Nah. I'm not in good shape."

Her gaze drifted down his body, then back up to his face. "You look to be in pretty good shape to me."

"Eh. It's all a facade. The moment you see me gasping

for breath after one hundred yards, you'll be on me." What did he just say? "*Onto* me. I meant onto me."

She covered her mouth, but he could see her smile in her cheeks and eyes.

"I should probably go inside before I say anything else dumb."

"Wait. I was thinking about you during this morning's run. You called this"—she motioned between them—"a partnership yesterday, right? I'm really stepping out of my comfort zone here, leaving my dad's home and all."

"Go on."

She studied his face. "Would you let me do some digging into your family name? The library has an archive listing every family who has ever owned property in the canyon."

"Haven . . ."

"What are you afraid of?"

"I have enough anger toward this town as it is. Every day I have to fight the hatred I feel for whoever hurt her. I guess I'm worried that if I ever match a face or a name to that hatred, I'll be consumed by it."

She moved a pinch closer and took his hands in hers. Her eyes shone with compassion as her thumb moved across his skin so delicately he barely felt it. "Then I'll be right here to help you sort it out. Trust me."

The last time a woman asked Jace to trust her, he'd fallen hard and fast. He still had the internal cuts and bruises to prove it. But Haven was nothing like Marjorie. She wasn't toying with his greatest fears to get what she wanted from him. "I trust you."

A smile was her only reply.

They lingered on the porch long enough for Jace to map the shape of her lips and commit it to memory—in case he ever found himself in a position to navigate them the way Sonny suggested.

Chapter Seventeen

Haven stroked the nail polish carefully from the cuticle to the tip. Of course, Rosalie had asked for bubble-gum pink with glitter. Such an innocent soul, that one.

"Don't you love this color, Haven?"

She peered up at Rosalie. "I do. I couldn't pull it off, though. You have the perfect skin tone for it."

Across the family room, Elijah applied layer after powdery layer of makeup to Sonny's face. The boy did not have a light hand, that was for sure.

"Do you think they have a lipstick to match? Without the glitter, I mean," Rosalie said.

"Probably. I could ask my sister Rarity. She's a makeup genius."

"Is she the one that owns the old dress shop?"

"She is. You know, there's a dance in a couple weeks. Maybe we could go to my sister's shop beforehand and pick out some fun dresses. What do you think, Sonny?"

Sonny waited until Elijah finished painting broad, mauve lines over and around her lips. "I'm not a big dress wearer, but a dance might be fun. As long as it doesn't get in the way of work."

Rosalie's cheeks flushed pink as she stared down at her nails. "Does everyone in town go to the dance?"

"For the most part. Although this year, the mayor announced a dress code that would prohibit anyone with excessive piercings, unnatural hair colors, or untraditional attire, whatever that means. Why?" Haven finished polishing Rosalie's pinkie nail.

"I didn't know if guys my age went."

Oh. Haven thought back to when Rosalie chatted with Jimmy Horst at the bookstore. "Yes. There will be plenty of guys there doing the cha cha slide and—"

"The what?" Rosalie asked.

"You know. One of those dances everyone learns in middle school. DJs love to play those songs to get everyone on the dance floor."

Sonny and Rosalie exchanged glances.

"It's more fun than it sounds."

Rosalie blew on her nails. "I missed out on that. Ya know, middle school wasn't the happiest time in my life."

"Me, neither," Sonny said. "Maybe if I'd gone to more middle school dances instead of going out with guys twice my age, I would've avoided a whole lot of trouble. Of course, I also wouldn't have this guy." She tucked Elijah into her lap and kissed him on the cheek, leaving a purplish-pink splotch on the boy's face.

"Sonny, I can't take you seriously with that makeup." Rosalie laughed. "Haven, now I'm worried. What if I don't know the . . . ?"

"Cha cha slide."

"Yeah, that. How will I even know what song it is?"

Haven held up her phone. "Let me find it." After a quick Internet search, she found the song. She pressed play and turned it up until the familiar beat begged her foot to tap.

"How does the dance go?" Rosalie asked.

"Yes, Haven. Please show us how the dance goes." Pure trouble shone from Sonny's blue eyeshadowed eyes.

"No way. I can't do it alone. I'll look silly."

"Do it. Do it," Rosalie chanted. Sonny and even Elijah joined in taunting Haven.

"I'm not a good dancer. I'm not even positive I'd get all the steps right."

"Please," Rosalie said. "If Jace lets us go to the dance—"

"That's a huge if," Sonny added.

"I don't want to be the only person who doesn't know. I'm tired of being so different from everyone else."

Haven groaned. "All right, fine. I can't believe I'm doing this," she mumbled as she restarted the song and stood in front of the television. If making a fool of herself would break through walls, she'd do it.

Sonny and Elijah scampered to the couch for a better view.

When instructed, Haven grapevined right a few steps, then left, and finally back. She hopped and stomped until her audience laughed themselves silly. Loving the joyful sound, Haven poured her whole heart into the dance. She'd just started cha-chaing toward the television when the front door opened. She spun around to find Jillian and Jace staring slack-jawed at her performance.

"What's this?" Jillian asked. "An exorcism?"

"Haven's teaching us some awful dance," Sonny explained.

Jace listened for a moment. "You're teaching them the cha cha slide?"

"Oh, sweet geezer, you know this dance, too?" Rosalie asked.

"I learned it at Terrence's wedding."

"Do it, do it, do it," Elijah shouted.

"Don't tempt me. You all can't handle my moves."

"Sure, cowboy. I bet you're a real great dancer," Sonny teased.

"Haven, restart the song."

Before Haven could spell *professionalism*, she and Jace were clapping a quick rhythm and crisscrossing together. Giddiness spilled from Haven in the form of laughter. And Jace? Well, his swagger brought a certain amount of heat to the dance that Haven didn't think was possible. And the way he smiled at her? Oh, sweet geezer.

Sonny, Rosalie, and Elijah joined them, making their dance floor quite crowded. When Haven tried to "get low," a bunny-hopping Elijah bumped into her backside, forcing her forward. Jace made a diving catch, saving her before the last of her pride hit the carpet.

"Are you okay?" he asked. Beneath her palm, his chest shook with the remains of laughter.

"I think I injured my self-respect."

Jace's hand slid into her hair at the back of her head, and he pulled her close, until his breath kissed her ear. "This was brilliant. I knew you'd find a way to get to Sonny and Rosalie."

Sonny and Rosalie. But what about—? A loud door-slam echoed through the house, making it shudder.

After church the following Sunday, Haven returned to Aspen Crossroads just as Jace's tractor chugged away from the barn. For the last few days, she'd searched high and low for any record of Jace's last name in Whisper Canyon's history. It wasn't in the library's archive, census records, or on file at the town clerk's office at Town Hall. She'd even called her grandparents in Arizona to ask if they had any recollection. All to no avail. Could his mother have changed her name?

In front of the farmhouse, Jillian lay on a blanket with her shirt rolled up to expose her stomach. For September in the Rockies, it was warm, and Jillian was making the most of the sun.

Haven grabbed the blanket from her trunk. She approached Jillian cautiously, the way a park ranger might approach injured wildlife. One wrong move and Jillian might ram, bite, or gore her. Haven tried to find her most casual tone. "Hey, girl." *Ugh. Awful.*

Jillian raised herself onto one elbow and peered in Haven's direction. "Oh, you're still here?" Then she plunked right back down onto the blanket.

Shaking it off, Haven released the folds of the quilt until it reached the grass. She positioned it next to Jillian, but not within a fist-strike in case Jillian got any ideas. Since they'd shared a house, Jillian had only spoken a handful of words to her. Haven crawled onto the quilt and mimicked Jillian's pose, facing the sun. She pictured Jesus lying out next to one of the folks he met, earning the right to be heard, and working on his tan. It was enough to crack her smile. Jesus, she was not.

The creak of the farmhouse door shook her from her daydream.

"You guys! Guess what!" Rosalie exploded off the porch and pounced on Jillian's blanket, holding her cell phone out for them to see. "I got asked out on a date!"

"No," Jillian said, sitting upright. "By who?"

"Remember that boy from the grocery store? The one with the super cute smile? It's him."

Jillian huffed and lay back down. "Better tell him no. Ain't no way Jace will let you go."

Haven shook her head but had enough wherewithal not to roll her eyes. "What's his name?"

"Jimmy."

"Reverend Horst's son?" Haven asked.

Rosalie's smile waned. "I didn't know his dad was a reverend. I just thought Jimmy was cute and nice every time I went to the store."

Afraid she'd allowed her own concerns to dampen Rosalie's spirit, Haven patted Rosalie's hand. "He's definitely cute and very nice. I think you two would make a great couple. When does he want you to go?"

"It doesn't matter," Jillian said, yanking off her sunglasses. "Jace doesn't want *his women* leaving the homestead for anything so dumb. Have you forgotten who we are, Rosalie? Do you honestly believe a reverend is going to allow his son to date you once he learns where you came from? I swear, sometimes I think I'm the only one of you that has any brains."

"What's all the yelling about?" Jace appeared behind Rosalie, his facial features washed out by the sun directly overhead.

"Don't you have work to do in the back fields?" Jillian asked.

"The tractor blew a belt. Now, what's going on?"

Haven buttoned her lips, and Rosalie's chin trembled slightly.

Jillian sighed. "Rosalie got asked on a date by the pastor's son, and I told her you wouldn't let her go."

Jace seemed to choose his next words carefully. "Jill's right. It's a terrible idea. You'll have to tell him no."

Rosalie jumped to her feet. "But I—"

"I said no," Jace said, sharp as a scythe.

Haven wasn't sure which sound was worse: Rosalie's sobs, Jace's boots swooshing angrily across the gravel to his truck, or Jillian's I-told-you-so laugh. Haven caught up to him as he climbed in his cab and pulled the door closed. Contemplating what to say, she rested her hands on the sill of the truck's open window. "Where are you going?"

"To get a new belt. Did you encourage that?"

"Rosalie wanting to date? I don't think so. I didn't *dis*-courage it, though."

"You don't know the kind of monsters who are out there waiting for girls like Rosalie."

"Jace, it's my reverend's son. He's anything but a monster."

"Great," he said with a scoff. "Even better. It's out of the question. As long as I'm here, there will be no dating for them."

"Fine. Fine. I'll talk to her and tell her about the importance of friendship over relationship. Is she allowed to have friends?"

Jace leveled a heated look at her. "Yes. She can have friends—within reason."

"Okay, then." Haven kept her focus on Jace until his angry expression finally broke. Still not a smile, but it was better than a death glare. "I've been looking. There's no record of a Leigh Anne Daring or any Daring at all."

He huffed, then fingered the edge of an old photo on his console. "No one other than me seems to remember her. It's like that tree-falling-in-the-forest riddle. If someone dies and no one remembers them, did they ever live at all?"

Jace needed a break before *he* broke. No record anywhere of his mother, and now Rosalie wanted to date? Could there be any worse idea out there? He searched the mountains as his truck sped down the highway toward the automotive store. Time and time again he'd seen what happened when the women he cared for got involved with a man. If he had the power to stop it, he would. Like he should have sixteen years ago.

He could still smell the musty scent of concrete in that New Mexican courthouse. He remembered thinking it ironic that a courthouse was where things were supposed to be made right, yet everything about that day in 2004 had felt wrong.

Jace had pulled at the sleeves of his ill-fitting shirt. Gus's shirt. Though freshly washed, it had still carried the smell of stale cigarette smoke and beer.

"Is my best man ready?" Mom's arm came around his waist. At only fourteen, he was already taller than her. Not gangly like the public school boys. He had more muscle than those jerks—the only thing that kept them from messing with him too much.

"Why do you have to marry him?"

"He promised to take care of us and keep a roof over our heads. And I won't need to visit with other men anymore. Besides, it's about time you had a male role model to look up to."

"I don't need any role model other than you."

"I'm no role model. Don't you like Gus?"

Jace shrugged. "He's not good enough for you. None of them are."

"You think too much of me."

"Can't we keep living in his house without you marrying him?"

"God values marriage. It's time I make things right."

"From what you've taught me, God would want what's best for us."

"You don't think that's Gus?"

Jace wrinkled his nose. "I can get a job to support us. The Laundromat might hire me."

"You need to concentrate on school. I don't want you dropping out like I did. With Gus, you'll get your diploma. Maybe you can even go to college. You'll be the first in the family to go."

"Did you drop out because of me?"

She took his face in her hands. "You are the greatest gift God ever gave me. And anything that happened after you came along is not your fault. Do you hear me?"

"Yes, ma'am."

"And I believe God brought Gus into our lives to take care of us."

A chill traveled beneath Jace's skin. "He's too . . ."

Concern etched her tired eyes. "He's what?"

"I dunno. He wants you all to himself." The guy didn't even like it when Mom paid too much attention to her own son. He'd wait until Mom would leave the room, then give Jace the stink eye.

"You only think that because of the men you've met in the past. Gus is different," she said with as much confidence as Jace when he answered a question in front of his geometry class.

"If you're so sure, then why aren't you getting married in a church so God can see over it?"

"What have I told you about church?"

"That church isn't the place for us, and no one will accept us there."

"God can look after us no matter where we are. His eyes search the land for ways to help his people. And he's watching over us now. I can feel it." She checked her watch. "Now, it's time for you to give me away."

Give her away? The words turned his feet to cement. How could he give his mother to a man he barely knew? All those times he'd watched her go off with men had been tough enough, but this felt even worse. She couldn't love Gus, could she? She didn't even seem to like the guy. If that was love, Jace didn't want anything to do with it.

His mom peeked inside the courtroom, then let the door slip closed. "Gus and the judge are waiting for us. How do I look?" She fussed with her golden hair. At least it had stopped falling out once she quit worrying about whether they'd eat that day. No mom should ever have to worry about that. Maybe college could teach Jace how to help people like him and his mom. So they wouldn't have to marry gross guys like Gus.

She wore a simple dress—light blue, thanks to a comment Gus made about her not being allowed to wear white. But it matched her eyes.

"How do I look?"

"Like an angel, Mom."

Only six months later, Jace's angel was gone.

Chapter Eighteen

J illian, are you in here?" Haven asked as she knocked on Jillian's bedroom door. While Haven didn't expect Jillian to want to go to Denver to look for restaurant decor, she still wanted to ask. After all, sitting in a car with the girl for ninety minutes both ways wasn't exactly Haven's ideal activity, either.

She knocked harder this time, and the door slipped open a crack. Haven saw a neatly made-up bed through the sliver. Although she desperately wanted to know more about her housemate, Haven wouldn't snoop. If Jillian didn't want her in her room, she would not go in. Downstairs, Sonny told Elijah they were going to The Mill to watch the appliances get delivered and installed. The front door opened and shut. The draft that carried through the old farmhouse swung Jillian's door open with a long creak.

Haven remained outside the threshold, but from where she stood, she got a great view.

While the floor, bed, and dresser were immaculately kept, every square inch of the walls displayed sketches of people—their faces or their hands. Sometimes their entire bodies. Beautiful drawings celebrating the human form, good enough to be in an art gallery.

Haven recognized a few of the faces. Rosalie with her inquisitive eyes. Elijah's chubby-cheeked grin. Sonny's regal stature. But where was Jace? Jillian clearly admired the man—who wouldn't?

Then she saw it. There was one picture, but Haven had to crane her neck to see it. The only drawing pinned to the ceiling hung directly above Jillian's pillow. This one was a landscape identical to Aspen Crossroads. Between the fields, a tall man wearing a cowboy hat held a woman in his arms.

"What are you doing in my room?" Jillian, smelling of sweat, earth, and hay, pushed past Haven, knocking her into the doorframe.

"I'm not in your room," Haven stuttered.

"You opened my door?"

"It swung open by itself."

"Oh yeah. It does that. I told Jace to fix it, but when he visits my room, he has more important things to do."

Haven kept her cool. "Speaking of Jace, he said you were in charge of the restaurant decor. If you want, we could go to Denver to look around."

"I don't need your help." With a leer, Jillian shut the door in Haven's face.

Haven threw her hands up. With Sonny busy at the restaurant and Rosalie checking out a GED prep class in town, Haven had nothing to do. For the next hour, she swept the main floor and dusted the furniture. After that, she visited the chick nursery. Audrey's toes had finally straightened out, so she no longer needed the cast. Haven found herself visiting her often. She fit Audrey and the others with Rosalie's hand-knitted sweaters in the evenings when the temperatures dipped. However, Haven could hang out with chickens for only so long. Pretty soon, she'd start seeing chickens in her dreams.

When Daniel's text came through offering her a lunch date, she jumped at the chance.

The Rusty Elk Steakhouse was empty at eleven o'clock—perfect for the gossip-laden Haviland twins. Daniel had already gotten a table when she arrived, but he rose to welcome her with an embrace, which she gladly accepted.

"Thanks for the invitation," she said before squeezing him as hard as she could.

"It's cute how you think you can hurt me, Have." He squeezed her back, though not nearly as hard as he could.

Still, her breath sputtered out. "Uncle, uncle. You win."

He kissed her on the forehead and then pushed her off him playfully. "Thanks for meeting me."

Haven took her seat across from him. "What's up?"

Her brother wiped invisible crumbs off the table. "Not much."

She eyed him suspiciously. "Daniel?" Every now and then, she caught a glimmer of the old Daniel. Of Oak. The confident, not arrogant, brother she'd always been able to count on when she needed him for a strong hand up or a perfectly timed word of encouragement. She could see him now.

"I've missed you. That's all."

Tears teased the corners of her eyes and a lump threatened to climb into her throat. "I've missed you, too. It's been a hard year, hasn't it?"

"It has. Between Grace leaving, you closing your practice, Nina . . ." Daniel hadn't called their mother *Mom* since she'd abandoned them. "It's been weighing on me."

"Will you tell me about it?"

He shook his head. "I guess I'm feeling a bit lost, but I'm fine. What about you? Are you doing all right?"

She nodded her head up, down, then in a circle—a childhood joke of theirs that meant *yes*, *no*, and *I have no idea* all at once. "I'm enjoying the new job even though there have been obstacles."

"What's the deal with Garrison? Why is he coming after The Mill so hard?"

"What do you mean?" she asked.

"Every time I go into Town Hall, I overhear him talking to someone about some new concern he has. Like, this morning, he was suggesting to the town engineer that the road leading to The Mill's driveway was at risk for falling rocks. You know the one part that nears the canyon wall? He wondered if the road shouldn't be gated at dusk to prevent accidents."

"What did the engineer say?"

"He said he didn't have the time or the budget for that."

Haven released her breath. "He does have an agenda. He doesn't want outsiders bringing any bad things into the town, not that anyone there would."

"I don't know. It seems like there's more to it than that. Like there's something there that he wants." Daniel pinned her with a look. "Is there anything you want to tell me?"

She pulled her bottom lip between her teeth and clamped down on it.

"Hey, folks. What would you like to drink?" The server handed them each a menu.

They ordered two ice waters, and the man left the table, leaving only awkward silence. After Daniel perused the menu, he tapped it on the table twice. "Why do you think Garrison is having Dad fix up that car?"

"Maybe he wanted a Corvette."

"Or maybe this is another part of his grand scheme." Daniel bent over the table. "Even though we aren't kids anymore, I'm still your brother, and if you need me—"

The restaurant's door opened, carrying a slight chill with it. The customer was none other than Lizzie Sautter, with Jace on her heel.

When they noticed Haven and Daniel, they shared a glance and a few whispers, then slowly approached the table. Lizzie spoke first. "Hello, Haven. Daniel, how are you?"

"Elizabeth," Daniel said, but instead of answering her question, his focus moved between Lizzie and Jace.

Jace's brow weighed heavily over his eyes. Even the half smile he offered seemed burdened. "The restaurant must be good if the locals choose it."

"It's great. The Rocky Mountain stew is a local favorite. Also, the prime rib sandwich is the best in town," Haven stammered. Why should she care that he was here with a woman? Lizzie was nice. He deserved to be with someone nice. It was all just so . . . nice.

"I'll seat you two right over here," the hostess said.

Lizzie and Jace were taken about ten yards away, toward the back, and were seated so that with a slight turn of her head, Haven could catch Jace's eye. Which she did, about ten times in the first two minutes.

"Are they dating?" Daniel asked after they ordered their food.

"Jace and I don't talk about that stuff." Haven pushed back from the table. "I have to go to the restroom. I'll be right back." She made a point of not looking toward Jace as she went to the back hallway of the restaurant. But instead of turning left into the restroom, she exited out the rear door. She'd barely taken two cleansing breaths when Jace appeared.

His mouth remained closed as he stood before her, but his eyes searched hers. "A couple of men from the county want to preview the restaurant on Wednesday. Lizzie thought it might be good to get them on board. On our side, if you will, in case Garrison pulls any stunts around the opening. This lunch is to help me come up with a game plan. I haven't said anything to you about it because I don't need you to worry."

"Why are you telling me now?"

The cool color of his eyes brought the Colorado sky nearer to her. "Because I want you to know Lizzie and I aren't on a date."

"It'd be okay if you were."

"Would it?" Jace looked hurt. He took a half step back. "Sorry. I'm not thinking. I'll let you get back to your lunch."

Did he just . . . ? No, he didn't like her. Not like that. They were colleagues. Coworkers. And sure, he was fun to flirt with, and she might have imagined him pulling her into a passionate kiss a time or two or ten, but it was harmless.

"Hey, Jace?"

"Yeah?" He turned, a glint of hope on his handsome face.

"Daniel works with the county and town officials on some of his projects. And although you two haven't had the best history, he'd be a great one to help you turn the tide in favor of the opening. If you and Lizzie wanted to join us at our table, we could help you with that plan."

"If you trust him, then I'll trust him." He held open the door for Haven, but she paused when she got directly in front of him.

"For the record, I'm glad you and Lizzie aren't on a date." She pursed her lips to keep any blush at bay and quickly entered the restaurant.

When they returned to the dining area, they both stopped short. Lizzie was sitting in a spare chair at Daniel's side. Haven suddenly doubted the wisdom of inviting Daniel into this meeting. "It looks as though they had the same idea."

Chapter Nineteen

On the street in front of the Rusty Elk, Daniel walked Lizzie to her car. Jace didn't love the idea of Daniel befriending Lizzie, but he could look out for only so many women at a time. Lizzie was smart. She could see through any of Daniel's come-ons.

"What are your plans for the afternoon?" Haven asked Jace.

"The appliances, counters, and shelving are being delivered to The Mill today. What about you?"

"Nothing really. I was thinking of stopping by Rarity's shop."

Jace glanced at his truck, then back to Haven. "Sonny could always oversee the delivery and setup. The kitchen is her domain anyway. I could join you if you want company."

"I'd like that."

They strolled north down the street, and when two women approached them, Jace gave way to let them pass, only to hear the whispers about "one of the Haviland girls." If Haven heard, she didn't show it. Instead, she kept her chin high.

"Tell me about Daniel," Jace said.

Haven looked out into the distance. "Daniel was the nicest kid. Everyone loved him. And while I was the one in my family that everyone went to when they were sad, we went to Daniel, or Oak, as we called him back then, when we needed strength and confidence. In fact, if it weren't for him, I never would have been able to study abroad."

"You studied abroad?" Jace asked.

"My sophomore year, I was struggling socially. My aunt offered for me to come stay with her in Australia. Daniel encouraged me to go. It was the one time I lived for myself. I discovered running and learned how to take care of my body. I even got to hold a koala."

He bumped her shoulder a bit. "I can picture you with a koala."

"It was the best year of my life." Haven's smile morphed into a frown. "While I was gone, Daniel caught our mother in bed with his married football coach. She made him keep her secret for nearly a year. And he did. When I came home that next summer, he didn't look like himself. He'd lost all his muscle. He wouldn't smile. He'd gone from straight As to barely passing. It took forever for me to get the secret out of him. I guess he was trying to protect me."

"Oh man." Jace felt a touch of pity for Daniel.

"I was the one who told our dad. My mother blamed him for destroying our family. And then she skipped town with the coach."

"How did you all handle it?"

"When she left, Valor moved to Fort Collins. Rarity took off to pursue fashion. Dash left to play soccer at this international academy when she was sixteen. Oak—Daniel—rebounded, but not in a good way. He demanded we never call him Oak again. He'd sleep with a girl, then act like he didn't know her. Almost like he was taking out his anger toward our mom on them. Then he went off to college, internships, and graduate school."

"What about you?"

"Me? I just . . . stayed."

"Why?"

"So my dad wouldn't be alone. So I'd be here when everyone else came home. The thing about Whisper Canyon is that all roads lead back here. They all returned with some new hurt for me to heal. Well, not Daniel. He returned with Grace Calhoun. They met during graduate school, and it was as if he'd never been hurt at all. He was good. Kind. Settled. However, she left him at the altar two months ago."

"Ouch," Jace said as they passed the spot where he'd pushed Daniel against the wall that day.

"As you might imagine, his trust issues put mine to shame. Now he's back to his old ways."

"Not with Lizzie, I hope. Can you talk to Daniel?"

"It's not that simple."

Haven stopped in front of a building with a *For Lease* sign in the window. In the reflection, her solemn expression lengthened her face.

Jace lifted his focus above the window. While the actual letters had been removed, Haven's last name ghosted the concrete's yet-to-be-repaired finish. "Haviland's Counseling. Do you miss it?"

"Sometimes. There's nothing else like watching someone find healing. It's like seeing a prayer answered right before your eyes." Haven gave him a smile, then nodded to the store next door. "Now, are you ready to meet my sister Rarity?"

"Is she anything like you?"

"Not at all."

A mannequin that appeared to be from the 1960s was dressed in a Woodstock-inspired outfit. Beyond that, a rack of clothes blocked half the sidewalk and a sandwich board spelled out *Fringe and Lace Vintage Dress Shop*.

"You aren't allergic to dust, are you?" she asked.

"Not that I know of."

"Good." Haven grabbed his hand and pulled him into the store. Bells rang out and a few customers looked their way. A man with hair down to his ribs glanced up, then knocked on a door. "Your sister's here. With a boy."

Before Jace could hightail it out of there, the back door swung open and one of the passengers from the *Titanic* burst through. Or at least, that's what it seemed, considering how she was dressed. As she neared, he recognized her as the sister who'd been at Haven's side on the street that day.

"Haven! Thanks for popping by." Rarity turned to Jace. "Hey, cowboy. Aren't you a dream?"

"Rarity, this is Jace Daring."

"Even your name is fine." Rarity grabbed two fistfuls of his shirt and pulled herself close to his chest. "And he smells good, too. Haven, why do you get all the good ones?"

"It's um, not, uh—"

Rarity released him. "Did you hear Garrison is trying to buy your old office? Word is he wants to fill it with some schmancy-fancy jewelry store. Personally, I think he's just trying to keep wifey happy."

"Good for them," Haven said without emotion.

"Good for them? I should lease it. We could turn it into a community space or a food bank. Or in winter, it can be a homeless shelter."

"Rarity, you know Garrison would never allow such a space right in the heart of downtown. He wants to drive out the town's population who need such services, not accommodate them."

So Aspen Crossroads wasn't the only organization being shut out by the rich and mighty in this town. Jace listened intently as Rarity continued about the mayor and his wife's vow to "clean up" the city. She believed it was all a scheme to turn Whisper Canyon into a ritzy resort town to compete with Aspen and Vail.

"What they're doing isn't right," Haven said. "But try to remember their perspective. To them, progress is the utmost."

"Progress means nothing if it changes the very heart of

Whisper Canyon. Prescott Garrison's grandson should understand that." Rarity slid her fist down her string of pearls so roughly, Jace expected them to break any moment. "I cannot believe my sister is defending that swine."

Haven stepped closer and placed a soft hand on her sister's shoulder. Her touch doused the fire in Rarity's eyes. "Not defending him. I'm on your side. Jace and I both face a similar battle. But Garrison is smart. If we want our voices to be heard, we have to start by understanding how they think they're acting heroically."

The two sisters chatted a bit longer, and Jace watched Haven's remarkable way of talking Rarity down from her soapbox. By the time a gaggle of teenage girls entered the shop, Rarity was able to give them her focus, and Jace and Haven snuck out. Once outside, they kept heading north toward the park.

"That's Rarity for you," Haven said. "All gas, no brake, as my father used to say. Would you believe she dated Trent's younger brother once?"

"He's got a brother?"

"Aidan Garrison."

"Like Aidan Garrison, quarterback for the Colorado Centennials?"

"The very one. Anyway, I think he and Rarity had something going a few years back. He must have broken her heart because she won't talk about it."

"Is Aidan more reasonable than Trent?"

Haven shrugged. "I don't think it matters. According to gossip, he wants nothing to do with Whisper Canyon or his family name anymore. He and Trent aren't even on speaking terms."

"You know, it's funny. I always thought everyone else had it so good being in a family."

"In my time as a counselor, families provide either the greatest protection or the fiercest harm. Sometimes both at the same time."

When they reached the traffic circle at the intersection of Main Street and Copper Kettle Way, Jace held her hand as they entered the crosswalk. Not the way a boyfriend might, but the way a mother might as she led her child across the street. Protective.

"What was your mother like?" Haven asked.

As they walked in the park, Jace sorted through miles of memories—some good and some horrendous, but all of them hidden deep within him. Haven was quiet beside him with perfect patience as he decided which memories to share and which ones to keep for himself. While a few children played on the new playground and their mothers chatted on the benches nearby with Jailhouse Roasters cups in their hands, Jace veered Haven toward the older, abandoned playground. Metal and wood combined to form a tangle of climbing equipment and swings that his mother had likely once played on. They paused by the gate, and Jace flicked a sign nailed to a post explaining that the old playground was due to be torn down next week. Aw, progress.

"She was a great mom. I mean, sure, we lived in homeless shelters, but she never let me doubt that I was loved." Jace walked to the merry-go-round. He gripped one of the chipped yellow bars around the edge. "She taught me to read before I was in kindergarten. And she'd recite Bible stories from memory along with all the set prayers." A tear formed in the corner of his eyes, and he knuckled it away. "She used to sing this song to me all the time, especially when I was scared. Like, if we were in a new town or a new shelter. She said she wrote it for kids she babysat."

"Will you sing it for me?" Haven asked, giving him the best doe eyes he'd ever seen.

"If you let me spin you on this thing."

"Never mind. No way. I'll either throw up my lunch or fall off and die underneath it."

"I won't spin you that fast. Come on. It'll be fun."

"Ugh." Haven stepped onto the faded red-and-gray base. She lay down on her back in the middle with a tight grip on one of the bars. "Okay."

Jace cleared his throat. "Here it goes:

"Brave one, brave one, time for bed,
Close your eyes and rest your head.
When you wake, the sun will, too.
There'll be much more fun to do.
Brave one, brave one, say your prayer,
Dreams come true for those who dare."

"That's sweet, Jace."

"Like I said, she was a great mom. Now, are you ready?"

Haven pressed her hands flat beside her. "Eek! Go ahead."

Holding on to the bar, Jace jogged in a circle, pulling the merry-go-round into a spin, not as fast as he could have gone, but enough for a rush. He hopped on and spread his body next to Haven's. Beside him, Haven rolled, grasping the crook of his arm and burying her face into his shoulder. He liked how it felt to have her hold on to him.

Too soon, the clouds stopped spinning, and the metallic groan from beneath the contraption quieted.

Haven still didn't let go. "Jace, what happened to your mother?"

Jace felt the tear return to his eye. "One of my mom's customers, Gus, offered to marry her. I think getting me into a stable home was all my mom cared about, so she said yes. I hated him. I hated how he treated her like a prostitute. One night, Gus threatened me. I wanted to fight him. If I could throw one good punch, I'd break his nose and show him he wasn't so tough. My mom told me to be the bigger man and walk away. So I left. I walked the city for hours. When I came back to the house at four a.m., the red-and-blue lights were everywhere, and the ambulance was leaving." Jace swallowed the stone in his throat. "They didn't even use the siren. She was too far gone."

Haven sniffled at his side. "What happened to Gus?"

"After he killed her, he turned the gun on himself. That's why I work so hard to help these women. There aren't a lot of ways out of the sex industry for those who want to leave, and there are way too many creeps like Gus who offer them the things they want most, only to hurt them worse in the end. If I can save even one person from that fate, it's worth it."

Haven set her chin on his shoulder, her earnest gaze settling on his eyes. "It's an honor to know you, Jace Daring." Her breaths came fast and went deep, much like his own. She'd said she was glad he and Lizzie weren't on a date. That, the hand touches, the way she looked at him now—she had to be feeling what he was. This yearning to bring his heart as close to hers as possible.

He had to repress it. To show restraint. Even if the ache threatened to engulf him. One touch. That's all. With his free hand, he grazed her cheek, yet that only brought his focus to her rosy lips. "I feel the same way about you."

Chapter Twenty

Jace paced across the main dining room of The Mill. At the meeting table, Haven, Daniel, and Lizzie watched him, but said nothing. With the restaurant due to open in less than three weeks, this had to work.

"Some cars pulled up," Jillian said as she peered through a window nearest the door. "Uh, was Garrison supposed to be here? Because he is."

Jace joined her at the window. "He wasn't supposed to be. I didn't think he knew about it." Sure enough, Trent led the two other men across the parking lot.

"I shouldn't be here." Haven stood. "Remember Trent's warning for me to stay away from you? If he sees me, the discussion will be over before it starts."

Jace went to her. "You don't have to leave."

"You know I do. Besides, you'll have Daniel and Lizzie to represent the locals, and I'll be listening from the kitchen. Remember the advice I gave Rarity. They are after progress and tourism revenue. Show them that this restaurant works for the town, not against it." She leaned closer to his ear. "I'll be cheering for you." Then she was gone.

At the hostess stand, Jillian's hands fidgeted.

"No need to be nervous, Jill. You'll be fine," he said.

"He . . . they know about my past."

"Only the mayor. And if he says even a word about it, he'll be walking out of here with a black eye and a lawsuit." Jace tried for a smile, but it didn't seem to ease Jillian's nerves. "Okay, everyone. Let's do this."

The door opened, and Trent slithered into the restaurant.

Jillian fixed a pleasant grin on her face that Jace had never seen before. "Hello, gentlemen. Welcome to The Mill. My name is Jillian, and I'll be your hostess and server this evening." Her focus lingered a bit too long on Garrison, and the creep noticed.

Finally, he unhooked his ogling eyes from her and perused the scene, doing a double take when he got to Daniel. "Haviland, what are you doing here?"

Daniel rose from his chair and extended a hand to Garrison. "I've recently become acquainted with Mr. Daring and his organization. With my interest in seeing Whisper Canyon thrive and my work with the town's planning commission, I invited myself to join the conversation."

"Are you the only Haviland here tonight?"

Daniel didn't miss a beat. "If you're worried that Rarity might show up and protest, well, you can rest easy. She's not here."

Scott Englevort, their local planning commission chairman, introduced himself to the group, followed by Bill Dreyer, the Summit County commissioner for Whisper Canyon's district. After a round of handshakes, they all took their seats.

"I have to say, Mr. Daring, you've done a remarkable job fixing up this old gristmill," Scott said. "Back in high school, I spent quite a bit of time here conjuring up scary stories and drinking toasts to the ghosts with cheap alcohol. Daniel, I remember that you were quite the partier. Tell me. Did you ever bring girls here?"

Daniel wasn't amused. "Let's keep this professional, Scott."

Jillian explained the evening's courses, then disappeared to get the appetizers.

As the group tried the poblano-stuffed mushrooms, spoon bread, and house salad with warm bacon dressing, Jace explained more about the mission of the restaurant: to provide modern comfort foods from sustainable farms no farther than five hundred miles from Whisper Canyon.

While Bill seemed interested in knowing about the ins and outs of farming in the mountains, Scott wanted to learn more about the renovation of the restaurant. Even Daniel seemed impressed with Jace's answers. With Daniel's knowledge of architecture, both new and classic, Jace had worried Daniel would disagree with some of the choices he'd made during the remodel.

Garrison, however, was as quiet as a brown recluse in the rafters, biding his time before he bit into Jace's work.

Jillian delivered the entrée. Bacon-wrapped filets, topped with cracked black pepper, grilled to perfection and paired with herb butter, garlic mashed potatoes, and sautéed spinach straight from Aspen Crossroads. Sonny's cooking didn't disappoint. Although the restaurant still needed to install Jillian's artwork on the walls and furnish the dining and bar area, it was already functioning better than any restaurant Jace had opened so far. He was proud of his team. He only wished Rosalie could be here, too, but she was babysitting Elijah back at the house.

"Why don't you tell the table more about your hiring practices, Mr. Daring?" Garrison said as he plunged his knife into the beef.

"The main team: my executive chef, Sonny; my manager, Jillian; and my hostess and trainer, Rosalie, were all hired this spring by the Secondly organization. The rest of the staff we've hired are locals. We start training next week."

"Do they have any background in restaurant management?"

Jace met Trent's eyes. "If you are asking if they are qualified for their work, then yes, absolutely."

"What's their previous work experience?"

Jace's frustration simmered in his veins. "Our organization vets our employees very well before hiring them."

"Tell us more about Secondly," Bill said.

"We give opportunities to hardworking individuals who haven't had the best chance in life. For instance, I was recruited when I was twenty years old. I'd been working on farms across the West for five years by that point. One of the farms was a Secondly farm. The operator, Terrence, took me under his wing. He still mentors me, although he no longer operates a farm. He procures real estate for Secondly. Mayor, I believe you had words with him when we were trying to buy this land. You also had words with him when you tried to block us from getting our business license."

Garrison huffed a laugh.

"Look," Jace said, "I shouldn't be where I am now. I should've died out there on the streets, but this organization stepped in so that didn't happen. They see the potential in a person, a run-down farm, or an old gristmill. They see how something as simple as a high-concept restaurant could bring even more money into a town like Whisper Canyon. They see the potential for progress. And isn't that what you're all hoping for?"

From the passenger seat of Jace's truck, Haven listened to the farm's night sounds. Jace had cut the engine several minutes ago, but neither one of them moved to leave the cab. Stars illuminated the moonless sky above, begging to be noticed. The passenger window cooled Haven's forehead as she peered up—a perfect complement to the warmth of the air between her and Jace.

"Isn't it beautiful?" She turned to find his focus on her.

He didn't answer. He simply released a heavy breath.

"Tell me again how great the night went," she demanded, angling herself to face him.

Jace grinned. "It couldn't have gone better, even if Trent hadn't crashed the party. Scott and Bill both raved over Sonny's food and the restaurant in general. They were taking selfies in front of it. Oh, I forgot to tell you this part. They came up with hashtags, BelieveTheWhispers and TastetheMill."

"I'm so glad, Jace. You're doing it." She reached over and squeezed his hand.

When she tried to release it, he held on. "*We* are doing it."Slowly, he turned his palm over until their fingertips matched up. Haven struggled to find enough oxygen, and her heart thudded so loud she was sure Jace heard it.

He swallowed hard, then delicately interlaced their fingers, worn and rough, until the heat from his palm nearly melted hers. A sweet, silent communion.

Yet Jace looked tortured, even as his thumb caressed her skin in small sweeping motions. She didn't understand. This was the best her heart had felt since . . . Trent first held her hand.

Jace let go with a flinch. "I should turn in. I have to be up early."

"Of course. It was a long night. Thanks for the ride home." Haven got out of the truck and, still processing what had happened, hurried across the drive to the farmhouse. Before she climbed the porch steps, she looked over her shoulder. Jace also stood at the foot of his steps, staring at her.

"Did your seat belt get stuck?"

Haven jumped. "Jillian. What are you doing out here?"

On the porch swing, Jillian sat cloaked in shadow. "Wishing on a star. Isn't that what girls like you did, before your mommy and daddy tucked you in and said your prayers with you?"

"Despite what you think you know about me, my childhood wasn't perfect. We had our problems like every other family."

"Not like every other family. Not like mine. Not like Jace's." Jillian stood. "He and I understand each other. After he talks to you about rainbows and kittens, he comes to me, and we talk about life. He might be attracted to your pretty face. He might even be telling you what you want to hear, but he'll realize one day that what you have isn't real."

The words scalded Haven's cheeks and ears. The house's facade seemed to bend around her, and the stars, which had before looked so beautiful, now felt like witnesses to her humiliation. "I'm tired. I think I'll head to bed." She trudged up the steps. With her hand on the doorknob, Haven paused. "One day, Jillian, I hope you can see me as something other than your competition. Not for my sake, but for yours. Good night."

Chapter Twenty-One

The brush slid through Rosalie's baby-fine hair, root to tip, without the slightest snag, so unlike Haven's thick tresses that tried to swallow brushes whole, especially in humidity. Hair like her mother's before she'd lost it all in her cancer treatment. Haven shoved away the throat-constricting memory of her mother's final days. Instead, she focused her eyes on the television screen beyond Rosalie's glossy locks, where the Pink Ladies and T-Birds arrived for their first day of senior year at Rydell High.

"People like this movie? It's so old." Rosalie settled back against Haven's shins. "And weird."

"Yep. There's even a sequel." Haven sectioned off the hair at Rosalie's crown, finger-combing the rest down past her shoulders. "Your hair is gorgeous. Is this your natural color?"

From where she sat curled up in the recliner, Jillian scoffed loud enough to make Elijah stir from his sleep next to Haven on the couch. She hadn't spoken to Haven in the two days since their late-night porch talk. Neither had Jace.

Rosalie's shoulders fell a touch. "Jill, why do you act so

mean all the time? When I first came here, my hair was blond."

"Fake blond." Jillian twirled a lock of her strawberry hair around her index finger.

Sonny threw a kernel of popcorn at Jillian.

"Teresa told me I needed to dye my hair blond because the men liked it better that way," Rosalie said.

"Teresa?" Haven separated the section of hair into thirds and crossed one over the other, careful not to tug any strands too tight.

"She owned the hotel and the agency, as she called it. She was the one who looked after us girls. Whatever Teresa said we should do to make the clients happy, we did. Sonny helped me get it back to my natural hair color. The box called it espresso brown? I think she did a pretty good job."

"Sonny, you did this? It's gorgeous."

"Hair coloring isn't any different than cooking. If you follow the recipe, it comes together. Jill helped, too. She's got a heart in there somewhere, even if it is the size of a peppercorn."

"Don't go tellin' anyone. You'll ruin my reputation," Jillian said.

"My hair's too thin. I wish I had thick hair like you," Rosalie said.

"We always want what someone else has, don't we?" Sonny shot a look at Jillian, who rolled her eyes in response and pulled a pillow against her stomach.

Rosalie turned her face a bit to look at Haven from the side of her eye. "Before I saw you, I was worried you'd be like Teresa. She'd be real nice until you disagreed with her."

Haven considered each syllable carefully as she lifted another line of hair with her pinkie and added it to the existing lock. "Was Teresa the one who brought you into that life?"

Again, Sonny stared down Jillian, but her eyes were glued to the television screen as Sandy and Danny took turns singing about their summer nights. Had the three women known one another in their former lives?

"Sorta. Sometimes she brought new girls in, but mostly she taught us what we needed to do when we were with a client."

Haven's fingers braided to the happy rhythm of the song, as did the pounding of her pulse in her temple. It would do no good to show anger or even pity right now. She needed to listen and understand. Even as her next question balanced on the tip of her tongue, Haven prepared herself for a gut-wrenching response. "How old were you?"

"When I started working at the hotel or when everything fell apart?"

"Whatever you feel comfortable telling me."

"I was a happy little girl, living in Denver with my mom and dad. My mom was the sweetest. She used to play with my hair just like you're doing. Except she would always put my hair in two French braids if I was going to school or softball practice."

Haven breathed in, then out. She wouldn't push Rosalie or the other women to share more than they wanted to.

"But my dad was super controlling. He never let her go anywhere unless he was with her. One day, she got real sick. I don't know what she was sick with. I was only twelve. My dad wouldn't let her go see a doctor until it was too late."

"Rosalie, I'm sorry." Haven's words came out a bit strained.

Yet Rosalie simply shrugged her shoulders. "This lady from the state kept trying to take me away from my dad but he wouldn't let her. A few months after my mom died, he stopped treating me like a daughter. More like a replacement for my mom, you know . . ."

Haven's fingers began to tremble, and she urged them to stay steady.

"After a couple of months, I told that social worker lady. My dad went to jail, and I went to foster care."

Good, Haven thought.

"The foster home I got put into was just as bad. Worse, even. When I told my foster mom what her teenage son would do to me, she started hitting me. I learned not to say anything. Just put up with it, you know?" Rosalie quieted.

"How long did you stay with them?" Haven asked.

"Until I was fourteen. Then I learned about this way to make money easily. All I'd have to do is watch TV with these lonely old men for an hour after school, and I'd get a hundred dollars. I used to do that with my grandpa when I was little, so it didn't seem so bad. Also, I always got teased at school for wearing ratty clothes. One hundred dollars could buy me a couple new outfits at Walmart." Rosalie reached forward and grabbed a behemoth-sized bag of Skittles off the coffee table. She picked through until she found a purple, orange, green, yellow, and red. Then she popped them all in her mouth at once. "The hotel was about a thirty-minute walk. The first time I went, I met Eddie. He worked for Teresa. I watched a movie with him. He asked me about my foster family and school and gave me snacks. Then he paid me the money, and I left."

Haven's eyes trailed across the room. Companionship, movies, snacks, friendship. Eddie and Teresa used all perfectly innocent things to work their way in.

"A couple of weeks later, Teresa texted me that Eddie wanted to see me again. She promised me a hundred and fifty dollars this time. So I went. He'd bought me this dumb dress from one of the mall shops. He asked me to change into it, and I did. It was sleeveless. And he saw a bruise on my shoulder from my foster mom. Eddie promised that my foster family would never hurt me again."

"Then what?" Haven finished the bottom of the braid and wrapped the braided tail in an elastic.

"That Friday, I came home from school and their house was burned to the ground. Eddie picked me up and told me I could live at the hotel. He moved me into a room and the closet was full of clothes. I thought it was heaven. Like God had finally brought a savior just for me."

Haven watched Sonny collect Elijah in her arms and carry him to bed.

"That first night, Teresa told me the police thought I'd started the fire. She said they'd hide me at the hotel as long as I remained grateful to Eddie. So she sent me to Eddie's room and demanded I show him how thankful I was." Rosalie handed a long blue ribbon to Haven and asked her to tie it on the end of her braid like her mother used to do.

Haven struggled to tie the ribbon as Rosalie unleashed all the details of what she'd been told thankfulness looked like. When Rosalie explained how Eddie began sending her to his friends' rooms, Haven found herself unable to speak even when she tried.

Sonny returned, and she and Jillian carried on watching the movie as if Rosalie's horrendous spiral into human trafficking and sexual exploitation was common. Rosalie spoke about the degrading, dehumanizing acts she was paid to do, describing them with such stoicism, like they'd been done to someone else in a faraway land.

When Haven finally found her voice, it was weak with exhaustion, and she hadn't even lived this tale. "Were you the only worker at the hotel?" She cringed at the word *worker* as if Rosalie had chosen to receive compensation for a fair and reasonable job. The truth was she'd been abandoned by the systems designed to protect her.

"No. There were other girls and women living at the hotel. Jillian was there."

Haven glanced at Jillian, who didn't seem too thrilled to be yanked into this conversation.

"We became sisters in a way. That's how they kept us from leaving. If I did something wrong or if I threatened to quit, the punishment got passed on to the person down the hall."

Rosalie ran a hand over her French braid, her fingers

lingering on the bow an extra second. Satisfied, she climbed onto the couch next to Haven and claimed Elijah's throw blanket.

"What made you finally leave?"

"Jillian."

Jillian looked everywhere but at Haven. Finally, she accepted the metaphorical microphone with a sigh. "One day, I was on the street in front of the hotel when Jace pulled up in his shiny truck. He asked me my name and my story. He told me about this job offer to help him start a farm and a restaurant with a good salary, benefits, schooling, food, and shelter. He said he could help every person who wanted a way out. I was the only one willing to go with him. And I pretty much dragged Rosalie into the backseat of his truck with me."

"You didn't want out?"

Rosalie's shoulders bounced in a quick shrug. "Not really. Up until then, each new place I tried was worse than the last. Besides, Jace wasn't the first one to try to 'rescue' us."

Jillian laughed. "Oh, baby, come away with me. I'll treat you real nice, and you'll never have to pull tricks again."

"I'll put you up in my Seattle apartment," Rosalie quipped in a deep voice.

"You were the one with all the businessmen and politicians. All I ever got was the dirty guys who'd just cashed their paycheck. It was all *You had a good time, didn't you? It's all yours if you want it*," Jillian cracked. "Look, Kenickie. I didn't want you when I was getting paid for it. I certainly don't want you for free."

Amidst the coarse jokes, questions tangled in Haven's mind. One stood out among the rest.

"What made Jace's offer different?"

"He was offering the women a way to rescue themselves," Sonny interrupted.

"And the others?"

Jillian stretched her legs out over the recliner's footrest. "Trusting others was what got most of us into that place. None of the others were willing to take that chance. They'd rather get Eddie's beating for my leaving than leave themselves. As for Rosalie, she didn't have a choice. I owed it to her to get her out."

"Why?"

Jillian blinked several times. "Because I was the one who invited her to the hotel in the first place."

Dreams and reality played tug-of-war with Jace's mind in his darkened bedroom. These days felt never-ending. He'd be up at five a.m. working again. The exhaustion held him captive. If it wasn't physical, it was mental or emotional. He'd never be free of it so long as men, women, and children were being used and abused. There was no peace. No haven. Or was there?

She walked to him between rows of cornstalks, her smile forcing the clouds above to unleash the softest summer rain on the plants. She wore a sundress, and as she passed by each stalk, her fingers caressed the striped leaves by her hip with the delicate touch he yearned to feel against his neck and chest. Her bare feet pressed into the earth, but strangely never muddied.

The rain dripped off his hat and cooled his aching back. It also wet her hair and kissed her rosy cheeks. She slowed as she neared him and secured her arms around his waist. "Kiss me, Jace."

The command drew his lips to hers. She tasted like the meeting of rain and earth. She smelled like the sunflowers on her dress, which had awakened to life against him. Heavenly. *Your lips drop sweetness as the honeycomb, my bride; milk and honey are under your tongue.* As the words from Song of Songs serenaded them, a sting pierced Jace's lip, and he broke the kiss. One bee, then another flew between them. Soon, they were swarmed by the creatures. Haven held tight to his chest, and her cries called to the part of him that wanted, needed, to save her.

I'm here, he tried to say, but the bees filled his mouth, muffling the sound. She was softening in his arms. When his hand reached for her hair, he found only his T-shirt. Where had she gone?

Jace's eyes shot open, finding no clouds, no bees. It was no longer summer, and he'd harvested the corn last week. Only darkness surrounded him now. A dream was all it was. Yet the echoing sobs remained. He sat up and looked toward his window.

His gaze moved to the closet where a safe held his Smith & Wesson, in case Eddie ever decided to come and reclaim what he considered his property. But this wasn't the sound of a threat.

No, someone was crying. Sonny worrying about Elijah's future? Rosalie crying over that preacher's kid? Or Jillian—no, Jillian didn't cry. No matter, Jace considered lying back down on the pillow. He didn't need to be entwined with Sonny, Jillian, and Rosalie. This was why he'd hired Haven. Still, the sound of the woman's sobs gutted him.

A minute later, Jace rounded the backside of the cabin to where the shadows layered deepest. He couldn't make out who it was yet, but Haven's flowery scent put the missing piece in place. "Haven?"

She turned and hurled herself against him.

"I'm here," he said as he rubbed his hands up and down her heaving shoulders. "Haven, I'm here."

Each racking sob pained him. Had he caused this? By bringing her here and subjecting her to Sonny's snark, Jillian's abuse, and Rosalie's drama, had he caused this? He was about to apologize when Haven's hands dropped from between her face and his chest and fell at her side. Although he didn't want to release her, he took her cue and stepped back.

"What they've been through . . . It's awful."

"They told you about the hotel?"

"Rosalie did. And the abuse before that. How could anyone do such things? She was a little girl."

"I don't know."

Haven surrendered to more sobs, and Jace took her in his arms once again.

"I'm so angry. I'm angry at those men who hurt them. I'm angry at women like Teresa who promised them one thing and gave them another. I'm angry at people like Trent Garrison who don't want them to get a fresh start. And . . . and . . ."

"Go ahead and say it."

"I'm angry at God for not protecting them from that evil." She buried her face in his shirt.

"Tell him."

"Who?"

"Tell God that you're mad. He's heard it from me. You don't have to hide from him. Or me, Haven. You can talk to me."

She looked up at him and shook her head. "After an entire lifetime of keeping everything inside, trust me, you don't want to be the one that I unleash on."

"You don't think I can handle it? I mean, I don't wanna brag, but have you seen my shoulders? I can carry burdens larger than yours."

She laughed. "Well, you are sturdy."

"Haven," he said, peering closer. "I'm strong enough to handle whatever you have to throw at me. And I tell you what. God is strong enough to handle whatever you want to take to him as well. Do you think he isn't angry? Angry at the people who hurt his children? Jesus overturned tables, and that was only because of some shady business dealings in the temple. One day, he'll make everything right. Until then, all we can do is try to stop evil in its tracks and find any joy we can."

It sounded a bit like an invitation. But had he meant it that way? His dream raced back to the forefront of his brain. *Kiss me, Jace*, she'd said. Now she wasn't saying those words with her lips, but her eyes? It certainly looked like it in this light.

He swallowed his desire. "Come on. I'll walk you home."

Jace kept his arm around her shoulder, and she looped her arm around his waist. As they walked, still mourning wrongs in the world, there was something right about this to Jace.

They turned the corner to face the farmhouse. Through the windows, a scene from *Grease* played on the screen. Jillian, Sonny, and Rosalie all stood hitting each other with blankets and throw pillows, laughing all the while. "See? Evil might rule the hour, but good will win the day."

Chapter Twenty-Two

You want me to put my child on the back of that beast? I don't think so." Sonny lifted Elijah onto her hip and turned back to the car.

"These horses are used for therapy. They're extremely gentle," Haven explained. This bonding experience wouldn't work if Sonny refused to go with them. And besides, if Haven had to conquer her fear of horses, then so would Sonny. At least Rosalie and Jillian weren't giving her lip.

"Look, I'm all for team-building exercises. Just not this one."

"Mommy, I want to ride a horsey. Pretty please," Elijah said.

"Sorry, baby, but I think Mommy has too much work to do at the restaurant. Maybe some other time."

The sound that emanated from Elijah's mouth could've sparked a stampede. Immediately, big crocodile tears dripped down his reddening cheeks.

Sonny glared at Haven as she patted her son's back. "Do you see what you've done? Okay, okay. We'll ride a horsey. How did Jace get out of this anyway?"

The rumble of Jace's truck spoke for itself. Leading a dust cloud, he parked next to the minivan, then jogged to catch up with them. "Sorry I'm late. Everything is under control at The Mill. The landscaping crew finished up. Did I miss anything?"

Jillian rested her hand on Jace's shoulder. She'd worn her checkered halter top beneath her jean jacket, and despite the nippy air, she hadn't bothered to button up. "Sonny's scared of getting bucked off a horse."

"You'll be fine. Haven said this place is highly reputable."

Colin Rivera greeted them outside the stable. "You all the group from Aspen Crossroads? Welcome to Alpine Ranch and Rescue."

"Hi, Colin. Thanks for squeezing us in," Haven said.

"Anything for you." He welcomed her with a hug.

Jace sized him up beneath his furrowed brow. He put forth his hand. "I'm Jace."

Colin accepted the handshake with a friendly smile. "Colin Rivera. Are you all new to town?" His gaze bounced from Jillian to Rosalie, and then landed on Sonny.

Jace quickly maneuvered himself between Colin and the women. "We are."

"How is Whisper Canyon treating you?"

"Eh. It's been hit-and-miss so far," Jace said.

Elijah peeked at Colin around Jace's right leg, and Colin responded by covering his face with his hands, then opening them in true peekaboo style. The game sent Elijah into a giggling fit and Sonny into a blush.

"We're just here to ride some horses, if you don't mind. Five adults, one child," Jace said.

Everything inside Haven wanted to scream *four adults*, but she was the one who set this up. She couldn't back out now. A horse whinnied inside the stable, and Haven wiped her sweaty palms on her jeans.

Colin eyed her curiously. "When did you get over your fear of horses, Haven?"

"Today," she said with an exaggerated smile.

After a tutorial on how to handle the horses on the trail, they were each fitted with helmets. As Colin adjusted Haven's, they were both aware of the way Jace watched them from across the space. When he moved close to her ear to inspect one of the straps, he whispered, "You must really like the guy to get on a horse for him."

"I have no idea what you're talking about."

"We dated for two years, and you never let me take you out riding. You used to rattle on and on about horses being able to kill with one swift kick."

"That was straight from my dad's mouth, and he doesn't lie."

"But the only horsepower your dad knows about is under the hood of a Ford Mustang." Colin patted the top of her helmet, then began pairing each person with their ideal horse.

Jace lifted Elijah in front of Sonny on the butterscotch mare. The boy looked even more adorable with his blond curls jutting out from the bottom of his toddler-sized helmet, and the smile he wore could move mountains. Slowly, Colin led the mare out of the stable and into the sun.

"You're scared of horses?" Jace came to Haven's side. With Jillian already saddled onto her horse and waiting behind Rosalie's steed outside, Jace was finally free to speak without any eavesdroppers.

Again, Haven tried to dry her hands on her pants, but it was no use.

"If you're that scared," Jace said, "you don't have to do this."

"Yes, I do. It'll be good." Now, if only her breaths would settle into a rhythm.

"All right, Haven. This one's yours. Her name is Serenade." Colin led a pretty brown horse with a black mane over to Haven. He instructed her to place her left foot in the stirrup, and then she swung her other leg up and over. "There you go, honey. I knew you could do it."

Jace's head whipped toward them. He stared hard at Colin. All because he'd called Haven *honey*? Haven couldn't worry about that now. Not dying was her goal for the day. As she settled in, getting used to the small movements of the horse beneath her, another horse brayed.

"All right, Jagger. You're next," Colin said to the black horse with a large head and fathomless eyes. He took the horse's lead from his assistant and brought the eager horse next to Serenade. So close that Haven's leg was pinned between the two horses, but not uncomfortably so.

Without need of help, Jace climbed on top of Jagger, squirming his leg in between the animals. "You okay?" he asked, patting her fisted hands.

Haven nodded.

"You're cute when you lie." Jace smiled.

Colin stroked Serenade's mane. "Jagger and Serenade are boyfriend-girlfriend. They like to be near each other on the trail, either side to side or one behind the other. They don't like for other horses to get in between them. Jace, you seem comfortable with horses. Will you bring up the rear and help Haven with Serenade so I can help Sonny and Elijah?"

Jace nodded.

The group started nice and slow. Serenade walked gracefully in step behind Rosalie's horse and next to Jace's. As Haven realized her chances of death weren't as high as her father had led her to believe, she was able to enjoy the scenery a bit. Although even the mountains with their golden yellow blanket of aspens couldn't keep her focus from returning to Jace.

"You don't have to worry about Colin, you know," she said.

"Nothing is going on between you, is there?"

"Not since high school. I meant, you don't have to worry

about Colin and Sonny's little flirtation happening up there."

Up ahead where the trail curved to the left, it was plain to see how easily Sonny and Colin spoke.

"Sonny, Jillian, and Rosalie don't need to date anyone in Whisper Canyon, remember?"

"I'm not even talking about dating. Just befriending. Venturing somewhere other than the farm and the restaurant. Allow them the chance to have community outside of Aspen Crossroads. I know you're trying to keep them safe, and they love that about you. *I* love that about you." Haven measured her words carefully. "Yet, at some point, you have to let them live the lives you promised them."

She let the words soak in during the silence that followed. Her brief glances revealed that Jace was considering the idea, though not happily.

"It's not that easy—letting them go out there on their own," Jace said.

"I'm sure it isn't."

"People can't be trusted. Like I said before, they'll either crush them with criticism about their pasts, or they'll try to consume them. Just imagine if they wandered into one of those churches. They'd be cut to shreds."

"Why do you think that?"

"Because that's what church people do."

"I go to church."

"You're different."

"My sisters. My father. They wouldn't judge them. Maybe you should give people, including churchgoers, a chance."

"Haven, I've heard what they say about you. Do you think they'd be any kinder to Sonny, Rosie, or Jill?"

The horses entered a meadow, and the trail widened. Serenade veered toward some flowers and began munching away.

"Serenade, Colin said no snacks." Haven pulled up on

the reins a bit as instructed, but the horse didn't obey. She tried mimicking the ticking sound out of the side of her mouth that she'd seen in movies. Still no response.

A loud bray behind them finally raised Serenade's head. Jagger was nipping at Jillian's horse, which stood between him and Serenade. The girl's horse turned in a circle, but Jillian yanked on the reins.

Colin yelled a warning, but it was drowned out as Jagger stomped the ground and bobbed his head. Jillian's horse reared up on its back legs, and Jillian lost her grip. She hit the ground hard, but fortunately rolled out of her horse's way before he backed over her. Instantly, Jace dismounted and was at her side.

Jillian remained still, her bare belly rising and falling with each breath, as Jace inspected her injuries. He asked her some questions, and Jillian either nodded or shook her head. Jace looked around at the group. "She's okay. Just got the wind knocked out of her."

"It's probably time to head back anyway," Colin said.

Jillian spoke into Jace's ear, and after tossing an apologetic glance at Haven, he nodded.

"Colin, she's too nervous to ride alone. Do you think Jagger could carry both of us?"

With Colin's permission, Jillian mounted Jagger. Jace climbed up behind her. Close behind her.

And if Haven knew how to make Serenade take off in a run, she'd do it, especially when Jillian looked her way and smirked.

The trail ride couldn't end soon enough for Jace. While some guys might love to have a girl like Jillian sitting so close, Jace wasn't happy with the turn of events. Sure, he felt bad that she'd fallen off the horse, but she'd been warned not to get in between Jagger and Serenade. And yet she hadn't listened. When would she learn?

And Haven thought he should let them go off into Whisper Canyon on their own, out of his sight, out of his protection? That had never ended well for him. Not in Tucson, and not with his mother. He couldn't do it. He couldn't lose anyone else.

Once the horses were stabled, Jace went into the ranch's restroom to splash water on his face. Haven was wrong this time. She didn't know the evil that lurked out there between church pews, with pastors' kids, or seemingly helpful ranch owners. He caught his reflection in the mirror. Deep lines surrounded his frown and crossed his forehead. Reminiscent of Eddie. Jace relaxed his expression and smoothed his skin with his fingers. They weren't alike at all.

Eddie kept the women locked away to use them, not protect them. Jace kept them locked away—

The taste of bile assaulted his tongue. He placed both hands on the cold porcelain sink to steady himself. Haven was right. This wasn't the life of freedom he'd promised them. Even if it opened them up to a little risk, he needed to make it right. They didn't need a gatekeeper, especially if that gatekeeper would be gone in six weeks.

Six short weeks. Then he'd move on to the next Secondly site and say goodbye to Aspen Crossroads. And he'd say goodbye to Haven Haviland. That ever-present exhaustion weighed heavily on his shoulders as he slumped before the mirror. Did she know he'd be leaving so soon? He'd explained his plans to move on when he'd first interviewed her, but he'd never said when.

He chugged half his water bottle, but the bad taste remained. After he dried his hands and face, he opened the door.

Haven waited in the open stable door, the late-afternoon light and Rocky Mountain landscape providing the perfect backdrop for her unequaled beauty and grace. Man, he liked her. He liked how she challenged him. How she cared for others. How she hadn't given up on reaching his team.

"Where's everyone else?" he asked.

"Sonny drove them back to the farmhouse so Jillian could get some ibuprofen. The soreness is settling in. You're stuck with me." She strolled toward him.

Jace swallowed his pride. "I owe you an apology."

"For what?"

"For shutting down the conversation on our ride. I was enjoying that time with you. I always enjoy my time with you, but I wasn't prepared to have you call me out about my rules for Sonny, Rosalie, and Jillian."

"I overstepped—"

"No, you didn't. I needed to hear it. I realized I'm acting far too similar to those men and women from their pasts. I promised them freedom, and I need to let them find it for themselves." Jace took a deep breath. "So, thank you."

"You're welcome."

He and Haven took a few steps toward the stable door.

"Does ZuZu's ice cream have milkshakes?" Jace asked. "I've been craving—"

Her hand latched on to his, yanking him to a halt. She wasn't speaking. She simply kept looking from Jace to the wall and back.

Curious what cat had gotten her tongue, he followed her gaze to the stable's dusty showmanship wall. Clearly, no one from this ranch had entered a competition of any sort in a long time. And then he saw her. A blond teenaged girl, holding a ribbon, in an eight-by-ten framed photograph. Jace's heart stuttered.

"She looks just like you," Haven said. "And just like that picture in your truck. Do you think—"

"It's her. My mom."

The girl stared directly at Jace through the camera lens, through the decades, even. Jace found himself leaning forward, and his fingers traced her cheek. The faded caption beneath the picture was difficult to read. *Lynn Chelsie takes 3rd place.*

"Lynn Chelsie? It can't . . . My mom's name was Leigh Anne Daring. But that's her. Do you think she would have changed her name?"

"It's possible. Especially if she was running from someone or somewhere."

A smaller frame displayed a yellowed newspaper article dated June 16, 1988. "Local Girl Wins Front Range Jump-off." Beneath the headline, in a black-and-white photo, Lynn Chelsie stood cheek to cheek with a horse. Jace skimmed the article as quickly as he could. At fifteen, Lynn had painstakingly trained a former racing champion to win a jumping competition to prove the beloved filly had more purpose. The horse's name? Lovely and Daring.

"Lovely and Daring. Leigh Anne Daring," Haven whispered, still holding tight to his hand.

He blinked back the tears clouding his vision as he tried to make sense of it all. Leigh Anne Daring was Lynn Chelsie. The stable around him warped, and Jace feared he might pass out until Haven put her hand on his jaw, steadying him. She pressed a bit closer until he could see the smudges of dust on her cheek.

"Jace, you *do* have your mother's eyes."

Chapter Twenty-Three

"Haven, I don't know about this." Jace's brows pinched together as his coffee sat forgotten on their table at Jailhouse Roasters. "Me and church?"

"That's why I set up the meeting here. I figured you'd be more comfortable. Your mother had to get her strong faith somewhere. If she grew up in Whisper Canyon it was either from St. Xavier's or Whisper Canyon Community. Since she never taught you the Hail Mary prayer, she probably grew up at my church. Reverend Horst may remember her and her family. Plus, he's a great man. He lives what he preaches. We can trust him to keep this conversation confidential."

"You can trust him. I'll trust you." Jace clasped his hands together tight next to his coffee cup. "Although, if my mom wanted to create a new name and leave Lynn Chelsie behind, maybe I should honor her wishes. I already betrayed her once by coming back to this town."

"Isn't there a small part of you that wants to know about her past? What if you have grandparents, aunts, or uncles? What if you have a . . . ?" Haven's words dropped off when she saw the hurt in Jace's eyes.

"A father? If I do, I can't imagine he's some upstanding guy with a strong moral compass."

"You never know. He might not have known about you. And back then, he might not have had any say in her leaving."

She gently placed her hand on his shoulder. When he didn't shy away, her hand slid to the muscle tying his shoulder to his neck. It strained beneath her touch, and she pressed the pads of her fingers into it. Jace's eyelids drifted closed, and with each small, massaging circle, he relaxed more. Soon, her fingertips had inched up the back of his neck, breaking into new territory. Intimate territory. Still, she didn't stop. She drew her fingernails up into the darker blond wisps of hair that grew even darker with sweat after his long days of work.

Jace leaned toward her ever so slightly. Coworkers didn't do this. One didn't play with their coworker's hair, and the coworker certainly didn't lean into it. And why on earth was she breathing so fast?

The bells from Jailhouse's door jerked Haven back to reality, forcing her hands into her lap. Likewise, Jace straightened up. Reverend Horst waved to Haven. Bypassing the counter, he headed straight toward their table.

Jace and Haven stood to welcome him, and Haven gave the introductions. After a bit of small talk, Haven dove right in, lest Jace turn a more sickly shade of green.

"Reverend, I'm helping Jace find out more about his mother. She used to live in Whisper Canyon back in the seventies and eighties. Do you remember Lynn Chelsie?"

The reverend's gaze drifted from Haven to Jace. "You're Lynn's son?"

Jace nodded slowly.

"Yes, I remember her. I haven't thought about her in ages, though. I didn't know her too well, but she was always nice to me even when other kids weren't." Reverend Horst pointed to the right side of his face where a large area of his brown skin had lost pigmentation due to vitiligo.

"She was very kind." Jace set his jaw and an emotion Haven couldn't pinpoint flickered over his features. Something grazed the side of her thigh nearest him. Her hand found his. It was cold, clammy, and it latched on to hers like she was the only thing keeping him steady.

"What can you tell us about her?" Haven asked.

"We were in Sunday school together. She was a quiet one. Very shy. She was homeschooled, I believe."

"Do you know what happened to her?" Haven prodded.

"I remember seeing her go up for prayer one day after the service when we were fifteen or sixteen. Her mother was crying, and her father was angry. Something about it stuck with me. Maybe because they were so distant. Like whatever she was going through affected them more than her. My father was the reverend at the time. I asked him about Lynn later that day."

"What did he say?" Jace said, his grip growing even tighter.

"He told me to mind my business. I never saw Lynn again. Her parents never came back to church, but I'd see them occasionally around town. Not anymore, though. They moved away."

"Could I speak to your father?" Jace asked.

"Reverend Horst's parents passed away," Haven explained. "Can you think of anyone else who might remember her or her family?"

"Not sure. They kept to themselves, but they did sell cheeses and jams for a while. Lynn's mom made the best chocolate pie ever. I guess that would've been your grandmother."

A tremor coursed through Jace's hand, and Haven ached for him. She aimed her focus back on the reverend. "Where did they sell them?"

"They had a stand on their farm."

"Farm?" Jace asked.

Reverend Horst seemed confused. "Their dairy farm. I

figured you knew. The Chelsies were the original owners of Aspen Crossroads."

Jace's hand went slack. Rather than dropping it, Haven cradled it between both of hers, caressing his palm with a featherlight touch. She could only imagine the thoughts running through his head. Since the previous owners had built Jace's cabin in 2012 as an in-law suite, his mother must have grown up in the farmhouse. Was he imagining what room was hers? Was he picturing her climbing the ladder in the barn to daydream about what her life might become? Or was he thinking of something more sinister that might have happened at Aspen Crossroads? Something that got his young mother banished from her home and her family?

"Thank you for meeting with us, Reverend," Jace stated in an almost robotic tone.

"I'm happy to help any way I can. Before I go, there was something else I wanted to discuss with you," he said. "Jimmy and Rosalie. He likes her quite a lot. I understand you're her caregiver."

Jace's mouth fell open slightly. "No. She's eighteen, so she's not required to have a caregiver."

"Oh, pardon. She told Jimmy that you're like a father to her."

Jace dropped his gaze to the table and said nothing.

"I assure you that my son has honorable intentions and would never harm Rosalie in any way. Honestly, I think she's the first girl he's liked enough to ask out. He's got a good head on his shoulders. He's hardworking and a good student. Still, I understand your trepidation in allowing her to date. It's a scary world out there."

Jace worked his jaw long enough to make Haven sweat. Finally, he pushed back his chair and stood. "Thanks again."

"Feel free to stop by for a church service sometime."

"Unlikely, but I appreciate the invitation. You have a nice day." Jace pulled some cash for a tip out of his wallet and dropped it on the table.

Haven had to scurry to keep up with him. "Jace, wait for me."

He paused by the bumper of his truck. "I can't believe that was her home. Terrence couldn't have known when he purchased Aspen Crossroads."

"God knew. Maybe it was providential," she said. "I have some ideas on where we can go from here, if you're willing to keep learning about her."

Jace took a moment to breathe. His crystal blue eyes implored her to lose herself in them. "I don't admit weakness often, but there's no way I could have gotten through that meeting without you. And there's no way I could go on learning about my mom's past without you."

"Lucky you. I'm not going anywhere." A breeze carried a few tendrils of her hair across her face.

Before she had a chance, his hand was there, smoothing the curls back behind her ear before coming to rest on the side of her neck. "Lucky me."

She cupped her hand over his and smiled. "What about the other topic? Rosalie."

Jace pulled away, but she grasped a fistful of his flannel near his waist to keep him close.

"Please, Jace. The Harvest Dance is in five days. And they have the reverend's approval. Why not give yours?"

Chapter Twenty-Four

Jace dug up the last row of root vegetables. He rubbed some dirt between his fingers. This very dirt used to be under his mother's feet. But now? He didn't even know where she was buried. He shouldn't have come here. Sonny, Jillian, and Rosalie would have been fine if he'd just quit Secondly when Terrence demanded he come to Whisper Canyon. He'd let his feelings get in the way of wise decision-making. Now he knew more than he cared to about his mother's previous life, all thanks to a nosy brunette.

Oh, Haven. If he wasn't careful, those personal desires would once again cloud his judgment. He'd already let her convince him this Harvest Dance was a good idea.

As if his thoughts had summoned her, Haven appeared in his periphery. She approached him without her normal confidence, like there was something she wanted to ask him. "A farmer's work is never done," she said.

"Shouldn't you be getting ready for the dance?"

"I wanted to give you a heads-up. Rosalie is pretty nervous about her date."

Jace hacked at the cold-hardened dirt with his trowel.

"Please don't call it that unless you want me to run the guy off with my gun."

"Aren't you tough?" Haven plopped herself down right in front of him and dug at the ground with her bare hands. "They're grabbing food at Sassy's Saloon beforehand. There will be plenty of chaperones there. The reverend's kid won't be able to get away with anything with all those eyes on him."

"I still can't believe you convinced me to break my no-dating rule. You and your influence . . ."

Haven tugged a beet from the ground and rubbed the excess earth off its ruddy skin. "You sure you don't want to go to the dance?"

"And watch the ladies dance with guys I want to strangle? Probably not the best idea." Even worse, Jace couldn't bear to watch Haven dancing with another guy. He'd barely handled it when Colin helped her fasten her helmet. But to see another man with his arms around her, when it's all Jace wanted to do ever since he felt her hand in his hair at Jailhouse? Who was he kidding? He'd wanted her long before that.

"Haven? Jace?"

There was no way the girl in the pink dress in front of him was the same one who climbed into his truck scared to death less than a year ago. Rosalie looked so grown, especially with the touch of lipstick and the curl in her hair.

"Rosalie, you look stunning!" Haven squealed.

"You think so?"

"Yes! Jace, what do you think?"

They both waited on Jace's words. Jace stood, and while he did his best to wipe the dirt off his hands, Rosalie fidgeted. When his words still didn't come, she slid into the coat she'd been carrying on her arm.

He cleared his throat, so the words came out nice and strong. "You look very pretty, Rosie."

She beamed. "Thanks, Jace. Jimmy should be here in a few minutes, but I wanted to talk to you both about something."

"What's that?" Haven asked, having caught on that Jace was having trouble with words at the moment.

"Um, well." Rosalie bent back the fingers of her right hand as she stammered. "Jimmy doesn't know about my past. He doesn't know that I've, you know. And I don't think he's even had his first kiss yet. What if I tell him, and he rejects me?"

Jace moved to hug the girl but stopped short. He wouldn't cover her with his dirt. The irony was glaringly obvious. "He won't reject you. And if he does, then he doesn't deserve you."

Her chin puckered. "I wish I had a different life. That I never was with anyone before. Not Eddie or any of his gross friends. I feel so dirty. I was watching this video the other day, and it said that once you've slept with someone, you're like a chewed wad of gum, and no one else will want you anymore."

Haven grabbed Rosalie's hands firmly and captured her focus with her own. "You are not dirty, and you are not some used piece of gum. To say that is to discount everything else that makes you a woman, everything that makes you beautiful and whole—your smile, your heart, your soul. And what those men did to you doesn't lessen your worth. It was their sin, not yours."

"How can you say that? There were plenty of times where I could've fought. I could've clawed their faces. I could have run away, but I didn't."

Haven's eyes softened even more. "You didn't choose that life. And even if you had, it wouldn't change anything. You're a gift to this world. I may not know Jimmy very well, but I know his family. They believe in grace and fresh starts. They won't reject you."

"Haven, have you ever slept with anyone before?"

As Haven struggled to speak, the color of her eyes deepened to emerald due to the reddening of her face.

"I have," Jace said.

Rosalie and Haven both turned to him. Was he really about to share this with them? It went entirely against that firm-boundaries plan. Yet if it would help Rosalie feel less alone in her struggles, he'd do just about anything.

"With an old girlfriend?" Rosalie asked.

"Not exactly. When my mother died, I fled town with no money and no possessions. I got work at a farm like this one, but much bigger. Right after my sixteenth birthday, the rancher's wife, Marjorie, offered to teach me how to drive. It seemed innocent enough. After a few lessons, she told me that if I was willing to take her on Sunday drives, then the old truck could be mine. On that first drive, she directed me to pull onto this dirt road. I knew it wasn't right—all she was asking me to do. She was married and twenty-nine years old. I was young and very inexperienced. But she warned me that I wouldn't get the truck if I didn't go along with it. To me, a truck was more than a vehicle. It was an escape plan. It was a shelter on a cold night." Jace couldn't bring himself to look at Haven as he spoke. "On the drive back to the ranch, she said if I told anyone, she'd tell her husband I forced myself on her."

"Seriously? I mean, I know that stuff happens to boys, too. I had no idea it had happened to you," Rosalie said.

"It did. I know what you mean. I could have fought her. Even though I was sixteen, I was bigger than her and stronger. These criminals—they don't just prey on the weak. They prey on the scared. They prey on the ones who have no one to turn to and nowhere to go."

"How long did it last?" Rosalie asked.

"Two years. Long enough for me to confuse what was love and what was abuse."

Rosalie rushed into Jace's arms. Although he didn't want to soil her party dress, he couldn't stand there all statue-like. And he didn't want to. He rested his chin on the top of her head, careful not to mess up her hairstyle.

She turned to Haven. "Would that stop you from dating Jace?"

Haven gathered her breath. "Not one bit. I don't think it would stop Jimmy from dating you, either."

"I love you, Haven," Rosalie said. "I love you, Jace."

The words whipped Jace's cheek with the sting of a fierce winter wind. He'd lost his foothold here and tumbled headlong into relationships he had no business forming. And yet, he wanted nothing more than to take Rosie back in his arms again and press into her how precious and loved she truly was.

"I need to touch up my makeup before Jimmy gets here."

Haven came to Jace's side as they watched Rosalie return to the farmhouse.

"You could've told me." Haven glanced up at Jace.

"Like I said before. I don't like admitting weakness."

Haven took his hands and tucked them under her chin. "You were not weak. You were a boy, two years younger than Rosalie. You were preyed upon by Marjorie. Like I was preyed upon by Trent. Neither one of us asked for what happened to us. Just like Sonny, Jillian, and Rosalie didn't ask for what happened to them. But I'm glad we found each other. And we shouldn't hide ourselves away. Come to the dance with me."

Within him, reason and logic warred with wants and misplaced hopes. In the end, he didn't have to answer. She saw it in his eyes. As he watched her leave to change into a dress he wouldn't see her wear, he'd never felt lonelier.

In his pocket, his phone buzzed. Jace checked the text message.

TERRENCE: Austin's approved. We're taking Secondly to Texas. How's October 31st for scouting land? That's a week ahead of what we'd talked about. Is that a problem?

Jace lifted his chin to see the woman who had his heart tied in knots disappear into the house. He had no right to do the same to her. Maybe leaving a week earlier would make things easier for everyone involved.

JACE: I'll make it work.

One more reason he should not attend this dance, even if he wanted to.

Chapter Twenty-Five

Haven combed her way through the room, smiling and nodding at those she knew, but avoiding unnecessary conversation. Despite the large crowd, she felt utterly alone. The Virginia reel began, and most of the attendees formed groups of couples on the dance floor. Rosalie and Jimmy were an obvious pairing with their small flirtations and shared blushes. Then Colin offered his hand to Sonny. She accepted only when Jillian offered to dance with Elijah. Daniel walked through the door in time to take Lizzie by the hand before Haven could warn him not to.

The dance hall bustled with residents, young and old. Unfortunately, not all of Whisper Canyon had been welcome at the dance. Rarity fumed when she'd seen security at the front door checking for dress code violations. Garrisonism, she'd called it. Between that and Jace's absence, Haven's favorite event of the year was quickly losing its place. At this rate, it was better than the Earth Day Litter Pick-Up and worse than the Summit County Rocky Mountain Oyster Fest, although the snacks were far more appetizing.

She'd hated to leave the farmhouse without Jace, especially after what he'd just confided. It felt a bit like she'd left a piece of her heart behind.

When the DJ played the first few notes of the "Cha Cha Slide," Rosalie and Sonny whooped. They refused to let Haven sit and mope. Soon, she was in the front line with them. Even Jillian learned the steps. When the song ended, Haven was left in desperate need of lemonade, but it was worth it, especially with the way the Aspen Crossroads women laughed.

Maneuvering toward the beverage station, Haven ignored the curious glances and whispers directed at her and the women. Wendy Hollingsworth seemed especially talkative tonight, and her smirk—

Haven smacked against a man's chest, bringing her to an embarrassing halt. "I'm sorry . . . Trent."

The grin on his face made her flesh crawl like one of Elijah's earthworms. "No apology necessary. How's life treating you, Miss Haviland?"

"Complicated, thanks to you."

"I'm not sure I understand what you mean. The Mill seems to be coming right along. I didn't see you there last week."

"What do you have up your sleeve, Trent? Other than blocking land purchases and construction permits, attempting to close roads—"

"Do you think so little of me?"

"Yes. Yes, I do."

"I simply want to chat with one of our fine residents. And"—he lowered his voice, but kept his distance—"offer to take this chat somewhere more private. My mansion's empty right now, and it's a short walk through the dark."

"You're a disgrace. Someone needs to rat you out, once and for all."

"So that's a no? Fair enough, but before you go squealing to someone, you should know I checked in at your father's shop. I'm not sure he's doing a great job with my

Corvette. It's a shame. I imagine a glowing review from me might help his business survive, while a negative one . . ."

"How do you sleep at night?"

"Easy." He crept too close, and his hot breath felt moist on her ear. "By thinking of you."

She wanted to yell, slap him across the face, or confess everything to his unsuspecting wife. Yet she couldn't risk a scene one week away from the restaurant's opening. Instead, she backed away, noticing too many sets of eyes on her already. She spun around to leave but found herself facing a starched white collar unbuttoned to show off a tanned, muscular neck. She followed the neck up past the clean-shaven jaw, full lips, and strong nose to those honest crystalline eyes.

One of Jace's arms slid around her waist and tugged her against his chest. He took her hand, holding it up in a dancing pose. Without a word and without taking his eyes off hers, he walked her backward to the dance floor. Once there, he led her in a two-step around the dance hall, riding the whispers of the spectators. Of course they were ogling. Jace was the gorgeous new face in town. And his lack of a wedding ring surely held every single gal's attention. Even Haven felt it—this magnetism pulling her closer to him than necessary. And it wasn't his good looks or even the muscular arms that held her now. No, it was the way he planted flowers with Elijah and mended baby chicks. And the way he worked sunup till sundown, all so three women who'd been mistreated by so many would have a second chance at life. Not to mention the way he looked at Haven— like she could single-handedly mend the world.

"I thought you weren't going to come," she said.

"I tried to stay away. But then I watched out my window as you all were leaving. Sonny said something that made you and Jillian smile. I couldn't miss this."

"I have a confession," she said. "I really wanted you here."

Jace grinned in the same mischievous way he had at the historical center. "I have a confession, too."

"Oh yeah? What's that?"

"My heart almost stopped when I saw you in this dress. Cherry red?" He squeezed his eyes tightly closed. "You're killing me, Haven."

Her cheeks warmed, either from blushing or smiling so big. She wasn't sure. "Do you like it?"

He nodded. "You're beautiful." With no warning, he spun her one and a half turns, then put his arm around her shoulder in a promenade. "Don't let it go to your head." He turned her again until she was once again facing him.

She pressed closer to him, hoping it might keep her thrumming heart from bursting through her chest. After several turns about the dance floor, she spied Rosalie and Jimmy chatting with Sonny.

"They seem to be having fun," Jace said, nodding to the group. "Maybe this wasn't such a bad idea."

"Whisper Canyon can become home for them. It isn't perfect, but what town is?"

"I don't want them to get hurt."

"I know. They'll be fine. The restaurant will be a raging success. The town will come out in droves to welcome them. Then the ski season will bring in the tourists. We'll have a great winter. And you'll finally get to relax a bit."

His expression tensed.

"Did I say something wrong?"

"No. Haven, there's something you should know."

"My turn." Jillian shoved herself between them, forcing Haven out of Jace's embrace before she could process what had happened.

For a moment, she considered denying Jillian the chance to cut in on her and Jace's dance, but that would only draw more attention of the negative sort. Instead, Haven secured a grin on her face and rejoined Rarity and Valor at their table, fully aware of their stares. It was one thing to have the town gawk at her, but her family?

"What are you all looking at?"

"You . . . and our future brother-in-law," Rarity snarked. "You're gorgeous together. Like Hallmark-should-cast-you-in-their-next-Christmas-movie kind of gorgeous. And the way you look at each other? Ugh. No wonder that girl is intimidated."

"Who?"

"The strawberry blond chick holding on tight to your man right now."

"Rarity, be nice. He's not my man." Haven's throat tightened as she watched them dance. Wes brought them all lemonade, and Haven chugged it in three gulps. The next song started, and Rosalie was the one twirling about with Jace. Wes asked Valor to dance, and before Rarity had a chance to tease them, Daniel had lifted her out of her seat and carried her to the floor. Those two had a history of wowing the crowd with their dancing skill.

"Who'd have thought Jace would be such a good dancer?" Jillian plopped down in Rarity's abandoned seat.

"Yep." It was all she could muster right now for the woman.

"What a shame he won't be here for the future dances." Jillian took off her high heel and rubbed her ankle. "Five weeks, and he'll be off to Texas."

"Texas?" Haven's throat caught on the second syllable.

"To start the next Secondly location."

There it was. She hadn't wanted to hear it, but Jillian had an agenda. And despite years of training herself not to show emotion when a client hit her with startling admissions, Haven felt it rising from her gut. He was leaving her? Like her mother? Like her siblings?

"Didn't he tell you?"

"Uh . . . I . . . he told me during my interview that he would go somewhere new. I thought it would be a few years." Across the room, she spied Jace chatting with Jimmy. When Rosalie tugged Jimmy back to the dance floor, Jace searched the room until his eyes locked on Haven's. His smile gave way to concern, and he began splitting the crowd.

"Funny that he wasn't honest with you."

The lemonade boiled in Haven's stomach, burning her from her feet to the tips of her ears. "Excuse me," she said before making a quick exit through the side door, welcoming the cool air into her lungs.

The night was blissfully dark the farther Haven walked from the dance hall, thanks to the moonless night. The stars that dusted the sky created a brilliant sight but didn't lend much light. If she tarried too much farther, she'd hit the glow of the Garrison mansion, which shared a boundary with the park on the northern side. Fortunately, the gazebo in the direct center of the park would keep her hidden, at least until Sonny and Jillian were ready to head home.

Haven sat on the bench inside the gazebo, not minding the fabric of her dress snagging on the splinters. Other than her breath, the only sound was the muffled music from the hall. Another square dance, it sounded like. "Tie a Yellow Ribbon," maybe.

He should've told her. If this was always the plan, he should've told her instead of withholding the truth. Then again, she'd known that he moved from place to place, setting up farms and restaurants. She'd never asked when he'd move on, perhaps because she didn't want to imagine Aspen Crossroads without him there taming the fields and offering a safe place for her own heart.

The floorboards creaked slightly, and Haven lifted her head.

"I talked to Jillian. I should've been more forthcoming about my leaving." Jace stopped in front of her, hat in his hand, his stature somehow penitent while still strong. "I was afraid if I told you, you'd be overwhelmed with caring for the women on your own. Then, once things settled at the farmhouse, I didn't want to tell you."

"Five weeks?"

"I have to be in Austin on October thirty-first."

The music from the dance hall grew louder. Someone had propped open the doors. The band played George Strait's "I Cross My Heart." Timeless and achingly true for how Haven was feeling in this moment.

"I never wanted to get attached. Not to the women. Not to you. Getting attached would only bring harm to those who have come to trust me. Only, with you, I couldn't help it. You were so kind and compassionate. You persevered despite the troubles we've given you. You're always giving grace to those who deserve it the least. And you're more devoted to helping others than anyone I've ever met."

Haven pressed a hand to her chest. How could her heart both bloom and break at the same time? She'd finally found her someone, and soon he would be gone.

"This may sound childish, but I like you, Haven."

The words were spoken so deeply she felt them reverberate through her skin and into her bones. "I like you, too, Jace."

"I don't know what will happen five minutes, five weeks, or five years from now." Jace tossed his hat onto the bench. "All I want in this moment . . . is to finish our dance."

He didn't need to say it twice. Haven entered his arms, pressing her cheek to his shoulder. If he minded the closeness, he didn't say so. He took Haven's hand and held it against his heart. Slowly, they began to sway to the melody. She should've been cold without a jacket, yet his warmth overtook her. Her nose dusted his neck, and his clean, fresh scent beckoned her closer despite the lack of space between them already. With a slow lift of her chin, the arch of her nose traced a line over his jaw. He lowered his head until they danced cheek to cheek, letting the melody lead them.

He turned his face a touch more, and his lips grazed the

corner of hers. "Austin is the only reason I'm not taking this any further. I hope you know that every moment I'm not kissing you, I'm wishing I were."

She released all her breath, collapsing her lungs as she pressed closer to him, the need to be as near as possible surpassing all rational thought except for how to make this feeling last forever.

"You humiliated me." The feminine screech pierced the air, bringing Jace and Haven's dance to a stop.

"Who is that?" Jace whispered.

Though they were mere shadows, it was clear who walked across the grass, not too far from the gazebo, toward their home.

"Trent and his wife. I don't think they can see us here," Haven said quietly.

"You can't keep doing this, Trent. I'm carrying your child—the one you wanted—and you wouldn't stop staring at that piece of Haviland trash the whole night."

"I was not staring at her, Elaine."

"Right. Not merely staring at her but whispering in her ear like no one could see you. What did I say when we got married? I don't care what you do or who you see, but do not humiliate me. You've heard the whispers. They all know you had an affair with that—"

Jace held Haven's ear to his chest, but it didn't do much to mute the curse Elaine called her.

"You even bought that dumb car. Like buddying up with her father will help get her back in your bed."

Elaine knew? Shame told Haven to back away—a physical sign that her lapse in judgment had alienated her—but Jace refused. He held her tighter still.

"I don't want her anymore," Trent said. "Tell me what I'm supposed to do. If I admit the truth, they'll kick me out of office. We'll lose everything: the house, the money, the cars. Even if I say she came on to me, I won't come away unscathed. They won't believe me."

"Yes, they will. Everyone knows what a floozy her mother was. She's just like her. I won't be made a fool. I'm tired of living in a town that caters to the worst society has to offer. For the last time, sweep the streets."

So Elaine wasn't as innocent as she seemed. She was the one leading the charge to change Whisper Canyon and boot out those they considered the "less desirables."

"Elaine, I'm sorry. Give me time, and I'll rid this town of the Havilands and everyone like them."

Jace took a step toward the Garrisons, but Haven clung to him. She shook her head and hoped he could see the plea in her eyes. Nothing good could come from a late-night altercation with Trent so close to The Mill's opening, especially when every person in Whisper Canyon was seventy-five yards away.

"Good," Elaine said. "Until then, feel free to sleep in one of the spare bedrooms."

Chapter Twenty-Six

Spelunking?" Jace said as they stood in the gift shop of Whisper Canyon Caverns and Cave Tours three days later.

"Oh no. We aren't going into the caves." Haven laughed. "The same family has owned this place ever since I can remember. Bo Radford is the current manager. He and my dad organize the town's classic-car event every spring. He's probably close to the age your mom would have been now, right? Since there's nothing between this place and Aspen Crossroads, maybe he knew her." Haven had quietly asked around about the Chelsie family. The only ones who remembered them said they mostly kept to themselves. This was their best bet.

Jace eyed the ceiling. "Okay, okay. I guess we can ask. The caves would be fun, though."

Haven pulled her shirt away from her neck. Why was this room so short on air? Maybe the little kids from the field trip had sucked it all up on their hunt for cheap souvenirs. Two busloads of them were swarming around her and Jace's feet while they waited to speak to Bo alone.

Two kids knocked into Haven while they attempted to

see the stuffed animals on the shelf behind her. She'd move, but there was nowhere else to go while they waited to speak to the manager. Shuffling her feet a few inches toward Jace wasn't enough, and when one of the children reached for a toy at her back, Haven did a quarter turn. Once again, they were chest to chest, just as they had been Saturday night in the gazebo during their dance.

In the three days since then, she hadn't stood anywhere near this close to him. He'd been busy with the restaurant, and at night, Jillian always found her way between them. It gave Haven time to hear more about Sonny's story. Finally, it seemed, the oldest of the women saw Haven as an ally, not an enemy. And, of course, Rosalie was never short on words about her budding relationship with Jimmy.

Jace's hand cupped her elbow, thankfully holding her steady. His nearness wasn't doing much to improve her oxygen intake. "Was this what it was like in the Haviland home when you were younger? Kids everywhere?"

She returned his smile. "You have no idea."

Once the little girl was done pulling the toy off the shelf, Haven reluctantly put space between Jace and herself again.

After another few minutes, the mass of kids followed their teachers through the door to the awaiting school bus, and a quiet filled the room. And this was what the Haviland home was like when everyone abandoned her to care for her father alone. She brushed off the thought. Today wasn't about her. If it were, she certainly wouldn't be standing so near to these wretched caverns. No, today's purpose was to learn more about Jace's mother.

Down at her side, his hand covered hers, his fingers securing her palm to his. Jace's brow wrinkled. "Why is your hand so sweaty?"

She tried to pull her hand away, but he held tight, his smile broadening.

"Seriously," he said, still playing tug-of-war. "Are you nervous about something? Is it me? It's me, right?"

"No." She couldn't help but laugh. "You don't make me nervous."

He grinned. "Want me to?" As he asked, he dropped both his head and the timbre of his voice until she was right back in that gazebo, hoping he'd kiss her despite every reason he shouldn't.

"It's not you. It's the caverns. The last time I came here, I got so nervous, I threw up all over myself."

He scrunched his nose. "Ew. Give me fair warning, will you? I know I told you I like you, but I like these boots more."

She playfully jabbed him in the stomach with the hand he wasn't holding hostage. Her knuckles spent way too many seconds pressed against the muscles they found.

Bo rounded the cash counter. "Uh-oh. It's a Haviland kid. I better check the security camera."

"Hi, Bo," Haven said, finally able to pull her slick hand away from Jace's grip. "I want you to meet a friend of mine. This is Jace Daring. He runs Aspen Crossroads, and he's helping to open The Mill restaurant."

"I heard people prattling on about you at the dance the other night. We're all excited about having a new restaurant in town." Bo was a good-looking man, with loose blondish-gray curls on top of his head and steel gray eyes that crinkled at the corners with humor. Haven had often wondered why he'd never married, especially with how much the ladies in town liked him. Her father always teased him about his nickname. Apparently, he'd looked so much like one of the *Dukes of Hazzard* guys, everyone in town tossed out his real name in favor of Bo.

"Don't tell me this guy is finally getting you down into the caverns, Haven," Bo said.

Haven ignored the stare Jace bored into her. "Um, no. We're here for something else."

"Oh, come on. Jace, have you ever seen the caverns?"

"Me? No. I've never been in any caverns, but I've always wanted to."

"There you go, Haven. No time like the present to get over your fear. You've got this big guy to help you through it."

"Jace is busy with the grand opening." Haven fought to keep her throat from closing completely. "Do you have time to answer some questions about someone who used to live in Whisper Canyon?"

"Hmm. I don't know. I do my best talking when I'm caving." Bo winked at Jace.

Bells rang out. Two college-aged guys and one girl entered the shop, still laughing from some joke they carried in from the outside.

"Are you guys my eleven thirty?" Bo asked, retracing his steps back to the cashier's desk. "I need you to sign a waiver, and then I'll set you up with gear."

"We have our own, thanks," the taller guy said. "We've been traveling around to all the caves in Colorado for our YouTube channel. We actually have a waiver for you to sign, saying you can appear on camera."

"Sign of the times, I guess," Bo said.

Haven stepped in front of the trio and gripped the edge of the counter. "Give us one minute? Please?"

Bo reached over Haven to disperse pieces of paper and pens to the group. "Name, address, and a promise not to sue if you get hurt."

"Do you remember a girl who used to live at Aspen Crossroads? Her name was Lynn Chelsie," Haven said.

Something hit the floor behind the counter. Bo's eyes rounded, and his focus landed on Haven. His lips parted, and the tan he'd always sported left his face. When the students held out their papers to him, he merely stood there.

Jace came to Haven's side. "You knew her? You knew my mother?"

"Yeah, I knew your mother. Is she here with you?"

"No," Jace said. "She passed away a long time ago."

The hope that had momentarily appeared in Bo's eyes splintered at once. "You have no idea how sorry I am to hear that. You said your name is Jace what?"

"Jace Daring. She changed her name to Leigh Anne Daring," Jace said.

"No wonder I could never find her. Daring? Like that horse of hers?"

"That's what we think."

"She did love that horse." The man nodded. "Hey, I'd love to talk more, but I'm the only one here who can lead this tour. Do you have time tonight? Dinner, perhaps."

Jace worked his jaw. "The Mill has an inspection. Could you come by the restaurant tomorrow?"

"I've got a full day of tours. What about tomorrow night?"

"We're training new employees." The disappointment on both of their faces was enough to mute the terror imparted by these caverns on her own field trip. And that was the kid-friendly tour with handrails, steps, and colored lights to make the killer stalactites hanging above their heads look pretty. But spelunking?

The very idea made her mouth go dry. Unfortunately, this was the fastest way to learn more about his mother's childhood. She could not let this moment pass. If she was able to overcome her fear of horses, she could do this. She *would* do this. For Jace. Unable to unstick her tongue, she didn't bother to try words. Instead, she grabbed two blank waivers from the stack.

We need to communicate better. If I knew you were *this* scared, I never would've let you do this." Jace wedged his foot at the base of the rock where, three feet up, Haven crouched like a rabbit caught in a snare. "We can go back."

"I told you about when I threw up. But it doesn't matter. We're here until we get the answers you need." Her voice still trembled. Not as bad as the first half hour as they plunged deeper into the earth, but the girl was terrified. And with her ability to mask most of her emotions, he knew this was only the surface of her fear. She glanced behind her. For the first time, he hadn't been right at her back, encouraging her through. Bo had instructed that for this element, Jace would need to go first.

"How do I get down?" she asked.

"Just like we watched Tariq and Kayla do. Slide down and put your foot on my thigh. Then you'll be able to worm yourself through."

One leg, then the other, stretched toward him. He guided her dominant right leg down. Slowly, the pressure increased until her entire body weight balanced on him.

His hands caught her around the belt. "I've got you. I've got you."

She rasped a thank-you.

"Careful, the ground is slippery. You can hold my hand if you want. I don't care if it's sweaty."

She let out a nervous laugh but took him up on his offer, fitting her hand against his.

"And to think, I thought you were nervous because you liked me."

"If I didn't like you, I wouldn't be climbing beneath tons of rock threatening to crush me in a nanosecond."

"Scared of horses. Scared of caves and caverns. Are you afraid of dying? Is that why you don't like taking risks?"

She paused. "It's more that I'm afraid of leaving my family without anyone to lean on. The one time I did something for myself and left to study abroad, my mom self-destructed and took Daniel with her. If something happens to me, who else can they count on?"

"So, they can head out on grand adventures and experience amazing things. Then, when it all goes wrong, they know they'll find you here in Whisper Canyon waiting to welcome them home?"

"It's my nature, my calling, my name even. And it's an honor to be there for someone in need. What else is there to live for?"

For the briefest moment, he imagined taking her in his muddy arms and kissing her in response. He didn't. Partially because her headlamp might scald his retinas. But mostly because that was a question she needed to answer for herself.

Jace turned sideways to fit through the cave's narrow hall. Spelunking, he'd discovered, was not designed for tall farmers with broad shoulders and less-than-nimble movements.

Haven, despite her trepidation, still moved with grace and waited for him to scrunch his body through the formations, releasing his hand only when necessary. So strange, this hand-holding. He couldn't remember ever doing it before, apart from a reassuring pat or a temporary clasp to comfort a woman daring to flee the only life she'd known. Marjorie, the rancher's wife, had held his hand only to tease him or signal her desire to meet with him. This was different. A physical expression of the emotional tether he'd felt for Haven that first day. He could hold her hand forever, sweat and all.

In a larger room, they found Bo and the others waiting for them. "I'm going to let our young digital nomads lead the way. Be careful not to touch the walls. The minerals there that look like snow are called aragonite crystals. It can cut through your skin, then shatter."

Haven's eyes couldn't get any wider.

Jace hugged her to his side. "I owe you big-time for this."

Bo allowed the students to go ahead of him, then turned to Haven and Jace. "Okay. What do you want to know about Lynn?"

Jace started with the basics. "How did you know her?"

"Lynn and I grew up together. Neighbors and all that. She was the best friend I ever had, though."

"Did she used to come here?"

Bo chuckled. "Not at first. She was scared as scared could be. Kinda like you, Haven. Real cautious. But, eventually, I got her in here. You could say it was our playground. She said that down here she could pretend to be brave and daring. We'd battle the Fratelli family and search for One-Eyed Willy's treasure. *Goonies* was big at the time."

"Do you know why she left?" Jace slowed his duckwalk even more, careful not to scrape his head on the low ceiling.

"To be honest, it's a mystery to me as well. As we got older, our friendship turned into something more. I thought I'd marry her after high school graduation." As he spoke, the light from headlamps bobbed and weaved through the cave, but it was still bright enough to see Bo's profile. Did his mother love this man once? Just how far had this love gone?

"The summer before she left, she became withdrawn. It only got worse as the school year started. Her parents thought it was something I'd done. They tried to keep us apart. One night in November she came to my house crying. She said she was sorry, and she had to go away for a while."

Why would strict, sheltering parents send their daughter away with no explanation back then? There was only one reason Jace could think of. "November. What year was that?"

"Nineteen eighty-nine."

Six months before Jace was born. Jace studied the sullen man's jaw—squarer than his—and eyes—darker than his. But a similar build and hair color. Bo could have gotten her pregnant then stood by while her parents sent her away to have Jace. If that was true, then Bo Radford was the first of many men willing to take from his mother without any concern for the consequences. Or maybe they were two kids in love, too sheltered to understand what a night together might lead to. Did Bo even know about the pregnancy?

"Did she tell you about me?"

"No, she didn't. After she left, I never saw her again."

"Did you ever try to find her?"

"I looked everywhere for her. For many years." The lines on Bo's face deepened. From guilt? Sorrow? Shame? "Can I ask you something? How was her life after she left Whisper Canyon?"

Anger and sorrow roiled inside Jace. He didn't know how to feel. Ever since he was young, he'd wondered who his father was. Part of him hated Bo Radford for what he might've done to Jace's mom. Yet part of him yearned to draw closer to the man he'd been missing his entire life.

"Not easy, but she was strong. There was never a day I didn't know that she loved me. I couldn't have asked for a better mother." His words ended in a rasp as the emotions got the better of him.

"I'm glad, Jace. I wish I could tell you more, but I can't."

Jace didn't know what to feel toward the man. If Bo was Jace's father, but never knew about him, he supposed he might be able to forgive him. If he had known of the pregnancy, but didn't man up, he was both a liar and a snake.

Haven put her arms around Jace's waist and hugged him. She'd followed through on her promise to be at his side so he didn't have to face his mother's past alone. Not only that, but she'd confronted one of her greatest fears for his sake. No matter what he was battling inside, he would stay close to her and hold her hand through her fear—the way a real man should.

Chapter Twenty-Seven

"D o you want to talk about it?" Haven asked with the same ease she'd stepped, climbed, and crawled through this death trap. None at all.

Jace seemed to chew his words. "After I've had time to process it all." He added a forced smile. "Are you doing okay?"

She nodded. "I'll be happy to see the sun and sky after this. You've made it better."

"This is the last element and the hardest," Bo said from the front of the group. He wasn't doing a great job of acting unaffected, considering the beads of sweat on his brow despite the cool temperatures. As he spoke, Jace's whole body appeared to tense. Haven narrowed the gap between them and rested her cheek against his shoulder. The movement made her headlamp flicker, then dim.

"One at a time, you'll be belly-crawling through a narrow C-shaped tunnel. It's about fifteen yards. Tight at the start, then it opens up a bit. You can take a moment to stretch and catch your breath. Then it narrows again. On the other side, there's a gate I'll have to unlock. That dumps us out into the main section of the caverns, and if you haven't seen it, you're in for a treat." Bo looked straight at Haven. "If you're prone to panic, this is the most likely spot for it. Keep your breathing steady and take your time. Jace, will you be the anchor?"

He gave no response other than a tilt of his chin.

"All right. Wait for the person ahead of you to finish and call out to you before you start. I'll lead."

Haven lost her breath. "One at a time?"

Her words shook Jace from his defiant stance. His arm came around her and rubbed her back. "I'll be right behind you. You won't be alone."

"But he said—"

"I don't care what he said. I'll be there with you." Then he held her against his chest as each person ahead of them disappeared into the hole in the cave wall. But was this embrace for her sake or for his? She couldn't tell, and she didn't care. He was warm in the cold, musty air and steady against her racing heartbeat.

When it was Tariq's turn, he waggled his brows in their direction. "See you on the other side, lovebirds." Then they were alone.

"In case I forget to tell you, thank you for doing this. And while I never would have asked you to do something that scares you this much, I'm proud of you for making it this far." He cupped her jaw with his strong hand.

Even in this terrible light, she could get lost in the blue of his eyes. But his gaze roamed her face instead, finally landing on her mouth. Possibly the only thing that could remove her from this nightmare of a place would be to feel his kiss. She ached for it.

Tariq's faraway voice echoed her name. It was time.

Jace leaned forward, his lips stopping just shy of hers. "Don't forget God's promise in Isaiah 41. *'Do not fear, for*

I am with you . . . I will strengthen you and help you.' You can do this, Haven."

Upon his release, she breathed a quick prayer, thankful there were no depths God couldn't reach, then began her crawl.

In front of her, she'd hoped to see a bright circle of light and Bo's face, but no luck. The light from her headlamp carried only so far, ending at a curve ahead. One breath, then another. Slow and steady. She bit into her lip to stop its trembling and pulled herself along the slippery rock, feeling it dig into her elbows with each move. Her jeans and light sweatshirt weren't the best spelunking attire. But bruised forearms were worth it if she could get out of here quickly.

Unfortunately, the panic was winning.

"Jace?"

A hand gently gripped her right calf. "I'm here."

"What was that song your mom used to sing to you when you were scared?"

"Do you want me to sing it for you?"

"Yes, please."

"Brave one, brave one, time for bed,
Close your eyes and rest your head.
When you wake, the sun will, too.
There'll be much more fun to do.
Brave one, brave one, say your prayer,
Dreams come true for those who dare."

Haven tried to match her breaths to the rhythm of the lyrics as she followed the tunnel's curve. There it was. The larger space Bo had mentioned. Halfway done with this cursed element.

However, *larger* was subjective. This spot was about as big as the trunk of her car.

"You're doing great," Jace said from near her feet. "If it makes you feel better, you could be hanging out with Jillian right now."

"Even that would be better than . . ." Something yanked her by the throat. She scrambled forward. Or tried to, but the hold tightened like a noose. She rolled to her side and clawed at her neck. The sweatshirt's drawstring was caught. After inching back and feeling her feet kick something with more give than the rock wall, she was able to catch a breath. Yet, even with some slack, the drawstring was still stuck. Her fingers followed the cord to a fissure she hadn't noticed. Was the rock opening beneath her? Would she soon be plunging into hell itself? She tugged at the string this way, then that way.

"Jace, I'm—I'm stuck."

"On what?"

She yanked again, but succeeded only in hitting the back of her head. Her headlamp once again flickered, then she was swallowed by instant darkness. *No, no, no.* She smacked the lamp with the palm of her hand to no avail. It was dead. "Jace! Jace!"

Her legs were pushed to the side, then bumped and nudged as Jace slithered right beside her, bringing his low light with him.

"My headlamp broke." She barely recognized her shrill voice. She tugged the headlamp off her head and threw it the best she could farther down the tunnel, where it narrowed again.

"You can share mine." Jace shimmied beside her, his body flush against hers. Not exactly the most modest positioning, but they had no choice. "I'm here with you."

Yes, he was. She swallowed—an attempt to rid her mouth of the taste of dirt her panic had stirred up. "My drawstring is stuck."

His hand found hers, then moved past to where the knot fused with the crack. He tried maneuvering the cord. When that didn't work, he pulled on it, his grunt echoing around them.

"Uh, you guys good?" Tariq said with a laugh from beyond.

"Haven's sweatshirt is caught. Do any of you have a Swiss Army knife?" Jace kept working the string in the hanging silence.

"No, but Bo said there's one in the gift shop. He said he'll take the elevator up and grab it. You guys sit tight."

Sit tight? Haven's breaths fought against her constricting throat, and her pulse throbbed in her ears.

"You're okay." Jace removed his headlamp with his free hand and placed it faceup ahead of them to illuminate the space as much as possible. "Does this help?"

"Just reminds me where I am. I don't want to die here, Jace."

"You won't. Can you take your sweatshirt off?"

Haven twisted the muddied cotton material, but like the tunnel, its neckline had tightened and trapped her. "Not without cutting it."

"We'll have to wait, then."

"Don't leave me."

"Never. You need to calm your breathing, Haven. If you pass out, this will be harder."

"How do I . . . do that?"

"Did you ever do visualization with your clients?"

"No."

"Oh. Well, we're going to do it right now. Close your eyes and pretend you're somewhere other than here."

"Where?"

"I don't know. Somewhere relaxing where cares and worries don't exist."

A whimper escaped her lips.

"Trust me. Close your eyes. Imagine we're at my cabin, watching a movie on the couch. How about that?"

She did as he asked, yet the cold earth still dug into her side. "This doesn't . . . feel much . . . like a couch."

"Okay, not a couch." He paused, then shifted his body. "Rest your head."

She stole a peek long enough to notice he'd placed his forearm between her and the floor of the tunnel. As she accepted his offer, she mused over the idea that the hard muscles he'd used to work the land at Aspen Crossroads, build a fortress for chickens, and defend Haven from an obnoxious brother, could now pillow her head so softly.

"Imagine you and I are lying just like this on the hardwood in front of my fireplace. Only the light from the flames separates us. And I have my arms around you."

His low, smoky voice soothed her. The picture came together easily in her mind.

"Nothing and no one else exists. It's you and me. That's all."

Her breathing had tempered to an easy pattern now despite the sense he was closer than even a moment ago.

"There's no cave. No Bo. No restaurant. No Jillian." He caressed her face from her temple down to her chin. "Only you and me."

"No Austin?" she asked.

His nose grazed the side of hers. "No Austin."

She inhaled the words he breathed. Without opening her eyes, she searched for his lips and found them lingering just above hers. The mere brush she'd intended bloomed into a perfect kiss as his mouth embraced hers with the tenderness of dew caressing the grass. Why had it taken so long for this to happen when it felt so completely natural? Like he was meant for her, and she for him. They held the kiss a few moments, and the next one began before the first ended. This time she followed his lead, and as he took their kiss to new depths, a mesmerizing warmth carried her away to a place she'd never been before.

A scuffling noise shook her back to reality. Jace pulled back as another beam of light neared, leaving Haven to grasp at the breath she'd lost.

"I've got the pocketknife," Kayla said as she squirmed toward them.

Jace cleared his throat and reached to take the knife from her. "Thanks."

Haven pressed her back against the wall, even as her heart strained toward him. But the string needed to be taut for Jace's sawing action to work. Soon, she was freed from the earth's hold, and relief swept over her.

"You go ahead," he said with a lazy smile. "I'll be on your heels. Try not to kick me again. That hurt."

For the briefest instant, she considered staying right here. She liked this place where nothing and no one existed but the two of them. What would happen when they got out of this tunnel? Pretend like that amazing kiss hadn't happened? That they hadn't just shared something more powerful than Haven had ever known?

"Take the headlamp," he said.

"I don't want to leave you here in the dark."

"Trust me, Haven. My thoughts are not on the darkness right now."

A few minutes later, she crawled through the opening, where Bo extended his hand to her. As promised, Jace was right behind her, but he denied Bo's offer of a hand up.

"Sorry about that, Haven," Bo said. "I'll have to mortar that crack, so that never happens again."

"I'm fine now. Jace was there for me." Haven examined the room. With the cave's high ceiling, the headlamps didn't show much.

Bo padlocked the grate covering the tunnel's opening. "We don't want any rascally kids to go missing. Like I said, you're now standing in the main caverns. There are a lot of nooks and crannies to explore. Take your time. Our next group isn't for another half hour. Once you're done, you can head toward the sign that says *Exit*. It will take you to the elevator that dumps you out in our gift shop. But first, before I turn on the cavern lights, I want to show you what true darkness looks like in the center of the earth. Go ahead and turn off your lamps."

Haven took one last look over her shoulder at Jace's sheepish expression before removing her borrowed head-lamp and handing it to Bo. Did Jace regret their kiss? Oh, she hoped not.

When Bo extinguished his own lamp, darkness drenched Haven, and she gasped. She gasped again when Jace's hands rested on her shoulders. Probably only being protective of her, knowing how she felt about these caverns. They'd need to talk about what happened back there before they returned to the farm down the road. Then they'd squash it . . . if that's what he wanted.

"Three, two, one . . ." Bo said.

Something clicked, and lights of every color gleamed across the ceiling and walls in the grand room, each one show-casing a different formation. Remarkable. And while Haven had been desperate to get back to the earth's surface minutes ago, she was more frightened of returning to the world and never discussing that kiss with Jace. So when the students and Bo headed toward the large chandelier-shaped stalactite bathed in orange light, Haven headed in the opposite direction and hoped Jace would follow.

She followed the wall where it forked into a new hall, lit with pink and purple hues. After a quick peek, Haven turned into a secluded spot overlooking a group of stalag-mites standing straight as soldiers. She steeled her heart in preparation to hear all the reasons this wouldn't, couldn't, and shouldn't work, then spun around. "Jace—"

His arms circled her waist, and he pressed his lips to hers without hesitation or apology. Haven swallowed her concerns. Despite everything she'd learned in her counsel-ing program, sometimes talking was overrated. Jace walked her backward until the cavern wall stretched cold and steady against her back. Her fingers slid up from the nape of his neck until they locked in the longer waves near the top. In case there was still any question in his mind whether she wanted this, her other hand clutched his shirt and tugged him against her. As she drank in his kisses, she finally understood what it might look like to live for something, to take risks, and to believe that even a Haviland deserved to be happy, if only for a few weeks.

Chapter Twenty-Eight

W hat in the world happened to you two?" Sonny looked them up and down.

Jace couldn't blame her. Haven looked like she'd been mauled by a jar of peanut butter. Still cute, though. He probably wasn't any cleaner. "We went spelunking."

"Gesundheit."

"We were sixty meters underground. I saw your text once we got topside. We raced over. What's wrong?"

"The building inspector came."

"No, we have an appointment for five o'clock. I've still got two hours."

"He said he needed to come earlier, but it doesn't matter. He refused to give us the occupancy certificate."

"Why?"

"He wouldn't say. In fact, he refused to believe that I have any authority here at all. Sexist pig."

Jace withdrew his phone from his pocket and faced Haven. "This may take a while. Why don't you take my truck back to the farm so you can get cleaned up? I can ride back with Sonny."

"Are you sure? I can wait for you."

"I'm sure." He lowered his voice so Sonny couldn't hear. They still had a lot to discuss, and it wouldn't help to have Sonny barging into the conversation with her strong opinions. "But it looks like my night just freed up. Can I make you dinner? Seven o'clock?"

"Sounds perfect."

Would he ever tire of seeing her eyes dance when she looked at him? He hoped not. "I'll see you later." He handed her the key to his truck, the transfer lingering long enough to earn him a smirk from Sonny afterward. He didn't give her a chance to rib him. He needed to settle this matter with the building inspector pronto.

After a few straight-to-voice-mail calls, the man finally answered.

"Tony here."

"Hi, Tony. This is Jace Daring from The Mill Restaurant. I heard you denied us our occupancy certificate after you showed up at a different time than we'd agreed on."

"Sorry about that. The mayor needed me tonight, and I had an opening at noon. I'm afraid The Mill hasn't passed all the necessary inspections."

"Which one are we missing?"

"The environmental site inspection."

"But that isn't required."

"We believe the structure is at risk for mold due to the proximity of the creek, so it is required."

"First of all, there is no evidence of mold spores. Second, why am I just now hearing about this? We open in five days."

"Which is why I suggest you arrange for an environmental site inspection soon."

Jace stifled the growl itching his throat. "Fine. I'll get the inspection. You'll be hearing from me. Oh, and for the record, Sonny Hollis is the general manager of the restaurant. I don't suggest underestimating her in the future."

He spent the rest of the afternoon trading phone calls

with different offices to find anyone who could perform an environmental site inspection. Half the people he spoke to had never even heard of the thing. Finally, he found someone.

"Crisis averted. Or at least delayed," he told Sonny in the kitchen doorway.

"Don't you step foot in my kitchen looking the way you do."

"Yes, ma'am. Inspection is Friday morning. Once we pass, we can rush the request for an occupancy certificate. As long as we get that, we're still on track for a Friday soft opening."

"And if we don't pass?"

"We'll pass. I personally checked every corner of the cellar for mold and we replaced every piece of wood that was even questionable. Oh, and I let Tony know who's the boss here."

"Aw, thanks. I'd kiss your cheek, but you're covered in mud. Plus, based on the way Haven and you were salivating over each other, I'm guessing you've had plenty of kisses today already."

"Is it that obvious?"

Sonny nodded.

"Jace likes Heaven." Elijah zoomed a wooden train across a small circular track in the corner near where Sonny was labeling shelves.

"Awesome."

"I think it's great. Just do me a favor and wait to tell Jillian until after the launch."

"Whoa. This is brand-new. Haven and I haven't even figured out what *it* is yet. Besides, it's not serious."

"Bull. Believe it or not, I know you, Jace. You wouldn't start something unless you were serious. By the way, that jerk-mayor stopped by, too. Right after the inspector left."

"He did? What did he say?"

"He was being all nosy, walking around the property.

When I approached him, he said to tell you and Haven he said hi. Then he said, *Good luck with the opening.*"

That explained the bogus inspection. Part of Jace wanted to take Haven to the front of the mayor's mansion, ring his doorbell, and kiss her like he did at the caverns, just to show the louse that he and Haven were done with his tricks. Of course, he'd never use Haven as a pawn in the mayor's game. He cared about her too much. *Way* too much. His head still swam with the memory of holding her. Maybe he shouldn't have asked her over for dinner. But how could he keep his feelings for her buried underground? Haven was the one who could mask her emotions. Not him. Sonny had seen right through him in seconds. Elijah, too, and he was three.

It wouldn't take Jillian long.

Sonny checked her watch. "'Lijah, are you ready to head home? Pack up your trains. Someone's got to get ready for his date."

The perfect evening. That's what this was. Outside, light snow fell across the farm in perfect snow globe fashion. Inside Jace's cabin, the soft melody of nineties country music provided the ideal soundtrack, and the firelight from the hearth bathed Jace's gorgeous face in the dreamiest glow. Not that she'd had her eyes open much ever since she and Jace finished dinner and moved their date to his couch.

She couldn't help it. Every soft kiss of his melted her. And the way his strong, hardworking hands caressed her cheek and cradled her jaw with a feather touch made her feel cherished. It was almost enough to make her believe this could last beyond this moment in time. Oh, how she wanted that. What she felt for him was more than a crush or an infatuation. And if she kept spending time with him and inviting kisses like these, she'd fall hard and fast.

"Jace," she whispered an instant before his lips were poised around hers again.

"Mmm?" he murmured without pulling away.

Her smile broke his hold on her. "We need to talk."

He sat back a bit and dropped his hands to hers. As he stroked her knuckles with his thumbs, his brow returned to its oft-furrowed nature. "Okay, what first?"

"Austin."

His shoulders rose and fell with a deep breath. "I'm willing to do the long-distance thing if you are. I know it won't be easy, but we can make it work. At least until something else comes about. Would you ever leave Whisper Canyon?"

The question unsettled her. "Would you ever leave Secondly?"

"You know what? We don't have to think about that right now. We'll deal with those decisions as they come. Fair enough?"

"Fair enough."

He leaned in, sweeping his upper lip across her cupid's bow.

"What about Trent?"

He groaned.

"I'm sorry to bring him up, especially like this, but he's already after The Mill. And if he finds out about this, who knows what stunt he'll pull."

"Okay. I won't kiss you like this in the middle of town."

"Jace, be serious."

"I am. We can keep this under wraps until the restaurant gets its rhythm."

"That leads us to the biggest issue."

"Jillian."

"She still doesn't trust me. Aren't you worried what she'll do?"

Jace sat back and rubbed his eyes. "Have I ever told you about Tucson?"

"No. That's where you were last?"

"Yeah. One of the women on our team—Gretchen—had a crush on me. If I led her to think I liked her in that way, I didn't mean to. All these women are like sisters to me. I was the person she came to with all of her concerns and joys. I hadn't brought in any mentors or anything. I even stayed three extra months, but that only made it worse when it was time for me to go. After I arrived here, I got a call from Alison—one of the other women at the farm. Gretchen went back to her old life. When the police found her body in an alley, I could only blame myself."

So much heaviness in his past. Far more than any one person should carry. Haven closed her eyes. "How awful."

"What if Jillian goes back?"

Haven pictured Jillian's strawberry mane soaking in the dingy puddles next to a Dumpster. "Give me a little more time with her. I'm hopeful that some expressive art therapy techniques might get her to open up. Meanwhile, she can feel the victory of a successful grand opening. She'll be great at managing the front of the house. After she has something else to focus on, I'll tell her about us. Until then, we'll keep our distance from each other."

"All the time?" He gulped in such a cartoonish way Haven nearly burst out laughing.

Instead, she moved to kiss him again. "We'll be sure to sneak in some moments here and there."

Chapter Twenty-Nine

Haven's arms ached beneath the weight of the shopping totes. She should've parked next to the barn to make her job easier. The two canvases she'd pinched under her arm slipped. Trying to save it from hitting the dirt, she dipped to the side and caught them against her leg, only to drop the totes in the process.

"I can already see how well this will go." Jillian kneeled beside Haven. Together, they scooped the acrylic paint tubes, brushes, and mixing boards back into the bag. "Are you planning on painting the Sistine Chapel? You got too much."

"I didn't want to miss anything. And whatever we don't use, you can keep here in your studio."

"Studio? You do realize this is a barn, right?"

"It can't be too comfortable, especially now that the temps are dropping so quickly."

"Once Jace leaves, he said I can use the cabin."

Jillian relieved Haven of the canvases and carried them to the barn. The walls had been lined with hay squares, stacked floor to ceiling. For insulation maybe? Dozens of paintings, drawings, and even a mosaic leaned against them. The wood floors were swept cleaner than Haven had imagined, but still, these works of art shouldn't be stored here.

"Jillian, these are extraordinary. When do you have time to do this?"

"I don't sleep very well at night."

One drawing stood out from the rest, and it made Haven blush. It appeared to be a nude self-portrait.

"You gonna judge me for that?"

"Why would I?"

"It doesn't align with your ideals, does it? It wouldn't hang in your church or your counseling office or your house."

"No, but that doesn't mean I'm judging you for it. Art is all about self-expression, right? What were you feeling when you drew that?"

"I don't think so. I'm not falling for that."

"All right. Can I tell you what I see?"

She shook her head dismissively. "Be my guest."

"Okay." Haven forced herself to focus on the artwork, the lines and the curves, the shadows and light. "I see a woman who has fought to survive. She's been to hell and back, but she's still here. There was a time when everyone had access to her body. Everyone but her." Her voice strained as she recognized a bit of herself in the drawing. "Finally, she gets say over what her body does. Her body finally belongs to her. Those are her eyes that get a new view of life. Her hands that get to touch the flowers, the paint, the dirt. For the first time, she is proud of who she is and hopeful for what she may become."

Jillian came near and stood silently. "Nah. My body looked hot one day. That's all."

Haven dropped her head in defeat.

There were two easels, one tall and one short. Jillian placed one canvas on each. Passing by the single bar-stool, Jillian took one of the hay bales off a stack and carried it to the spot in front of the short easel. "Here's your spot."

"Perfect," Haven said, wondering if it would be rude to grab her quilt from the car trunk to pad her seat.

After Jillian clicked on the electric heater between their stations, she pulled the barn doors shut.

Haven withdrew each of her purchased supplies out of their bags and added them to the wooden shelving unit, making sure she didn't mess up Jillian's neat organization.

"Why do you want to learn how to paint again?"

"My father's sixtieth birthday is in February. I'd love to paint something for him. Maybe the mountains or the canyon. But I don't know anything about painting techniques."

"And you assume it's something you can simply pick up? I hope you aren't expecting me to Bob Ross you."

"No, but some basics would be helpful."

"Yeah, okay. We'll do a basic mountain-and-valley landscape. First, come over here and choose four or five colors."

"What colors would be best?"

Jillian didn't look up as she scrolled on her phone. "It's up to you. When you look at the mountains or the canyon, what colors do you see?" She pressed the on/off button on the Bluetooth speaker, and suddenly, a familiar song Haven couldn't pinpoint filled the barn.

"Is that how you choose?"

"Yeah. Landscapes aren't my favorite scenes, but when I started the one for the restaurant's main dining room, I could've focused on the light when the sun is high and everything is fresh, clean, and new. I would have chosen lighter colors. Or, I could've focused on the shadows that overtake the canyon in the night. I would have chosen

dark." Jillian pointed to a large sheet-covered rectangle behind them.

Haven closed her eyes and pictured the surrounding mountains and this town. Simple. She grabbed bright green like the
park's grass, royal blue like the sky above, and a combo of
light gray, pink, and red to match the red brick and concrete in
town. Jillian squirted blobs of white paints on Haven's mixing
board and directed her to start with a thick brush, painting
broad white strokes until the top of the canvas was covered.
Haven did as instructed. "Did you grow up in Denver?"

When no answer came, Haven glanced at Jillian's canvas. The top half of her canvas was dark gray, not white.

"Why are you using dark colors?"

"My mountain scene will be at night."

"Why is that?"

Jillian snickered. "I get it. This is your attempt at counseling me."

"No—"

"I'm not a fool." Jillian's eyes narrowed on Haven. "But
since you asked, my mountain scene is set at night because
I don't see life in rainbows."

"I don't, either."

She rolled her eyes. "Come on. Tell me one thing that
isn't perfect about your life." Jillian stared at Haven while
a song by the Smiths came on. She knew this one thanks to
one of Rarity's phases. "How Soon Is Now?"

Haven went back to the supply table and perused the
acrylics. She picked out a few and returned to her easel.
One splatter of Mars Black later, Haven was smearing
gloomy streaks through the white paint until her sky looked
like something out of a sci-fi show. Following Jillian's example she added a gray to the middle of the canvas and
blended it with the monstrous darkness above to give an
illusion of a horizon that Haven hadn't yet seen.

"Once you've been here awhile, you'll hear the stories,

so I'll go ahead and tell you. When I was little, I thought my mom was the most beautiful woman in the world. The most beautiful and yet the saddest. Ever since I could remember, she would come into my room and lay beside me in bed. I'd awaken to the sound of sobs. She'd say, *I messed up again* and *What's wrong with me?* and *I don't want to hurt your daddy anymore.* You see, my mother had a reputation for sleeping around. She would go to Sassy's Saloon, get drunk, and end up in some tourist's hotel room or the car of one of the married men in town. Then she'd come home in tears and it was my job to comfort her. I remember being eight years old and she told me we'd be better off if she killed herself." Haven placed a dollop of midnight blue on the board. Again, following Jillian's example, she dragged a thin brush through the paint and created angles for the mountaintops.

Jillian had slowed down working on her own painting.

Haven had no idea if she was even listening, but she continued anyway. "I carried her burdens for her. I'd see my father in pain, and I'd hug him and tell him it wasn't his fault. I carried his burdens. I felt like I'd crack under the pressure, so I left to stay with my aunt when I was fifteen. When I returned, we learned Mom had been having an affair. Before she left to run off with the guy, she told me that if I'd been here, it never would have gone so far."

"She blamed you? That's shady."

After Haven filled in the mountains, she stepped back to get a new perspective on her work. "We didn't see her again until last year."

"She came back?"

"Only because she didn't want to die alone. She had cancer." With her brush, she dappled the mountains with black.

"Did she apologize for what she'd done?"

"Not once. My sisters and I took care of her anyway. My dad showed her so much undeserved love. It wrecked me."

"Let me guess. You stole a sip of alcohol? Smoked a cigarette?"

"I slept with a client during his counseling session."

Jillian's brush dropped from her hand, landing on the barn floor.

"My mom had just died, and I needed an escape from all the conflicting feelings I had. I found out afterward that he was still married."

"Was it Mayor Garrison?"

Haven whipped her head toward Jillian. "How'd you know?"

"I heard people gossiping at the dance."

Haven sucked in an audible breath.

Jillian laughed. "I'm joking. I saw him gawking when you and Jace were dancing. How did you not know he was married?"

"I fell for lies. Jace said the man exploited me, but I didn't say no."

Jillian dipped a brush into Haven's leftover midnight blue paint and began quickly creating vertical lines of varying heights along the base of the mountain. "I bet you asked for it as much as I asked for it from my fifth-grade gym teacher."

"Oh, Jillian. What did your parents do when you told them?"

"It was only my grandmother, and she didn't care about anything as long as she got her next fix." Jillian switched to a dark green and went back over the pine trees in the distance. "You know who pretended to care? My brother's best friend. He was twenty. I was twelve." Jillian tossed the small brush on the tray and went at the canvas with the largest brush she had, pushing and smearing the paint until it covered the rest of the blank space. "For the longest time, I thought there was something wrong with me and that was why people would hurt me. Use me. Consume me. But you're Miss Perfect and you got used, too. Maybe they're the messed-up ones."

Haven traced the basic outline of buildings along Main Street. When she got to the town hall, she switched to a bloodred shade. "I think you're onto something."

Chapter Thirty

W e got it!" Jace yelled the moment he entered The Mill.

Rosalie and Jillian stopped setting the tables, and Haven leaned the broom against the wall.

"The certificate of occupancy?" Jillian asked. They gathered around the powerful piece of paper as if it couldn't be real.

"The signed approval letter from the environmental site inspector was the last thing they needed."

"Such a waste of time," Jillian said. "That inspector this morning didn't have to take samples or anything."

"Yeah, well, there are no more hoops for us to jump through. I'll hang this up, and we're good to go."

"I'll put it in a frame!" Rosalie took the paper from his hand and headed to the office on the third floor.

He shared a smile with Haven, and she nodded to the large wall where Jillian's watercolor mural now hung. Jace put his hands on his waist and took in the artwork she'd kept hidden until now. It was far more abstract than her pencil drawings, but still recognizable as Aspen Crossroads and the mountains beyond it. "Jillian, this looks incredible."

"You really think so?" A proud grin fixed itself to her face—a nice change from her typical smirk-and-glare combination.

"Absolutely." And he meant it. "You're gifted. Sonny will have to start looking for a new front-of-house manager. As soon as people around town see this, they'll be contracting you for custom artwork. We'll be small potatoes."

"No one's ever thought I was good at anything before."

"I doubt that's true."

"Well, nothing outside of a hotel room." In the past, Jillian had used those types of comments to come on to him. He'd brush them off, not wanting to shame her. This time was different. She looked sad, and it punched him in the gut. More than anything, he wanted to tell her until the words soaked into her flesh and bones that she was worth much more than what she's been told in the past. "The mural is perfect. Thank you for working hard on it."

"You got it."

"I'm going to see if Sonny needs a hand prepping in the kitchen." Jace checked his watch. In only three hours, fifty guests would be seated, and the newly hired and trained staff would go to work. Strangely, sorrow tinged the joy he felt. It was always difficult to leave after working so hard and building a solid team. This time, though, the idea that he'd be leaving hurt something awful. Jace rubbed the heel of his hand against his chest, hoping the ache would disperse as quickly as it arrived. It didn't.

"Sonny, put me to work," he said as he headed for the sink to wash up.

"How would you feel about chopping a bag of onions?"

"I've been waiting for you to ask me to do that."

"Smart aleck. Where's your girlfriend?"

"Stop."

"What? You may be trying to keep it quiet, but to me, it's clearer than springwater. You should see her during the day. No one blushes when they get a text, except for Haven. You must be pretty schmoopy in those messages you send."

"Schmoopy?"

"Lovey-dovey. Romantic. You know."

Jace shook his head and reached for a cutting board and knife. "Haven's family is in town passing out flyers and hanging advertisements about tomorrow's grand opening. I hope our parking lot can handle the crowd."

Sonny paused her work of stuffing chicken breasts with a spinach, artichoke, and breading mixture. "It all seems too easy. The farm. The restaurant. It fell into place perfectly, didn't it? I kept waiting for the town to find out about us. No way did I think that sicko-mayor would keep this on the down-low."

"Maybe he found an ounce of integrity when we weren't looking. Would it be the worst thing for God to bless The Mill and honor all the hard work we've done?"

"The God I know allows man's evil to reign on this earth. Reckoning might be coming, but until it's here, the devil rules the roost."

Jace cut the end off the onion, then sliced it in half. "Hey, Sonny, did you go to church as a child?"

"My grandmother used to take me. I haven't been in years."

"Would you go back?"

"Why are you asking?"

"Haven's invited me to the church in town."

"And?"

"I told her no. My mom taught me the stories from the Bible. But she also taught me that church is no place for . . ."

"For people like us?"

"Yeah."

"Maybe. Maybe not. As I said, I haven't been in years. But since the beginning, people have done a good job of bringing bad to what the Lord meant for good. Church is no exception, but then again, what is? Now, get to chopping. We've got a crowd to feed tonight."

Welcome to The Mill," Rosalie said with a beaming smile. Her dark hair was slicked back in a sophisticated high ponytail. Between that and her crisp blouse and black slacks, she looked older than her eighteen years.

If the sight of Rosalie filled Haven's heart with joy, the ambiance of The Mill's dining room nearly caused it to burst. The team at Aspen Crossroads had done a marvelous job. From Jillian's art to the high-end table settings complete with candlelight, and everything in between. And the smell? Haven's mouth had started watering as soon as they'd turned onto the driveway, and she'd picked up the first hints of seared beef in the air.

Tears wet her lashes, and she tried to wipe them away before her mascara left an inky path down her cheeks.

"How many are in your party?" Rosalie's plastered and poised smile splintered into her childlike grin. "I'm sorry. I'm trying to be professional, but I'm so excited."

"You should be excited! You've all worked hard for this night. And there are seven in my party. Elijah will need a booster seat, won't you, buddy?"

Elijah held tight to Haven's pinkie finger. He looked up at her. "Can I see Mommy now?" Thanks to Rarity, he looked like a little Danny Zuko in his jeans, white T-shirt, and mini black leather jacket. She'd even used pomade to slick his curls down, with one perfect curlicue hanging down his forehead.

Haven lifted him onto her hip. "Just a peek, but remember, Mommy is super busy."

Rarity, in her favorite red-and-black polka-dot rockabilly dress, feigned confusion. "Where are you taking my new best friend?"

"To the kitchen. We'll meet you at the table." Haven carried Elijah past the staircase to the hallway that led to the kitchen, nearly ramming into Jace.

"Whoa. Note to self. Add a mirror, so we have no server collisions," he said. "Hi, guys. 'Lijah, you look handsome, man!"

"Rockin' and rollin'." Elijah let loose a giggle.

"Rarity taught him that. Hopefully, that was all he learned from her." Haven readjusted the boy's weight on her hip. "Can he say hi to Sonny?"

"Sure. The kitchen is in good shape. They're waiting for the first orders to come in." Jace took Elijah from her and brought him into the kitchen.

Haven peered back to the dining room. Guests were still filtering into the restaurant in pairs and small groups. Haven recognized most of them. A few influential folks, like Reverend Horst, his wife, Deanne, and Jimmy. Some older ladies and gentlemen from the senior center, most with money to spare, followed Lizzie and her grandfather to a table. Were they donors to this venture? Invitations went out only to those who had supported The Mill from its inception, so they must have been.

Jace ducked out of the kitchen without Elijah. His gaze took a brisk walk down Haven's dress to her sandals and back up. "You're beautiful."

Haven fidgeted with one of the pleats on the skirt of the dress. "Thank you. And you look . . ." She couldn't finish the sentence. Every part of her ached to press herself against his plaid-shirted chest and feel his charcoal sportscoat–clad arms surround her. She now clutched the skirt's fabric in her fist when she wanted to grab hold of his tie and lead him to the cellar. The man had officially muddled her brain.

His soft laugh teased her even more. "I don't get dressed up too often. If you can call this dressed up."

"I like it." Haven coiled a lock of her hair around her finger. "The place looks and smells amazing."

"Thanks. They've been finessing the dishes for the last couple of hours. I don't want to take credit or anything, but I cut up all the onions."

"Then I'll order everything with a garnish of onions since you can't sit next to me."

"I'll try to stop by. Who did you bring?"

"My dad, Rarity, Daniel, Valor, and Wes."

"I'd like to meet your dad. Where is he?"

Haven nodded toward the dining room, and he followed her to the end of the hall. When he placed his hand gently on the small of her back, she nearly forgot who she was looking for in the first place. "The big table over by the windows. He's the one talking to . . ."

Bo Radford stood next to her father, and the two men shared what appeared to be casual conversation, same as they always had. But this was not the Haviland home, the car shop, or even the site of the classic car show. This was Jace's restaurant.

"Why is Bo here?" Jace's jaw muscle flexed.

"I can ask him to leave if you want." She gently palmed his cheek until his eyes met hers. "Maybe he wants to get to know you."

A throat cleared from down the hallway, and Haven dropped her hand. Jillian, dressed in head-to-toe black, glowered at Haven. "You mind? I need to talk to Jace."

"Not at all. I should rejoin my family."

"Yes, you should." The edge in her voice made Haven wonder if all their progress would be undone when Jillian learned the truth about her and Jace.

After Haven retrieved Elijah from Sonny's arms, she escorted him to her family's table amid a series of comments like *How adorable* and *Simply precious*. Elijah soaked in the attention, even waving to the ladies in the place. The joy ended when she noticed Bo seated at their table. "Where did Daniel go?"

"Shocker. He found a girl to sit with," Rarity said. "Bo

took his spot, and he's trying to convince Dad to buy an old motorcycle."

"Not just any old motorcycle," Bo said. "A 1950 Triumph Thunderbird 6T like the one Marlon Brando rode in *The Wild One*."

Rarity rested her chin on her folded hands. "Marlon Brando? I'm coming around. Keep talking."

Haven helped Elijah into his booster seat, but before taking her own seat, she perused the restaurant. Daniel sat near the front door right beside Lizzie and the seniors. She caught his eye and shook her head. He responded by resting his arm on the back of Lizzie's chair.

A fresh-faced server delivered drinks and a basket to their table. He explained the different types of bread and pointed out two crocks on the table, one holding hand-churned butter and the other, honey from Aspen Crossroads.

The evening's special menu featured four main courses. Haven chose the pepper-crusted filet mignon over the spinach-and-artichoke-stuffed chicken breast. Having learned more about the farm-to-table movement, she now worried she might be eating someone else's Audrey Henburn. Her father opted for the braised lamb chops, and both of her sisters chose the vegetable tagine.

"You would've been proud of your daughter the other day, Michael," Bo said while he buttered his pumpernickel slice. "She took on those caverns like a warrior. And not the easy caverns. The caves."

Haven felt all the eyes on her as she unwrapped a pack of saltine crackers for Elijah to snack on.

"I've been trying to get you to go with me since you were ten," Valor said. "You always refused. What changed?"

"I know what changed." Rarity's singsong voice grated on Haven's nerves. "Jace Daring moved to Whisper Canyon."

"What's this?" her father asked.

"Remember? Jace is the man I work with at Aspen Crossroads."

"And he's a dreamboat," Rarity said.

Bo cleared his throat. "He was great with Haven in the caves. I used to know his mother. Her son seems to be a good deal like her. Softhearted. Thoughtful."

Haven could continue with the traits Jace had exhibited in the couple of months she'd known him. Hardworking, loyal, patient, playful, and romantic. But she'd rather hear more about Lynn. She opened her mouth to speak, but Bo beat her to it.

"Haven, there's something I wanted to talk to you about. You and Jace seem close. Do you think he'd care to—I don't know . . ." Bo scratched his nose with his knuckle. "Losing Lynn was the hardest thing I've ever gone through. I'd love to have even a piece of her in my life. Would Jace be open to going fishing with me or something? I don't mean to take the place of any father he has . . ."

"I think you'd have to speak to him about it. But do it quick. He's moving on soon."

Chapter Thirty-One

Lights off. Candles out. Customers and staff gone. To Jace, as he stood in the darkness, The Mill resembled a skeleton more than Whisper Canyon's newest restaurant. The ghostly tables and chairs might as well be its ribs. The staircase, its spine. As an old body might crackle and pop, this old building creaked and moaned in its transition back to life. And life is what Whisper Canyon's gristmill would have once again.

The night had gone without a single hitch. Too good to be true. Would they have the same fortune tomorrow night when customers rotated throughout the dinner service or when they stayed for late-night dessert and drinks?

"Good night, you ol' gristmill. Until tomorrow," Jace called out before opening the front door.

In the middle of the parking lot, Haven's car sat alone, away from his truck in the farthest employee parking space. She reclined on her hood and windshield, covered with a quilt up to her chest.

He smiled to himself. He'd hoped to see her tonight. After locking and double-checking the front door, he pocketed his keys and strolled to her car.

"Haven, it's nearly midnight. What are you doing here?"

"I wanted to tell you congratulations."

"You could've texted that."

"Not good enough. Come on up. I saved you a spot."

"I'll dent your hood."

"I thought your name was Daring. Besides, my dad owns a car shop, and this car isn't exactly new."

"Okay, then." He crawled up as carefully as he could to the place next to her. As she draped the quilt over his body, he reclined on the windshield and exhaled for what felt like the first time since he'd arrived in Whisper Canyon. "I could fall asleep right here."

"And miss this?" She waved her hand at the sky, where star upon star riddled the darkness. "How did it go, from your perspective?"

"Flawless. First time that's ever happened."

"The team did great. Rosalie and Jillian rocked the front of the house. And the food? Oh, Jace. Sonny's amazing."

"Right? We'll see how tomorrow goes. I have a weird feeling about it in the pit of my stomach."

"Here?" Haven dug her fingers into his ribs, and he curled around her hand, grunting at the attempted tickle attack.

He wrestled her hand away, then held her tight to his side. A long kiss against her forehead was all he had the energy for tonight, but it was enough. "Thanks for bringing your family out."

"They were excited to see a little of what I've been working on. And they wanted to see you, too."

"I'm glad I got to meet your dad. Even if it was brief. I thought he'd be intimidating. Like Daniel times one hundred."

"No, my dad is a softy. Sometimes I wish he wasn't that way. It would've saved him a good deal of heartache."

"You don't look like him."

"Daniel and I take after my mom."

Jace's thoughts remained on the dinner table, including

the Haviland family's unexpected guest. "Do you think I look like Bo?"

"Maybe a little. He wants to spend time with you. He said something about fishing, but I think he wants to get to know you. You might get a call."

He caressed her brow with his lips. "I'll think about it." Just not tonight. He was tired.

Haven traced circles on Jace's chest where his coat lay unbuttoned.

He could stay here all night, cold windshield and all. Haven was warm enough for them both. How great would it be to decompress with her after every long day? Swim in that flowery scent of hers? Kiss her breathless and feel her soft skin against his.

You'll never find someone like me. Marjorie's warning crashed his thoughts. She'd been so angry the day he broke things off with her and left town. But she'd also been right. Haven was nothing like Marjorie.

Chapter Thirty-Two

Jace toed a stone with his boot. In front of him, waves of white and gray peaks stretched as far as he could see beneath the morning's clear blue sky. At least he hadn't tried to hike Chapel Peak this morning. Not that driving it was any easier or safer this time of year even on dry, sanded roads. But he needed to come here. To the only church he felt comfortable near.

Last night's soft opening might have been a success for Secondly and his Aspen Crossroads team, but he felt like he'd swallowed the entire menu in one sitting. After hearing that Bo wanted to get to know him, he needed to clear his head.

Another car climbed the mountain, the driver as foolish as he was. He couldn't see the person on the far side of the church, but he heard the ignition cut off, followed by the foot-steps. Lizzie appeared, wearing the unflattering, large coat of an older man. "Jace? Good heavens. You must be freezing! Are you out of your mind?"

"Are you?"

"I have a reason to come up here. I have to shut down the chapel for the season."

"Need any help?"

"If I did, I wouldn't ask you." Lizzie pulled the coat tighter around her. Her normally peaceful expression was missing.

"I saw you last night. You had interesting company," Jace said.

"That's what you're concerned about most right now? My company?"

"You need to be careful with Daniel. Haven knows him better than anyone and—"

"Jace, do you get the paper?"

"No."

"So you haven't heard?"

"Heard what?"

"On the front page, a reporter cites an anonymous source, outing Aspen Crossroads for what it is, and he didn't hold anything back."

Jace's truck screeched to a halt between the cabin and the farmhouse. He leapt out of the cab and threw the door closed with all his might. Nothing could quell the blaze burning him from the inside out. But this town would rue the day if any harm came to his team because of this article. His shaking hand knocked on the farmhouse door.

After a few seconds, Sonny peeked through the sidelight curtain. Then the door opened, and her red-rimmed eyes bored into his.

In her arms, Elijah hugged his mother's neck. "Rosie's got a boo-boo," he said.

The cries reached through the opening and clutched his heart. Sonny opened the door farther, and Jace stepped inside, not even bothering to remove his boots. Nothing mattered anymore except these women who had trusted him to guard and protect them. He'd failed.

On the couch, Rosalie clung to Haven, and her whole body racked with each sob.

Haven cradled Rosalie, brushing the girl's hair off her tear-pummeled face again and again. Yet Haven's expression was stoic. Counselor mode. When Rosalie saw Jace, she left Haven's embrace in favor of his. She locked her arms around his waist and melted against his chest.

"Rosie, I'm sorry. I should've done more."

Sonny deposited Elijah back in the middle of his circular Thomas the Tank Engine track, then grabbed the newspaper off the coffee table. "Haven's sister brought a copy over. You want to read it?" She held the front page of the *Whisper Canyon Chronicle* so he could see it over Rosalie's head. The title read "Lust, Greed, and Prostitution on a Platter: The Canyon's Newest Restaurant Invites the Rabble In." A full spread. Front and center, an image of The Mill with its impeccable landscaping and impressive facade were surrounded by words like *abhorrent*, *criminal*, and *sinful*. Chef Sonny, Manager Jillian, and Hostess Rosalie were all named, though thankfully, not pictured. The article implied they were still sex workers, using the restaurant as a ruse to gain clients. Jace was painted as a hotheaded pimp for them, eager to corrupt the town's good moral character so he could fill his pockets.

"That's not all." Sonny let the bottom half of the paper unfold, revealing a picture of Haven—the one from her counseling practice's website.

A Counselor with Secrets to Spare

Once voted Whisper Canyon's favorite counselor, Haven Haviland has taken the town for a ride. Numerous sources describe Ms. Haviland's practice as a scheme to wreck happy homes. According to a source, she regularly attempted to seduce married men who sought out counseling to become stronger fathers, husbands, and community members . . .

Farther down, it tied Haven to Jace in a purported collaboration to use the townsfolk's trusting nature for their
gain. The article then reminded readers about her mother,
Nina Haviland's tryst with Whisper Canyon High's married
football coach that led to a town scandal. It even tossed her
sister Rarity under the bus, citing her outspoken opposition
to the town's status quo.

Finally, at the bottom, a bold-printed call to action: *Boycott The Mill Restaurant.* Jace's stomach might as well
have dropped through the farmhouse floor.

"What's Jimmy going to say?" Rosalie asked between
heaves. "Why would he want me now?"

Jace made a shushing sound against her hair. Not to
quiet her as much as to soothe her pain. If only that were
possible. To take away the pain from everyone in the room.
To promise them it would all be okay. That this would blow
over in time. But he knew better. "Where's Jillian?"

"Gone," Sonny said in resigned defeat.

Fresh panic seized Jace. "Gone where?"

"Don't know. After she read the article, she grabbed the
keys to the van and took off. If I had to guess, I'd say she
knows that so-called collaboration between you and Haven
is a personal one."

Haven lifted her eyes to his, and they glinted with the
shame Jace felt in his heart.

Sonny tossed the paper onto the table. "We aren't going
to sit here crying all day. We need a plan."

"A plan?" Rosalie sniffled.

"Yes. We have a restaurant to open tonight."

Rosalie loosened her grip on Jace and turned to face
Sonny. "But the boycott."

"So what? Some hoity-toity, thinks-they're-better-
than-us people won't come to the restaurant. Others will
come out of curiosity. And there have to be people around
who don't believe this nonsense, which sounds like it was
written by an overdramatic teenager. No offense, Rosie."

"None"—sniff—"taken."

"What do you suggest?" Jace asked.

"First, find Jillian. And we can't send Haven to do that. If looks could kill, we'd be digging a grave in the beet field. Second, we get Jimmy to work things out with Rosalie. Third, we egg this reporter's house. Fourth, we get a list of Haven's past clients and egg their houses." Sonny jutted out her chin defiantly. "Fifth, we make the best food people have ever eaten in their lives. But we don't apologize for who we are or who we've been."

Haven fumbled with her car key, failing to fit it into the door's lock. *Hold it together for one more minute.* That's all she had to do. Then she could drive farther into the mountains until a curtain of pines shielded the meltdown she'd been holding in for the past two hours.

A masculine hand covered hers. "Where are you going?" Jace asked.

"Away." Her chin trembled.

"Haven."

"Please. I can't do this here."

"You can't do what? Show them you're human. Let them know that you don't just share in their pain, but you have pain of your own?"

"I caused this. It's all my fault."

"That isn't true."

"It is. This is Trent's doing. If I'd never accepted him as a client or if I'd never believed his lies, he wouldn't have cared one lick about this place."

"First of all, you didn't lead him astray. He sought you out. Second, Garrison opposed our presence in Whisper Canyon long before you and I ever met."

"When I got involved, it became personal. It's my fault they are in danger. And those accusations about my practice? And poor Rarity?"

Jace placed a hand on her back, but she didn't dare face him.

"Haven, let me hold you."

"We can't. Jillian."

"She isn't here, and besides, she knows about us now." He eased her around until his eyes met hers.

"I'm supposed to help people, not hurt them." The emotional gates broke open. Now she was the one crying into Jace's chest while he shushed her. And as her world, profession, and reputation crumbled around her, she let someone else shelter her.

Chapter Thirty-Three

D on't worry about a thing, sis." Rarity paced their father's kitchen with steps so powerful that Haven worried she might crack the tile. "All of my friends will be at The Mill tonight. They can take their boycott and shove it where—"

"Rare," her father warned.

"Oh, I'm supposed to be nice? I have watched this same group of people move along Main Street 'cleaning' up the businesses. They are erasing the town's heritage, its soul! And all for what? So we can be more like those other ski towns and charge a thousand dollars for a one-night stay in our ski lodge?" She pounded her fist onto the palm of her other hand like a judge with a gavel. "Now they come after an organization trying to give new life to people who have already been abandoned by society. And don't get me started on the lies they told about Haven."

"Are they lies?" Daniel asked from the darkest corner of the kitchen.

In the quiet that followed, whatever part of Haven's heart that hadn't already broken, shattered.

"Oak Haviland, you apologize to your sister right now," her father said, rising to his full height from his seat at the table.

"Look, Haven, I'm sorry, but you haven't denied the allegations against you, as ridiculous as they are."

"Of course she denies them," Valor said. She placed an arm around Haven's shoulders and squeezed. "Haven's the best one of us. While we were all off making our mistakes, she was here, taking care of Whisper Canyon, Dad, and each one of us when we came straggling back home."

Haven dropped her focus to her tissue-twisting hands in her lap. She debated the wisdom in holding on to the last missing piece or going public with it. Admitting her short-lived dalliance with Trent would serve only to convict her in the court of public opinion, and it would officially kill her chance of ever returning to counseling in the professional sense. However, if she explained Trent's lies, it might blow a hole in his attempt to sanctify this town. Even those at the top wouldn't appreciate their leader's tumble down the rabbit hole of sin. With the mayoral election a few weeks away, it might make him drop out of contention, leaving room for someone more worthy to lead the town. She'd be willing to sacrifice her happiness if it could save Rarity, other business owners, and The Mill. But would anyone believe her?

Rarity's phone buzzed on the counter. She glanced at it, then snapped her fingers toward the family room. "Turn on the TV. To the local station. Hurry."

Valor got to the remote first and turned it to Channel One. Typically, the channel showed high school football games and town council meetings. Not much else. Right now it displayed Trent Garrison, standing behind a podium.

"To answer your first question, no, I don't condone prostitution anywhere. Especially not in our community. I assure you that myself and the town council will not stand idly by while criminals and degenerates move in. As for your second question, I support the boycott of The Mill Restaurant, absolutely."

Trent wore one of his designer suits and was perfectly groomed as always. Unnaturally tanned skin. Wavy, dark blond hair that had tinged gray at the temples combed and gelled back off his face. Gray eyes that roamed the press conference room with intention and calculation. The same way he'd first entered her office and claimed he was desperate to save his fledgling marriage and yet found excuses to touch Haven's hand, knee, and shoulder throughout the session.

Trent pointed to a reporter off camera.

"It's been reported," a deep voice said, "that you were a client at Haviland Family Counseling. Did you ever experience any inappropriate advances by Miss Haviland?"

Haven sank onto the couch and pulled her knees to her chest. When Daniel sat down and put his arm around her, she leaned into him.

Trent dipped his head a moment. Regret? Would he admit to his affair? No way. Haven steeled herself for what he'd say next.

"I was afraid this might come up. There have been many times I've considered coming forward with this, but out of respect for my lovely wife, I never did. But the time has come. After Elaine and I began thinking about having a child, I decided to do all I could to become the best husband and father Trent Garrison could be. And so, I did seek counseling from Miss Haviland."

"How heroic . . ." Rarity said sarcastically, and Valor hushed her.

"After a few months, Ms. Haviland's interest in me became clear. Personal interest, not professional. She admitted that she'd fallen in love with me."

"That's not true," Haven said. She'd never loved him, even when she was drowning in the deepest pool of his lies.

"She begged me to leave my wife. My Elaine." The camera panned out to show Elaine Garrison, in a white maternity dress with a blush-colored bow around the bodice, take Trent's hand and stand close by his side. "She threatened to close the counseling practice if I didn't run away with her. She stood by her threat, which was why Haviland Family Counseling is no longer open. Of course, I was never even tempted. I love Elaine, my unborn child, and Whisper Canyon too much to throw it all away for a seductress. That's exactly what Miss Haviland and the women at The Mill are."

Haven clenched her teeth so hard that she feared she might break them. How could he be so vile?

"I'm afraid that after this, there might be anger toward Miss Haviland. In times like this, I lean on what my father taught me." Trent nodded behind him to his father, Samuel Garrison, who had been mayor before him, as had his father before him. Blast that tradition that kept the Garrison family in power since the town's founding. "If you want to understand a child's ways, look to the parents. Miss Haviland and her siblings are products of their home life. They can't help but take after their mother, Nina Haviland, God rest her soul. That's enough questions for now."

Rarity pushed past Valor and headed toward the front door.

"Where are you going?" their father asked.

"To make sure Mom's name never comes out of his filthy mouth again."

Valor caught her. Rarity couldn't compete with Valor's paramedic strength. Soon enough, Rarity gave up her fight and wept on Valor's shoulder.

"Haven?" Daniel asked.

"It wasn't like he said. He told me he and Elaine had quietly divorced, but they weren't going to say anything until after the election."

"Quietly divorced? Oh, Haven . . ." Valor sighed.

"I know, I know. It all happened in the last few months of Mom's life. I did like him. He was funny and charming. I guess I needed some kind of escape. That's what he offered for one hour a week."

"Did you two . . . ?" Daniel asked.

Haven met his eyes.

"Are you serious?"

"It was only once. I never asked him to leave the wife he said he no longer had. Or abandon the child I knew nothing about. Once they announced the pregnancy, I understood that I'd been played, and I stopped all communication with him."

"I knew he was full of it from the start, but then when he said you asked him to run away with you? That's not something you'd do—leave Whisper Canyon for a man," Daniel said.

"I never should have taken on his Corvette's restoration," her father said. "I poured my best effort into that car. All the while, he was working behind the scenes to tear this family and Aspen Crossroads apart."

"Is it still at the shop? I can find my old baseball bat," Daniel offered.

"He picked it up yesterday afternoon." Her father placed his hand on her shoulder. "Why didn't you tell us, love?"

"Every one of you would have done something to defend my honor, and every one of you would have lost something in that process. Besides, I knew what I'd done was wrong. I'd gotten too personal with a client. Married or not, I broke the oath I made to help, not harm."

"That's why you closed the doors on your practice?" Rarity asked.

"Yes. And if I'd gone public with Trent's lies, I figured no one would believe me. I'd only heap more shame on our family. But here we are. I'm so sorry for letting you all down."

As she shuttered her eyelids to block out the mess she'd caused for all those she loved, she felt four sets of arms wrap around her.

J ace's head throbbed. How on earth could they run the restaurant with only half their staff? Many had already given their notice. Could he blame them for wanting to avoid the stigma now associated with The Mill? Depending on how widespread this boycott got, they might not even need the staff that arrived.

Embers of resentment glowed red inside him, waiting for a breath to awaken them to a full-fledged flame. This town. It had done these women wrong the same way it had with his mother. And now Haven was in its crosshairs, thanks to that good-for-nothing Garrison.

He rubbed circles on his temples. The Mill. Keep focus on The Mill. Don't think about all the things you'd like to do to that man for the lies he splattered across the television screen earlier. It wouldn't do his team any good for Jace to get arrested. And then there was that turn-the-other-cheek nonsense his mother had taught him. But if God was keeping score on Jace's life, this one might be worth having a point taken away. Maybe two points. One for each busted cheek, since Jace's left hook was just as strong as his right.

Haven had spent the day with her family. She and Jace had spoken over the phone after the press conference, but he hadn't yet seen her. He'd had his hands full with comforting Rosalie over Jimmy and working out a survival plan with Sonny. Jillian was still nowhere to be found.

Two hours until the grand opening, and his manager was missing.

His focus fell to the boy seated across from him at the restaurant table. With Sonny and Rosalie prepping food in the kitchen, he was left on babysitting duty. Elijah focused on his drawing, which mostly consisted of wonky circles with three dots and a line that formed a Picasso-esque face. What kind of life would the kid have if The Mill shut down? Where would he and Sonny go? Would another restaurant give her a chance to shine the way she does? And what about Rosalie? She had her next GED test in a couple of weeks. What if she couldn't pass it? How could she support herself? And Jillian? He didn't have to imagine what Jillian would do. He'd seen it before with Gretchen.

"Look it!" Elijah held up the paper for Jace to see. "It's 'Lijah, Mommy, Jace, Rosie, Jillian, and Heaven." His family. His strange, unconventional, broken family. But Elijah didn't see it as broken. He had five people who loved him like crazy. Was that *broken*?

"That looks awesome, buddy."

The door to the restaurant swung open, and the place brightened with the added daylight. The man who stepped across the threshold was the last person Jace expected to see.

"Bo? What are you doing here?"

"Hi, Jace. Hi, Elijah." He spoke to the boy like he was a full-grown man. Didn't he have any experience with little kids? "I saw everything hit the fan today. It's a crying shame what they've gone and done. I wanted to see if you needed any help."

"Can you manage a restaurant?"

Bo snickered. "Doubtful. But I know my way around a kitchen."

"You don't have to."

"I want to. I cared about your mother more than I can say. I owe it to her to help you any way I can."

"You don't owe her anything."

He nodded. "Maybe I owe it to myself, then. If it's the same to you, I'd still like to help."

"Fair enough. There are aprons in the kitchen."

Jace watched the man disappear down the hall, then

withdrew his phone and called Jillian for the twentieth time. And for the twentieth time, his call went straight to voice mail. Through the window, Jace watched Haven's car pull into a parking spot. "Hey, 'Lijah. You keep coloring, okay? I'll be right back."

He met her on the front stoop and didn't hesitate to take her in his arms.

"I'm okay, Jace."

"Don't pretend. Not with me, remember?"

"I'm devastated, and I'm sorry."

"We'll get through this together. I have no idea how, but that answer will come."

She lifted her face. Free of makeup, her eyes were a more tender green, and her skin glowed with innocence and freckles the size of pinpricks. Her hair was still wet from a shower and hung in untamed waves around her face. Her flowery scent had been washed away, leaving a slightly soapy smell in its place. He still had her. He rested his forehead against hers and closed his eyes. If everyone got ripped away, he'd still have her. If towns rejected him and his teams here, in Austin, or who knows where else, he'd still have her. If men in power continued to use and abuse women, he'd still have her. His Haven. Finally, he'd found something praiseworthy in this dreadful situation.

A familiar squeal of turning wheels yanked his focus away. The minivan the women used at the farm came to a stop in the employee parking area. He stepped back from Haven, but it was too late. Jillian had seen them. He bit back a curse.

Jillian approached them with her chin held high. And while Haven seemed to have softened from the day's events, Jillian walked with a hardened air. Even Jace was intimidated. He couldn't imagine what Haven was feeling.

"You're here," he said.

"I have a job to do, don't I?"

"Jillian, we need to talk," Haven said.

"Trust me, counselor, you don't want to hear what I think about you right now." She turned her glare on Jace. "And you? I thought you were different. You're the same as the rest of them."

Chapter Thirty-Four

Haven pushed back the shades in the restaurant's third-floor office. She couldn't read the signs the protesters held. Perhaps that was a good thing. Now, if only she could make their words invisible to any guests that did come to the grand opening tonight.

"I don't get it," she whispered to the God she'd tried to honor ever since she first gave her life to him at seven years old. "I made one mistake. I thought your grace was supposed to be sufficient."

"Who you talking to?" Elijah sat behind the desk, his stature dwarfed by the high-back leather chair better suited for Sonny or Jace. An episode of *Paw Patrol* streamed on the tablet he held.

"I was praying."

"No. You pray like this. 'Now I lay me down to sleep.'"

"That's right. I'll try that one tonight."

Haven had gladly volunteered to watch Elijah tonight. She was the only one without a job at The Mill, and there was no way she'd add to the controversy by appearing in the dining room. If anyone showed up. Five minutes until six, and no customers had arrived. Only protesters.

The clock on the wall ticked away while Haven debated how she should best defend herself from the allegations. She could gather counternarratives from clients that attested to her professional demeanor. Her clientele leaned heavily toward females or couples, but over the years, there had been a few men who came to her for one reason or another. Would they defend her? Or would that old stigma against counseling keep them from coming forward?

A low roar emanated from outside. The protesters were more vocal now. Her father's beloved Shelby Mustang cruised through the crowd and into the parking lot. But it wasn't just him. Wes's truck came next. Then Rarity's vintage Beetle. And Lizzie's Cadillac with Daniel in the passenger seat. An entire train of cars spilled into the lot. As the drivers shut off their cars and everyone climbed out, she recognized most of them. Several business owners on Rarity's side of the street—the ones who'd also been targeted by the mayor and his wife. Some of the quirkier townsfolk—mostly Rarity's friends—also arrived. Wes had brought his friends from the medical community, many of whom Haven had worked beside to promote wellness for the town's most underserved population.

Her heart, which had taken quite a beating today, thudded optimistically. Maybe there was hope. Another car pulled in, and Haven's breath caught as Reverend Horst and Jimmy got out. They each held a rolled posterboard as they rounded the front bumper of the car and took a stance closer to the restaurant, away from the other protesters and directly in front of the door. Haven's reverend unrolled his sign first and held it above his head. Written in dark, prominent, no-nonsense lettering, it read, *You belong in Whisper Canyon.*

A few blinks helped to clear Haven's tear-blurred vision just as Jimmy lifted his sign. *You belong with me.*

Down below, Rosalie appeared and ran to Jimmy. He dropped his sign and hugged her. The reverend turned away from the two teens, either to let them have a moment's privacy or to show his sign to the protestors. Slowly, the crowd began to disperse until only posterboard signs littered the drive.

A re you worried?" Haven's question came out on a yawn. They were all exhausted after The Mill's emotional opening. While there had been protestors only on Saturday, the boycott was still going strong. Sales for the first week were the lowest Jace had ever experienced at a Secondly restaurant. Was he worried? Absolutely.

"We need more customers."

"The ones you have will tell their friends. And the winter sports crowd will pick up. We can advertise at the ski lodge and focus on . . ." Haven yawned again. "Focus on the tourists."

"I should let you go to bed."

She leaned forward and cuddled against him. "I'm not even tired," she said drowsily. Earlier that day, she'd admitted she hadn't been sleeping well. Tensions weren't high only at the restaurant, but on the farm, too. Jillian had been ice-cold to Jace and Haven. In fact, the only peace they'd both been able to find was during the little time they spent together on his couch at the end of the day.

"Right. You'll be snoring louder than a combine harvester any minute."

"I do not . . . snore . . ." Her breaths lengthened, and little rumbles tickled his neck.

He allowed himself a few moments to soak in the feel of her before he tipped her back and awakened her with a kiss. And awaken her he did. Not the best idea on a night when he could easily give in to small pleasures and simple temptation. He pulled her hand out of his hair and ended the kiss awkwardly, leaving her reaching for him. "Time to walk you home."

Minutes later, he waited on the porch while she locked
the farmhouse's front door and he debated patting himself
on the back for sticking to the most important of his prin-
ciples. Going forward, it would only get more difficult as he
fell deeper in love with the girl right across the drive.
Maybe long-distance would be good for them after all. Or
perhaps he just needed sleep. He turned back to his cabin,
but a faint light caught his attention over by the barn. More
than once, Jillian had worked on a piece until late in her
makeshift art studio. In his training, he'd learned to encourage creative pursuit for those who'd left the industry,
especially for those who didn't express their struggles ver-
bally. And if that didn't describe Jillian . . .

As he neared, he recognized her music spilling through
the closed barn doors. Jillian liked The Cure and Morrissey
best. It all sounded the same to Jace.

"Everyday Is Like Sunday." The moody lyrics prepared
Jace for what he might find inside.

He was right. Jillian's focus shifted from the canvas to
Jace as soon as he slid the door open a crack. Her eyes
rolled before she brought them back to her work. Her hand
held what looked like a dark piece of chalk, and it moved
with precise, tiny movements.

"Kind of late to be working."

"Thanks, Dad."

"What's this piece?"

She smirked. "A self-portrait." Jillian dropped the chalk-
thing, revealing black smudges across her fingers and thumb.
She stood and turned the canvas and its easel around for
Jace's perusal.

Shaded with charcoal, Jillian's likeness was apparent in
the delicate facial features. His gaze followed the long
locks of hair down to the bare body he found less recognizable. Quick as he could, he returned his focus to the portrait's face.

"It's like something in a museum," he said.

Jillian dragged her inky hand across the portrait's eyes, leaving a long smear all the way to the edge.

Jace grabbed a milk stool and sat with his back to the wall of the barn where he couldn't see the revealing portrait. "Can't sleep?"

Outside, an owl hooted. Some small critter skittered in the loft overhead. Still, Jillian didn't answer. She yanked a baby wipe out of a package and began cleaning her hands.

"She's one of them. It may not seem like it, but she is. They'll forgive her and welcome her back. But they'll never accept us in their clean-cut world." She tossed that wipe onto the ground and grabbed another. "You and I? We're the same. We should leave Whisper Canyon."

"And go where?"

"Cincinnati, Jace," she deadpanned. "No, my point is we can't keep trying to act like we'll be accepted here."

Jace's thoughts jogged back to the reverend's sign. "We belong in Whisper Canyon."

"Cute. So what's the plan? Are you two going to elope? Build a white picket fence around your cabin and live in marital bliss for the next three weeks?" Jillian shook her head and tossed the soot-covered wipe onto Jace's lap. "She'll hurt you. Sooner or later, she'll choose this town over you. I'd bet my soul on it."

Chapter Thirty-Five

Haven pushed through the cold freezing her lungs and ran harder down Main Street.

"Hav . . . en, slow . . . down."

She'd almost forgotten Valor had joined her. Her sister had been several steps behind her since they started down by their father's house. Against her instinct, she backed off her killer pace to a more reasonable one. "Sorry. I'm worried about The Mill. And hoping I don't run into any slimy politicians."

Ahead of them, Rarity wheeled a clothing rack onto the sidewalk and placed it by her shop window. Then, before returning inside, she ripped down every red, white, and blue streamer in the immediate area of her shop.

"At least Rarity has your back," Valor wheezed. "Hold up. I need to stretch."

Perfect. They'd stopped right in front of a flyer taped to a newspaper rack. *Mayor to Lead Founder's Day Parade.* Next Saturday, the Garrisons would host the annual celebration that touted Prescott Garrison's "courageous" efforts to settle the canyon. And every year, the town named the Garrison mayor grand marshal of the parade and pretended it was some surprise.

She felt like she'd swallowed a mouthful of sand just seeing Trent's photo. "I'm going to ask Rarity for a bottle of water." She held open the door to Rarity's shop, allowing Valor to enter first before ducking in herself.

"Hey, girls," Rarity said. "Don't get sweat on the dresses, remember."

"Can I snag some water?" Haven shrugged. "I have an awful taste in my mouth."

"I think we all do." Rarity nodded to the Culligan jug near the counter. "I still can't believe you let a Garrison kiss you. Tell me. Does he have a forked devil tongue, or is that a rumor?"

"Come on, Rarity," Valor said. "We all know you and Aidan had a thing."

"Aidan Garrison is the absolute last person I'd allow near my lips. If I've said it once, I've said it a thousand times. I don't—"

"Date football players," Valor and Haven said in unison.

"All I care about is that Aidan stays far away from Whisper Canyon. His brother has enough Garrison arrogance to fill this whole canyon. Haven, are you ever going to speak out against him?"

Haven chugged back the paper cup, then refilled it and chugged it again. "What good would it do? No one would believe me. I look like Mom, and now people think I act just like her, too."

"Even if it does no good, it will let Trent know that our family won't roll over." Rarity's voice climbed as she spoke. "He shouldn't come out of this unscathed. We have to do something. How's The Mill?"

"A couple of the employees came back after the protests stopped, but the customers simply aren't there. Jace is supposed to leave in three weeks, and I don't think he likes taking off when things aren't going well."

"I imagine there are other reasons he doesn't want to leave, too. How are things between the two of you?" Rarity removed a sign from above a rack and replaced it with a *10% Off* card.

Haven tailored her disappointment. "We're still walking on eggshells to not hurt Jillian."

"Please," Rarity scoffed. "She can get over it."

"Jace is afraid she'll go back to her old life. I wish there was a way to make this new life worth sticking around for, even if she can't have him."

"What we need is redemption all around," Rarity said. "The fact is, Whisper Canyon is a great town. But it's been taken over by a small-minded aristocracy that believes our only worth is our ability to draw in rich tourists. We need to show Trent we won't let him destroy our town or our people simply because they don't fit into his plan."

"Great idea." Valor dipped down into a runner's stretch and groaned. "Now, how do we do it?"

Rarity scrutinized the ceiling of her shop while working her lips in concentration. "The parade is in one week, right?"

"Yeah," Haven said, drawing the word out. Rarity's ideas were never small.

"I think it's time we bite back."

Exactly one week later, Haven lifted handfuls of black velvet fabric to ease the weight pulling her shoulders down. "They didn't actually wear this, did they?"

"Not that one specifically. Siva from the Community Theater is letting me borrow these. I think it's from their *Shakespeare in Love* production."

"I saw that one. It was good."

Rarity tugged a sixteenth-century-style headdress on Haven's head.

"I feel silly."

"I gave you a choice between Hester Prynne and Anne Boleyn. You chose this. A queen falsely accused of treason and adultery by a powerful king who once claimed to care for her? It's perfect."

"Will anyone understand it?"

"They will when they get this flyer we're handing out." Rarity handed Haven a piece of paper, then proceeded to apply royal costume jewelry.

"A poem? *Poor imprisoned Anne, who put her trust in a man. He lied when he said his marriage was dead, now her blood stains his hand.*" Haven winced. "Oh, Rarity . . ."

"Not my best work, but it gets the point across. Plus, on the back, there's a coupon for a free appetizer from The Mill!"

"What if this backfires?"

"And what? The restaurant closes? The Havilands' reputation is tarnished? People think I'm an awful poet?"

"Rarity, I don't know if I'm strong enough to do this."

"You are! And if you get scared, I'll be right there with you." Rarity swooshed her own Tudor-style dress around her legs.

"You don't have to."

"Yes, I do. In Édouard Cibot's painting we're re-creating, Anne isn't alone. And you aren't, either." Rarity pulled Haven into an embrace. "You know you're not the only one that wants to take down those Garrisons."

"Haven, Rarity," Wes called. "The float is parked inside of your dad's shop. Everyone is ready. The parade starts in twenty minutes, so you should head over."

"Is Jace with you?"

"He's meeting me by the theater in a bit. He's in for a surprise, I think. Haven, you look pretty, even if you are playing the role of a decapitated queen. You, too, Rarity."

"Thanks, Wes," Rarity said. "Now, if you could give those kinds of compliments to Valor, maybe you guys would finally move closer to *Will they?* than *Won't they?*"

Wes shook his head as he backed out of the shop.

Fifteen minutes later, they arrived at the car shop. A

large crowd had gathered, mostly Rarity's friends. And while the number of piercings, tattoos, hair colors, and attire might be shocking to others, Haven had gotten to know many in the crowd through her sister. *Good people*, her dad would say. And coming from him, that meant a great deal.

The float was fairly simple. Red and black silky fabric had been draped over a trailer. The edges sported signs saying, *Bruised, not broken; Down, not out. The Mill Restaurant.* Silver-covered food trays formed stacks on either side. Whatever Sonny had cooked up smelled unbelievable. Even if the crowd hated them for barging in on the Founder's Day parade, they couldn't be mad at whatever was inside those trays. In the middle of the float, there was a stage of sorts and more dark fabric. A mock-gold picture frame, large enough for someone to stand in, rested upright with dark brocade curtains spilling down behind it. An intricate side table displayed an open book. And a single chair was stationed directly in the middle of the frame under the sign that shared the name of the painting: *Anne Boleyn in the Tower of London.*

A frown threatened, and Haven fought it.

Rarity climbed onto the float and garnered everyone's attention with a whistle. "Remember that as much as we're here to support my sister and defend her from Garrison's slander, we are also here to back The Mill Restaurant and those who work there. These strong women have endured the unimaginable. Yet they're here marching with us, even as some in our town are trying to victimize them all over again. Whisper Canyon is better than that. It's love and grace. It's community and family. It's unique, and it is home to anybody who needs one. Arrive a stranger; stay a friend—right?"

Haven looked around for the best way to climb up. Sonny reached down her hand. Down by her legs, a sign in Sonny's handwriting said, *Trafficked at 16.* She was telling her story. Shouting it, really.

Dear God, don't let her be rejected.

Rosalie neared, holding her own sign: *Trafficked at 14*. She extended her hand as well, and the two women helped Haven onto the trailer. Haven took her place on the framed seat, feeling her cheeks burn at the attention.

Rarity continued. "We'll sneak into the line behind the high school marching band. The Alpine Ranch and Rescue knows about the plan, and Colin Rivera is expecting us to go ahead of them. Once we get to the crowd, some of you can hand out the flyers that feature the Anne Boleyn poem and a coupon for The Mill. The others can pass out food samples."

She took her seat at Haven's feet, draping herself across Haven's knees, just like in the painting. Her sister was nothing if not dramatic. Her father raised the garage door, and the truck hauling the trailer shifted into gear. No turning back now. As they pulled onto Copper Kettle Way, Haven spied a mane of strawberry blond hair walking alongside the float and holding a sign of her own. *Trafficked at 11 years old.*

Tears pricked Haven's eyes as she locked gazes with the girl who had been a nemesis for too long. Jillian offered a quick nod, but no smile. No promise of mutual respect or collaboration, either. But it was something.

Patriotic music bellowed from the high schoolers' instruments on Main Street.

"Rarity, do you think it was wise to go immediately after the marching band? The parents won't be happy."

Her sister looked up at her, squinting in the sunlight. "I did that on purpose. Look at how old these women were when they were taken. They were no different than those boys or girls. I hope it opens eyes."

"Me, too, Rare. Me, too."

The float turned onto Main. Colin rode on Jagger. Beside him, his younger sister commanded Serenade. They directed the remaining Alpine Ranch horses and their riders to yield until Haven's entire group emerged from the side street. Colin tipped his cowboy hat to Haven, but then he turned his focus on Sonny and . . . was that a wink?

On either side of the street, people stopped their clapping at the sight of the float. Curiosity turned to confusion. After reading the flyer and realization came, a few glared. But some—yes, some—stood and resumed their applause. At least until they were offered one of the plates holding a quarter of an elkburger. Not many refused that. A few brave souls even caught up to their float to grab seconds, prompting more than a few laughs. Even Jillian smiled. An honest, nontilted smile.

Still, Haven's face burned with humiliation. The longer the parade lasted, the tighter the bodice of her dress felt.

"Hey, love." It was her father's nickname for her, spoken from Rarity's lips.

Haven looked down into her sister's eyes.

"I'm proud of you," Rarity said. "No matter what comes from this, you were right to stand up for yourself and these women."

"Thank you for helping me find a way to do so."

Once they got to the last block of the parade route, she spied Jace leaning against a light post, a scowl marring his model-worthy face. Wes hit his arm, and Jace perked up. Like the rest of the crowd, it took a solid ten seconds for the scene to register, but when it did, he locked eyes with Haven. He laughed and shook his head. He sidestepped through the crowd, then hiked himself up on the trailer next to the stack of empty trays, stopping directly in front of the Boleyn tableau. "You Haviland sisters are trouble, you know that?"

"Jace," Rarity said. "That's the nicest thing anyone's ever said to me." As if on cue, she traded places with Jace.

He helped Haven to her feet. "Anne Boleyn? You're positively scandalous."

She scrunched her nose. "I was going for daring."

He smiled. "And you did it without me holding your hand."

"I wanted to show you that we'll be okay when you go to Austin. You don't have to worry."

"Thank you, Haven." With a knuckle beneath her chin, he raised her lips to his and kissed her for all to see.

Chapter Thirty-Six

The following Saturday evening, after they'd finished their frozen hot chocolates from ZuZu's, Jace held Haven's hand and they strolled down the sidewalk. Since the parade, Main Street had gotten a face-lift. In front of many stores, either a sign or a piece of art displayed the town's reversal of perspectives, thanks to the spectacle at the parade. Signs varied widely. *You belong in Whisper Canyon. Muffled no more. Call me a sinner, too. Imperfect, yet loved. Saved by Grace. Be Kind. Come inside for a hug.*

"Hi, Haven," a blond woman said as she stepped out of the passenger side of an SUV.

"Hey, Delilah. How are the girls?"

"Good. We saw you at the parade. You're so brave."

"Thank you." The past few days, Haven's eyes shone brighter than he'd ever seen. She'd taken back her story, even if some would never believe her. But she was no longer ashamed of her mistake.

And Jace couldn't be prouder of her. "You are brave. And your sister is a genius."

In front of Fringe and Lace Vintage Dress Shop, a sculpture of a man with the head of an alligator donned a polka-dot shirt with a butterfly collar and bell-bottom jeans. Next to him, a sandwich board read *Embrace Your Weird*.

"Yes, she is, in her own quirky way."

"Do you want to stop in and say hi?" he asked.

"No. She's probably closing up. Plus, we've had enough issues with third wheels. This date is ours alone."

"I see. This is a date, huh?"

"Our first date," she stated proudly. "Spoiler alert. I'm hoping for a kiss at the end of the night."

"Why wait until then?" Jace spun her around, before pulling her into an alcove where they'd be slightly hidden from public view. Not that many people were out. Apparently, most were spending their Saturday night south of town. According to Rosalie, The Mill had a two-hour wait for a four-top table. What was that saying? Everything was turning up roses? And he had the most amazing woman he'd ever met locked in his arms.

Jace traced the line of Haven's cheek. He needed to memorize the curve of it. The softness. The way it bloomed in color after a run or a few minutes of kissing, enriching the green in her eyes. He lowered his face to hers, teasing her a bit by sweeping his lips over her cheeks and brow. Her skin was as cold as the late-October air, and she shivered in his embrace. A good shiver. He was doing something right. When he finally brought his lips to hers, he found them already parted, waiting for him. Her mouth was as warm and rich as coffee. Likewise, it spread liquid heat through his veins until his body burned with desire. He forced himself to break the kiss, then touched his forehead to hers. He wanted her, that was clear. For a moment, his thoughts crashed into each other. Did he love her, or was it lust that tied him to her in this way?

"Jace." She released his name on a breath. "I love you."

His breathing stilled.

"You don't have to say it back. It's just important that I tell people what they mean to me."

Jace looked into her eyes. "Why?"

"So if they leave me, at least they know."

"No. I meant, why do you love me?"

Haven locked her arms around his waist. "Because you're heroic, brave, kind, funny, and even romantic when no one's looking. You see people for what they could be, not for the mistakes they've made. And you're caring. You plant flowers with Elijah. You've become a father to Rosalie. And you rescue baby chicks with crooked toes that no farmer would want."

"Haven . . ." He knew better than to leave those words hanging, but it wasn't so simple for him. "Do you remember when I told you about Marjorie, the rancher's wife?"

Haven's smile fell. "Yeah."

"And do you remember when I said that I would get confused? Sometimes I felt used by her, but sometimes I felt loved by her?"

She nodded slowly.

"I think that messed with my head. Because sometimes I wonder if I could ever care for someone more than I care for you. In a matter of months, you've become my closest friend and the best partner I could ask for. Yet, other times, I wonder if it's too good to be true. I wonder if I've conjured something out of nothing. Or if my desire for you—and I think you know how much I desire you—is confusing things in my head. I don't want to be Trent. I don't want to be Marjorie. I want it to be real."

Outside the alcove, snowflakes began to fall. Jace was about to punch himself in the face for ruining this moment for Haven, this night when they had only a week's worth of them left. Yet Haven, with her delicate touch, ran her hand across his jaw, lifting it until he looked into her eyes. "I desire you, too. But I'm not confused, because in addition to that attraction, I am absolutely, positively, unimaginably in love with you, Jace Daring. And I will tell you that every day until you understand without a doubt that what you feel right here"—she placed her palm against his pounding heart—"is real."

Chapter Thirty-Seven

The knocking was so loud it might as well have been directly on Jace's skull. He opened one eye and peered at his clock: 7:08. He'd grown used to sleeping in since harvest ended. Who in their right mind would try to wake him up so early on a Sunday? Had something gone wrong? Had one of the women been hurt? Or was it something with the restaurant?

Jace stumbled out of his bed, nearly tripping on a fallen pillow. He unlocked the door and yanked it open to find Rosalie, Sonny, and Haven standing on his welcome mat.

The blast of Rocky Mountain air, along with their widening eyes, reminded him that a simple pair of boxer briefs was not the best attire for answering the front door. Rosalie threw her hands over her eyes. Sonny laughed. Haven turned her back to him, then started smoothing her hair in her nervous way.

"Uh, sorry. Come in." Jace snagged a quilt off a chair and wrapped himself in it. "Is everything okay?"

The three women stepped inside. Rosalie kept her eyes covered until Sonny gave her the all clear.

"Why wouldn't it be?" Sonny winked. "Gracious, Jace. How many muscles does one man need?"

Jace rolled his eyes. "If nothing is wrong . . ."

"We've decided to go to church," Rosalie said.

His parched mouth craved water, and not just because of the long night of sleep. "Really?"

"Jimmy has invited me a few times. I want to go."

Sonny stood tall and determined. "And I want to see just how accepting Whisper Canyon is."

"You're going to . . . what? Walk in and sit in the front row?"

"Probably not the front row. Jimmy says his dad sometimes spits when he preaches," Rosalie said. She lunged forward and tugged Jace's arm, nearly making him lose his grip on the blanket. "Come with us, Jace."

"Maybe I'll stay back with Jillian."

"Can't. Even Jillian is going," Rosalie said. "Well, not to church. She's Jewish. Rarity's coworker offered to bring her to his synagogue for brunch and a concert they're hosting."

Haven stepped forward. "Can I speak to Jace alone?"

"Sure thing. We need to find our Sunday-best dresses. Don't we, Rosie?" Sonny said, linking arms with the girl and then leading her out.

Once they were gone, Haven ran a hand down Jace's arm. "You don't have to go with us. You are invited, though. I'd love to have you by my side."

"What if you stay here with me, and we can read through Philippians or something? We can even turn on some worship songs."

"God wants us to have community. In the Bible, the church is a group of people, not a building."

"I've seen that group of people my whole life, and trust me, they won't want me there, or the women."

"Jace, I'm one of those people, and I want you there." Haven worked her jaw. "Or are you saying I'm one of the unwelcomed? Because I don't care whether Wendy or

Elaine or anyone else welcomes me. My savior didn't die on a cross so one man can tell another whether he's welcome to join the Lord's church. The church is full of sinners like us. We all need mercy. We all need grace. Come stand at my side to receive it."

Jace shook his head. "I can't. As far as I know, that group of people turned its back on my mother."

"But you don't know that. Maybe they were innocent. I know you don't want people making assumptions and judgments about you. Why is it okay for you to do it to them?"

No words. He had no words.

"Just think about it." Haven kissed his cheek, then retreated to the door. She paused with her hand on the knob. "Don't you get cold sleeping in just your boxers?"

"I sleep under heavy blankets."

She gathered a deep breath. "It's a good thing I'm heading to church. It's not good for a girl to have that image just sitting in her head all day."

Two hours later, Jace stood at the bottom of Whisper Canyon Community Church's front steps, staring up at the doors. Inside the sanctuary, worship had already started.

Sanctuary. The word felt like a misnomer if he'd ever heard one.

He'd watched Haven, Sonny, Elijah, and Rosalie load up in the minivan and drive away from Aspen Crossroads after he'd refused their invitation. They must be in there now, and so far, the ceiling hadn't caved, and the townsfolk hadn't thrown them out. Maybe, just maybe, there was a place for Jace as well.

"Jace Daring, right?" An older man in a three-piece suit and a striking resemblance to Trent climbed the first two steps before turning around to face him. "Samuel Garrison. I've heard quite a bit about you from my son."

"I bet you have."

"Trent—he has strong opinions like his grandfather. When he gets an idea about something or someone, well, he can be quite stubborn."

"Perhaps he would heed advice from a father like you. You could advise him to leave The Mill alone and take back the lies he told about Haven Haviland."

The man wiped his brow with the back of his hand. "Indeed. I am sorry about the Haviland girl being brought into this. The Havilands are a good family, despite what people might say. There are rumors about a feud between our families, but don't listen. That was resolved long ago. You've grown close to them, have you?"

"Yes, sir."

"Sir? Where are you from?"

"Here. At least my family was. The Chelsies. Any recollection?"

"The name scratches my memory. They left a while back. Oklahoma, was it?"

Jace bit his tongue. No one had been able to tell him where his grandparents had gone when they sold Aspen Crossroads and left town in 2000.

"Then you know that this town has one hundred and forty-six years of fascinating history. I had the fortune of serving as the mayor for quite a few of those years. There's no place better anywhere on earth."

"I have it on good authority that this place wasn't always such an Eden. At least not for all its residents. May I ask you a question? If Whisper Canyon was so great under your guidance, then why is your son trying so hard to change it with his 'clean-up' initiative?"

The elder Garrison scratched his beard. "I suppose every man wants to make a difference. He wants to take this town to new heights."

"See, I think there's a place for The Mill in that plan."

"Off the record, I don't disagree with you. All I'm saying, son, is there's no point in riling everyone up the way you're doing." The man clamped a rigid hand on Jace's shoulder. "One thing I know. Trent doesn't like to be made a fool. Right or wrong, he doesn't like you. The sooner you separate yourself from the restaurant, the sooner he'll let it lie. That Haviland girl, too. I don't know what transpired between them, but she still has a chance to remake herself. Maybe regain her career if she stays out of controversy from here on out. If you haven't noticed, your presence in Whisper Canyon invites controversy." Samuel climbed the steps of the church as the warbled lyrics of "Amazing Grace" seeped through the walls.

After a brief hesitation, Jace followed until the former mayor reached the door. He looked back at Jace. "Better get on your way. The sooner you're gone, the sooner this town and those women you care about will find that peace they deserve."

Garrison disappeared inside, letting the door shut behind him. Frozen in place, Jace attempted to blink the sting away from his eyes. It was no use. This was why he didn't want to come here and learn anything about his mother or her hometown. He didn't belong here, and she knew it. And this was why he'd wanted to keep firm boundaries. A glimmer of belonging, of family, of community, of love, and he'd allowed himself to hope for something that was meant for someone else. Not him.

Chapter Thirty-Eight

"I was hoping you'd join us at church." Haven dug her hands deeper into her pockets as she watched Jace scribble in a notebook on his kitchen table. "There was a lot of support there. For all of us. Afterward, people were eager to introduce themselves to Sonny and Rosalie. Jimmy acted like Ol' Sixclaw with a tummy full of huckleberries."

"What?"

"It's a saying around here. He was happy. The guy is head over heels for our Rosalie."

"*Our* Rosalie?" Suspicion marred his expression.

"Yes, *our*." Haven smiled. "What are you working on?"

"Trying to make a schedule for next year. That way, the team will know what tasks have to be done around the farm and when."

"Oh. I hoped to spend time together. We could go to the hot springs. They're heavenly on a cold day." Haven certainly wouldn't mind eyeing Jace in swim trunks now that she'd seen him shirtless. Immediately, she kicked herself for remembering the image she'd promised God she'd push out of her mind.

"I can't. I'm sorry." He nodded to a cardboard moving box on the floor. "I have a lot to do before I leave Saturday."

Haven forced a swallow as he kept his eyes glued to the notebook. Following her recent pattern of pushing beyond her comfort zone, she moved behind his chair and hugged his shoulders. "What can I do to help?" She placed a gentle kiss on his neck just beneath his earlobe. Experience had taught her that was his quit-work-early button. And his forget-your-stress button and his who-needs-to-finish-dinner button.

As always, his tension loosened, and he turned into her, his lips finding hers. Just as Haven was starting to think the hot springs trip might happen after all, he broke free. "Haven, I need to focus right now."

While she deciphered his mixed messages, a knock sounded at the door. Through the window, she recognized Bo's face.

"Great. More distraction," Jace said.

Haven absorbed the words like a punch to her gut as Jace rose from his seat to answer the door. Had what she said last night scared him? Or had the invitation to church been too forward? She hadn't meant to push him in any way. Hadn't he wanted her to share more of herself with him? Or so she thought.

He opened the door to Bo, but his stature was anything but welcoming. "Bo."

"Hey, Jace. How are ya?"

"Fine."

"I was hoping to talk with you some more."

"It's not a good time."

"It's about your mother. I—I have a letter." Bo fished a worn envelope from his inside coat pocket and handed it to Jace.

Jace returned to his seat without taking his eyes off the envelope and held it in front of him. "Why is it addressed to Jason Radford? Who's that?"

Bo remained at the door and shot a questioning glance at Haven. She gave a slight nod to invite Bo inside, then she pulled a chair close to Jace's and sat down.

"That's my given name. In high school, I picked up the nickname Bo from kids at school because of the *Dukes of Hazzard*, but Lynn always knew me as Jason. Or Jace, for short. That's why I acted so funny when we first met. I'm honored she named you after me."

Jace's brows pinched together, and his Adam's apple appeared to catch at the top of his throat for a second. The remainder of Bo, er, Jason's address was written in bubbly letters, as was the return address:

Lynn Chelsie
8612 Oakwood Way NE
Sweetwater, TX

"When did she write this?" Haven asked.

"A couple of months after she left Whisper Canyon. She was staying with her aunt and uncle in Texas."

"I thought you said you didn't know what happened to her after she left," Haven said.

"I don't. Not after she left her aunt and uncle's house."

Jace removed the yellowed notebook paper from the envelope and smoothed it on the table between him and Haven, an apparent invitation for her to read along. At least he hadn't closed her off completely. They both began to read silently.

Dear Jace,

I'm sorry I left so quick and didn't get to say bye. My parents wanted me to stay with my cousins in Texas for a while. It's okay, I guess, but I miss you. I would give anything to go caving with you. Can you believe I'm saying that? Please tell Lovely and Daring I'll be back.

My parents said I can come home in July. We can pretend I was never gone.

Love,
Lynn

"According to this, I would've been born in Sweetwater, Texas, but my birth certificate says Santa Fe."

"When were you born?" Bo asked.

"May twelfth, 1990."

Bo dropped his gaze to the floor but said nothing. He appeared to be working out a math problem in his head. "She was pregnant?"

"That can't come as such a surprise. Teenage girl disappears for nine months. I'm pretty sure that was a common tale back in the 1980s. She really never told you about me?"

"No, she didn't. You were born in May 1990? Were you premature?"

"Not that I know of. Do you have any clue why she didn't come back here in July?"

"Maybe she was afraid to tell me about the pregnancy. She had to know I would've been there for her no matter what."

"I'd hope so. You got her into that mess. A good man would've been there for her. I don't care if you were sixteen."

Understanding dawned on Bo's face even as Jace glared at him. "You think I'm your father."

Jace was silent, but his shoulders heaved with each breath.

"Jace, I'm not your father."

"You said she named me after you."

"And that means the world to me. I promise it does. Only your mother and I never did anything other than kiss. By the time she left, we hardly did that. Whenever I would try to touch her, she would squirm away. I'd never force myself on a girl for a kiss or anything else."

"Are you saying my mother cheated on you?"

"No. The sixteen-year-old girl I knew wouldn't have done that with anyone. Not willingly."

The sound of Jace's teeth grinding was painfully loud. Soon, the first tears formed above his bottom lashes.

Haven grabbed his hand. "Did you write her back?"

A visible tremor rolled through Bo's shoulder. It took time for Haven's question to register. Finally, he met her eyes. "I did. Many times, even though I never got another letter from her. I was worried, and her parents wouldn't speak to me. They must have blamed me, too. The day after school ended, I borrowed my dad's truck and drove to that address. She wasn't there. Her aunt didn't say much. Just that she'd left in May."

A single tear spilled over Jace's lashes, not even bothering to touch his cheek before it landed on the back of Haven's hand.

"After I met you, I called my parents to talk to them about it. They said that sometime in the midnineties, Lynn showed up on our doorstep looking for me. You see, after years of waiting for her to return, I'd moved to Denver to attend the Colorado School of Mines. I even tried dating a girl for a while. My parents told Lynn as much, and she left." Bo's nostrils flared at the admission.

"What color is your front door?" Jace asked.

"Blue. Why?"

"Nothing. I thought I remembered something."

"It was a burnt orange back then, though."

Haven gasped. Jace was right. Lynn had wanted help, and she'd been turned away. "Why didn't they tell you?"

"They said they believed I was finally getting over losing her, and they didn't want to see me get hurt again. I never got over losing her."

Each grizzled word cut into Haven's heart. She couldn't imagine what Jace was feeling.

"I wish she'd have come back here. I would've done all

I could to take care of the two of you. I would've made you my business." Bo's voice cracked, and he fought to finish his words. "I would've made you my son."

J ace's truck sped down the highway. He'd avoided almost all conversation since Bo's visit yesterday. Although Haven had pulled out her best tactics to get him to talk, he'd refused.

"Jace, can you slow down, please? You're making me nervous."

The truck sagged as he took his foot off the gas. Haven's head whipped forward as the seat belt caught and held her body firm against the passenger seat.

"I'm sorry. Haven, I'm sorry. Are you okay?" Thrashed with guilt, Jace brought the truck to a reasonable speed, before turning onto the restaurant's private drive.

"I'm fine. I wish you'd talk to me."

"About what?"

"Bo's visit. Austin. The Mill."

"There's not much to say. Bo isn't my father, after all. My father, whoever he is, assaulted my mother." He fought to clear his throat. "It was bad enough that she changed her name and decided that sex work and homelessness were better than coming back here for good."

"Even if Bo isn't your biological father, it isn't too late for him to be a father figure to you now. He said it himself. He would've made you his son."

Jace slowed as he entered the parking lot. "And on the subject of Austin? The sooner I get there, the better."

"This isn't because I told you I love you, is it?"

Jace jerked his head toward her. "No. Of course not."

Sonny, holding Elijah in her arms, stood next to Jillian and Rosalie by The Mill's front door, which now displayed a bright yellow rectangle that hadn't been there yesterday. Dread washed over him.

He pulled the truck to a stop and shifted it to park before hopping out and jogging straight to the notice tacked on the door.

"'Notice of Closure by the Summit County Health Department due to reported violations,'" Jillian read aloud. "This is bunk. Sonny runs an immaculate kitchen. She'd never violate any health or safety codes. And we were inspected less than a month ago."

"This is Trent's doing," he seethed. "I'll deal with him once and for all."

"What are you going to do, Jace?" Rosalie asked. "March into his office and ask him to apologize? It won't work." She sniffled, then buried her face into Jillian's shoulder. Other than swinging an arm over Rosie's shoulder, Jillian stared unseeingly at Jace's boots.

"I have to confront him," Jace said. "What's next? Suspending the liquor license? I've known men like Garrison my whole life. They use, they abuse, they take advantage, simply because they can. I'm tired of it."

Sonny turned to Jace. "You deal with Garrison. Meanwhile, I'll call the inspector and demand they come out this afternoon to reinspect. We won't miss a beat if I can help it."

Chapter Thirty-Nine

Fifteen minutes later, Jace was still fuming as he parked the truck where the courthouse, town offices, and luxury apartments overlooked the heart of town. He hadn't wanted Haven to come along, but she refused to get out of the passenger seat. She had a few things she'd like to say to Trent herself.

"Do you think . . . ?" She trailed off.

"What?"

"Do you think Terrence would let you stay in Whisper Canyon a bit longer, considering all this mess?" So selfish. Then again, maybe it wasn't completely selfish. Jace was in no state to move on right now. He needed time to process all he'd learned about his mother and his paternity. The last thing he needed was to isolate himself.

"I can't stay."

"Have you asked?"

"I can't stay!" Jace shut off the engine. "I'm sorry for yelling. Haven, I . . . I was going to go to church yesterday, but I had a run-in with Samuel Garrison on the steps. He said that Trent wouldn't rest until I was far away from The Mill and you. This is proof."

Haven closed her eyes and counted to ten before opening them. This wasn't news. She'd known Trent would never give up until she and Jace were apart. Of course, she'd thought *she* was the one who needed to step away. Not Jace. "What's your game plan?"

"I don't know yet. Knocking him out probably won't do much good, will it? But I have to say something."

Two minutes later, Jace was arguing with Trent's administrative assistant, a mousy woman whose voice Haven recognized from when she'd book counseling appointments for her boss.

"I'm sorry, Mr. Daring. Mayor Garrison is booked all day."

"Find time, or I'll march straight in and interrupt whatever joke meeting he has."

"I don't suggest you do that. Besides, the mayor isn't even in the office today."

"Where is he?" Jace asked.

"Denver, if you must know. But I will leave him a message that you stopped by. Good day to you both," she snapped.

Defeated, Jace took Haven's hand, and they left.

Haven checked her watch: 9:25 a.m. "Since we can't meet with Garrison today, how about this? Daniel's apartment is over there. He works with these guys from the town all the time on his projects. Maybe he can help us strategize."

"Your brother isn't my biggest fan."

"But he's mine, so as long as you're with me, he'll help. Daniel's a good guy underneath."

"Fine. If you think it will help."

As they walked one block down, Haven clung to Jace's arm. "Do you think there will ever be a time when we can just stroll down a street without needing to save the world or fight the villain?"

Jace didn't say anything.

"Despite it all, I think we make a good team, don't you? I don't know what I would've done without you by my side these past couple months. You're the best thing that's ever happened to me. No matter what happens after this, I love you, Jace," she whispered as they reached the exterior door to Daniel's apartment. But would the sentiment be enough to cut through all the stress, hurt, and anger he carried?

It was. He drew Haven into his arms and peered down at her. His blue eyes swam with emotion, and his lips parted, perhaps to speak the words that Haven longed to hear from him alone for the rest of her life. But the sound of a door opening on their right killed the moment, especially as recognition collided with understanding.

"Lizzie?" Jace spoke her name with astonishment.

The girl—the sweet, innocent, naive girl who had done so much for Aspen Crossroads and The Mill—stood before them with eyes as round as radishes, unbrushed hair, and wearing Daniel's Princeton sweatshirt. She blushed brighter than Haven had ever seen anyone blush.

"Elizabeth," her brother's voice called from inside. "You forgot your necklace." For the instant before Daniel saw Haven and Jace, she caught his familiar grin. The one he'd used to charm women all across town.

"Excuse me," Lizzie said, ignoring the cross necklace Daniel held out to her. She skirted around Haven. Should she follow her? Talk to her. But what to say? Had her heart already been broken, or would that come later when her brother didn't call?

When he saw them, Daniel sheepishly looked from Haven to Jace. Then he slinked back inside to close the door, only Jace caught it and pushed himself inside.

Haven followed, trying to call Jace off. She climbed both flights of steps and caught up to the two men just as Daniel entered his private studio apartment that reeked of self-indulgent bachelorhood. On the far end, she noticed his bed's mussed sheets, and her heart dropped. "Daniel. What did you do?"

"He took advantage of her," Jace said. "All so you could, what, get another notch on your belt?"

"Well, if that's what you think of me, then you'll be happy to know I paid her with a nice dinner."

Jace lunged at Daniel, his right fist moving double-time until it cracked against her brother's face.

Haven moved forward but stopped. Was she supposed to coddle her womanizing twin? Scold her boyfriend for defending the weak and innocent?

Weak and innocent . . . Did that even describe Lizzie? She was an adult when she came here last night. Daniel had no authority over her, and he'd never ask her to do anything she wasn't willing to do. From what Haven could tell, she chose this. Haven's thoughts grew muddier as she stood watching what would happen next.

Daniel straightened up and pressed his fingers to his brow, where blood trickled into the crease of his eyelid. Haven waited for Daniel to match Jace blow for blow, but instead, he returned to his spot before Jace, as if he would willingly accept another punch.

Jace reared back with his fist clenched.

"Stop. Please." Haven felt woozy.

Jace turned his attention to her, his eyes wild with a swirling mix of fury, concern, and regret. He left Daniel and came to her with his hand extended.

Despite her best efforts, she recoiled and stepped around the couch until she was equally distant from both of them. "I can't, Jace."

"What do you mean?" Jace asked. "You can't condemn his actions? Or you can't let me hold your hand?"

"We can't expect everyone to act or believe the same way we do about these things. Lizzie isn't a child. She made a choice."

"I can't believe what you're saying. After all you've learned from Sonny, Jillian, and Rosalie about the nature of man. After what you experienced with Trent. Daniel did to Lizzie exactly what Trent did to you. He exploited her."

"No. It's different. Trent is evil. You don't know what Daniel went through with our mother, and then with Grace. Their actions caused a lot of damage."

"You're defending him?"

"He's my family. You don't under—" Haven clamped her mouth shut.

Jace frowned. "I don't understand because I don't have family, right? I may not have had a father or siblings, but at least I had a mother who loved me."

The sting of his words lanced her throat so that no words, only memories, came. Her mother crying in her bed. Haven getting shoved down on the middle school playground because of her mother's actions around town. Her mother blaming Haven for not being there when she needed her. Haven caring for her mother between counseling appointments and throughout every night until her last day, leaving Haven physically, mentally, and emotionally exhausted.

Jace's shoulders dropped, and he twisted his hands in front of him as he searched the floor. Finally, he raised his gaze to hers. "That came out wrong. I wasn't saying your mother didn't—"

"No, I get it." Haven put her fingers into her hair, combing it back off her face. "Maybe she didn't. But I loved her. That's what I do. Love those who don't love me. Stay when others go." She shrugged.

Cavernous lines formed between Jace's brows, and he shook his head. "Haven."

Her heart pleaded with her to go to him. To apologize and to forgive. Only if she did that right now, she'd be turning her back on her twin brother. Daniel . . . Oak, despite his height and muscular frame, was still the boy who promised not to push her too high on the swing, stood by her side when no one asked her to dance at the eighth-grade formal, and encouraged her to go find her wings in Australia. Oak was still the boy she came home to find splintered and up-rooted. He couldn't have another woman he loved turn her back on him. So, she betrayed the heart she'd promised to Jace and stayed.

Jace nodded but said nothing. He headed back to the open door, paused, then continued into the hallway and down the steps.

Haven and Daniel didn't move. The only proof that time moved at all was the dabbing of his hand against his cheek to catch the blood before it dripped on his overpriced rug.

"Are you angry at me?" he asked.

"I'm disappointed. I've stood by while you've broken heart after heart. I've sat across the counseling office from some of the women you've hurt. And I've held my tongue because I love you, and I believe there's a good man in there underneath all the muck." Haven's chin quivered. "Now you've gone too far."

"I love her. I love Elizabeth. I have for a long time—"

A lifetime of captured emotions and insults waged battle inside her until she lost all control of her tongue. "If you loved her, you would have honored her beliefs. You wouldn't have treated her like she was a goal to achieve. No, the only person you love is yourself."

Haven didn't want an apology or an excuse. She needed air before she made things even worse. Without another look, she followed Jace's path out Daniel's door, but when she made it to the parking spot in front of the town offices, Jace's truck was gone.

Chapter Forty

Jace tossed the last of his possessions in a box. He'd already spent most of the last week packing. Of course, at the time, he'd still been wavering on whether Austin was the right place for him to be. Now he was sure of it. He glanced around his cabin. All that remained were the old furnishings that had come with the place when Secondly purchased it. Except for one thing.

Jace stalked to the kitchen table and grabbed the envelope with his mother's handwriting on it. Bo had let him keep it. Not that there was any point. His mother was gone. All traces of her were gone. He'd never know what happened to her in this awful town. But one thing was obvious. He wanted out, and as soon as possible. After tucking the envelope into his back jeans pocket, he heaved the last moving box up and carried it out the front door to his truck. With the bed full, this one needed to go in the back of the cab. He balanced the box between his hip and the side of the truck while he opened the door.

Elijah's spare car seat was still buckled onto the bench. He flashed back to that first day he'd met Sonny. She was sitting on a street corner behind a cheap folding card table and selling the best chicken cutlet sandwich Jace ever ate. Elijah, just two years old, was asleep in his stroller. One long conversation later, Jace was in a Target parking lot fumbling to install this car seat in his truck while Sonny gathered their possessions from the shelter. He'd questioned his sanity for taking in a toddler. The need for babysitting alone gave him a headache, but they'd made it work.

Once he'd untethered the seat, he turned with it in his arms and nearly rammed Jillian with it.

"You're not leaving now, are you?" she asked.

"It's for the best."

"No goodbyes?"

"I was going to knock on the door before I left. And stop at the restaurant on my way out of town to see Sonny and Rosalie."

Jillian's cold expression nearly made him drop the seat. He walked it to the farmhouse porch and leaned it against the brick beside the door. When he returned to the truck, he caught Jillian forcing the box roughly into the back. She slammed the door with the might of a bodybuilder before she faced him. "I thought you were brave, but you're running."

"You know the plan was always to move on. I no longer have a role here. I work for Secondly. Not Aspen Crossroads. Not The Mill."

"Jace, you never once disrespected me . . . until now. You're taking me for a fool." Jillian stared up at the sky. "I know what it's like to try to stay detached from everyone. Letting people in gives them easy access to hurt you. But aren't you tired of running? I am. Some of the people in this town may be giving us trouble, but won't they all? And this little family of ours isn't one I'd choose, but it's the only one I got."

"You're no fool. You're a big part of the reason why I feel I *can* leave. You're tough, and you won't put up with anyone coming in and trying to hurt Rosalie, Elijah, or Sonny. I can't stay."

"Does Haven know you're taking off?"

Jace looked away. "Since when do you care about Haven?"

"Since I realized it wasn't her keeping us apart. It was you and the love you have for her."

The words pricked his very soul. "I don't love her."

"Oh, sweet geezer, yes, you do. You're better than this."

"You've always thought I was better than I was. I need to go." Jace opened his arms to Jillian. It took a few seconds, but cautiously she entered them. He kissed the top of her head. "Goodbye, Jill."

He cursed the emotion trying to get the best of him as he released her and then hopped in the driver seat. He wasn't running. He was going somewhere new. There was a difference. And this time, he'd make positively sure he didn't get entangled with anyone.

And when I got to the parking spot, Jace was gone." Haven forced out a shaky breath.

Valor pressed her lips into a line in that big sister know-it-all way of hers.

"What, Val?"

"Jace might think you want him to leave."

"I don't want him to leave, but I also can't stop him. I can never stop anyone from leaving me."

Rarity and Valor exchanged glances. Was that guilt?

"Haven, when I left for Milan, I wasn't leaving you," Rarity explained. "Maybe that's how it felt, but I was leaving Whisper Canyon. I was leaving the gossip about mom. I hated her for what she did to us. But more than that, I hated how everyone talked about us."

"It was the same for me when I left. I was angry at the world, at Wes, at myself. Not you. Never you."

"Wes?" Rarity asked, but Valor kept her eyes steadied on Haven.

"Why are you telling me this now?"

"Because," Rarity began, "Jace is dealing with a lot of stuff right now. Trent's fixation on you and The Mill. That new information he discovered about his mom and his paternity. I bet Austin will feel like a vacation after this. He's not leaving you. He's leaving Whisper Canyon."

"When does he go?" Valor asked.

"Saturday. Why did this have to happen now when I have so little time to smooth things over? And what am I supposed to do about Daniel?"

Rarity paced in front of the dressing rooms. "I'm calling him. And then I'm calling Jace. I may as well throw Trent in there. Some men are going to get a piece of my mind." She withdrew her phone from her skirt pocket.

After tossing her balled-up tissue onto the mountain of discarded Kleenex, Haven rose off the chaise and took Rarity's phone from her. "I don't need you to be my crusader right now. Just my sister."

Rarity sighed. "I guess I can be that." Rarity put her arms around Haven and squeezed.

"And so can I." Valor hugged Haven's back.

The bells to the shop's front door rang out and footsteps grew louder.

"What did I miss?" Dash Haviland dropped her duffle bag on the ground and grinned.

Chapter Forty-One

I'm sorry I wasn't here." Dash wasn't the most emotional Haviland sister, yet sorrow warped her pretty face.

"No, you're not. You had a gold medal–winning tour to complete. I'm glad you're here now, though. Thanks for the ride back to the farm." Catching up with her sister would be a wonderful distraction, but she had more pressing matters to attend to. Like, first, where was Jace? As Dash pulled her Jeep next to the farmhouse, Haven couldn't see his truck. The minivan was gone, as well, but Sonny was at the restaurant already with Rosalie. When Sonny called the county, she was told the notice had been a simple clerical error. The women didn't buy it for a second. At least they got it removed. Hopefully, word of the closure hadn't gotten too far.

"Call me later," Dash said.

Haven didn't bother to watch her sister drive away. Perhaps one of the women had borrowed Jace's truck for an errand. That would be good. They'd need some uninterrupted time to sort this out. She climbed the steps and pounded on Jace's door.

"He's not there." Jillian stood in the farmhouse's doorway.

"Where is he?"

"You better come inside."

Acid pooled in Haven's stomach and climbed up her throat. He wouldn't have left for Austin. He wouldn't have. She walked slowly across the gravel drive, all the while finding Jace's contact on her phone and calling him.

Straight to voice mail.

Inside the house, Jillian sat on the recliner with a mug in her hand and a book splayed out on the armrest. *Persuasion*. Haven wouldn't have taken her for a Jane Austen fan, but then again, she didn't know much about Jillian.

"There's tea on the stove if you want some."

"I'm okay." Haven took a seat on the couch, casually tucking her legs beneath her. She must stay composed. Professional. Jillian was her client. No matter what came out of her mouth next, Haven could handle it with grace and strength.

"Jace left for Austin two hours ago."

Haven kept still, but if there was air in the room, her lungs struggled to find it. A rush of heat blanketed her, and she considered bolting to the porch. Although she lifted her chin and blinked up at the ceiling several times, those stubborn Texas-sized tears still came. "I'm sorry for crying."

"You don't have to be sorry. It's not like you're the only one who's ever cried over that man. Besides, it's nice to know you're a real person."

"Did he say anything?"

"No. I said a lot, though. I told him he was a coward for leaving. Do you know how many times I've wanted to take off? I mean, I knew it was always the plan for him to move on. I just thought we'd be different. Especially now that I've seen how he feels about you. But in the end, it didn't matter anyway. He's gone."

A deep ache dug into the left side of her chest, and Haven closed her eyes against the hurt. The last time she'd been this hurt, she'd allowed it to destroy her counseling practice. She couldn't do that this time. Not when three women, and one little boy who called her Heaven, needed her. No matter what happened from this point on, she wouldn't spend any energy on regret. She was brought to Aspen Crossroads for a reason. It did matter. Her time with Jace and these women did matter. And she couldn't waste any time being heartbroken. She had a job to do.

"Jillian, what was it about Jace that made you so fond of him?"

"You've seen him," Jillian said while rolling her eyes. "He's hot."

Haven snort-laughed.

Jillian cracked a smile. Haven wasn't even sure the girl had teeth for the first month they lived together. Now here they were, sharing a moment. Jace would be so proud.

"We do agree on something," Haven said.

Jillian sobered, and she ran the tip of her index finger around the rim of her mug. "I know y'all think I was hoping Jace was some Richard Gere type come to take me away, but that wasn't it. At least not entirely. I'd been in the business for so long, I didn't know there were men who could show respect to women. Or value them for something other than pleasure. Jace saw me. Like HaShem watching over Hagar in the desert. The rabbi probably wouldn't like to hear that comparison."

"I think he'd be okay with it. We all have moments when we exhibit the character of God. Like the other day when 'Lijah bumped his shin, and you rocked him in the recliner until he stopped crying. You comforted him like God comforts us."

Jillian nodded. "And you standing up on that float. You were a bit like Queen Esther, standing up for her people."

"I didn't feel like Queen Esther, though. And as long as Trent Garrison is mayor, *my people* are still at risk."

"That mayor needs to pay for what he's done, and not just to you." Jillian stared even harder into her tea. "He takes from those who have nothing left to give."

Haven nodded, torn between the desire to understand Jillian's thoughts and not wanting to push her. "I can cook dinner tonight. I have an overly complicated enchilada recipe that may take my mind off things."

Jillian looked up, seemingly surprised that Haven was speaking. "Hmm?"

Haven repeated herself.

"I'm not hungry. Tea fills me up. I think I'll read a few more hours and head to bed a bit early." Jillian picked up her book and stared at the page, but her eyes didn't scan the sentences. They remained dreamily fixed on the seam until her patented smirk returned.

O utside Haven's window, the wind howled, and some-where in the old farmhouse, a whistle rose and fell with each gale. Haven pulled her blanket higher on her neck, but she couldn't shake the chill. Perhaps it was know-ing that Jace's cabin sat dark and empty tonight. An un-usual yipping sound forced her upright in her bed. Her clock showed no glowing digits. A power outage? She felt around for her phone, yet found nothing. Strange.

Yip, yip.

Haven jumped out of bed and peered outside her win-dow. All that pierced the darkness was blowing snow. The sound continued outside near the chicken coop. The yip-ping had turned to growls. Audrey. Without another thought, Haven raced out her bedroom door. She flew down the stairs, not bothering to keep the creaking at bay the way she usually would in the middle of the night.

At the front door, she fumbled with the security locks. Why did there have to be so many? She felt helpless. How could she help the chickens and goats if she was trapped inside? One swift jerk loosened the door from its jam, and Haven ran into the night, the snow biting her bare feet with each step.

She was almost there.

The growls grew louder and came from every direction. She had to be daring. She had to save Audrey. She slammed into the chain-link fence, and her eyes tried to focus.

The coop—it was gone. All that remained of it were scraps of wood and metal fencing. Destruction everywhere. And blood, so much blood melting the snow. One night in her care and Audrey and the others were dead.

Above the wood heap, a shadow began to roll like a cornfield swept by a canyon breeze. Only, rather than cornstalks, the shadow showed lines of black and gray fur.

The shadow turned until all Haven could see were the glowing red eyes fixed on her.

Haven tried to back away, but her feet wouldn't move. The beast leaped directly at her, sinking its claws between her ribs and biting her shoulder.

"Haven, wake up."

Morning light filtered through her curtains, half blinding her. After her eyes adjusted she read 7:21 on the clock.

"I'm sorry to wake you." Rosalie sat on the edge of her bed, her hand still resting on Haven's shoulder. "Where's your car?"

Haven rubbed her eyes, finding them wet with tears. "Are the chickens okay?"

At the window, Sonny pushed the curtains to the side. "They're out there clucking around. Why?"

Haven gathered her breath. "Nothing. Why are you asking me about my car?"

"Because it's not here," Sonny said.

She glanced between Sonny and Rosalie, trying and failing to interpret their worried expressions.

Rosalie frowned. "Neither is Jillian."

Chapter Forty-Two

Jace adjusted himself for the hundredth time in the reclined driver seat. He should've bitten the bullet and gotten a hotel room. His idea of sleeping in his truck in a
grocery store parking lot wasn't his best. Dreams of Haven
marred the little sleep he did get. He lifted his phone off the
console. Seven calls yesterday from her, followed by one
text:

> **IF I'D KNOWN YOU WERE LEAVING, I WOULD HAVE
> TOLD YOU I LOVE YOU ONE LAST TIME.**

Then nothing all through the night.

His phone began to vibrate, and for a moment, he was
thankful he had another chance. Yet, in the next, he was
thankful it was only Sonny's name on the screen. "Hello?"

"Have you heard from Jillian?"

"No. Why?"

"She left, and she took Haven's car. No note or anything. I figured there was a chance she was coming after
you."

"She hasn't called. You don't think she'd have gone back to the hotel, do you?"

"We aren't sure. But we'll deal with it. She's not yours to care for anymore. Sorry to bother you."

"Sonny, wait." Jace licked his dry lips. He was dehydrated, starving, and his entire body ached from this road trip. He obviously wasn't caring for himself anymore, either. "How's Haven doing?"

"What do you think? You broke her heart, Jace."

"She told you what happened?"

"Sort of. She wouldn't tell us a lot of the details. Just that you and her brother got into it, and you left without telling her goodbye."

"It was more complicated than that."

"I don't know what could complicate it enough to make you leave the way you did."

Jace's foot itched for the gas pedal. The sooner he was in Austin, the better. "Let me know when Jillian comes home, will you?"

He placed his phone in the cupholder. A few more hours until Austin. Maybe he could check in early to the hotel and grab a good nap. Or search his Bible for a verse to help him let go of the past. Let go of the team at Aspen Crossroads and The Mill. After all, he was the start-up guy. It was theirs to carry. He'd let go of Haven. Even if they could get over that speed bump of a twin brother, she would never leave Whisper Canyon. In her eyes, it would mean turning her back on her family. And she'd made it clear that if she had to choose between him and her family, he'd lose.

No way would he return to Whisper Canyon. That was the easiest thing to let go of. What a wretched place, full of wretched people, wretched leaders, and wretched memories that weren't even his.

Jace pulled out of the lot and onto the road. Soon he was

coasting down Route 84 and trying not to think about all he'd left behind.

"Thanks for the guidance, God," he said to the blue sky above the road. He felt only slightly guilty about the sarcasm. He figured the Lord of the universe could handle a bit of criticism, especially after all the ways he'd turned a blind eye thus far in Jace's life. "For the life of me, I don't know why you, Terrence, and Haven thought I needed to know any of that information about my mom. What good could come from me knowing I'm a child of rape? Is that better than thinking I had a father like Bo Radford who didn't want me?"

His phone's directions app alerted him to a merge onto I-20 east. Jace obeyed.

"I used to believe you were everywhere except the churches where people were shunned for their pasts. Now I'm wondering if you're anywhere at all."

Ahead of him, he saw a sign for Exit 244 and followed the app's advice to merge onto the access road.

"Turn right on TX-70S," the robotic voice said.

He brought his truck to a stop at the intersection. All around him, signs hailed the town of Sweetwater, TX. Where had that envelope gone after he took it out of his back pocket? He spied it on the floor beneath the passenger seat, and he bent over to grab it.

A car honked, and he jerked back up in time to see a bigger pickup truck than his speed around him. Jace pulled his car into the Schlotzsky's Deli parking lot and then stared at the return address where his mother had once lived. Sweetwater, Texas. "Is this what you call guidance? What a wise guy you are. Okay. I'll try it. What else can I lose?"

Ten minutes later, Jace stood before a one-story brick home with a yard of weeds and a gutter hanging off the front of the roof. Of course, he knew better than to judge someone's home. Anything was better than being home-less. Still, it was hard to imagine his mother going from the farmhouse with its tall ceilings and charming appeal to this. Then again, it was thirty-one years ago. A lot had changed. What were the chances his mom's aunt and uncle still lived here?

"Hey, mister. Why are you staring at my Gigi's house?" A little girl called from the corner two dozen yards away. She had a blond ponytail and wore a winter coat over her dress. On her back, she carried a book bag far too heavy for a girl who couldn't be more than seven.

"I'm looking for someone I used to know." He felt strange yelling across like this, but he wouldn't dare approach the girl at what was probably her bus stop. He didn't want a worried neighbor thinking he was a kidnapper. "What's your Gigi's name?"

Again, chances were that it wasn't Chelsie. But if it was . . .

"Gigi."

Jace chuckled under his breath. "Right."

"Well, I gotta go to school now. Bye, mister," she said as a yellow school bus pulled up to the corner.

Jace watched her board then turned back to the house. A woman stood in the door's opening, no doubt wondering who this stranger was chatting with the child.

"Is she your granddaughter?"

"Great-granddaughter, yeah. Can I help you with some-thing?"

"I'm not sure." Jace rounded his truck's back bumper but didn't step on the woman's lawn. "I'm looking for a family who used to live here a long time ago. My mother stayed with them for a bit. Her name was—"

"Lynn Chelsie," the woman finished. "She's my niece. You look just like her. You may as well come in. Your stuff will be fine out here. No one here wants anything that don't belong to them."

His feet failed to move. His mother's aunt. So this woman was his great-aunt? He glanced back to where the young girl had been. Would that make them cousins? Living family members. Kin. For better or for much, much worse. There had to be a reason his mom left their kin behind. Jace had a feeling he was about to find out. He took a deep breath and followed his great-aunt inside.

Although the house lacked stylish furnishings, it was clean. The family room had a dollhouse in the corner and a sign reading *Happy Harvest* on the mantel. In the kitchen, the refrigerator displayed kid drawings and schoolwork, and a blue-and-white-checkered dress lay on the table next to a sewing machine.

"Her name's Ricki. She wants to be Dorothy for the Fall Festival on Sunday."

"She lives with you?"

"Since she was born. She reminds me a lot of your momma. Sweet as strawberries at pickin' time."

"Can you tell me about her? My mother?"

"What do you know?"

"I know she left Whisper Canyon when she was sixteen. I know I spent the first few years of my life in New Mexico."

The woman pulled out a chair at the kitchen table, then lowered herself into the seat across from it. "New Mexico? Is that where she went? Where's your momma now?"

"She passed away in 2005."

Her face soured. "Tragic. I'm sorry, boy. She loved you very much."

Jace accepted the invitation to sit. "Yes, ma'am."

"Look at you. Handsome and respectful. Funny to think you were almost mine to raise."

That's right. Lynn told Bo she'd be returning to Whisper Canyon in July, after Jace's birth. Was the plan to leave Jace here? "You were going to adopt me?"

"That's what we'd agreed to. We'd help her through her pregnancy, and then you'd be ours."

"What happened?"

Gigi's countenance darkened. "My first husband was not a nice man. I know we ain't supposed to speak ill of the dead, but I figure where he is, the truth ain't the most painful thing. He scared your momma with his yelling and hitting."

"He beat my mother?"

"No, I wouldn't let him touch her. I always put myself between them. Took the blows myself."

Jace remembered how his mother pushed her way between him and Gus, taking the shot aimed at him. He pictured Haven placing herself between Jace and her brother physically at the farmers' market and figuratively only yesterday. Who had Jace become? "I'm sorry you had to go through that. I guess, in a strange way, I should thank you."

"No need for that. I was just doin'. But she always saw it. With me or the other children. We had three girls of our own. I suppose she didn't want you taking those kinds of hits." Gigi rose from her chair. She went to the fridge, took out two cans of Pepsi, and then slid one in front of Jace. She didn't retake her seat, though—just leaned against her counter. Most of her hair was dyed a rich red that paled her wrinkled skin. Her two-inch roots, however, were a peppered gray. The woman, who appeared to be in her seventies, looked tired.

He obliged her by cracking the Pepsi open and taking a sip, even though it was still before nine in the morning.

"She told me once that she wanted to keep you. I reminded her that her parents wouldn't take her back with a baby in her arms." Her eyes glassed over as she spoke. "You were a big baby, and she was such a tiny thing. I don't know how she did it. Your momma was strong. Stronger than I was back then. You know what? You wait here. I'll be back in a jiffy." Gigi left the kitchen.

It didn't make sense. He'd been born in Santa Fe to Leigh Anne Daring. It said so on his birth certificate. Unless the birth certificate in his possession had been forged. It wouldn't have been the most desperate thing his mother did to protect him.

Rummaging sounds from the back of the house paired with the rhythmic drip of the kitchen faucet and the annoying clicking of the family room's wobbly ceiling fan. No matter where Jace went, he found himself surrounded by disrepair.

Once Gigi returned, she handed him a paper.

Certificate of Adoption.

"Lynn stayed with us long enough to fill out the adoption paperwork. But one night, you were crying, and my husband told me to shut you up or he would. I think that was what did it. The next morning, Lynn had taken you and all the cash in my cookie jar. Never heard from her again."

The letters on the paperwork crossed over each other until Jace blinked several times. *Henry Chelsie, Jr.* That was Jace's birth name.

"Hank wanted to name you after him. He was mad as can be when he found you gone. He'd wanted a son so bad. That devil of a man vowed to find you, but he never did. Your momma must've hidden you well."

"She changed our names. Leigh Anne Daring and Jace Daring."

"Smart girl. Strong girl."

"What about my grandparents? Are they still alive?"

"They died a long time ago on their farm in Kansas. First him. Then her. If you ask me, it was their grief that killed 'em. They never did forgive themselves for sending Lynn here."

"Did my mother ever tell you about my father?"

"She got letters from that one neighbor boy. Jason? He wrote her all the time, but Hank guarded that mailbox like it held his life savings. None of those letters made it to her hands, I'm sad to say."

"Jason wasn't my father. I've spoken to him. Their relationship wasn't physical in that way."

"I had a feeling."

"What do you mean?"

"According to Hank's brother—your grandfather—Lynn told them she'd had a man force himself on her."

Jace steeled himself. "Who?"

"Lynn used to babysit in the summers. She said it was one of the fathers. That's all I know."

The sip of soda burned in his stomach.

"When her parents didn't believe her, she went to the police. They didn't believe her, either. They told her she shouldn't keep spreading those lies, or she'd be branded a liar and a, well, certain kind of girl."

"Why didn't they believe her?"

"Times were different. Your grandparents were pretty strict. If Lynn wore her hair or dressed a certain way, they'd accuse her of trying to get attention from men. They didn't like her spending time with the neighbor boy, especially when they'd go down in those caverns all alone. When she ended up pregnant, they were convinced he was the father and she'd lied to protect him. They demanded she keep the pregnancy a secret or she couldn't come back home. She wasn't even allowed to tell Jason. We let her send one letter to him. Even then, she could only say a little bit. You know that crazy boy drove all the way down here to see her?"

"He loved her. Eleven hours is nothing if you love someone," Jace said. "Why didn't my mom keep writing to him? Or go back to him after she left?"

"Probably scared Hank would come get you. That and

your grandparents convinced her that she was too soiled, too broken, for anyone to love her. Even that boy." Gigi's gray eyes tinted green as tears formed. "I wish I'd been strong enough to tell her what a lie that was. But I believed the same lie about myself back then."

Jace reached across the table with his palm facing up. Gigi eyed it for a few heartbeats, then gave him her hand. He stroked the feather-thin skin with all the gentleness he could muster.

"What happened when Lynn took you to New Mexico?"

He considered telling her the hard truth of what her and Hank's actions had led to, but compassion tethered it within him. "She loved me. And she did what it took to take care of me."

"And how are you, Henry? I'm sorry. Jace?"

"I'll be okay." Jace's focus returned to the certificate in front of him, where it said *Mother's Name.* "Your name is Alice?"

She nodded. "You can call me that or Gigi. That's what my grandchildren call me. The ones who are still around anyway. Most left Sweetwater to chase dreams and whatnot."

"Gigi, how long did you stay with Hank?"

"Until the night our oldest girl told us she was pregnant. She was only fifteen. He vowed to beat the child out of her, so I grabbed his Colt and shot him."

Jace froze.

"Only in the hand. It slowed him down until the police showed up. He died in a prison fight a few years after that. Now, my second husband? He was good to me and the girls. He died five years ago from heart disease." She fiddled with a plain gold band on her trembling ring finger.

"I'm sorry for your loss." Jace thumbed a drop of condensation on the side of the Pepsi can, only to divert his gaze back to the sink. "How long has that faucet been dripping?"

"Oh my. I don't know. I reckon awhile."

He took another sip. "I could fix it for you if you want."

"Don't you have somewhere to be?"

"Gigi, I think I'm exactly where I'm supposed to be in this moment."

Chapter Forty-Three

Three days after their fight, Haven stood outside Daniel's apartment like her boots were frozen to the sidewalk—something that might happen on a wintry day like this if she didn't make a decision soon. A big part of her wanted to hold on to the grudge she'd formed against him, but she also wanted to make things right. They were twins. They were family.

Daniel hadn't spoken to anyone in the three days since their fight. Not even their father. Apparently, Daniel had borrowed the Shelby the night before and hadn't yet returned it. Their father was worried. Not about the car as much as his son.

That settled it. She'd march right up there and demand that he straighten himself up and get his act together. She wouldn't stand by silently anymore. But most important, she'd remind him that she loved him no matter what.

She took out her key ring and found the spare key he'd given her when he'd first moved in, then used it on the downstairs door. Two flights up, she unlocked the door to his apartment where she'd last seen him and last seen Jace. It was quiet inside. And clean. There was no sign of life at all. Like a morgue, and as cold as one, too. She peered at the thermostat. It had been lowered to sixty degrees.

On the table, a single sheet of paper caught her eye. Beside that, she found Daniel's cell phone and a set of keys to his truck. As she drew nearer, her blood chilled to the temperature of the apartment.

Haven,

You're right about everything. I need time to clear my head, and I can't do that here. I guess I'll see you when I see you. Do whatever you want with my possessions. The lease is paid through next month. My truck's in the garage behind the apartment. Keep it. Sell it. Send it off Chapel Peak. I don't care. Tell Dad I'm borrowing the Shelby for a while. I'll take good care of it. I'd tell you I love you, but you wouldn't believe it.

Daniel

P.S. Please tell Elizabeth I'm truly sorry.

Haven pressed the paper to her heart and cried.

Where she sat on the farmhouse couch, Lizzie stared at Daniel's note without even a hint of emotion. After a few minutes, she lowered the paper to her lap so she could sip her chamomile. Then she read the note again.

"Well," Lizzie said, "there isn't much to say, is there? It's for the best. I moved my grandpa into hospice on Sunday. I should focus on spending as much time with him as I can. Daniel would have just complicated everything. At least now I can forget about him."

"You moved him in Sunday? I had no idea."

Lizzie nodded. "I was too upset to drive myself home

afterward, so I called Daniel. He dropped everything and came to get me. We grabbed some sandwiches from Sassy's and took them back to his apartment. I didn't feel like eating, but Daniel said I needed to get something in my stomach. You may not believe it, but he was caring."

A flurry of anger and sympathy roiled Haven's gut. She and Jace had been right. Lizzie had been going through an emotional time, and Daniel had taken advantage of that.

"It got late, and Daniel offered to drive me home. I didn't want to go to that house without my grandpa there. I got upset all over again. I wanted to feel something other than fear and pain. That's why I kissed Daniel for the first time. Only I didn't want to stop there."

Despite her mix of emotions, Haven fixed her counselor expression on her face and listened.

"I know you think Daniel was using me, but he kept saying we needed to take things slow. I kept pushing. Eventually, he gave in. I'm not proud of it. I always wanted my first time to be with my husband." A hint of sadness flickered over her brow.

Haven knew that feeling too well. She grabbed Lizzie's limp hand, where it had fallen away from the note. "Lizzie, your wedding night will still be special, and your husband, whoever he may be, will see you as an absolute treasure. This doesn't change that."

"Thank you, Haven. How is your family taking Daniel's leaving?"

"My sisters are angry at him. That Shelby is worth over two hundred thousand dollars and although my father promised to one day leave it to Daniel, it wasn't his to take. My father, though, is only worried about Daniel."

"Have you spoken to Jace?"

"No. If he needs time, I'll let him have it. I've grown used to people leaving. They almost always come back. Daniel, Jace, even Jillian. I can pray for them and do my best to carry on without them. And without my car." Haven shook

her head. It was about time she got rid of that clunker anyway. Jillian could have it. Who knows? Maybe it would provide her shelter on this cold night, wherever she might be.

"Well, I plan to do more than simply carry on. I will love
my grandpa well until he takes his last breath. And then,
who knows? I love running the chapel, but I've never been
anywhere other than Colorado. Maybe I'll travel."

"Good for you, Lizzie."

On the coffee table, Haven's phone rang. A quick peek
displayed an incoming call from Jillian. She scrambled to
answer it. "Jill?"

"Um, no. This is Kitty. I used to work with Jillian.
You're the first person in her primary contacts to answer."

"Is she okay?"

"She's alive, but she's at the hospital. Denver Health.
She got beat up pretty bad."

Haven moved to the edge of the couch.

"Do you know what happened?"

"She came back to the hotel where we, um . . ."

"I know. Go on."

"She said she needed to get something out of the room
she used to stay in. Something important. Eddie wasn't
happy to see her. Not at all. He told her to get lost unless she
was willing to bring Rosalie and come back to work. She
hit him good, and she got to search the room before she left.
Teresa sent a guy after her, though. When I found her, she
was lying next to the car."

"Is she alone?"

"I'm here with her."

"It will probably take me two hours to get there. Can
you stay with her until then?"

"Yeah, of course."

"And Kitty? Thank you." While Haven put on her shoes,
she relayed the information to Lizzie. She tried calling
Sonny and Rosalie on their cell phones, but they kept them
off when working. Even the restaurant's main line was busy.

What to do? Haven couldn't bring Elijah to the hospital with her. Besides, he'd been asleep for two hours already.

"I'll stay here with Elijah," Lizzie said. "And I'll keep trying to call the restaurant."

"Thanks, Lizzie."

While Haven waited on the front porch for her sisters to appear on the drive with Dash's Jeep, she looked down at Jace's picture and contact information on her phone screen.

He'd want to know, wouldn't he? Even if this was his biggest fear. Even if he'd left them behind? Even if he didn't want to speak to Haven? Without another hesitation, she tapped his number and held the phone to her ear. After a few rings, his voice mail picked up.

"I know you don't want to talk to me. There's something—"

A beep interrupted her. She glanced at her phone. Jace was calling her. She ended the voice mail and answered.

"Jace?"

"Hi, Haven." His voice was soft enough to make her want to crawl through the phone and rest against his chest. "I—"

"Something's happened to Jillian."

"She went back, didn't she?"

"She did, and she got attacked. She's going to make it, I think, but she's at a Denver hospital. I'm heading there now."

"Should . . . should I come back?"

The million-dollar question. He was asking her opinion. Oh, how she wanted to say yes, except she didn't want him to act out of obligation or that protective instinct of his.

"I can call after I see her and talk to the doctor."

"Please do."

"All right." Haven didn't want to hang up, but she didn't know what to say, either. Would he care that Daniel left? Or that Lizzie wasn't shattered? Or that Elijah had asked ten times a day why Jace went away?

Jace didn't end the call, either. "I should have said good-bye to you."

Thick clouds blocked all the light from the stars and moon. It was only because of the porchlight that she could see the falling snow. "Yes, you should have. I deserve more respect than that."

"You do. I'm sorry, Haven. Forgive me? Please?"

The glow from headlights stretched into the air over the hill, ahead of the Jeep. Haven exhaled a slow breath. "You're already forgiven."

Even with a borrowed pillow and blanket, the hospital couch felt like a hospital couch. Haven wasn't the tallest girl, but her legs were too long to curl up in front of her. Then whenever Haven closed her eyes in Jillian's room and pictured her lying alone and unconscious in a snowy parking lot, she'd remind herself this couch wasn't so bad.

Thank you, Lord, for Kitty.

They'd spoken briefly in the waiting area before the nurse walked Haven to the room. Kitty couldn't be older than twenty herself. If she'd known Jillian and Rosalie, then she'd had the chance to escape to Aspen Crossroads last winter. She hadn't, though. Haven shivered, imagining the girl waiting for the ambulance in only shorts and a T-shirt. She'd risked more than cold temperatures to save Jillian. Would she pay the price when she returned to the hotel?

Jillian's legs kicked in the bed. The thrashing must have hurt her broken ribs, considering how she cried out.

Haven rushed to her side. "Jillian, you're safe."

Her gaze, narrowed by the swelling around her eyes, darted wildly before settling on Haven. Fear quickly turned to confusion.

"You're in a hospital, and you're safe."

Her body settled beneath the blanket, and she tried to speak. Already, the skin on her throat was splotched black, purple, and red.

"You don't have to talk if it hurts. Are you thirsty?"

She shook her head, then winced at the motion. Her split lips rounded slowly to form a word. No, words. Two of them. Jillian mouthed them again.

Haven couldn't place them, but Jillian seemed determined to be heard. She strained to make sound. Haven pressed the nurse call button, then leaned her ear close to Jillian's mouth.

"Note. Book."

"Notebook?"

Jillian tried to nod.

"You need one?"

My *notebook*, she mouthed.

"You're looking for your notebook?" Haven searched the room. She hadn't seen anything when she first came in. "I don't know where your notebook is."

Jillian closed her eyes. A tear rolled down her temple and into her bloodied and soiled hair.

The nurse came in—a cute guy named Emilio that Jillian might bat her eyelashes at in normal circumstances. "Our girl's awake," he said. "Jillian, my name is Emilio, or Leo for short, and I'm at your beck and call." As he went through his protocol, Haven continued to look for a notebook of some sort.

"Excuse me. Where are her belongings?"

"Probably taken as evidence since this was a crime. I'll ask when those will be returned. Which is a good thing because I'm going to personally make sure whoever did this to her goes to jail for a long time."

With Jillian's permission, Haven stepped out of the room and retreated to the waiting area. It was dim, but Haven quickly found who she was looking for. Valor and Dash slept awkwardly in adjoining chairs with Dash's head rested on Valor's shoulder. Rarity was curled into a ball on the chair next to them. Meanwhile, Kitty slept on the same type of couch that had been in Jillian's room, and Valor's coat covered her like a blanket.

Haven gently touched Kitty's shoulder. "Kitty?"

The girl roused. "Yeah?"

"Jillian is asking for her notebook. Do you know what she means?"

Kitty frowned. She seemed to be sizing Haven up. For what, she couldn't be sure. Eventually, she wrestled her sleepy body into a seated position, then pulled a satchel-style purse from behind her legs. "She'd hidden it in her shirt. I found it when I was looking for her phone. I didn't want the cops to take it." She pulled a six-inch spiral note-book from her purse. "I think it's why she came back."

Haven accepted it. She considered flipping through it, but she'd worked tirelessly to earn Jillian's trust. She wouldn't destroy that now.

She returned to the room as Leo was finishing up. He sang "My Girl" by the Temptations under his breath and grinned reassuringly at Jillian. "How about another blanket? I'll get you a nice, warm one, okay?" Then he was gone.

Haven held up the notebook for Jillian to see, and her chin quivered in response. "Is this it?"

Jillian mouthed *Open*.

The first page showed a pencil sketch of a man's face. Not the kind that covered Jillian's walls, displaying life, joy, personality. Or the art at The Mill that evoked feelings of comfort, home, and community. No, these were more like the work of a police sketch artist. The man had a rounded face with a small nose, pockmarks, and unkempt hair. Above it was a date from nearly two years ago.

She showed Jillian, who lifted her chin, like a nod. "Keep going?" Haven flipped to the next page. A different man this time, one day later. "Is this . . . a record of johns? Purchasers?"

Jillian blinked.

Leo came back through the door, blanket in hand, and Haven sank down onto her couch. She carefully flipped through the book, careful not to smudge any of the pictures.

Why would Jillian risk her life to get this? Leo spread the blanket over Jillian's broken body the way an angel might cover a child with a shield of protection, but Jillian kept her eyes glued to Haven.

The face on the very next page stilled Haven's fingers. Trent stared up at her from the page. It was unmistakable. The date read October 8th, thirteen months ago. No wonder Jillian had eyed Trent so curiously. She'd recognized him.

Chapter Forty-Four

For the next two days, Haven debated how the notebook might best be used as she stayed at Dash's Denver apartment, a quick light-rail trip away from the hospital and the impound lot where her car was residing until Jillian's release. Meanwhile Haven's sisters returned to Whisper Canyon with a new friend in the back of the Jeep. When Kitty had asked if there was room for her at Aspen Crossroads, the celebration might have been heard across the Rocky Mountains. Rosalie was especially excited to have her best friend joining her in the canyon.

In between visits with Jillian and phone calls to Sonny with updates, Haven gave in and called Jace to get advice about the sketch.

"I don't want to play down Jillian's efforts," he said. "What she did was incredibly courageous. I only wonder how much good it will do. As far as I know, there's no way to validate that was drawn that date. Or that Garrison actually solicited sex from a prostituted woman. It's circumstantial, I'm afraid."

"It would cast doubt on his character. And he was drawn in her notebook on three different dates between October and January. Maybe Elaine remembers him taking a business trip those days. There might be ATM withdrawals from their bank account."

"It's possible. I doubt she would corroborate after what we heard the night of the Harvest Dance, though."

Haven's skin warmed at the memory of their time in the gazebo right before they'd heard the Garrisons' true nature.

"Haven, are you still there?"

"Sorry. I was thinking. Elaine may be as power-hungry as him, but I don't think she'd put up with him spending their money on this."

"Whose money would he spend?" Jace asked.

"You know, when Trent first took office, he promised authenticity. He said that all the spending reports from his office would be made public on request. What if there's a clue on one of those reports?"

"Do you honestly think he'd be dumb enough to pay for this with Whisper Canyon's money?"

"I think he'd be arrogant enough to. I could have Sonny or Rosalie look into it."

"He'd block it the second they showed up at his office."

"He's not in his office. My dad said Elaine had the baby yesterday. He's either with her or out campaigning."

"There's no rest for the wicked, is there?"

"Get this. They're introducing the newest Garrison at a press conference tomorrow evening. They're making it a big event, even bringing Trent's brother, Aidan, back for it. Honestly, I think he's worried about Tuesday's election. There's buzz around town that people may write in Rarity's name."

"Do you think she has a chance to win?"

"Not unless we get these sketches into the right hands."

There was a long silence.

"Tell me about Texas."

"On my way down, I stopped at my mom's aunt and uncle's house. The one she sent Bo the letter from."

"And?"

"I met my great-aunt Alice. Or Gigi, as I call her."

"You call her Gigi already?"

Jace recounted the details of the visit and how he'd stayed all that day and the next helping her fix things around the house. He told Haven about the adoption. That legally Gigi was his mother and about all she'd overcome through the years after leaving an abusive marriage. He talked about Ricki, the coolest seven-year-old he'd ever met.

"Oh, Jace, you do have family." Haven dabbed her eyes with a tissue.

"I do. I'm hoping to keep in touch, maybe visit them occasionally and help her do more to fix up her house if she lets me."

"You're such a good man, Jace Daring."

"Thank you, Haven. Look, I hate to do this, but I have to go. I'm meeting with a Realtor to look at property around here. Terrence is joining us, and he just pulled up."

"Yeah, I have to pick up Jillian and drive her home."

"Would you mind if I call you later?"

"I'd like that."

J ace pocketed his phone and approached the rental car, but there were three people in the car instead of one. A man and woman Jace had never seen before joined Terrence in front of the sedan. The woman, who reminded him a bit of Haven, hugged the man's arm as they peered up at the farmhouse. So far in Jace's Internet searches, this was the best property to support this next venture, except that there was only the one living space. He'd be sharing the house with the team this time. Fortunately, it was large, with six bedrooms and two kitchens. Still, there would be no boundaries here.

"Daring, how are you?" Terrence paired the question with a firm handshake that might intimidate another man.

Jace, however, knew the man had a heart as soft as one of Rosalie's oatmeal chocolate chip cookies. "Did you just get in?"

"Got here yesterday. I spent a few days in Sweetwater with . . . family." The word sounded strange rolling off Jace's tongue.

Terrence's brows hiked to the middle of his forehead. He knew Jace's story. When they'd met, Jace was a twenty-year-old field hand with no high school diploma, no home, and no path. "Family. Hmm. So my Whisper Canyon plan worked?"

"Not quite. I'll fill you in later. Who'd you bring with you?"

"This is Mark and Lindsey Campbell. And this is Jace." As they exchanged handshakes, Terrence continued with the introduction, first telling them about Jace's eleven-year history with the organization. "The Campbells both went through our training program to establish new properties. They ended up falling in love and getting married last month. I wanted them to join us as we scouted this property, so they'd understand what to look for when they seek out their own."

"When will that be?" Jace asked.

"Unfortunately, not soon. Counting Austin, we have twelve ventures starting up in the next year, all with established operators. We can't carry any more than that. Mark, Lindsey, why don't you go on and check out the peach orchard? Jace and I will meet you over there once the Realtor arrives."

An orchard? That was different. Jace would have to learn a new crop. Different and new didn't mean bad, though. Who would want to stick with familiar, easy, and comfortable?

Jace. That's who. For the first time in his life.

"How are you feeling about leaving Colorado? I half thought you'd put down roots there."

"It's complicated."

"Does complicated mean workable?"

"What do you mean?"

"You've been doing a great job for us. You've helped a lot of people over the years. But you've also moved, what, nine times in eleven years?"

"Your point?"

"You don't have to keep doing this. You're allowed to settle down and have a personal life."

Jace looked at the young couple holding hands as they approached a line of trees. "Are you firing me?"

"Actually, quite the opposite."

Chapter Forty-Five

"You've been talking to Jace? Does he know what happened?" Jillian asked. Her voice still rasped, and the bruises she sported from head to toe had darkened considerably.

"Yes. He thought about coming back, too. He was worried about you," Haven said.

"Is he coming back?" Sonny paused her brushing of Kitty's hair. That morning, Sonny helped her dye it back to Kitty's natural color, ash-blond.

"No." Haven focused on the television screen, trying to pretend that everyone in the room wasn't staring at her.

Rosalie took Haven's hand and held it. "Did you ever ask him to stay?"

"Of course not." Haven laughed at the absurdity. Asking someone to stay . . . "I can't control whether people leave."

"What if the people who leave do so because they don't know you want them to stay?" Rosalie asked.

Sonny pointed the hairbrush at Haven. "Or here's an idea. Have you ever considered going to Austin with him?"

"Sure, I've considered it, but my job is here with you."

"Haven, we love you, but we can hold our own now,"

Rosalie said. "You've encouraged all of us. You went to get Jill. You and Sonny are kind of friends. And me . . . Oh! What time is it?" Rosalie ran to the kitchen counter and opened her laptop. She tapped away on it for a moment.

Her GED test. Haven had forgotten about it. Rosalie had been scheduled to take it Saturday morning while Haven was still in Denver with Jillian. And now her results should be available. The group watched Rosalie as she clicked through a couple screens.

"I passed all the sections. I'm a high school graduate!"

Haven didn't need to get up. Rosalie came to each one of them and squeezed them hard enough to hurt. Except Jillian. She received a gentle kiss on the cheek.

"See, Haven," Sonny said. "You've made a big difference here. If you wanted to go be with Jace, we wouldn't stop you."

"But my family."

Sonny pinned her with a look. "Would your family want you to keep sacrificing your happiness for them? No way."

"Jace would want you to take a chance. Be daring," Rosalie said, still beaming from her news. She continued texting on her phone. Probably Jimmy.

"Yes, he would." Haven chewed her lip. Could she really leave Whisper Canyon? Who would she be if she wasn't everyone's haven? That wasn't a simple answer.

"Haven, what do you want?" Jillian asked quietly.

That was simple. "Jace."

Jillian lifted her lips into a small grin. "Then, go get him."

After one more glance around, Haven was convinced. "I'll leave after the press conference. I need to pack."

Thirty minutes flew by as Haven shoved everything she needed and nothing more into one suitcase and a few grocery totes. Her family all planned to attend the press conference so she could say goodbye to her father and sisters there. Then she'd get a few hours under her belt before stopping for the night at a hotel.

Haven looped the bags over her arm and steered her rolling suitcase backward down the stairs, one thump at a time.

"Need a hand with that?"

Haven froze with her back to the masculine voice she'd grown to know so well. On the landing, she balanced the suitcase on its wheels and let the totes slip off her wrist. She turned slowly, praying she hadn't imagined him.

Jace stood at the base of the stairs. Although he had bags under his eyes, a severe scruff, and messy hair, he was the handsomest she'd ever seen him. "Where are you going?"

"To you. Why'd you come back?"

He grinned. "For you."

"What about Austin? Secondly?"

"There was another couple looking to start a farm. Terrence and I thought it might be better if I let them serve Austin, and I came back here and worked to train future operators."

"But you loved going to new places, new towns."

"No, I *love* you, Haven." He climbed the steps, stopping one step below her. "I know what I feel for you is real because it didn't go away when I was apart from you or angry with you. And when I met my adoptive mother and little cousin, I wanted more than anything to have you there with me. When I pray, you are the one I thank God the most for. The fact is, I don't want to live the rest of my life without you. That's why I came back. You're worth staying for."

Haven touched his cheek and let the cool blue of his eyes wash peace over her. "And you're worth leaving for. I love you, Jace Daring."

"For all time." He placed a promise-filled kiss on her lips, and she welcomed it the way sunflowers welcome the sun after a dark night.

Chapter Forty-Six

Your aunt was wrong." Bo ran his hand over his jaw, pulling his skin down with it. The man had fire in his eyes. "Lynn didn't babysit for several families that summer. There was only one family. Only one man that it could be. Why didn't I see it? I knew something was happening. You said she reported it to the police, but they dismissed it as a lie?" Bo cursed. "I know why."

Jace hid his frustration with a nod and squeezed Haven tighter against his side. Luckily, she didn't seem to mind. They'd barely let go of each other since they'd reunited one hour ago.

Bo placed a strong hand on the back of Jace's neck. "I'm glad you're home, son. You are home, correct?"

Haven grinned. "We're staying in Whisper Canyon."

"Good. We need more upstanding men like you here. I'll talk to you after the press conference. After I've made things right." Bo left them and headed straight for an older policeman. He pulled him away from the gathering crowd and questioned him.

"That's Police Chief Singleton. He was probably on the

force when your mother went to report the assault." Haven hugged Jace's waist. "Your mother must have been strong to report such a thing when she had no support. And then to protect you from her uncle the way she did?"

"She was strong, for sure. I wish you could have met her."

"Me, too. But you can introduce me to her through your memories." Haven glanced at the rows of the chairs in the town hall that were quickly filling up. "We should take our seats."

Jace allowed Haven to lead him by the hand to the Haviland row, which included Sonny and Rosalie. Jillian and Kitty stayed back at the farmhouse with 'Lijah. Between them all, only one seat in the row remained untaken. The one on the aisle next to Rarity.

A man plopped down on it without asking if it was reserved.

Rarity took one look at him, then laughed awkwardly loud, as her fair skin turned to a blazing pink. "I know you don't plan to sit here next to me."

Jace leaned close to Haven's ear. "Is that—?"

"Aidan Garrison? Yes. Trent's little brother."

"Scarity Haviland, you hurt my feelings. I expected a kiss on my cheek from you."

"Scarity? Aren't you hilarious. It's amazing you went the football route. Was a birthday party clown not prestigious enough for a Garrison?"

"Babe, you know I didn't go into the NFL for prestige. I went for the money and fame. Oh, and the women. Are you jealous?" Aidan put his arm around Rarity and rested it on her chair back.

"If you don't move your hand, I'm going to bite it off."

Aidan snickered. "Nice to see time hasn't changed you." He looked past Rarity, settling his sights on Haven. "Hello. It's Haven, right? I'm Aidan."

"Yes, I'm Haven." She placed a hand on Jace's knee.

"And this is Jace Daring. It's nice to meet you. Shouldn't you be up there with your family?"

"That isn't the spotlight I like. I'm not a fan of the Garrison political machine. I came to meet my nephew. Poor kid's going to need an awesome uncle. Besides, the company here is far more pleasant. Your sister is like an ice cream sundae. She's so sweet I don't even mind the way she sends shooting pain to my brain."

Trent climbed the stage and took his place behind the podium. He smiled across the crowd until he got to Jace. He scowled even more when he looked at his brother. Elaine entered the room with a blanketed bundle in her arms. A wave of *aww*s welcomed her. Jace couldn't help but feel joy for the new life, even if he was stuck with pretty heinous parents. At least kids are resilient. He'd learned nothing if not that.

"Thank you all for coming out. Elaine and I would like to introduce our son, Oswald Trent Garrison."

"Oy," Aidan said loud enough to catch Jace's ear before the crowd clapped.

The baby didn't like the applause and started shrieking. Elaine bounced the baby back and forth. Trent stole the child from his wife and positioned himself directly behind the microphone. "I've got this, honey. I've been saving up a special song for my first child."

"Not this song. He'll do anything for votes," Aidan mumbled under his breath.

Trent grinned at the crowd, then sang:

"Brave one, brave one, time for bed,
Close your eyes and rest your head.
When you wake, the sun will, too.
There'll be much more fun to do.
Brave one, brave one, say your prayer,
Dreams come true for those who dare."

The lyrics pierced Jace straight through. That was his mother's song. The song she made up for the kids she babysat.

Haven recognized it, too, because she leaned across Rarity and asked Aidan where they'd learned that song.

"From a sitter we had when we were little. She'd sing it to us before she'd put us to bed."

"What was the sitter's name?" she asked.

"I'm not sure. I was only four or five. I think I called her Lynnie. Why?"

Jace felt ill as his attention shifted to the man standing behind Trent on the stage—Samuel Garrison. It was him. He was the one who had assaulted his mother when she was only sixteen. And he'd gotten away with it for all these years.

Haven squeezed Jace's hand. When she looked at him, it was clear she'd had the same revelation. Is that what Bo had figured out, too? No wonder her family and the police hadn't believed her. The town had spent too long catering to this wretched family. Well, no more. In his head, Jace assembled words to proclaim.

Meanwhile, Trent, having failed to calm the child, handed him off to his wife, and she took the baby through the back door. "It truly is an honor to celebrate this day with four generations of Garrisons. Thank you to our past mayors, my father and grandfather, for joining us today. Tomorrow, the voters' voices will be heard, and my time as mayor of this great town will carry on. I'd like to start the press conference by—"

"Mayor, what do you have to say about the report detailing criminal activity in your office?" a reporter asked.

"I'm sorry, could you say that again?"

"We at Channel One have received a report that includes secretive plans to replace local businesses with high-end retailers, including a luxury ski resort at the current location of The Mill restaurant. It states you plan to destroy Whisper Canyon's unique character in favor of commercialization."

Trent tensed, grabbing the podium with both hands. "There is nothing wrong with trying to bring tourists and new business to Whisper Canyon."

"But there is something wrong when the town's mayor is an investor in those specific businesses, is there not? It says it right here in the Colorado Code of Ethics for Government Officials."

Trent smirked. "Who, may I ask, offered this *report*, as you call it?"

"Daniel Haviland, one of the town's contracted architects."

Jace thought he heard Haven's heart stop. Daniel might be long gone, doing who-knew-what while he found himself or whatever, but he'd done one last thing before he left. And it would cost him. If he hadn't already quit, he was sure to lose his job over this leak of nonpublic information.

"That explains it," Trent said. "The Havilands have a history of problematic behavior in this town. They caused trouble for our great founder, Prescott Garrison, back in the 1800s. With her scandalous behavior, Nina Haviland showed how completely derelict they are. That alone should prove to everyone here that the word of her children cannot be trusted."

"Does that same logic apply to the Garrison family?" It was Bo's voice. He stood on the far side of the crowd. "In 1989, a sixteen-year-old girl who babysat for Samuel Garrison's children was raped. The girl told her parents and reported the crime to the police, but the case was dismissed before an investigation took place."

Samuel stepped forward, knocking Trent out of the way. "Hogwash. Thirty-year-old hogwash."

"There's proof. I've been assured that the report is still in the police station's archives, and if that isn't enough, the assault resulted in a pregnancy for the girl, whose name was Lynn Chelsie. That child may be willing to do a DNA test to prove paternity."

"May be willing? Take your lies somewhere else," Samuel said.

Jace rose from his seat. "I'm that child, and I'm willing to undergo DNA testing to prove Mr. Garrison's guilt. My birth name was Henry Chelsie, although you all know me as Jace Daring. My mother, Lynn, was banished from Whisper Canyon for speaking out against the mayor's attack. That banishment led to a difficult life—something that inspired me to partner with the Secondly organization and The Mill Restaurant. For many victims of sex trafficking, there are people like Samuel Garrison who forced them there."

Rosalie stood. "And there are people like Mayor Trent Garrison who pay for their services. They pay to *abuse* them. On the night of October eighth, last year, Trent Garrison stayed at the Stargaze Hotel in Denver and paid three hundred fifty-nine dollars of taxpayers' money for a room and 'extra entertainment,' as you can see on this expense report I requested from the mayor's office. Thanks to my GED classes, I can tell you that's two hundred fifty-nine percent more than a hotel room alone. Oh, and we also have a sketch of his gross face from that day, too. According to this report, the mayor visited the Stargaze Hotel at least seven times in the past year—all paid for with taxpayer money." Rosalie sat down triumphantly.

"Don't listen to that—" Trent spoke a word away from the microphone, but it was clear what sexist slur he'd used.

Jimmy jumped onto the stage and pushed Trent back, forcing him to land hard on his backside. "Don't ever call my girlfriend that again!" Bo got in Samuel Garrison's face, backing the sleaze up until he hit the wall. The police chief got in between them and escorted Samuel off the stage, noticeably swinging a pair of handcuffs in his hand.

The entire scene devolved into a madhouse. Everyone in the crowd was soon on their feet, likely excited they no longer had to whisper about the sins that had taken place in the canyon. As most of them headed toward the stage, the Haviland and Aspen Crossroads families headed out onto the street. Only Jace and Haven remained in their seats.

Haven grasped his hand tight. "I don't know how you're holding it together."

"It's only because you're here with me. Otherwise, I would have been up on that stage throwing fists."

"I wouldn't blame you if you did. At least, the town won't reelect Trent now. God willing, Trent and his father will go to jail for their crimes."

"Samuel may not. This state has a statute of limitations. It's been too long. He'll get away with it." Heaviness threatened, and he looked up at the ceiling.

"Not in this town. And even if he does get away with it now, he'll have to account for his evil one day. His punishment isn't for us to decide. We can only choose to live each day with purpose and with grace."

"I have Garrison blood in me," he said, scarcely believing it.

"That doesn't make you his son. You are the son of God the Father. You are the son of Leigh Anne Daring. And you are my love. I'll never let you doubt it."

Once Jace was able to compose himself, he and Haven left the town hall's auditorium in each other's arms. He paused in front of the statue of Ol' Sixclaw, remembering the day his mother brought him here. Only this time, his mother's voice spoke.

"What you meant for evil, God used for good. If you don't believe that, look at this child. I will raise him to be the kind of man who protects and doesn't harm. He will have honor and courage and strength—all the things that you lack. And I feel sorry for you because you'll never know him. Maybe no one believes me, but you'll pay for what you've done. I can only hope you won't destroy this town or any more lives until then."

His mother had picked Jace up and carried him to the front door. Peeking over her shoulder, five-year-old Jace had seen the face of Samuel Garrison glaring like an angry bear.

She'd stood up to him. She may have been young, ignored, and cast out, but she'd stood up to the beast and followed through on what she vowed, raising Jace to protect others and to be daring.

"Is something wrong?" Haven asked.

He smiled at her. "Not anymore."

Once they hit the streets, Aidan Garrison approached. He looked between Haven and Jace. "You'll never get an apology from the rest of the Garrisons, but you have one from me. I'm sorry for all the hurt and trouble my family has caused you both. If there is anything you need, don't hesitate to reach out. I mean that." He seemed sincere enough.

"Thank you, Aidan," Haven said on both their behalves.

Aidan turned to Rarity. "What do you say, Scarity? Want to go grab dinner somewhere?"

"About as much as I want to eat a plate of Rocky Mountain oysters."

"Ha. You're so weird."

"And you're so normal. Now go on back to your celebrity football world."

"Hmm. I was thinking of sticking around. This place is finally getting interesting. See ya later, doll." Aidan winked at Rarity, then gave a more sober nod to Jace before walking away with his hands in his pockets.

Rarity rolled her eyes and turned to the rest of the family. "Jace, I'm glad you came back. Whisper Canyon isn't perfect, but maybe now it will get better. Everyone else, I say we head to The Mill for a pre–election day dinner."

Sonny linked arms with Rosalie. "And our family will

serve it to you. We should head over before the dinner rush picks up."

Haven's father stepped forward. "Ladies, please know you'll always have the Havilands if you need anything at all. And that goes for you, too, Jace. You're family now." He shook Jace's hand.

"Thank you. That means more than you know."

Jace put his arm around Haven, and together they walked south down the street, past Daniel's vacant apartment, toward Jace's parked truck. A gust of wind, inexplicably warm, dipped into the canyon.

It's all right, boy.

The words, carried on the breeze and spoken in the faintest of whispers, brought him to a standstill.

"Jace? Is everything okay?" Haven's caring and curious eyes settled on him. She hadn't heard the whisper.

"Yes, everything is more than okay. You know, it's funny. When I came to Whisper Canyon nine months ago, I had no family at all. Now I have more than I know what to do with."

"And you were what brought us together. You have a gift for that. Bringing good out of pain. New life out of what was broken."

"Well, I have an excellent counselor." Jace looked at the storefront on their right. "This was where I tried to defend you that first day we met. In a strange way, God was directing my path even then."

"I believe he was."

"Speaking of that day, I have a confession. At the farmers' market, I only wanted five chicks. But I needed an excuse to talk to you, so I bought six."

"If we're making confessions, then I have one," Haven said, turning to face him. "I know how to drive a tractor. I pretended I didn't so you'd have to get close to me."

Jace's laugh was loud enough to echo off the canyon's

walls. It felt good to laugh, especially when Haven was in his arms. True to her name, she had become his place to rest. But more than that, she was his place to laugh, love, and truly live daringly, the way his mother always wished for him to.

Epilogue

All down Main Street, painted eggs hung from tree limbs beside new buds announcing the arrival of spring. Soon, the winter tourists would be on their way out, and the summertime mountain bikers and hikers would swoop in. As always, the year-round residents of Whisper Canyon would be there to welcome them into the quirky shops and restaurants run by folks with questionable pasts and huge hearts. Haven loved them all. Thank goodness she and Jace had decided to stay. She cherished every moment she was able to spend with the ladies of Aspen Crossroads. They were busy. Jimmy had helped Rosalie apply to online colleges for hospitality studies. Sonny was balancing her working-single-mom act spectacularly. Of course, it helped that Colin had offered to teach Elijah more about horses whenever Sonny needed an extra hand.

Thanks to Jillian's and Kitty's efforts, the traffickers Eddie and Teresa were arrested in December and awaiting trial. The Stargaze Hotel was shut down, and all the prostituted women received resources to help them move forward if they wanted. All but one accepted the help. Nurse Emilio was true to his word and provided support to Jillian through the whole investigation. He'd even reached out to Wes about working at the pediatric office in Whisper Canyon so he could continue spending time with her. When Jillian wasn't making excuses about why she and Emilio weren't official yet, she taught Kitty the ways of the farm.

Haven spied Rarity out in front of her shop. She studied a newspaper article hanging on the light post. "Aidan Garrison Officially Moves into the Mayoral Mansion."

"What are you doing?"

Rarity jumped, dropping what was in her hand. A capless, black permanent marker rolled across the sidewalk, finally coming to a rest next to a roll of tape. On the article's picture, Aidan sported poorly drawn Harry Potter–style eyeglasses and a villainous mustache.

"Rarity," Haven scolded.

"What? Just because he's our new mayor doesn't mean I have to respect the guy."

"What do you have against him anyway? Or are you simply bitter he got more write-in votes than you?"

"First of all, he barely got more votes than me." Her sister shook her head. "And second, that is a story for another time, my dear. We're late for the candlelight service."

"Do you think it's strange? Whisper Canyon has had enough changes with Samuel's exile and Trent's arrest. Now the main church in town is adding a service that's typically done at Christmas. I've never even heard of Palm Sunday Eve."

"I don't know," Rarity said.

"Jace said he may go. Like, he may step into a church for the first time ever. I'm so proud of him," Haven said, fully aware of the dreamy look on her face whenever she spoke about her boyfriend. They'd spent the last five months healing together, and Haven fell more in love with him every day.

"I know. I've been telling him that if anyone even looks at him funny, I'll hurdle the pews and escort them out myself."

"He appreciates that offer, too. He's come so far in opening up to the community. Church is the last step."

"Then what?"

Haven felt her cheeks heat. "I'm not sure." She glanced up and down the street. "Where is everyone?" All of the people she knew had planned to attend this service, except for Daniel, of course. He was still traveling, but his occasional postcard from various cities across the United States let them know he was alive, well, and not wanting to be found. Lizzie hadn't been around much due to her grandfather's decline, but she seemed to be handling Daniel's disappearance with as much grace as one could.

"I told you we're late. Let's go." Rarity jogged up the steps in her seventies-era platform shoes. She grasped the handle of the church's front door, then turned to Haven. "Are you ready?"

"Ready for what?"

Rarity smirked, then pulled the door open and held it. A violin began to play. Not a church song, though. No, it was a George Strait song. "I Cross My Heart"—the song she and Jace danced to in the gazebo so long ago. Definitely strange.

There was indeed candlelight. As she took her first step down the aisle, she noticed a candle on every pew where her community usually would be sitting. Other than the violinist, whom she couldn't see, she was alone here. Even Rarity had disappeared.

A noise drew her focus to the front, where a chicken clucked its way past the front pew in her direction.

"Audrey?" she said as if the hen might perk to its name. But it was her, although she wore a new outfit, probably thanks to Rosalie. A black, knitted dress. Haven scooped her up and noticed an elastic string of fake pearls around Audrey's neck, accented by a diamond ring hanging from the necklace.

Boots thudded a rhythm against the hardwood floor. Jace

appeared, illuminated by the candlelight. He was here in a church, without shame and without fear. He met Haven in the center aisle, wearing the same outfit from the Harvest Dance, as well as that smile of his—the one that appeared whenever he vowed to love Haven well beyond their last sunset at Aspen Crossroads. He slipped the necklace off Audrey's neck, then took her from Haven's arms and placed her on the ground. While down on bended knee, he glanced at Haven, his eyes filled with promise and the slightest glimmer of tears. "Excuse me, miss. I have a question for you."

ACKNOWLEDGMENTS

First and foremost, I'd like to thank my husband and my children. There is no one I'd rather be quarantined with during a global pandemic than you all. Writing this book might have fallen off the priority list without all your support. Thanks to my mother, Shirley, for stepping in with dinners and babysitting when deadlines loomed!

Tamela, you continue to be a great encourager to me. Thanks for all you do. To my Berkley team, specifically Anne, Fareeda, and Brittanie: I couldn't manage this writing gig without your dedicated help. I appreciate you!

To my writing colleagues, especially Janyre and Rachel: you are lifesavers! It's an honor to brainstorm, laugh, and cry with you! Amanda Gopal, thank you for lending your knowledge and experience to this novel. I so admire the work you do to help trafficking survivors and former sex workers get a fresh start. Judy Christian, your help brought Haven to life and I appreciate your sweet soul! Zach Berry, thanks for helping me with the ins and outs of city leadership and civil engineering. Any mistakes I made were my own.

To my children's 2019–2020 and 2020–2021 teachers: you are amazing. Thanks for caring for my kids and teaching them during this strange time. Without your patience, understanding, and willingness to go above and beyond, this book would still be on my laptop, unfinished.

Finally, thank you, Lord. You are the God of new beginnings and unconditional love. You see the lost, the discarded, the lonely, and the broken-hearted and provide a haven for them to rest. For that, I will exalt your name forever.

Ready to find
your next great read?

Let us help.

Visit prh.com/nextread

Penguin
Random
House